Dime Novel Roundup

Dime Novel Roundup

Annotated Index 1931-1981

Michael L. Cook

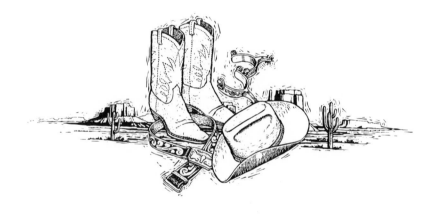

Bowling Green University Popular Press
Bowling Green, Ohio 43403

Acknowledgements:

The article quoted within the chapter "The Dime Novel Roundup and the Editors," written by Ralph F. Cummings and published in the July and September 1968 issues of e The Dime Novel Roundup, is printed with the permission of the editor.

Dedication

To Ralph F. Cummings and Edward T. LeBlanc
for their unceasing interest and devotion in
publishing The Dime Novel Roundup

Contents

Introduction   3

The *Dime Novel Roundup* and the Editors   5

The Dime Novel and the New American Literature   15

Chronological Listing of Issues of
The Dime Novel Roundup   21

Index to Contents of *The Dime Novel Roundup*,
January 1931 - December 1981   25

INTRODUCTION

The dime novel represents an important facet of the popular fiction field, being the first wide-spread publishing venture that distributed "escape" literature. Many of these were greatly successful with each issue selling in the hundreds of thousands of copies. While frowned upon by many parents, educators and librarians of the period (roughly 1867-1925), they were widely read and portrayed tales of adventure, detection, and even moral virtues that appealed to all ages. The dime novel was not a strikingly original development, but rather the culmination of a trend that began in the 1830's. The majority of readers were denied access to popular literature by the relatively high cost of the hardbound books and the limited number and access to libraries. New printing methods and subsequently new methods of marketing allowed the success of the dime novel, and these stirring adventures of pirates, detectives, outlaws, bootblacks and soldiers concerned with adventure, history, romance, war, the west, city life and rural life were immediate successes.

The Dime Novel Roundup, although aimed at collecting of these magazines and story papers, includes much information of considerable value to researchers and scholars of all facets of life for the period covered. Interviews and articles on outlaws and western heroes, and on the authors (many of whom contributed articles) of early fiction are included. Many valuable bibliographic listings appear, as well as thoroughly researched articles on early publishers. The majority of this information

appears nowhere else, and the availability of back issues adds to the value.

The Dime Novel Roundup is unique, also, for its long span of publication. The first issue was January 1931, and through the end of 1981 there have been 552 issues published. This Index is intended as a key to the material contained therein and opens it to researchers and scholars as well as readers and collectors in many fields - those of Western Americana, outlaws and bandits, early publishing history both in the United States and England, mystery and detective fiction, boys' books study and collecting, early authors, and students of life both in the city and rural areas. And, of course, bibliographical data on over 150 dime novels and story papers. Annotations describe the nature of the entry indexed where the title does not adequately do so.

Indexing is by title, author, and subject matter. Index references refer to issue number and page number (i.e., 348:98 would indicate issue number 348, page 98). Identification of issues published appears in a listing immediately preceding the Index.

Appreciation and thanks are extended to Ralph F. Cummings for the interest and friendly correspondence over a number of years, and to Eddie T. LeBlanc for his interest and help in making this Index possible.

There have been but two editors of the *Dime Novel Roundup* during its fifty-one years of publication, Ralph F. Cummings and Edward T. LeBlanc. Their interest and dedication, even through the depression years and World War II, has been somewhat phenomenal and much is owed to them for their untiring efforts.

The beginning of the *Dime Novel Roundup* can be traced back as early as 1922 when Ralph F. Cummings published a small paper titled *Cummings & Clark's Flyer* in December of that year. This was a combination of an advertising flyer and of news and comments on dime novels and story papers. In September 1925 Cummings published a similar paper, *The Book Hunter,* changing the name to *The Novel Hunter* with the second issue and this continued until May 1927. Commencing in 1926 he published *The Novel Hunter's Yearbook* for six years. He then assumed editorship of the *Happy Hours Magazine,* the journal for the Happy Hours Brotherhood (a group of dime novel collectors in which Cummings was one of the founders); the last issue of this was November/ December 1930 and this was supplanted by the *Dime Novel Roundup* in January 1931.

A reminiscent article in the *Dime Novel Roundup,* July and September 1968 issues, by Ralph F. Cummings can best relate the early history of the Brotherhood and the magazine and at the same time provide the proper nostalgia for the period when the dime novels and story papers were still a staple part of the

reading material readily available:

"It was the latter part of 1913 or 1914 that I read my first novel and I believe it was an old Secret Service about the Bradys, old and young. If I remember correctly, the story was an underground adventure with snakes and good sized ones at that.

"I was on my father's milk route at the time, and there used to be several boys that wanted to help out in peddling the milk. We peddled milk in Farnumsville, Fisherville and Saundersville, small mill towns just south of Worcester, Massachusetts. As we made the rounds by horse and team and later by mule and milk wagon, the youngsters would talk about the wonderful adventures of Young Wild West, Old and Young King Brady, the Liberty Boys of '76 and others.

"After a while I became interested and asked if I might have the loan of one of these novels; so sure enough, I had one and it was the Secret Service mentioned above.

"There was a newsstand in town run by Eugene J. Lemaire and his father. There I started to buy the Frank Tousey big six, that is the ones I liked to read. My father, Ernest W. Cummings ran the Riverside Farm. My mother used to help him as well as raise us kids. I was the oldest and there was my sister, Mildred and my brother, Harold. A little later my father made ice cream and sold it both wholesale and retail, and believe me we were all busy. No dull moments and none

of us could go anywhere, as we didn't have the time to go.

"Of course my father had hired men who were paid by the month. They did the farming such as milking, planting, etc.

"Along early in 1917 I believe it was, I saw an ad of Ralph P. Smith, Lawrence, Mass., that said he had old novels for sale at 20 for $1.00 sent postpaid as they came. Believe you me, it didn't take me long to send him the $1.00 and when I got them, oh boy, I had a picnic. And it wasn't long before I sent for more of them. And such novels as I had never even heard of, such as Tip Top, Nick Carter, Buffalo Bill, Diamond Dick, Beadles Dime and Half Dime Libraries. No matter what they were, I enjoyed reading them. My father and mother were too busy to investigate my reading, and I'm glad they didn't although some years later my father got after me for reading the Dalton Boys, Far West Bandits and I laid off reading for 6 to 8 months but came right back at it again, full force. He never said anything after that.

"Coming back to novels again, I happened to see ads of other dealers stamped on the novels I was getting. I loved it at the time and every new ad I'd see, I'd write to the party and a few letters came back, but not many. And those I did hear from, I was able to get more old novels. I sure got some dandys at times. And so it went along. In the meantime Ralph Smith started to pay me visits every little while, and I was sure glad to see him. I read novels by the hundred and how I

loved them. I read them on the milk route every chance I got. I read them while milking cows. I read them anywhere I could. You may wonder how I milked cows and read at the same time, well to make a story short, I had milking tubes and I used them on the poor cows while I read novels. If my father had caught me doing that, my sitdown would of gotten warmed up good, as it doesn't do a cow any good for tubes to be used all the time. It's O.K. if there aren't any sores on them. Year in and Year out it should not be done. Some time in 1918, William J. Benners of Philadelphia, Pennsylvania came up to Lawrence to visit a doctor friend of his and while up there, somehow or other, he was told about Ralph P. Smith. As Billy loved to read and collect these old novels and story papers, he paid Ralph a visit and then Ralph told him about me and it wasn't long before he got down here. Ralph Smith and his wife came down with him as Billy didn't have a car. We sure had a fine time all around.

"Along about 1923 I had gotten some small papers sent to me by the late L. C. Skinner of Pawtucket, R.I. These little pagelets or booklets, whatever you want to call them, were, I should judge, 3x4 inches in size with 8 or 10 pages. The name of the little paper was called the "Novel Exchanger's Union." Mr. Skinner was a member of the Union, as was J. P. Guinon of Little Rock, Arkansas.

"When Ralph Smith came down on one of his visits, I asked

him what he thought of starting a dime novel club and have
a magazine to go with it. He jumped at the idea, so in 1924
we had it all planned to start the Happy Hours Brotherhood
and to publish the Happy Hours Magazine as of the official
organ.

"Ralph Smith was to be the publisher and I was to be the
president. The late Robert H. Smeltzer of Philadelphia was
vice president and William M. Burns of Rockland, Maine, and
J. Edward Leithead were to be on the advisory board.

"No. 1 of Happy Hours Magazine came out and was dated
January - February 1925 and was published every two months.

"The printer lived in Wisconsin and if I'm not mistaken
the name was Pine Hill Printers. We started with only a few
members, Ralph P. Smith, myself, Robert M. Rowan, John Ferguson,
Robert H. Smeltzer, John Matula, J. R. Kohrt, Ralph F. Adimari,
Earl Farmer and C. H. Blake. The first membership list was
published in the May - June 1925 issue of Happy Hours Magazine.
In June George Sahr joined up and he is still with us. Bob
Smeltzer died a few years ago. C.H.Blake died quite a long while
ago. He was a great story paper collector.

"In the July - August 1925 issue, Thomas Kelly, William
M. Kreling and William L. Beck joined up. They are all dead now.
The September - October issue announced memberships of George
Kreling, Sam Nathan, James T. Adams, C. Young and Henry C. Ludwig,
also all gone now. During November - December 1925 new members

were Bob Frye, Richard Zorn, Frank T. Fries, C. A. McCarthy and Robert Burns. All are gone except Bob Frye and Robert Burns.

"So you see since we started with only a few members back in 1925 we have grown some. I see by the current listing that there are now 283 members. If all members were counted, the list would come close to 1500. As of the end of 1925, there are still 7 of the old members still with us.

"Somehow or other, William J. Benners didn't join the Brotherhood until late 1927. If I'm not mistaken he was traveling abroad when we started. He was a great traveler.

"Way back in 1925 when Tom Kelley used to publish little papers for me, such as The Novel Hunter, The Novel Hunter's Yearbook, which started in 1926 and ended in 1931, I was in my seventh heaven knowing I had become a publisher.

"Tom printed everything by hand in those days, set the type and what not. I used to have anywhere from 200 to 500 printed at a time. I would get them flat and I assembled them, got them into envelopes and off to the post office. I was in my prime in those days. Now that I am 70 years old I'm not so fast as I used to be.

"Even further back in time, December 1922, Bob Smeltzer published my first paper. This was the Cummings and Clarks Flyer, printed only on one side and about 7x8 inches. Nos. 2, 3 and 4 were issued as one issue and printed by Lessor & Call, printers,

Dover-Foxcroft, Maine. The size was 6x9 inches. Nos. 5, 6 and 7 were printed by Ernest Biggs of Indiana. With No. 8, December 1923, Thomas Kelley began printing them for me, size 8x5½ inches, 2 columns to the page, and a poem by Jack Harkaway was featured in Vol. 2 No.4, April 1924. I published my first poem, "Reckless Ralph, the Dime Novel King" and I thought I was something. I had quite a collection of old novels and story papers at that time, which I don't have now. In the May 1924 issue Tom Kelley had a poem "Wanted A Prize Poem." He wanted to help me all he could so he offered a Zane Grey book for the best poem he could get. George Sahr of Kenosha, Wisconsin wrote the first prize winner which appeared in the June issue. In addition to the poem, each issue contained ads for dime novels.

"James C. Morris wrote "Memory of Days Gone By" that was a real bit of poetry. Then Bob Smeltzer came along with "Boyhood Heroes." In Vol. 2, No. 11, November 1924 my second poem was published, "Dime Novel Days in Massachusetts." At that time Albert E. Clark and myself went up into our attic where my folks used to have old farm magazines as well as newspapers, church and school papers, etc. We got to hunting through the old papers when Albert Clark came across a Buffalo Bill Stories and as he was a great lover of Buffalo Bill and had a long run of Buffalo Bill Stories and New Buffalo Bill Weekly, but he did not have the one he found, it was a prize. My turn came next

when I dug out No. 4 of Paul Jones Weekly. It was the first
Paul Jones either of us had ever seen, and we both read it in
a hurry after we finished hunting. How these dime novels got
up there or where they came from, no one knows, but as my
folks had hired men from time to time, we think they must have
bought them at a newsstand and brought them home to read. When
they were finished with them, they had thrown them in with
the other papers. The Paul Jones Weekly was in pretty poor
condition, but I prized it for a good many years until I was
able to get a set of 1 through 18 from Charles Austin of
Philadelphia.

"Albert Clark used to come to our old place, The River
Side Farm on the old Providence Road in Grafton. Albert was
a little younger than I was, but he liked to read the old
timers the same as I did. We were together quite a lot. He
was well educated. He had attended Worcester Academy and was
attending Brown University. While there he contracted some
kind of disease, I never knew what kind it was, and died a
terrible death. He went down to nothing before he died. His
folks turned his collection of old novels over to me.

"The Cummings & Clarks Flyer continued to feature poetry
about dime novels and old dime novel days. Robert M. Rowan,
James C. Morris, George Sahr and Earl Farmer all were contributors.
Other writers for the Flyer were Ralph F. Adimari, John Ferguson,
and Pearl A. Knece. Pearl is a man, although Pearl sounds like

a girl's name. But as it was the name given him he just had
to take it. It is a good name just the same.

"In October 1929 I brought out the Novel Hunter's Year
Book Supplement with articles by Knece, Vernon Lemley, W.B.
McCafferty and Bob Smeltzer and George Sahr. This Supplement
is very scarce today. Guess I didn't have too many printed.
The Novel Hunters' Yearbook started December 1926 and featured
articles about dime novels much as the Dime Novel Roundup
does. The last number was published in 1931. At that time I
took over publication of the Happy Hours Magazine which after
two months became the Dime Novel Roundup.

"If my memory serves me correctly it was in 1920 that I
first started collecting in order to accumulate a file of
these novels, story papers and certain kinds of old books,
magazines, etc. This fascinating hobby has been the means of
bringing me many good friends, the most of whom I have never
met. Of the 40 or so original correspondents there are only 7
left, Ralph Adimari, Ed Leithead, George Sahr, Ralph Smith,
Robert Burns, P. J. Moran and Bob Frye.

Ralph F. Cummings, born January 4, 1898, Uxbridge,
Massachusetts, was editor of *The Dime Novel Roundup* for the
first 237 issues, until July 1952. At the time of this writing,
he is alive and in ill health, living in Grafton, Massachusetts.

With the July 1952 issue the editorship was assumed by
Edward T. LeBlanc, and he has continued as editor to the
present. Under his able guidance and devotion, *The Dime Novel*

Roundup has prospered and grown, both in subscriber/members and in size. With the October 1975 issue the magazine became bi-monthly, but with an increased number of pages. Except for a period of a few months in 1932 and 1933 when Ralph F. Cummings was ill, and six months in 1940, the magazine has been published on schedule for fifty one years.

Edward T. LeBlanc was born in Georgiaville, Rhode Island, eight miles north of Providence, on August 31, 1920. At the age of fifteen he became an avid collector of dime novels. An advertisement in *Wild West Weekly* by Ralph P. Smith started Eddie and his father collecting in earnest and with membership in the Happy Hours Brotherhood; much correspondence, exchanging, and buying ensued. The interest has never waned. He graduated from business college in 1939 and shortly thereafter commenced working for the Navy Department in Washington, D.C., later being transferred to the Naval Torpedo Station, Newport, Rhode Island in April 1941. He was drafted into the armed services in October 1942, and spent "3 years, 3 months, 3 days and 15½ minutes" with the air force. Eddie and his wife Florence, after twenty eight years of married life, have six children and three grandchildren, and a continuing special affection for the old dime novels.

THE DIME NOVEL AND THE NEW AMERICAN LITERATURE

It was not until the War of 1812 that American authors transcended the spiritual blight that had gripped the nation. One of the first to produce readable fiction set in the rich activity of the then still young United States was James Fennimore Cooper, and his bold, imaginative stories of the frontiersmen and Indians dared to break the traditional European scene and set the stage for the future. At about the same time, a young Southerner, Edgar Allan Poe, migrated to the North with pen in hand and with the publication of "Murders in the Rue Morgue," "The Gold Bug," and "The Purloined Letter" gave a new meaning to the short story. This rebirth was again somewhat of an innovation in lieu of the pompous, long-winded European novels. Poe's real contribution, of course, was the detective, a pure American character. It is interesting to note that Poe's first stories were at first published in dime novel form, the size being about five by eight inches, with paper covers, and thus relegated to being considered second-class literature not worthy of a clothbound book.

It is indeed a tragedy that many of the American authors of this period followed religiously the "New England school of literature," overlooking the rich material of everyday life in the United States, and instead seeing the American Scene through an Englishman's eyes.

One notable exception was Ralph Waldo Emerson, a rebel with a cause, espousing the nobility of man and his new heritage, and his creative youthful philosophy met a ready response with the youth of the country. While others admired the genuine English character found in the large cities, and felt that the rest of the country represented, at best, an uncouth and inferior England, Cooper, Poe and Emerson found and presented an enthusiastic new approach. Walter Whitman was another who represented a purely native American view, disregarding tradition, taste, and morals, and although his poetry discarded previous standards it reached a new heigth in understanding; a new kind of literature was born, portraying this young nation and its Western frontier.

There were a few earlier attempts to write genuine native literature, and for the most part, the authors have been forgotten. One of the earliest was Royall Tyler who published an early book of adventure, *THE ALGERINE CAPTIVE* (1797). An early sea and adventure story, *FORTUNE'S FOOTBALL,* by James Butler appeared that same year. Soon after, George Brockden Brown, although his novels were crude in construction, wrote about frontier life in *EDGAR HUNTLEY* (1799), one of the earliest stories wherein fair maiden was rescued from the Indians.

By the 1830's the new generations eagerly sought this type of material; the West had been opened to the extent that

the mysteries of the new land were of intense interest, and reminiscences of Indian warfare still fresh enough that tales of the conflicts were acceptable and desired.

The December 1833 issue of *The Western Monthly Magazine* carried an essay, by Isaac Appleton Jewett, addressed to the writers of America being an eloquent plea for the new and distinctly national literature based on the richness of the wilderness and the West. He stated "The thirst for works of the imagination is as strong and universal at the present time as at any former period; and we trust that of the floods which annually pour in upon the reading world, there are some fountains at which the soul may drink and feel itself refreshed and invigorated." The late thirties, forties and fifties brought forth an ever greater amount of writing utilizing the frontier landscape, characters and incidents. Several notable examples are Robert Montgomery Bird's *NICK OF THE WOODS* (1837) and William Gilmore Simm's *THE YEMASSEE* (1835) and *BORDER ROMANCES,* the latter in several volumes published from 1834 to 1840. A number of lesser writers were also beginning to grind out the western fiction that was immediately popular.

The first crude story-paper appeared in 1839, the *Brother Jonathan Weekly,* a mammoth sized news and story paper measuring 22x32", aimed at the mass audience. With nearly twenty million population, most of whom were literate, this was a ready-made audience that could now be satisfied with reading material

produced at low cost. With introduction of the steam rotary press and new means of distribution by utilizing the railroads, the market promptly attracted many more experiments in cheaply produced papers. For the most part, consisting of several short stories (some pirated from English publications), chapters from serial novels, and a few news items, organized in newspaper format on crowded pages, such papers met success and the public eagerly awaited the next issues.

The popularity of the story-papers encouraged Erastus and Irwin Beadle in 1860 to publish what is now considered to be the first dime novel, "Malaeska: The Indian Wife of the White Hunter," written by Ann S. Stephens. With this the concept of publishing the entire story in one issue was presented and within a few months more than 65,000 copies had been sold. The stirring action, albeit often padded prose, all in one "book" for a dime, immediately attracted other publishers (as well as many would-be authors) and the flood of dime novels was upon the American public in a seemingly never to end parade. Stories of pirates, detectives, soldiers, highwaymen, outlaws, bootblacks and villains galore! With tales of history, adventure, love, war, urban and rural life, and, above all, the West, the acceptance was phenomenal. By April 1864 Beadle's Dime Books alone had sold more than five million copies.

For approximately sixty years the dime novels represented the low cost fiction that the public demanded, but competition

arose in the attempt to give the reader more for his nickel or dime and the pulp magazine was born. As early as 1888 the thick *Argosy* appeared, an outgrowth of the juvenile story-paper *The Golden Argosy,* and in 1903, *The Popular Magazine. Blue Book* commenced in 1904 under the title *The Monthly Story Magazine,* and *All-Story* in 1905. These were followed in rapid succession by a host of others. The 32-page dime novel had passed into history.

CHRONOLOGICAL LISTING OF ISSUES

Year	Jan	Feb	Mar	Apr	May	June	July	Aug	Sept	Oct	Nov	Dec
1931	1	2	3	4	5	6	7	8	9	10	11	12
1932	13	14	15	16	17	18	19					
1933					20		21		22	23	24	25
1934	26	27		28	29	30	31	32	33	34	35	36
1935	37	38	39	40	41	42	43	44				45
1936	46	47	48	49	50	51	52	53	54	55	56	57
1937	58	59	60	61	62	63	64	65	66	67	68	69
1938*	70	71	72	73	74	75	76	77	78	79	80	81
1939	82	83	84	85	86	87	88	89	90	91	92	93
1940						94	95	96	97	98	99	100
1941	101	102	103	104	105	106	107	108	109	110	111	
1942	112	113	114	115	116	117	118	119	120	121	122	123
1943	124	125	126	127	128	129	130	131	132	133	134	135
1944	136	137	138	139	140	141	142	143	144	145	146	147
1945	148	149	150	151	152	153	154	155	156	157	158	159
1946	160	161	162	163	164	165	166	167	168	169	170	171
1947	172	173	174	175	176	177	178	179	180	181	182	183
1948	184	185	186	187	188	189	190	191	192	193	194	195
1949	196	197	198	199	200	201	202	203	204	205	206	207
1950	208	209	210	211	212	213	214	215	216	217	218	219

*Special Birthday Issue, January 1938 also issued, unnumbered (indexed as "81A").
Special Supplements are numbered with issue number they accompanied, and "SS" for page number

Year	Jan	Feb	Mar	Apr	May	June	July	Aug	Sept	Oct	Nov	Dec
1951	220	221	222	223	224	225	226	227	228	229	230	231
1952	232	233	234	235	236	237	238	239	240	241	242	243
1953	244	245	246	247	248	249	250	251	252	253	254	255
1954	256	257	258	259	260	261	262	263	264	265	266	267
1955	268	269	270	271	272	273	274	275	276	277	278	279
1956	280	281	282	283	284	285	286	287	288	289	290	291
1957	292	293	294	295	296	297	298	299	300	301	302	303
1958	304	305	306	307	308	309	310	311	312	313	314	315
1959	316	317	318	319	320	321	322	323	324	325	326	327
1960	328	329	330	331	332	333	334	335	336	337	338	339
1961	340	341	342	343	344	345	346	347	348	349	350	351
1962	352	353	354	355	356	357	358	359	360	361	362	363
1963	364	365	366	367	368	369	370	371	372	373	374	375
1964	376	377	378	379	380	381	382	383	384	385	386	387
1965	388	389	390	391	392	393	394	395	396	397	398	399
1966	400	401	402	403	404	405	406	407	408	409	410	411
1967	412	413	414	415	416	417	418	419	420	421	422	423
1968	424	425	426	427	428	429	430	431	432	433	434	435
1969	436	437	438	439	440	441	442	443	444	445	446	447
1970	448	449	450	451	452	453	454	455	456	457	458	459

Year	Jan	Feb	Mar	Apr	May	June	July	Aug	Sept	Oct	Nov	Dec
1971	460	461	462	463	464	465	466	467	468	469	470	471
1972	472	473	474	475	476	477	478	479	480	481	482	483
1973	484	485	486	487	488	489	490	491	492	493	494	495
1974	496	497	498	499	500	501	502	503	504	505	506	507
1975	508	509	510	511	512	513	514			515		516
1976		517		518		519		520		521		522
1977		523		524		525		526		527		528
1978		529		530		531		532		533		534
1979		535		536		537		538		539		540
1980		541		542		543		544		545		546
1981		547		548		549		550		551		552

*Page references refer to Issue Number
and page number. Thus, "313-131" is
to be identified as Issue No.313, page
131. Date of that particular issue may
be determined by referring to chronological listing of issues table.*

A Bangup Vacation (reminiscences), by
Charles Duprez. 313-131

A BIBLIOGRAPHY OF HARD-COVER BOYS BOOKS,
REV.ED., Harry K. Hudson, changes
and additions by author. 529-31;
531-78; 532-89; 539-82

A Bit on Nick Carter Library, by
Harold C. Holmes. 90-1

A Book Grabber's Gripes (on collecting
boys' books), by Jack R. Schorr
475-50

A Defense of the Dime Novel (literary
and entertainment value), by Edward
Hamlin, 151-2

A Curiosity of Horror (discussion of
horror stories), by G.H.Cordier,
47-1·

A Dime Novel Graduate (reminiscences),
by J. H. Armbruster, 77-1

A Famous Old English Boys Journal
(on BOYS OF ENGLAND), by Henry
Steele, 134-1

A Few Do's and Don'ts (advice and
tips on collecting), by Don S.
Learnard, 342-22

A Few of the Less Known Series (on
boy's books series), by Jack
Schorr, 464-47

A Few of the Non-Series Books (on
boy's books not in series), by
Jack Schorr, 467-85

A Final Word on the Pseudonyms of
Edward S. Ellis, by Denis R.
Rogers, 363-108

A Fine Little Anecdote (on dime
novels), by L.S.Patterson, 186-3

A Fragment on George A. Amy, Illustrator for Young Sports, by
Stanley A. Pachon, 371-76

A Half Century of the Hardy Boys, or
Clues to an Obscure Chronology
(Hardy Boys series by Franklin
W. Dixon); bibliography, by
Robert V. Riordan, 530-35

A Handsome Harry Episode (character
in Diamond Dick stories), by
Harold C. Holmes, 71-3

A Librarian Who Unearthed History
(Florence E. Wheeler's efforts
on Johnny Appleseed), by Nicholas
Zook, 224-38

A List of Alger Titles (bibliographic
checklist),Morton S.Enslin, 467-74;
468-90

A Little Dime Novel Chat (reminiscences)
by Ralph Cummings, 22-3

A Lode of Golden Hours (on pseudonyms),
by Harry A. Weill, 215-59

A Lost Novel by G.W.M.Reynolds? (on
THE GIPSY CHIEF), by E.F.Bleiler,
499-38

A Lurid Record (on collecting), by W.E.
Bennett, 60-1

A Meeting with Gilbert Patten, by P.J.
Moran, 397-104

A Memory (verse), by J.P.Guinon, 256-7

A Memory (reminiscences). by Eli A.
Messier, 102-7

A Merry Chase After "Merry" (on Frank
Merriwell), by Frank T. Fries, 3-5

A Monument for Deadwood Dick, news item,
31-1

A New and Interesting Phantom Title (on
never published boys' book), by Harry
K. Hudson, 537-47

A Note on D.W.Stevens, by Wm. L. Beck
12-4

A Novelist in the Legislature (news of
Oll Coomes), 85-1

A Partial History of the Brett Publications,
by Ralph Adimari, 368-42

A Plea for Unity, Brotherhood and
Cooperation (Happy Hours Brotherhood)
by William M. Burns, 54-3

A Publication Pattern of Edward S. Ellis
(study of the Porter & Coates/Henry T.
Coates/John C.Winston editions of boys'
books by Ellis), by Denis R. Rogers and
J. Edward Leithead, 480-80; 481-95

A Quick Synopsis of the Merriwell Saga
(in TIP TOP WEEKLY), by Ralph P. Smith,
537-48

A Sad Calamity (humor), 108-4

A Sensation of the 60's (on dime novels),
38-4

A Short Short Mystery (on reading dime
novels; reminiscences), 111-2

A Sketch of Hezekiah Butterworth (author
of early boys' books), by Jack Scorr,
539-77

A Story of India (dime novel style fiction)
by Harold C. Holmes, 84-2

A Thrice-Told Tale on "Golden Hours" by
Harry A. Weill, 148-1

A Time of Lively Fiction (survey and discussion of popular literature from dime
novels to present),by Robert Sampson,
540-93;541-8; 542-33; 543-52; 544-71;
545-87; 546-104

A Tribute to Der Roundup (verse), by "Heinrich Knoodles" 326-94

A Tribute to Charles Hamilton (author) by W.O.G.Lofts, 355-33

A Tribute to Gil Patten (author), by James E. Knott, 150-4

A Two-Gun Bluff (reminiscences), by J.H.Armbruster, 255-94

A Vacation Trip 1973 (boy's book collecting), by Jack Schorr, 495-137

A Visit with Don & Grace (Don and Grace Learnard), by Harold Poore, 352-2

A Weaver of Romances (on Mrs. Alex. McVeigh Miller, author), by Ethel Clark Lewis, 110-1

A Yankee Hater: A Regular Dime Novel Story (dime novel style fiction) by J.H.Armbruster, 221-9

Aaron, Frances: letter of comment, 381-52

Abandoned Farm House, The (fiction on collecting dime novels), by "Noname," 106-1

ACE-HIGH MAGAZINE, 15-7; 17-7

ACE-HIGH NOVELS, 17-7

Acker, Frank C.: Cap'n Wiley, Maine's Merry Munchausen (dime novel character discussed), 494-126

Acker, Frank C.: Frank Merriwell's Stage Setback (review of Frank Merriwell or Honor Challenged, stage production), 466-68

Acker, Frank C.: Gilbert Patten, The Man and the Magic (discussion of author), 409-96

Acker, Frank C.: letter of comment, 404-52; 515-120

Adams, Dan: letter of comment, 389-18; 404-53; 522-142

Adams, David C.: Frank Merriwell's Father (death of Gilbert Patten, author, and on dime novels in general), 150-1

(Adams, William T.), Chronological checklist of books (Oliver Optic), by Janet R. Lillibridge, 517-28

(Adams, William Taylor), Oliver Optic (Adams as author and editor with definitive checklist), by S.E. Wallen, 511-26; 512-38

(Adams, William Taylor), William Taylor Adams: A Literary Retrospection (literary discussion; Oliver Optic) by Peter C. Walther, with checklist, 548-26

Adimari, Ralph: A Partial History of the Brett Publications, 368-42

Adimari, Ralph: The Alger Fakes (Alger books by Stratemeyer), 349-105

Adimari, Ralph: Cecil Burleigh, One of the Comic Writers, 296-36

Adimari, Ralph: Clara Augusta Jones 1839-1905 (author), 297-5

Adimari, Ralph F.: The Dime Novel, It's Place in American Literature, 12-6; 13-1; 14-3; 15-2; 16-2; 17-2; 18-4; 19-2; 23-4; 25-3

Adimari, Ralph: Ellen Price Wood (1814-1887), English Juvenile Writer, 366-22

Adimari, Ralph: Facts About "Peter Pad" (dime novel character) 12-3

Adimari, Ralph: The Frank Tousey Authors, 293-10

Adimari, Ralph: J. Edward Leithead collection of pseudonyms, 329-10

Adimari, Ralph: James Perkins Tracy - A Self-Made Man (author), 277-82

Adimari, Ralph: letter of comment, 380-45; 390-30

Adimari, Ralph: The Library of Congress Pseudonyms, 321-50

Adimari, Ralph: Miscellaneous Pseudonyms 341-10

Adimari, Ralph: The Ralph Adimari Collection of Pseudonyms, 324-74

Adimari, Ralph: Report on Robert Emmett Owen, Illustrator of Street & Smith publications, 333-50

Adimari, Ralph: Upton Sinclair, Last of the Dime Novelists, 285-42; 286-51

Adimari, Ralph: William J. Benners - The First Historian of the Dime Novel, 312-121

Adimari, Ralph, William J. Benners Pseudonyms, The, 317-14

Adimari, Ralph & C. Arthur Neetz: Wolff and The Tousey Reprints (on Tousey Publishing Co.), 332-43

Adimari, Ralph & Gerald J. McIntosh: Frank Merriwell on Radio & Television 410-112

Adimari, Ralph & Edward T. LeBlanc: Checklist of Street & Smith Dime Novels and Related Publications, 299-60

Adley, D.J. & W.O.G.Lofts: Favorite Boyhood Characters on the British Screen, 525-66; 528-122

Admirable Arlington, The, (Chester Arlington, dime novel villain), by J.P. Guinon, 70-1; 71-5

ADVANCE TEN CENT NOVELS (sketch), 4-3

ADVANCE TEN CENT NOVELS, Dime Novel Sketches #160, 488-49

ADVENTURE, 49-2

(Adventure Series, Arthur Westbrook Co), The James Boys in the Saddle Again, with checklist, by J. Edward Leithead, 280-2

(adventure, worldwide), The Anatomy of Dime Novels, No.15, Stories of Worldwide Adventure, by J. Edward Leithead, 440-42, 441-50

ADVENTURE WEEKLY, Dime Novel Sketches #25, 346-75

Adventures in Dime Novel Land (reminiscences), by F. Fred Orphal, 57-1

Advice to Collectors, by Charles Bragin, 245-14; 342-21; 405-63

Ages of Beadle Authors, by Albert Johannsen, 212-39

Ah, Those Holden Years (boy's books collecting comments), by Jack Schorr, 508-5

(Aimard, Gustave), Gustave Aimard (French author), by George Froncal, 411-132

Akers, Paul E.: letter of comment, 389-17

(Alamo, The, stories), The Anatomy of Dime Novels, No.18: The Alamo and The Mexican War, ju J. Edward Leithead, 450-24

Alas, That Truth Must Prevail (on Buffalo Bill Cody), by "Seajay," 158-4

ALDINE LAND AND SEA LIBRARY, 123-3

ALDINE LIFE AND ADVENTURE LIBRARY, with checklist, by Denis R. Rogers, 533-98

Aldine Papers, 174-17

Aldine Publishing Co., 175-28

(ALDINES NEW BOYS PAPER), Old English Journals for Boys, by W.M.Burns, 331-34

(Aldine Publishing Company), The Early Publications of the Aldine Pub.Co. (with special interest to Alger series), by Denis R. Rogers, 532-82; 533-98

Alfred Bronaugh Taylor, a Beadle Author, by Albert Johannsen, 303-104

Alfred D. Hynes, Beadle and Munro Author, by Denis R. Rogers, 386-94

Alger, Horatio, Jr., letter published November 25, 1872, 123-2

Alger: Facts and Fancy (Brandeis Univ. Alger Seminar), 387-110

Alger Fakes, The (Alger books by Stratemeyer), by Ralph Adimari, 349-105

Alger Heroes, The Merriwells, et al!, by Ralph D. Gardner, 445-100

Alger is Out (claims no longer popular among readers), by Ernest L. Meyer, 92-1

ALGER SERIES, Dime Novel Sketches #221, 549-49

Alger, Horatio, Society: letter of comment, 407-81

(Alger, Horatio, Jr.), A List of Alger Titles (bibliography and checklist) by Morton S. Enslin, 467-74;468-90

(Alger, Horatio, Jr.), Alger: Facts & Fancy (Brandeis Univ. Alger Seminar) 387-110

(Alger, Horatio, Jr.), The Alger Fakes (Alger books by Stratemeyer) by Ralph Adimari, 349-105

(Alger, Horatio, Jr.), Alger Heroes, The Merriwells, et al!, by Ralph D. Gardner, 445-100

(Alger, Horatio, Jr.), Alger is Out (claims no longer popular among readers), by Ernest L. Meyer, 92-1

(Alger, Horatio, Jr.), An Overlooked Alger Weekly, by Stanley A.Pachon, 498-30

(Alger, Horatio, Jr.), Bibliographical Essay, by Marjorie Heins, 506-131

(Alger, Horatio, Jr.), Books recorded in Book Auction Records, 546-102

(Alger, Horatio, Jr.: CAST UPON THE BREAKERS), Horatio Alger's Last Hero, 495-141

(Alger, Horatio, Jr.), The Early Publications of the Aldine Publishing Co. (with special interest to Alger series) by Denis R. Rogers, 532-82; 533-98

(Alger, Horatio, Jr.), THE GARFIELD LIBRARY (English novel series), by Denis R. Rogers, 470-124; 471-138; 472-5

(Alger, Horatio, Jr.), Horatio Alger Goes Greeley: From Wretches to Riches (literary sketch), by David Soibelman, 539-79

(Alger, Horatio, Jr.), Horatio Alger,Jr. After Seventy Years (reminiscences), by Morton S. Enslin, 451-40; 452-50

(Alger, Horatio, Jr.), HORATIO ALGER, JR., AN ANNOTATED BIBLIOGRAPHY OF COMMENT AND CRITICISM, by Gary Scharnhorst and Jack Bales, a review by John T. Dizer, Jr., 550-74

(Alger, Horatio, Jr.), Horatio Alger, Jr. and Ragged Dick: Reality and Myth, by Ken Donelson, 525-58

(Alger, Horatio, Jr.), The Horatio Alger Paperback First Editions, by Frank Gruber, 259-26

(Alger, Horatio, Jr.), Horatio Alger Society meeting on 67th anniversary of Alger's death, report, 407-83

(Alger, Horatio, Jr.), Horatio Alger: Symbol for Success (influence of Alger upon his and succeeding generations) by Marjorie Heins, 505-118; 506-130

(Alger, Horatio, Jr.), In and Out of Books: Nostalgia, Ltd., 303-105

(Alger, Horatio, Jr.), In Defense of Horatio Alger, Jr. (discusses the immoral charges against Alger), by Max Goldberg, 552-114

(Alger, Horatio, Jr.), In Defense of Listing Current Alger Values (discussion on values and scarcity), by Ralph D. Gardner,472-2

(Alger, Horatio, Jr.), The Many Faceted Alger (on his humorous sketches), by Stanley A.Pachon, 548-37

(Alger, Horatio, Jr.), The New York Sun and Those Elusive Alger Serials, by Stanley A. Pachon, 492-98

(Alger, Horatio, Jr.), The Newsboys Lodging House: Impetus for an Immortal, by Jack Bales, 521-116

(Alger, Horatio, Jr.), Paging H. Alger - His Stuff Works, 94-5

(Alger, Horatio, Jr.), ROAD TO SUCCESS, THE BIBLIOGRAPHY OF THE WORKS OF HORATIO ALGER by Ralph D. Gardner, review by Kenyon C. Rosenberg, 488-57

(Alger, Horatio, Jr.), Those Alger Days (verse), by Frank Eisenberg, 543-56

ALL AROUND WEEKLY, Dime Novel Sketches #62, 390-21

ALL SPORTS LIBRARY, Dime Novel Sketches #35, 358-67

ALL STAR DETECTIVE STORIES, 15-7
(Allen, Frank, series), Garden City
    Publishing Company's paperback
    juveniles (boys' series), by Bob
    Chenu, 531-72
(Almard, Gustave), The Lunatic Novelist,
    127-3
(Altshelter, Joseph A.), Now They're
    Collector's Items (boys' series
    books), by J. Edward Leithead,
    417-54
AMAZING ADVENTURES OF LYIN' BOB HAGUM
    AND FIDDLIN' JIM, by Charles
    Clark, review by Edward T. LeBlanc,
    390-30
(AMERICAN BOY), Hess Collection
    acquires complete set, news item,
    515-120
(AMERICAN BOY), comments in letter
    from Louise Harris, 516-150
American Indian, or Whose Top Is He
    Blowing Now, The, by Nameless Joe,
    (reminiscences), 217-73
(AMERICAN INDIAN SERIES, Arthur West-
    brook Co.), Dime Novel Sketches
    #84, 411-127
(AMERICAN INDIAN WEEKLY), Dime Novel
    Sketches #65, 392-43
AMERICAN INDIAN WEEKLY, photo article,
    262-49
(AMERICAN LIBRARY, THE), Dime Novel
    Sketches #122, 449-13
(American News Company), Edward S.
    Ellis Stories Published by the
    Mershon Complex, by Denis R. Rogers,
    490-70; 491-86; 492-104
(American News Company), Sinclair
    Tousey, President, American News
    Co. (biographical sketch), 344-60
AMERICAN NOVELS (Wm. H. Chaney), 42-3
(American Revolution), The Anatomy of
    Dime Novels, No.7: Novels of the
    American Revolution, by J. Edward
    Leithead, 418-64; 419-76
(American Revolution), The Anatomy of
    Dime Novels, No.17: Frontier and
    Revolutionary War Stories That
    Missed "Pluck and Luck", by J.
    Edward Leithead, 446-110; 447-122
(AMERICAN TALES, 2nd series), Dime
    Novel Sketches #181, 509-9
AMERICAN UNION, THE, 144-3; 175-25
(Amy, George A.), A Fragment on George
    A. Amy, Illustrator for YOUNG SPORTS,
    by Stanley A. Pachon, 371-76
An Artist Recalls Nickel Novel Days
    (Charles L. Wrenn), by J. Edward
    Leithead, 87-1
An Interview with Jesse James, by P.J.
    Moran, 191-66
An Oddity (Beadles Half Dime Library
    No.5), by "Seajay," 96-2
An Open Letter on the Writers of
    GOLDEN HOURS, by Willis E. Hurd,
    130-1
An Open Letter to Mr. Flaum (dime
    novel reminiscences) by Harold C.
    Holmes, 178-51

An Overlooked Alger Weekly (STAR STORIES),
    by Stanley A. Pachon, 498-30
Anatomy of Dime Novels, The, by J. Edward
    Leithead:
    No.1, Nick Carter, 384-76; 385-85
    No.2, Buffalo Bill, 389-10; 390-22
    No.3, Railroading, 398-114; 399-126
    No.4, Spanish-American War Novels,
        402-24; 403-36
    No.5, The Firefighters, 407-74; 408-86
    No.6, Kit Carson, 413-14; 414-14
    No.7, Novels of the American Revo-
        lution, 418-64; 419-76
    No.8, Civil War Novels, 422-106; 423-114
    No.9, Wall Street Stories, 427-34;
        428-44
    No.10, The Arthur Westbrook Company,
        429-56; 430-68
    No.11, Bootblack Detectives, 431-78
    No.12, Novels of the Circus, 432-88;
        433-96
    No.13, Temperance Stories, 434-108;
        435-118
    No.14, West Point and Annapolis Stories,
        437-18; 438-30
    No.15, Stories of World Wide Adventure,
        440-42; 441-50
    No.16, Stories of the Klondike Gold
        Rush, 443-76; 444-88
    No.17, Frontier and Revolutionary War
        Stories That Missed "Pluck and Luck"
        446-110; 447-122
    No.18, The Alamo and The Mexican War,
        450-24
    No.19, Stories of Boarding School and
        College Sports, 454-72; 455-80
    No.20, Stories of the Stage, 458-112;
        459-120
    No.21, Stories of Polar Exploration,
        461-14; 462-24
Anderson, David: Thinking About Popular
    Literature= The Example of the Dime
    Novel (response to J. Randolph Cox'
    The Detective-Hero in the American Dime
    Novel), 547-13
(Annapolis stories), The Anatomy of the
    Dime Novel, No.14, West Point and Anna-
    polis Stories, by J. Edward Leithead,
    437-18; 438-30
(ANNIE OAKLEY OF THE WILD WEST, by Walter
    Havighurst), review, 266-66
(anon.), Buckskin Bill Rides Again Down the
    Dime Novel Trail (verse), 423-119
(anon.), How I Got Acquainted with the Dime
    Novel (reminiscences), 52-8
(anon.), We Plead Guilty, Its the War (on
    dime novel collectors), 108-3
Another Old Timer of the West Passes On:
    Maj. Gordon Lillie (Pawnee Bill), by
    Edwin Brooks, 114-9
Any You Boys Met George French? (biog.
    sketch), by Charles Duprez, 338-89
Applause Column in TIP TOP WEEKLY, The, by
    J.P.Guinon, 328-2
(Appleseed, Johnny), A Librarian Who Un-
    earthed History (Florence E. Wheeler),by
    Nicholas Zook, 224-38

(Appleton, Victor), The Publication History of Tom Swift (boys' series books by Appleton, with bibliographic checklist), by William R. Gowan, 536-22

(Appleton, Victor), Shopton, Home of the Swifts (Tom Swift series locale), by John T. Dizer, Jr., 449-14

(Appleton, Victor), Stratemeyer and Science Fiction - The Swifts (science fiction aspects of Tom Swift series of boys' books), by John T. Dizer, Jr., 520-73

(Appleton, Victor, II) Tom Swift, Jr., (boys' series books, bibliography, checklist), by William R. Gowan, 538-56

(ARGOSY), GOLDEN ARGOSY, by Stanley A. Pachon, 382-58; 383-69

Arietta: Heroine of Wild West Trails (dime novel heroines), by J. Edward Leithead, 367-32

(Arlington, Chester), The Admirable Arlington, (dime novel villain), by J.P.Guinon, 70-1; 71-5

Armbruster, J.H.: A Dime Novel Graduate, (reminiscences), 77-1

Armbruster, J.H.: A Two-Gun Bluff (dime novel reminiscences), 255-94

Armbruster, J.H.: A Yankee Hater - A Regular Dime Novel Story (dime novel style fiction), 221-9

Armbruster, J.H.: Early Bicycling Days, (reminiscences), 260-34; 261-45

Armbruster, J.H.: Hospitality on the Range (reminiscences), 243-90

Armbruster, J.H.: Soapy Smith ("cheap imitation of a dime novel hero"), 86-2

Armbruster, J.H.: Western Pioneer Days, (reminiscences), 132-2

Armbruster, J.H.: When the Mounties Did Not Get Their Man - a Real Dime Novel Story, 107-1

(Armbruster, J.H.), Obituary, 308-36

(ARMY AND NAVY LIBRARY), Dime Novel Sketches #124, 451-39

(ARMY AND NAVY WEEKLY), Dime Novel Sketches #55, 380-39

ARMY AND NAVY WEEKLY, 148-5; 402-24

(Arnold, Maj. Henry), Bill Bruce Books Background (Bill Bruce boys' series by Arnold), by Julius F. Chenu, 474-41

Art of Repairing Novels, The, by George T. Flaum, 211-25

Art of Robert Emmett Owen, The, (cover artist, dime novels), by J. Edward Leithead, 421-94

At Long Last - The Real Buffalo Bill Cody (review of THE LIVES AND LEGENDS OF BUFFALO BILL by Don Russell), by J. Edward Leithead, 340-2

Austin, Charles, 178-52

Austin Collection and Exhibit of Extra-ordinary (dime novels), by Robert H. Smeltzer, 41-1

Author and Artist of the Street & Smith Staff: W. Bert Foster and Charles L. Wrenn, by J. Edward Leithead, 361-92; 362-99; 363-110

Author Who Lived What He Wrote, The (Ned Buntline), by John Hix, 77-4

Authors of Old Weeklies, by Joe Gantner, 136-1

(authors), Concerning Old Authors, 109-5

(aviation, juvenile series), Notes on World Syndicate Juvenile Aviation Fiction (various series), by Rick Crandall, 552-124

(aviation stories), Early Juvenile Aviation Fiction (boys' books, various), by Rick Crandall, 545-82

BAD BOYS PAPER, THE, by W.O.G.Lofts, 313-134

(Badger, Joseph E., Jr.), Wedding Bells for J.E.Badger,Jr., (news item), 30-1

Bales, Jack: Charles Pierce Burton, The Father of the Bob's Hill Boys (boys' series, scouting background), 541-2

Bales, Jack: letter of comment, 517-30; 543-58

Bales, Jack: The Newsboys Lodging House, Impetus for an Immortal (Horatio Alger association item), 521-116

Bales, Jack: Standard Library Reference Books for the Book Collector, 504-112

(Bales, Jack, and Gary Scharnhorst: HORATIO ALGER, JR., AN ANNOTATED BIBLIO-GRAPHY OF COMMENT AND CRITICISM), review by John T. Dizer, Jr., 550-74

Ball, John P.: letter of comment, 380-44; 394-72; 425-19

Ballad of Dead Dime Novels (verse), 135-5

Ballad of Dime Novels (verse), by George S. Barton, 86-5

(Ballou, Maturin Murray), Checklist of Published works, 25-3

Ballou, Maturin Murray (publisher), 17-2; 18-4; 19-2; 23-4

Bandit Brothers of Old Missouri (James & Younger gangs), by J. Edward Leithead, 276-70

Bandit on the Stand: Frank James Giving Testimony, 326-94

Bang! Bang! Bang! (reminiscences), by "Frisco Bert," 251-60

(Banta, Deane), Obituary, 497-25

(BAKER STREET JOURNAL), Odds and Ends - Sherlock Holmes, by W.B. McCafferty, 216-70

Barney, Ralph T.: letter of comment, 367-38

(Barr, Amelia E.), Favorites of Yesterday, Amelia E. Barr (author), by Hermon Pitcher, 326-95

Barred by the Post Office (ESQUIRE ruled as obscene, and other postal regulations), by Ralph P. Smith, 145-1

Barrett, Jean: Prize Novelist John T. McIntyre Rises to Defense of Pot-Boilers, 93-1

Barry, Beatrice: Did Mottern Commit
  Murder from Reading Dime Novels?
  (explores link of popular fiction
  to social scene), 204-73
Barton, George S.: Ballad of Dime
  Novels, (verse), 86-5
Barton, George S.: letter of comment,
  92-2
(baseball), Boston Pitcher Threw Double-
  Shoot in Game Against Baltimore in
  '96, by Burt L. Standish, 165-2
(Beadle publications), A Complete File
  of the STAR JOURNAL, 217-75
(Beadle publications), Ages of Beadle
  Authors, by Albert Johannsen, 212-39
(Beadle publications), Alfred D. Hynes,
  Beadle and Munro author, by Denis R.
  Rogers, 386-94
(Beadle publications), The Buffalo Bill
  Stories Published by Beadle, 123-2
(Beadle publications), Early Adventures
  with the House of Beadle, by Roland
  D. Sawyer, 45-2
(Beadle publications), The Forgotten Men
  of the House of Beadle, 141-3
(Beadle publications), Hon. William
  Adams Brodribb, Beadle author, by
  Denis R. Rogers, 353-12
Beadle & Adams, 172-2; 280-5
(Beadle & Adams), Beadles in England
  (London publications of Beadle & Co.)
  by Denis R. Rogers, with checklist,
  496-2; 497-14; 498-33
(Beadle & Adams), 98 William Street in
  1872, by "Deadwood Dick, Jr. (pseud.
  of Orville J. Victor), 14-4
Beadle and His Wooden Types (wood print
  fonts), by John C. Kunzog, 169-1
Beadle Brothers, The (Erastus and Irwin
  Beadle), by John C. Kunzog, 415-34
Beadle, Erastus F., 14-4; 68-7
(Beadle, Erastus), Beadle and His Wooden
  Types (wood type fonts), 169-1
(Beadle, Erastus), The Beadle Brothers,
  by John C. Kunzog, 415-34; 416-46
(Beadle, Erastus), Blunder and Thunder
  Novels for Boys, by M. Bertrand
  Couch, 68-7
(Beadle, Irwin), The Beadle Brothers,
  by John C. Kunzog, 415-34; 416-46
Beadle Reprints in Iver's and Westbrooks's
  Deadwood Dick and Frontier Novels,
  by Albert Johannsen, 123-6
(BEADLES AMERICAN LIBRARY), Dime Novel
  Sketches #26, 349-104
(BEADLES BOYS LIBRARY), Dime Novel
  Sketches #78, 404-57
(BEADLES BOYS LIBRARY), Those Iver's
  Reprints of "Beadles Boys Library,"
  by Willis E. Hurd, 37-1
(BEADLES CLASSIC STORIES), Dime Novel
  Sketches #163, 491-85
BEADLES DIME BIOGRAPHICAL LIBRARY,
  Checklist, 542-40
(BEADLES DIME BIOGRAPHICAL LIBRARY),
  Dime Novel Sketches #214, 542-33
BEADLES DIME CLASSICS STORIES, 114-13

(BEADLES DIME FICTION), Dime Novel Sketches
  #177, 505-117
BEADLES DIME LIBRARY, 240-66
BEADLES DIME LIBRARY No.517, by W. M.
  Burns, 104-1
BEADLES DIME LIBRARY, Dime Novel Sketches
  #97, 424-1
(BEADLES BOYS LIBRARY, Octavo edn.), Dime
  Novel Sketches #107, 434-107
BEADLES DIME LIBRARY OF CHOICE FICTION,
  118-5
Beadle's Dime Novel, The, (verse), by
  Stuart Close, 20-3
BEADLES DIME NOVELS, 119-6
(BEADLES DIME NOVELS), A Sensation of the
  '60's, 38-4
(BEADLES DIME NOVELS), Dime Novel Sketches
  #123, 450-23
(BEADLES DIME TALES), Dime Novel Sketches
  #184, 512-37
(BEADLES 15¢ NOVELS), Dime Novel Sketches
  #165, 493-113
BEADLES FRONTIER SERIES, by Denis R.
  Rogers, 507-136
(BEADLES FRONTIER SERIES), Dime Novel
  Sketches #31, 354-19
BEADLES HALF-DIME LIBRARY, 63-1
(BEADLES HALF-DIME LIBRARY), Boy Detectives
  by J. Edward Leithead, 240-66
(BEADLES HALF-DIME LIBRARY), Dime Novel
  Sketches #93, 420-85
(BEADLES HALF DIME LIBRARY), My Collection
  of "Beadles Half Dime Library" by
  W. M. Burns, 174-1
(BEADLES HALF DIME LIBRARY, No.5), An
  Oddity, by "Seajay," 96-2
(BEADLES HALF DIME LIBRARY, no.1090),142-4
BEADLES HALF DIME NOVELETTE, 113-9
BEADLES MONTHLY, THE, by Roland D. Sawyer,
  163-2
BEADLES NEW DIME NOVELS, Dime Novel Sketche
  #148, 475-45
(BEADLES POCKET LIBRARY), Dime Novel
  Sketches #102, 429-55
BEADLES POCKET LIBRARY, Reprint of BEADLES
  BOYS LIBRARY, by Deadwood Dick, Jr.,
  117-3
BEADLES POCKET NOVELS, 119-6
(BEADLES POCKET NOVELS), Dime Novel Sketche
  #150, 477-63
(BEADLES POPULAR LIBRARY), Dime Novel
  Sketches #109, 436-1
Beadles STANDARD LIBRARY OF ROMANCE, by
  Roland D. Sawyer, 296-41
(BEADLE & ADAMS 20 CENT NOVELS), Dime Novel
  Sketches #146, 473-17
Beadles Abroad (foreign language editions
  of Beadles novels), by Denis R. Rogers,
  347-86; 348-96
Beadles in England (London publications of
  Beadle & Co.), with checklist, by Denis
  R. Rogers, 497-14; 498-33
Beck, William L.: A Note on D.W.Stevens
  (author), 12-4
Beck, William L.: Norman L. Munro, Publishe
  26-1
Beddow, M.S.: letter of comment, 369-58

(Beeton Publications), Old Boys' Magazines and Journals, by Frank Jay, 109-1

Believe It or Not, an Eye Opener (visit with Lurana Sheldon, dime novel author), by George French, 193-84

Bender, Stewart H.V.: My First Novel (reminiscences on reading dime novels), 53-2

Bender, Stewart H.V.: What I Know About Assorted Novels (dime novel comments), 54-1

Bengis, Nat: review of JULES VERNE, THE BIOGRAPHY OF AN IMAGINATION by George H. Waltz, Jr., 158-1

Benners, B.: Novelist Fooled by Innocent Face (author John T. McIntyre), 71-2

Benners, William J.: The Bertha M. Clay Mystery Cleared Up (identity of author as William J. Benners), 95-3

Benners, William J.: Fortunes Left by British Writers (dime novelists), 81-5

(Benners, William J.), $446,000 Estate Left (obituary), 98-6

Benners, William J.: The Golden Age of English Boys Literature, 14-2; 15-5; 16-4

Benners, William J.: Nick Carter? Let 'em Read It, Says Scientist (social significance), 74-1

Benners, William J.: Notice to Our Readers (on Edwin J. Brett and BOYS OF ENGLAND storypaper), 80-1

Benners, William J.: One Road to Heaven, (dime novel style fiction), 100-4

Benners, William J.: William Benner Says (re: Bracebridge Hemyng), 74-3

(Benners, William James, Jr.), In Memorial to, 151-1

(Benners, William J.) William J. Benners, The First Historian of the Dime Novel, by Ralph Adimari, 312-121

(Benners, William J.), The William J. Benners Pseudonyms, by Ralph Adimari, 317-14

(Benners, William James, Jr.), William James Benners, Jr., by E. Burke Collins (tribute), 108-1

(Bennett, Arnold), obituary, 5-8

Bennett, W.E.: A Lurid Record (on collecting dime novels), 60-1

Benson, T.R.: letter of comment, 389-90

Bertha M. Clay Mystery Cleared Up, The, (identity of author as Wm. J. Benners) 95-3

(bibliographical essay), Horatio Alger, Jr., by Marjorie Heins, 506-131

(bibliography), NEW BUFFALO BILL WEEKLY, by J. Edward Leithead, 452-SS

(bibliography), NEW NICK CARTER WEEKLY, by J. Randolph Cox, 516-SS

(bibliography), THE NEW SENSATION (and THE SPORTING NEW YORKER), by Ross Crawford, 521-SS

(bibliography), NICK CARTER LIBRARY, by J. Randolph Cox, 502-SS

(bibliography), NICK CARTER STORIES and Other Series Containing Stories about Nick Carter, by J. Randolph Cox, 526-SS (Pt.1); 542-SS (Pt.2)

(bibliography), OUR BOYS and NEW NEW YORK BOYS WEEKLY: The Great Tousey-Munro Rivalry, by Ross Crauford, 535-SS

(bibliography), ROUGH RIDER WEEKLY and TED STRONG SAGA, by J. Edward Leithead and Edward T. LeBlanc, 478-SS

(bibliography), TIP TOP WEEKLY, by Robert McDowell, 532-SS

(bibliography - see also "Checklists")

Bibliographical Reflections (research in the story papers and dime novels), by Denis R. Rogers, 509-10; 510-17

Bibliography of Custer Dime Novels (General Custer stories) by Brian W. Dippie and Edward T. LeBlanc, 442-66

(bibliography), Oddities of Dime Novel Days (bibliographical mystery items), by Denis R. Rogers, 526-85

(bibliography) Recently Published Articles Concerning Dime Novels and Boys' Book Collecting, 381-52; 390-30; 392-51; 395-84; 402-30; 408-90; 409-109; 412-11; 413-20; 415-43; 416-51; 425-22; 427-40; 428-50; 429-64; 430-76; 431-82; 432-94; 435-125; 437-27; 438-46; 441-63; 443-85; 447-131; 448-4; 449-21; 451-46; 452-57; 453-68; 454-75; 455-89; 457-106; 459-126; 461-19; 463-41; 465-58; 467-86; 469-119; 470-136; 472-16; 473-31; 474-43; 475-52; 477-69; 479-74; 480-92; 482-116; 483-117; 485-24; 486-38; 489-66; 490-76; 500-60; 502-88; 505-126; 507-139; 508-6; 509-14; 511-33; 514-85; 515-121; 517-26; 518-53; 519-65; 520-96; 521-124; 522-143; 523-21; 525-72; 526-91; 528-133; 529-28; 530-49; 531-75; 532-93; 533-110; 534-124; 535-10d; 536-35;537-46; 538-68; 540-97; 542-43; 543-59; 544-74; 545-86; 547-21; 549-65

(bicycling), Early Bicycling Days (reminiscences), by J.H. Armbruster, 261-45

Bill Bruce Books Background (discussion of Bill Bruce boys' books written by Maj. Henry Arnold), by Julius R. Chenu, 474-41

(Billy the Kid) Claim He is Still Alive, by Ralph F. Cummings, 219-89

(Billy the Kid) The Last Days of Billy the Kid, by J.P. Guinon, 104-6

(Billy the Kid) Movies Checklist, by Arthur N. Carter, 520-93

(Billy the Kid) The Photo of Billy the Kid, by W.B.McCafferty, 2-4

(Billy the Kid), Wyoming's Wild Riders and Other Hunted Men (in dime novels), by J. Edward Leithead, 294-20

Biographical Data (Mrs. Alex. McVeigh Miller, dime novel author), 114-7

Biographical Mysteries of George Alfred Henty (biog. essay), by W.O.G.Lofts, 524-44

Biographical Sketches of Famous
Frontiersmen, by Clyde F. Wake-
field:
Kit Carson, 158-3
James Bridger, 160-4
James Butler (Wild Bill) Hickock,
161-4
Biographies of Pioneers, by Arlie
Kinkade:
Col. Daniel Boone, 2-1
Col. David Crockett, 3-4
Biography of Lu Senarens (author and
editor who used pseudonym "Noname")
114-10
Bird, Robert Montgomery, 15-2
Bisch, Louis E.: The Value of Friend-
Ship (essay), 161-1
Bischoff, Murray: letter of comment,
548-41
"Bits" Regarding Dime Novels, by Harold
C. Holmes, 81A-11
BLACK BESS SERIES, 25-8
(BLACK HIGHWAYMAN NOVELS, THE), Dime
Novel Sketches #154, 482-111
BLACK HIGHWAYMAN NOVELS, THE, sketch,
2-3
(Blake, Sexton), British detective,
reference to article in SAINT
MAGAZINE, 395-84
(Blake, Sexton, Detective), Exit
UNION JACK (demise of British
storypaper), by William M. Burns,
17-5
(Blake, Sexton, Detective), Jeff
Clayton - Sexton Blake, or Another
Mystery Solved (Jeff Clayton dime
novel detective in Arthur Westbrook
paperbacks, and Sexton Blake) by
J. Edward Leithead, 449-21
(Blake, Sexton, Detective), Nick Carter
in Another Man's Shoes, by J.Edward
Leithead, 350-112; 351-120
(Blake, Sexton, Detective(, Sexton
Blake, by W.O.G.Lofts (discussion),
439-40
Bleiler, E.F.: A Lost Novel by G.W.M.
Reynolds? (speculation on THE GIPSEY
CHIEF, dime novel), 499-38
Bleiler, E.F.: letter of comment,
527-115; 537-47
Blood and Thunder Novels for Boys (dime
novels), by M. Bertrand Couch, 68-1
Blood and Thunder Novels of the Gay
Nineties Period, by "Frisco Bert,"
105-1
Blood-and-Thunder Novels Were Well
Liked in Last Century (discussion),
by William Sidney Hillyer, 165-2
BLUE AND GREY WEEKLY, 54-2
(BLUE AND GREY WEEKLY), Dime Novel
Sketches #17, 337-81
BLUE DWARF, 165-3
(BOB BROOKS LIBRARY), Dime Novel
Sketches #89, 416-45
(Bob's Hill Boys series), Charles
Pierce Burton, The Father of
the Bob's Hill Boys (boy's scouting
series of books), by Jack Bales,
541-2

(Bonaparte, Napoleon), Unfinished Novel
by Napoleon Published, 92-5
(book dealers), Willard Thompson, Book
Dealer (sketch), by John Guernsey,
480-90
Book Hunting with Reckless (collecting
adventures with Ralph Cummings), by
Eli A. Messier, 73-9
Book I Had the Hardest Time Finding, The,
(comments of various collectors in
boy's book field), by Jack R. Schorr,
444-95
(book prices), In Defense of Listing
Current Alger Values (discussion on
values and scarcity), by Ralph D.
Gardner, 472-2
(book prices), Used Book Prices (essay
on values of books and why), by Denis
R. Rogers, 469-114
Booklet Novels versus Black & Whites
(pocket size vs. dime novel size), by
Ralph Cummings, 52-1
Books for the Campfire: The Redpath Novels,
by Roland D. Sawyer, 198-20
Books He Remembers (reading reminiscences),
by A. Jay See, 186-2
Books of William Heyliger (boys' series
books by Heyliger), by Bob Chenu,
519-62
(Books), The Cobwebbed Bookshelf (books
reviewed in journal that are still
available), by Michael L. Cook, 551-104
(Books), Well, What Have You?, (old book
collecting), by U.G.Figley, 148-2
(Boone, Daniel), Biographies of Pioneers,
Col. Daniel Boone, by Arlie Kinkade,
2-1
(Boone, Daniel), Buckskin Men of Forest
and Plain, by J. Edward Leithead,
246-18; 248-33; 249-43; 250-50; 253-74;
254-86
(Boone, Daniel), Movies, Checklist, by
Arthur N. Carter, 520-93
BORDER BOYS LIBRARY, 413-16
(BORDER BOYS LIBRARY), Dime Novel Sketches
#96, 423-113
Boston Pitcher Threw Double-Shoot in Game
Against Baltimore in '96 (baseball
reminiscences), by Burt L. Standish,
165-2
BOUND-TO-WIN LIBRARY, 50-3; 115-3
(BOUND TO WIN LIBRARY), Dime Novel Sketches
#222, 550-73
Bowery Bill's Our Oyster Now (comments on
BOWERY BOYS LIBRARY dime novels), by
"Nameless Joe," 202-57
BOWERY BOYS LIBRARY, 241-76
(BOWERY BOYS LIBRARY), Bowery Billy's Our
Oyster Now, (comments on dime novel),
by "Nameless Joe," 202-57
(BOWERY BOYS LIBRARY), Dime Novel Sketches
#12, 331-33
Boxes L-179 and L-180, (Publishing records
of Street & Smith), by J. Randolph Cox,
551-94
Boy Actor, Author and Dramatist: Master
T.W.Hanshew (biog. sketch), 137-1
Boy Avenger, The, (fiction), by H. O.
Rawson, 126-1

Boy Detectives, (in dime novels), by
J. Edward Leithead, 240-66; 241-74;
242-85
BOY PARTNERS, An Edward Edson Lee
Publication, (index and summary of
periodical), by Willis J. Potthoff,
550-83
Boy Scout Series Book Mess, (discussion
of various boys' books pertaining
to scouting background), by Bob
Chenu, 486-34
Boy Scouts in a Great Tangle, or
Unraveling the Saalfield Puzzle
(Boy Scout boys' series books),by
Bob Chenu, 499-42; 505-124
(Boyd, Felix, detective), Half Nick
Carter and Half Sherlock Holmes
(Felix Boyd stories in THE POPULAR
MAGAZINE), by Robert Sampson,552-118
Boyhood Heroes, (reminiscences), by
Don Buchan, 422-110
BOYS AND GIRLS PENNY MAGAZINE, 277-84
(BOYS BEST WEEKLY), Dime Novel Sketches
#77, 404-47
(BOYS BEST WEEKLY), Memories of BOYS
BEST WEEKLY, (discussion), by Howard
B. Silsbee, 311-116
Boys' Book First Editions, (difficulty
in determining first printings), by
Harry K. Hudson, 525-71
(boys' books), A Book Grabber's Gripes,
(on collecting), by Jack R. Schorr,
475-50
(boys' books), A Few of the Less Known
Series, by Jack Schorr, 464-47
(boys' books), A Few of the Non-Series
Books, by Jack Schorr, 467-85
(boys' books), A Half Century of the
Hardy Boys, or Clues to an Obscure
Chronology, (bibliography of the
Hardy Boys boys' series of Franklin
W. Dixon), by Robert V. Riordan,
530-35
(boys' books), A New and Interesting
Phantom Title, (discusses boys'
series books announced but not
published), by Harry K. Hudson,
537-47
(boys' books), A Publication Pattern
of Edward S. Ellis (study of the
Porter & Coates/Henry T.Coates/
John C.Winston editions by Ellis),
by Denis R. Rogers and J. Edward
Leithead, 480-80; 481-95
(boys' books), A Sketch of Hezekiah
Butterworth (author of early boys'
books), by Jack Schorr, 539-77
(boys' books), A Vacation Trip 1973,
(collecting adventures), by Jack
Schorr, 495-137
(boys' books), Ah, Those Golden Years,
(collecting experiences), by Jack
Schorr, 508-5
(boys' books), Ben Lightbody series -
Question and Comments on Existence,
514-84

(boys' books), The Book I had the Hardest
Time Finding (experiences by various
collectors), by Jack R. Schorr, 444-95
(boys' books), Books of William Heyliger,
(discussion), by Bob Chenu, 519-62
(boys' books), The Boy Scout Series Book
Mess (various Boy Scout series), by
Bob Chenu, 486-34
(boys' books), Boy Scouts in a Great
Tangle, or Unraveling the Saalfield
Puzzle (Boy Scouts boy's book series)
by Bob Chenu, 499-42; 505-124
(boys' books), Boys Books and the American
Dream, (influence), by John T/ Dizer,
Jr., 425-12; 426-29. See also 427-42
(boys' books), Boys' Book First Editions,
(difficulty in determing first printings)
by Harry K. Hudson, 525-71
(boys' books), Browsing Around, (collecting
experiences), by Jack R. Schorr, 473-23
(boys' books), Censorship and Early Adolescent Literature: Stratemeyer, Mathiews
and Comstock, (attempts to discredit
Stratemeyer), by Ken Donelson, 534-119
(boys' books), Changes by author to A BIBLIO-
GRAPHY OF HARD-COVER BOYS' BOOKS, REV.
EDN., by Harry K. Hudson (revisions by
author), 529-31; 531-78; 532-89; 539-82
(boys' books), Charles Pierce Burton: The
Father of the Bob's Hill Boys, (Bob's
Hill Boys series of boys' books), by Jack
Bales, 541-2
(boys' books), Chronological Listing of
Boys Books by Edward Stratemeyer First
Published as Serials, by John T. Dizer,
Jr., 515-118
(boys' books), Disposing of Your Collection,
(problems encountered), by Jack Schorr,
503-103
(boys' books), Displaying One's Collection,
(on the collection of Willis Potthoff),
by Edward T. LeBlanc, 518-46
(boys' books), Displaying Your Collection,
(methods and ideas), by Jack R. Schorr,
465-57
(boys' books), Early Juvenile Aviation
Fiction, by Rick Crandall, 545-82
(boys' books), Edward Stratemeyer's Appeal
to Contemporary Young Readers, by Peter
C. Walther, 535-2
(boys' books), Ellis' Ten War Chief Tales
(hardbound Indian Chief novels by Edward
S. Ellis), by Denis R. Rogers, 539-74
(boys' books), The Elusives, (hard-to-find
boys' books), by Jack Schorr, 494-130
(boys' books), Exasperations of a Book
Collector, (collecting experiences), by
Jack R. Schorr, 448-2
(boys' books), The First Tom Slade Book, or
Movies to Print, (Tom Slade, Boy Scout
series books), by Julius R. Chenu, 514-83
(boys' books), 4500 - All Mint, (collection
and experiences of Jack R. Schorr),
469-118

(boys' books), From Boxes to Shelves, or How to Know What You Have (collecting boys' books), by Jack R. Schorr, 479-76

(boys' books), G & D Every Boys Library Boy Scout Editions (Grosset & Dunlap boys' series Boy Scout books), by Bob Chenu, 536-33

(boys' books), Garden City Publishing Company's Paperback Juveniles, by Bob Chenu, 531-72

(boys' books), Going, Going, Gone, (boys' books becoming scarce), by Jack R. Schorr, 488-56

(boys' books), H. Irving Hancock: A Romanticized View of Sports and Boys, by Ken Donelson, 522-138

(boys' books), Hard Ones to Find - Do They Really Exist? (scarce or non-existent boys' series books) by Bob Chenu, 468-107

(boys' books), The Hard-Cover Merriwells (hardbound Merriwell series), by Harry K. Hudson, with checklist, 541-15

(boys' books), Harrie Irving Hancock's Boys Series Books (discussion with checklist), by Bob Chenu, 538-64

(boys' books), Hybrids, Oddities and Freaks, (variations in editions of dime novels and boys' series books), by Denis R. Rogers, 475-46, 476-56

(boys' books), Jack Straw Series - Question and Comments on Existence, 514-84

(boys' books), Land of the Heroes (boys' books series locales), by John T. Dizer, 465-52, 465-62

(boys' books), The Lawrenceville Series by Owen Johnson, (boys' sport series) by Bob Chenu, 517-11

(boys' books), Magazine Serial and Book Relationships in Leo Edwards Books (discussion), by Bob Chenu, 534-122

(boys' books), The Most Popular Boys Series of Books, (various series discussed), by Bob Chenu, 540-98

(boys' books), News Note from the University of Missouri, by D. C. Dickinson, 437-26

(boys' books), Notes on World Syndicate Juvenile Aviation Fiction (various series), by Rick Crandall, 552-124

(boys' series), Now They're Collectors Items, by J. Edward Leithead,
#1: Edward S. Ellis and Harry Castlemon, 405-58; 406-66
#2: Optic, Otis, Tomlinson, Stoddard and McNeil, 411-128
#3: Stratemeyer, Munroe, Graydon, Henty, Rathborne, Sabin, Altshelter, 417-54
#4: Various authors, 420-86

(boys' books), Old Time Boys' Books, by J. Edward Leithead (discusses the older books and series), 227-58; 228-69; 231-91; 233-11; 234-22; 236-35; 238-55; 239-61

(boys' books), Optics Serials as Books, (Oliver Optic), by J. R. Chenu, 518-50

(boys' books), Paperbacks, Dime Novels and the Virtues of Reading Series Books, by Jack Dizer, 483-122

(boys' books), Poisoning Your Child (former attitude and criticism against boys' books), by Gil O'Gara, 540-91; 541-8

(boys' books), Promises, Promises, Promises, (mentions of future books in boys' series books advertising), by Ken Donelson, 550-77

(boys' books), The Publication History of Tom Swift (boys' series by Victor Appleton, with bibliographic checklist), by William R. Gowan, 536-22

(boys' books), The Rolt-Wheeler/Gilbreth Letters (correspondence between Francis Rolt-Wheeler, boys' book author, and Lillian M. Gilbreth, with checklist of Rolt-Wheeler books), by John T. Dizer, Jr., 500-56

(boys' books), Scout Master G. Harvey Ralphson's Triplets (Boy Scouts series books pub. by Donohue Co.), with checklist, by Bob Chenu, 498-32

(boys' books), Serials and Boys Books by Edward Stratemeyer, by John T. Dizer, Jr. 516-126

(boys' books), Shopton, Home of the Swifts, (locale of Tom Swift books discovered), by John T. Dizer, Jr., 449-14

(boys' books), Some of the Boys' Books from Britain, 471-150

(boys' books), Stoddard, Saltillo Boys and Syracuse, (W.O.Stoddard and his books for boys), by John T/ Dizer, Jr., 490-77

(boys' books), Stratemeyer and Science Fiction (early science fiction and Tom Swift; Stratemeyer's role), by John T. Dizer, Jr., 514-66; 520-73

(boys' books), Stratemeyer and the Blacks, (attitude toward and treatment of Blacks by the Stratemeyer Syndicate), by John T. Dizer, Jr., 515-90

(boys' books), Tom Swift, Jr., (later Tom Swift series by "Victor Appleton II" with bibliography and checklist), by William R. Gowan, 538-56

(boys' books), Travels of a Book Collector, (collecting adventures), by H.W.Miller, 483-121

(boys' books), Travels of a Book Collector (collecting adventures), by Jack R. Schorr, 483-120

(boys' books), Two Boys' Books Writers from Wisconsin, (Leslie Quirk and Everett McNeil), by Marge Dahl, 494-131

(boys' books), "Wanted: A Hero" (heroes in the boys' series books), 482-112

(boys' books), The Winnetka Graded Book List and Its Supplement (rating childrens books 1924-25), by Deidre Johnson, 549-61

(boys' books), Winning World War I, (exploit of boys' book heroes), by Bob Chenu, 543-50

Boys Books and the American Dream, by
    John T. Dizer, Jr., 425-12; 426-29;
    See also 427-42
BOYS' BOOKS OF ROMANCE AND ADVENTURE,
    Dime Novel Sketches #179, 507-135
Boys Books Written by Capt. F.S. Brereton,
    by William M. Burns, 263-57
BOYS CHAMPION JOURNAL, THE, 13-5; 21-4
BOYS' COMIC JOURNAL, 8-3; 279-104
BOYS COMIC JOURNAL, by W.B.Lawson,
    262-52
(BOYS COMIC JOURNAL), A Partial History
    of the Brett Publications, by Ralph
    Adimari, 368-42
(BOYS FAVORITE, THE), A Partial History
    of the Brett Publications, by Ralph
    Adimari, 368-42
BOY'S FRIEND, 15-4
BOYS HALF HOLIDAY, 13-5; 21-4
BOYS' HERALD, 16-5
(BOY'S HOME LIBRARY), Dime Novel
    Sketches #220, 548-25
(BOY'S HOME WEEKLY), Dime Novel Sketches
    #80, 407-73
BOYS' JOURNAL, 14-2
BOYS JUBILEE JOURNAL, THE, 118-5
BOYS LEADER, 26-2; 58-7; 322-60; 358-72
BOYS LEISURE HOUR, 13-5; 13-7; 21-4
(BOYS LEISURE HOUR), Old English Story
    Papers for Boys: THE BOYS LEISURE
    HOUR, by W. M. Burns, 325-84
BOYS LIBRARY, 147-5
(BOYS LIBRARY), Dime Novel Sketches
    #133, 460-1
BOYS MAGAZINE, 295-30
Boys, Meet Dewey Miller, (biographical
    sketch), by Charles Duprez, 284-33
BOY'S MISCELLANY, 14-2; 15-5
BOY'S MONTHLY MAGAZINE, 15-4
BOYS NOVELIST, THE, (photo article
    and checklist), 247-26
BOYS OF AMERICA, 117-7; 197-11
BOYS OF AMERICA: A Twentieth Century
    Story Paper, (discussion), by
    Ralph F. Cummings, 7-2
(BOYS OF AMERICA), Dime Novel Sketches
    #41, 365-11
BOYS OF ENGLAND WEEKLY, 8-2; 15-5; 16-4;
    59-3; 75-5; 76-1; 80-1; 88-5; 121-6;
    279-103
(BOYS OF ENGLAND), A Famous Old English
    Boys' Journal, (discussion), by
    Henry Steele, 134-1
(BOYS OF ENGLAND), A Partial History of
    the Brett Publications, by Ralph
    Adimari, 368-42
(BOYS OF ENGLAND), Notice To Our Readers,
    (cessation), by William J. Benners,
    80-1
(BOYS OF ENGLAND), Putting Long Trousers
    on the Eighteenth Century (literary
    discussion), by Henry Steele, 8-2
(BOYS OF LONDON), (photo article),
    242-81
BOYS OF THE NATION, THE, 13-6
BOYS OF LONDON AND NEW YORK, 121-7

BOYS OF NEW YORK, 26-2; 30-3; 42-6; 58-7;
    58-8; 88-6; 117-8; 118-3; 147-5; 407-76;
    413-16
BOYS OF NEW YORK, by G.H.Cordier (literary
    discussion), 133-1
Boys of New York, The, (verse), by Ernest
    C. Page, 235-27
(BOYS OF NEW YORK), Dime Novel Sketches
    #62, 389-9
(BOYS OF NEW YORK), Famous Tousey Story
    Papers, (discussion), by Edward T.
    LeBlanc, 508-2
(BOYS OF NEW YORK), Notes by a New York
    Boy, 42-6
(BOYS OF NEW YORK), Old Story Papers #5:
    BOYS OF NEW YORK, (discussion,history),
    by William B. Burns, 306-18; 307-28;
    308-37
BOYS OF NEW YORK POCKET LIBRARY, 58-8
(BOYS OF NEW YORK POCKET LIBRARY), Dime
    Novel Sketches #117, 444-87
BOYS OF NEW YORK WEEKLY, 138-3
BOYS OF THE BRITISH EMPIRE, 8-2; 279-104;
    295-29
(BOYS OF THE EMPIRE), Old English Journals
    for Boys: BOYS OF THE EMPIRE, (history
    and discussion), by W.M.Burns, 321-52;
    322-60
BOYS OF THE ISLES, 313-135
BOYS OF THE NATION, 21-4
BOYS OF THE WORLD, 90-5
(BOYS OF THE WORLD), A Partial History of
    the Brett Publications, by Ralph
    Adimari, 368-42
(BOYS OF THE WORLD), Valedictory, (cessation),
    90-5
BOYS OWN, THE, 73-10
BOYS OWN LIBRARY, by Denis R. Rogers,
    453-60
BOYS OWN LIBRARY, Author's Index, by Denis
    R. Rogers, 453-63
(BOYS OWN LIBRARY), Dime Novel Sketches
    #128, 455-79
BOY'S OWN MAGAZINE, 14-2; 15-4
(BOY'S OWN NOVELS, THE), Dime Novel Sketches
    #155, 483-119
BOYS' OWN READER, 15-5
BOY'S PENNY MAGAZINE, 15-4
BOYS OF 76, 64-2
BOYS STANDARD, THE, 13-5; 16-5; 21-4; 279-103
BOYS' STAR LIBRARY, THE, 3-4; 25-2; 157-4
(BOYS' STAR LIBRARY, THE), Dime Novel
    Sketches #87, 414-23
BOYS' SUNDAY READER, 16-5
BOYS WEEKLY, 58-8
BOYS WEEKLY NOVELETTE, 13-6; 21-4
Boys Who Never Grow Up, (dime novel
    characters), by Arthur T. Rich, 163-1;
    192-75
(BOYS WILL BE BOYS by E.S. Turner), review,
    "The Giants March Past," by J.V.B. Stewart
    Hunter, 197-9
BOYS WONDER, 21-1
BOYS' WORLD, Dime Novel Sketches #45,
    369-49
Bradshaw, Walter H.: letter of comment,
    395-85

(BRADY'S CHAMPION STORIES), Dime Novel
    Sketches #193, 521-105
Brady's Champion Stories, with Check-
    list, by J.C.Dykes, 156-1
BRADY'S MERCURY STORIES, Dime Novel
    Sketches #202, 530-34
BRADY'S MERCURY STORIES, List of
    Titles, 530-49
BRADY'S PEOPLE'S NOVELLETTES, Checklist
    of Titles, 527-115
(BRADY'S PEOPLE'S NOVELLETTES), DIme
    Novel Sketches #199, 527-97
(Braeme, Charlotte M.), World Famous
    Author, by Hermon Pitcher (dime
    novelist), 112-3
Bragin, Charles: Advice to Collectors,
    (dime novel collecting), 245-14;
    342-21; 405-63
Bragin, Charles: Dime Novel Collecting,
    (advice), 365-12; 402-28
Bragin, Charles: Dime Novel Prices
    Hold, (discussion on values), 19-4
Bragin, Charles: Experiences and Thoughts
    on Gilbert Patten (on "Burt Standish"),
    409-107
Bragin, Charles: Francis Worchester
    Doughty, Uncrowned King of the Dime
    Novel Writers (sketch), 44-1
Bragin, Charles: letter of comment,
    372-86; 391-39; 395-86; 396-99;
    401-21; 404-52
Bragin, Charles: Pluck & Luck, (dime
    novel discussion), 25-2
Bragin, Charles: Protect Your Novels,
    (preserving dime novels), 340-7
Bragin, Charles: Voice of the Collector,
    (collecting experiences), 12-3
(Bragin, Charles), obituary, 517-20
(Brand, Max), obituary 143-3
BRAVE AND BOLD WEEKLY, 241-75
(BRAVE AND BOLD WEEKLY), Dime Novel
    Sketches #13, 333-49
(BRAVE AND BOLD WEEKLY), Likes and
    Dislikes in BRAVE AND BOLD, by
    W. M. Burns, 368-45
Brazil Thrilled by Buffalo Bill and
    Nick Carter, (foreign editions),
    2-4
(Brereton, Capt. F.S.), Boys Books
    Written by Capt. F.S.Brereton,
    by William M. Burns, 263-57
(Brereton, Capt. F.S.), Now They're
    Collectors' Items, (boys' series
    books), by J. Edward Leithead,
    420-86
Brett, Edwin J., (publisher, dime
    novels, storypapers),76-1; 80-1
(Brett, Edwin J.), A Partial History
    of the Brett Publications, by
    Ralph Adimari, 368-42
(Brett, Edwin J.), Notice to Our
    American Readers - BOYS OF ENGLAND
    Story Paper, (cessation), by William
    J. Benners, 80-1
(Brett, Edwin J.), The Rival Rangers
    of Fleet Street (British dime novel
    publishing), by A.W.Lawson, 279-102

(Brewer, Don), obituary, 331-37
(Bridger, James), Biographical Sketches of
    Famous Frontiersmen #2 - James Bridger,
    by Clyde Wakefield, 160-4
BRIGHT DAYS, 311-114
(BRIGHT DAYS), Dime Novel Sketches #38,
    361-91
BROADWAY LIBRARY, 42-3
(BROADWAY LIBRARY), Dime Novel Sketches
    #129, 456-91
(Brodribb, William Adams), Hon. William
    Adams Brodribb, Beadle Author (biog.
    sketch), by Denis R. Rogers, 353-12
Brooks, Edwin: Another Old Timer of the
    West Passes On: Maj. Gordon Lillie
    (Pawnee Bill), 114-9
Brooks, Edwin: Chicago Dime Novels (with
    Chicago locales), 108-3
Brooks, Edwin: Scientost Collects Dime
    Novels (collection of Albert
    Johannsen), 82-2; 83-1
BROTHER JONATHAN WEEKLY, 279-102
BROTHER JONATHAN WEEKLY, First Story
    Paper, 17-2
(Brown, Jane), Song Author Died Before
    Its Birth (sketch), 94-3
Brown, Mrs. John W.: letter of comment,
    380-44
Brown, Walter E.: letter of comment,
    382-64; 395-85; 405-62; 453-68
(Browne, G. Waldo), obituary, 6-6
(Browning, Bruce, dime novel character),
    Bruce Browning's Seven Years at Yale
    in TIP TOP WEEKLY, by Gerald J.
    McIntosh, 390-28
Browsing Around, (boys' book collecting),
    by Jack R. Schorr, 473-23
(Bruce, Bill), Bill Bruce Books Background,
    (boys' series books by Maj. Henry
    Arnold), by Julius R. Chenu, 474-41
Bruce Browning's Seven Years at Yale in
    TIP TOP WEEKLY, by Gerald J.McIntosh,
    390-28
Buchan, Don: Boyhood Heroes, (reminiscences)
    422-110
Buchwitz, Lyle J.: letter of comment,
    547-19
("Buckskin"), Identity of Scouts of the
    Wild West using This Name, by C.D.
    Randolph, 245-14
(BUCKSKIN AND SATIN) review of book by
    Herschel C. Logan on Texas Jack,
    266-86; 268-5
Buckskin Bill Gallops Thru the Pages of
    Beadles Dime Novels, (verse), by
    Charles D. Randolph, 457-105
Buckskin Bill Recalls Famous Iowa Neighbors
    and a Trip to Old Missouri (memory of
    Buffalo Bill Cody and the James Gang),
    by J. Edward Leithead, 291-94
Buckskin Bill Rides Again Down the Dime
    Novel Trail, (verse),anonymous,
    423-119
Buckskin Bill Story, The, (Col. Charles
    Daniel Randolph), by J. Edward Leithead,
    270-18

Buckskin Men of Forest and Plain, (biog. sketches), by J. Edward Leithead, 246-18; 248-33; 249-43; 250-50; 253-74; 254-82

(Buckskin Sam), Leominster, Mass. Man Wrote Many Famous Dime Novels (biog.sketch, Samuel Stone Hall), 180-1

Buffalo Bill, by Roland Sawyer, (biog. reminiscences), 66-12

Buffalo Bill and His Pards of the West, (reminiscences), by J. Edward Leithead, 43-1

Buffalo Bill and Ned Buntline (dime novel connections), by Sam E. Conner, 161-1

Buffalo Bill, Hero of Dime Novels, (verse), by Col.Charles D. Randolph, 526-94

Buffalo Bill in Bound Book Fiction, by Don Russell, 320-40

BUFFALO BILL LIBRARY, 195-101

Buffalo Bill, Multi-Storied Border King, (bibliography of storypaper serials and novels), by J. Edward Leithead, 168-2; 171-6; 173-1; 174-18; 175-26

Buffalo Bill Novels in Paperback Book Format, with checklist, by J. Edward Leithead, 201-49

Buffalo Bill Once College President, (news item), 186-3

Buffalo Bill Reprints, by J. Edward Leithead, 342-18; 343-26

Buffalo Bill Slept Here, (reminiscences), by Joseph J. Myler, 388-1

BUFFALO BILL STORIES, 43-2

(BUFFALO BILL STORIES), The Anatomy of Dime Novels, No.2: Buffalo Bill, by J. Edward Leithead, 389-10; 390-22

(BUFFALO BILL STORIES), Buffalo Bill and His Pards of the Old West, by J. Edward Leithead, 43-1

(BUFFALO BILL STORIES), Dime Novel Sketches #29, 352-1

(BUFFALO BILL STORIES), English Reprints of Buffalo Bill Novels, by J.Edward Leithead, 392-44; 393-56

(BUFFALO BILL STORIES), More About the BUFFALO BILL STORIES, by J. Edward Leithead, 58-1

(BUFFALO BILL STORIES), The BUFFALO BILL STORIES Published by Beadle (dime novels), 123-2

(BUFFALO BILL WEEKLY), Colonel Prentiss Ingram, by J. Edward Leithead, 376-1; 377-10

Buffalo Bill's Benevolence, or Col. Cody's Church Dollar (spiritual life of Cody), by Gerald J. McIntosh, 484-2

Buffalo Bill's Birthday, (verse), by Col. Charles D. Randolph, 221-15

Buffalo Bill's Life on the Border, by Paul T. Nolan, 383-68

Buffalo Bill's Wild West Show, (verse), by Buckskin Bill, 247-29

Bullfrog Ben Describes Yreka Jim, (verse), by H.O.Rawson, 157-3

BULLS-EYE, 21-1

Bundza, Daniel: letter of comment, 372-86; 409-108; 456-97

Buntline, Ned, (mention), 15-3; 175-25

(Buntline, Ned), The Author Who Lived What He Wrote, (biog. reminiscences), by John Hix, 77-4

(Buntline, Ned), Buffalo Bill and Ned Buntline, by Sam E. Conner, 161-1

(Buntline, Ned), Facts About the "Two Bills" and Buntline (Wild Bill, Buffalo Bill, and Ned Buntline0, by Roland D. Sawyer, 160-4

(Buntline, Ned), How Ned Buntline Turned from Runaway Boy to Writing Genius: His Relations with Buffalo Bill and the "Know Nothings" by Leon Mead, 101-1

(Buntline, Ned), Ned Buntline's Centenary, by Roland D. Sawyer, 175-26

(Buntline, Ned), Review of THE GREAT RASCAL: THE LIFE AND ADVENTURES OF NED BUNTLINE, by Jay Monaghan; the review by Lewis Gannett, 235-25

Burgess: Gelett: Confessions of a Dime Novelist, (Eugene T. Sawyer, author of many Nick Carter stories), 105-2

(Burleigh, Cecil), Cecil Burleigh, One of the Comic Writers (dime novels), by Ralph Adimari, 296-36

(Burnham, Maj. Frederick Russell), obituary, (Indian scout), 184-3

Burns, William M.: A Plea for Unity, Brotherhood and Cooperation (re: Happy Hours Brotherhood),54-3

Burns, William M.: Beadles Dime Library No.517, (discussed), 104-1

Burns, William M.: Boys Books Written by Capt. F.S.Brereton, 263-57

Burns, William M.: Dime Novels at Last Recognized in High Places, 27-1

Burns, William M.: The Dime Novel Must Go, (wane of the dime novel), 151-3

Burns, William M.: Exit UNION JACK, (cessation), 17-5; 23-1

Burns, William M.: Frank Leslies BOYS OF AMERICA, (historical discussion), 139-1; 141-1; 149-1

Burns, William M.: In Refutation (regards Col. Prentice Ingraham), 177-43

Burns, William M.: Likes and Dislikes in BRAVE AND BOLD, 368-45

Burns, William M.: Likes and Dislikes, Then and Now, (reminiscences), 102-1

Burns, William M.: Long Stories in My Collection (dime novels), 273-47

Burns, William M.: My Collection of Beadles' HALF DIME LIBRARY, 164-1

Burns, William M.: My "Pets" in WIDE AWAKE LIBRARY, 168-1

Burns, William M.: Old English Journals for Boys: ALDINES NEW BOYS PAPER, (historical discussion), 331-34

Burns, William M.: Old English Journals for Boys: THE BOYS LEISURE HOUR, (historical discussion), 325-84

Burns, William M.: Old English Journals for Boys: BOYS OF THE EMPIRE, (historical discussion), 321-52; 322-60

Burns, William M.: Old English Journals for Boys: COMRADES, (historical discussion), 323-66

Burns, William M.: Old English Journals for Boys: Those Special Christmas Issues, (historical discussion), 326-92

Burns, William M.: Our Old Story Papers, (historical discussion)
No.1, ARGOSY, 184-1
No.2, GOLDEN ARGOSY, 185-9
No.3, NEW YORK WEEKLY, 200-37
No.4, HAPPY DAYS, 214-49
No.5, BOYS OF NEW YORK, 306-18; 307-28; 308-37

Burns, William M.: Reckless Ralph and Wild Bill Visit the Grave of General Henry Knox, (travel visit), 170-1

Burns, William M.: Reminiscences in Novelania Past and Present (dime novel reminiscences), 183-96; 189-3; 190-58; 193-82

Burns, William M.: "Strikes" That I Have Made in Noveldom, (collecting finds), 4-1

Burns, William M.: To Collectors of Frank Reade Stories, (dime novels), 322-62

Burns, William M.: Up-to-Date History in HAPPY DAYS, (current events coverage), 302-96

Burns, William M.: The Works of Bracebridge Hemyng, (early author), 152-1; 153-1

(Burns, William M.), Biographical Sketch, by Charles Duprez, 268-4

(Burns, William M.), obituary, 373-101

(Burrage, E. Harcourt), The English Giant, (early author), by Ross Craufurd, 12-2

(Burrows Gang), Wyoming's Wild Riders and Other Hunted Men (in dime novels), by J. Edward Leithead, 294-20

(Burt, A.L., Company, Publishers), Edward S. Ellis Stories Published by the Mershon Complex, by Denis R. Rogers, 490-70; 491-86; 492-104

(Burt, A.L., Company, Publishers), Survey of the Probable Publication Pattern of the Books of Edward S. Ellis under the Imprints of A.L. Burt, by Denis R. Rogers, 524-26

BURT L. STANDISH LIBRARY, 3-5; 271-32

(Burton, Charles Pierce), Charles Pierce Burton: The Father of the Bob's Hill Boys (boys' series Boy Scout books), by Jack Bales, 541-2

Butcher, Stanley E.: letter of comment, 429-64; 448-4

(Butterworth, Hezekiah), A Sketch of Hezekiah Butterworth, (author of early boys' books), by Jack Schorr, 539-77

"By the Author of Buffalo Bill," (notes on var. authors), by J. Edward Leithead, 308-34; 309-42; 310-100

C.H.Forbes-Lindsay, A Famous India Author, (biog. sketch), by Roy B. Van Devier, 386-97; 387-104

Cadbury, Warder: letter of comment, 409-109

(Calamity Jane), Movies: Checklist, by Arthur N. Carter, 520-93

Caldwell, Ray: J.R.Musick, (biog. sketch), 90-4

CAMPFIRE LIBRARY, 42-2

Cap'n Wiley: Maine's Merry Munchausen, (dime novel character discussed), by Frank C. Acker, 494-126

CAPTAIN HERON SERIES OF HIGHWAYMAN TALES, Checklist, 537-46

(CAPTAIN HERON SERIES OF HIGHWAYMAN TALES), Dime Novel Sketches #209, 537-39

Captain Jack: The Relentless Foe of the Dime Novel, (John Wallace Crawford), by Paul T. Nolan, 374-102

Captain Walter Wiley, The Windjammer and the Marine Marvel, or The Terrible and Terrific Teller of Tall Tales in TIP TOP, (dime novel character), by Gerald J. McIntosh, 435-123

Carlay, Carlee: Guerilla, (fiction on Jesse James), 148-3

(Carson, Kit), The Anatomy of Dime Novels No.6: Kit Carson, by J. Edward Leithead, 413-14; 414-24

(Carson, Kit), Biographical Sketches of Famous Frontiersmen: Kit Carson, by Clyde F. Wakefield, 158-3

(Carson, Kit), Buckskin Men of Forest and Plain, by J. Edward Leithead, 246-18; 248-33; 249-43; 250-50; 253-74; 254-86

(Carson, Kit), Kit Carson: An Eye Witness Word, (historical reminiscences), by Roland D. Sawyer, 296-40

(Carson, Kit), Kit Carson's Rifle, 239-64

(Carson, Kit), Movies: Checklist, by Arthur N. Carter, 520-92

(Carter, Ad: Just Kids Comic Strip), Too
   Much Blood and Thunder, and A Matter
   of Price, (episodes), 2-7; 3-3
Carter, Arthur N.: letter of comment,
   398-120
Carter, Arthur N.: Movies Featuring
   Real and Fictional Characters
   Made Famous by Dime Novels,
   Checklist, 520-91
Carter, Arthur N.: TIP TOP WEEKLY
   Locations, (locales of dime
   novel stories), 352-8
(Carter, Nick), A Bit on NICK CARTER
   LIBRARY, by Harold C. Holmes, 90-1
(Carter, Nick), A Letter from the Last
   of the Nick Carter authors (S. C.
   Spalding), 329-11
(Carter, Nick), The Anatomy of Dome
   Novels, No.1: Nick Carter, by
   J. Edward Leithead, 384-76; 385-85
(Carter, Nick), on authors, 136-2
(Carter, Nick), Chapters from the
   Chronicles of Nick Carter (discussion
   on the exploits of Carter), by J.
   Randolph Cox, 500-50; 501-62
(Carter, Nick), Confessions of a Dime
   Novelist, (Eugene T. Sawyer, author
   of many Carter stories), by Gelett
   Burgess, 105-2
(Carter, Nick), Death of author Frederick
   W. Davis, 48-10
(Carter, Nick), Davis, Nick Carter's
   Ghost Writer, Dies in New Bedford,
   (1933), 35-1
(Carter, Nick), Did Mottern Commit
   Murder from Reading Dime Novels?
   (possible dime novel social
   significance), by Beatrice Barry,
   204-73
(Carter, Nick), Dime Novel Days (on
   author Frederick Van Renselaer Dey),
   112-2
(Carter, Nick), Dime Novel Reviews:
   The Coming of Dr. Quartz (foe of
   Nick Carter), by J. Randolph Cox,
   522-130
(Carter, Nick), Doctor Quartz and Other
   Nine-Lived Villains (villains in the
   dime novels), by J. Edward Leithead,
   380-40; 381-48
(Carter, Nick), The First Nick Carter,
   by Harold C. Holmes, 79-1
(Carter, Nick), First Nick Carter Story
   was Accepted (by author Eugene T.
   Sawyer), 73-7
(Carter, Nick), Frederick W. Davis, Nick
   Carter author, obituary, 449-19
(Carter, Nick), The Greatest Sleuth
   That Ever Lived (discusses Nick
   Carter stories), by J. Edward Leithead
   272-38
(Carter, Nick), Letter from J. Randolph
   Cox pertaining to Nick Carter,
   482-115
(Carter, Nick), More About the NICK
   CARTER LIBRARIES, by J. Edward
   Leithead, 245-10

(Carter, Nick), My Search for Old Nick
   Carters (collecting the dime novels),
   by Joe Gantner, 111-1
(Carter, Nick), NEW NICK CARTER WEEKLY,
   Bibliographical Listing, by J.
   Randolph Cox, 516-SS
(Carter, Nick), Nick Carter? Let 'em Read
   It, Says Scientist, by William J.
   Benners, 74-1
(Carter, Nick), Nick Carter and Buffalo
   Bill items, by J. Edward Leithead,
   61-1
(Carter, Nick), Nick Carter Again, by
   Robert H. Smeltzer, 22-1
(Carter, Nick), Nick Carter and the Shadow
   Woman, by W.B.McCafferty, 118-3
(Carter, Nick), Nick Carter Detective
   Tales in MAGNET and NEW MAGNET LIBRARY,
   Checklist, by J. Edward Leithead,
   212-33
(Carter, Nick), Nick Carter in Another
   Man's Shoes (Carter stories by Samuel
   C. Spalding: Sexton Blake), by J.Edward
   Leithead, 350-112; 351-120
(Carter, Nick), Nick Carter in Print
   (Bibliography 1886-1936), by J. Edward
   Leithead, 181-75
(Carter, Nick), Nick Carter in the Movies
   (discusses var. film productions), by
   J. Randolph Cox, 534-114
(Carter, Nick), NICK CARTER LIBRARY,
   (Bibliographical listing), by J.Randolph
   Cox, 502-SS
(Carter, Nick), Nick Carter on Radio
   (Mutual Network programs), 136-4
(Carter, Nick), Nick Carter 100th Anniver-
   sary Book (Nick Carter Killmaster
   paperback series), by Edward T.LeBlanc,
   511-33
(Carter, Nick), Nick Carter Reprints, by
   J. Edward Leithead, 337-82; 338-92
(Carter, Nick), Nick Carter Stories and
   Other Series Containing Stories About
   Nick Carter, (Bibliographical listing),
   by J. Randolph Cox, 526-SS; 542-SS
(Carter, Nick), Nick Carter Studies, (the
   exploits of the Great New York Detective)
   by J. Randolph Cox, 517-22
(Carter, Nick), NICK CARTER WEEKLY, by
   L.H.Larmon, 59-1
(Carter, Nick), NICK CARTER WEEKLY, Nos.
   91 and 92, (discusses the large size
   issues), by Harold C. Holmes, 55-1
(Carter, Nick), Nick Carter, Jr. Stories
   Proposed, by Joe Gantner, 153-4
(Carter, Nick), Old Nick Carters, (on
   dime novels), by Joe Gantner, 129-1
(Carter, Nick), On Stage, Mr. Carter,
   (Frederick Van Rensselaer Dey as writer
   of Nick Carter stories), by J. Edward
   Leithead, 314-140; 315-151; 316-9
(Carter, Nick), Rome Bans Nick Carter,
   Buffalo Bill, and Lincoln, 89-1
(Carter, Nick), Sherlock Holmes Exhibit
   (Philadelphia Free Library 1968: Nick
   Carter), 429-61

(Carter, Nick), Some Notes Toward a Study of Nick Carter, by J. Randolph Cox, 439-44

(Carter, Nick), Strange Encounter (with Nick Carter?), by J. Randolph Cox, 394-70

(cartoons), Dime Novels in cartoons, (Jim Williams and other artists), by Gerald J. McIntosh, 412-2

(cartoons), Merriwelliana in Cartoons, (Frank Merriwell in the comics),by Gerald J. McIntosh, 442-73

(Cary, Alice), obituary, 25-9

(Cary, Phoebe), obituary, 25-9

(Cary, Rosa N.), Favorites of Yesterday No.4, Rosa N. Cary (early author), by Hermon Pitcher, 203-66

(Cassell & Co., Publishers), The Edward S. Ellis Stories Published by the Mershon Complex, by Denis R.Rogers, 490-70; 491-86; 492-104

(Cassidy, Butch), Wyoming's Wild Riders and Other Hunted Men (in dime novels), by J. Edward Leithead, 294-20

(CAST UPON THE BREAKERS: Horatio Alger, Jr.), Horatio Alger's Ladt Hero, 495-141

Castlemon, Harry: How I Came to Write My First Book, with Checklist, 100-1

(Castlemon, Harry), Now They're Collectors' Items #1: Edward S.Ellis and Harry Castlemon, (discusses boys' books by these authors), by J.Edward Leithead, 405-58; 406-66

Cecil Burleigh: One of the Comic Writers (in early works), by Ralph Adimari, 296-36

Censorship and Early Adolescent Literature: Stratemeyer, Mathiews and Comstock, (attempts to discredit Stratemeyer), by Ken Donelson, 534-119

(censorship), Introduction to SETH JONES OF NEW HAMPSHIRE by Edward S. Ellis, 172-1

CHAMPION, THE, 49-2

CHAMPTION LIBRARY, THE, 10-7; 21-4

(CHAMPION LIBRARY, THE), Dime Novel Sketches #126, 453-59

(CHAMPION NOVELS), Dime Novel Sketches #171, 499-37

CHANEY'S UNION NOVELS, 115-3

(CHANEY'S UNION NOVELS), Dime Novel Sketches #157, 485-17

Chap Books (1780-1830), 24-1

Chapters from the Chronicles of Nick Carter (discussion of the exploits of Nick Carter as detective), by J. Randolph Cox, 500-50; 501-62

Charles Lamb's Forerunners of the Dime Novel (early popular fiction novels 1805-1808), by J.E.Riehl, 533-109

Charles Pierce Burton: The Father of the Bob's Hill Boys (Boy Scout boys' series), by Jack Bales, 541-2

Charles Rothstein Collects Florida Dime Novels, by Jane Hamlin, 434-115

(Chase, Josephine), Josephine Chase and Her Pen Names, by Roy B. Van Devier, 382-61

(Chatterton, A.L., Company, Publishers), Edward S. Ellis Stories Published by the Mershon Complex, by Denis R. Rogers, 490-70; 491-86; 492-104

(Chatterton-Peck Company, Publishers), Edward S. Ellis Stories Published by the Mershon Complex, by Denis R. Rogers, 490-70; 491-86; 492-104

Cheap, But Not Trashy, (mail-order periodicals), by Fred T. Singleton, 224-34

CHEAP EDITION OF POPULAR AUTHORS, Checklist, 540-90

(CHEAP EDITION OF POPULAR AUTHORS), Dime Novel Sketches #212, 540-89

Checklist -
 Adams, William Taylor, (Oliver Optics), by Peter C. Walther, 548-26
 ADVANCE TEN CENT NOVELS, 4-3 (partial)
 Adventure Series, Arthur Westbrook Co., by J. Edward Leithead, 280-2
 ALDINE LIFE AND ADVENTURE LIBRARY, 533-98
 Aldine Publishing Company, (early publications), by Denis R. Rogers, 532-82
 Alger, Horatio, Jr., Titles (bibliographic), by Morton S. Enslin, 467-74; 468-90
 Appleton, Victor: Tom Swift books (Sr. & Jr.), by John T. Dizer, Jr., 520-88
 Ballou, Maturin Murray, works, 25-3
 Beadle Publications in England, by Denis R. Rogers, 496-2; 497-14
 BEADLES DIME BIOGRAPHICAL LIBRARY, 542-40
 Black Bess series, (partial), 8-6
 Black Highwayman Novels, (partial), 2-3
 BOY PARTNERS, An Edward Edson Lee Publication (boys' paper), by Willis J. Potthoff, 550-83
 Boy Scouts series, boys' books pub. by Donohue Co., by Bob Chenu, 498-32
 BOYS NOVELIST, THE, 247-25
 BOY'S OWN LIBRARY, (Author Listing) by Denis R. Rogers, 453-63
 BOY'S STAR LIBRARY, (partial), 15-5
 BRADY'S CHAMPION STORIES #1-19, by J.C.Dykes, 156-1
 BRADY'S MERCURY STORIES, (list of titles), 530-49
 BRADY'S PEOPLE'S NOVELETTES, (list of titles), 527-115
 Buffalo Bill bibliography of story-paper serials and novels, by J. Edward Leithead, 168-2; 171-6; 173-1; 174-18; 175-26
 Buffalo Bill Novels in Paperback Book Format, by J. Edward Leithead, 201-49

Checklist (cont.)

CAPTAIN HERON SERIES OF HIGHWAYMAN TALES, 537-46

Carter, Nick, Detective Tales in MAGNET and NEW MAGNET LIBRARY by J. Edward Leithead, 212-33

Carter, Nick, in Dime Novels and Storypapers 1886-1936, by J. Edward Leithead, 181-75

Carter, Nick - Stories and other series containing stories of Nick Carter (bibliography), by J. Randolph Cox, 526-SS, 542-SS

Castlemon, Harry, works 100-1

CHAMPION LIBRARY, THE, (partial, 10-7

CHEAP EDITIONS OF POPULAR AUTHORS, 540-90

Circus stories: Tanbark and Spangles in the Five-Cent Libraries, by J. Edward Leithead, 223-25

Cleek, Hamilton, Detective series by T.W.Hanshew, by J. Randolph Cox, 487-44; 490-81

Cook, William Wallace, works, by Mabel Cooper Skjelver, 518-34

Coomer, George H., (dime novel author & poet), works, by S.E. Wallen, 502-94

Custer, General, Dime Novels, by Brian W. Dippie and Edward T. LeBlanc, 442-66

Dalton Gang, in Dime Novels, by J. Edward Leithead, 289-79; 290-87

DAWLEY'S CAMP & FIRESIDE LIBRARY, by Edward T. LeBlanc, 238-49

DAWLEY'S NEW WAR NOVELS, (partial), 5-7

Dewitt Publications (dime novel series), by Edward T. LeBlanc, 520-97

DEWITT'S GOOD BOOK SERIES, 515-123

DEWITT'S HANDSOME JACK SERIES, List of titles, 526-92

DEWITT'S ROMANCES, List of titles, 522-141

DEWITT'S STORIES OF THE SEA, List of titles, 524-49

DEWITT'S TWENTY-FIVE CENT NOVELS, 529-30

Diamond Dick, Jr. & Diamond Dick, Sr., bibliography, by J. Edward Leithead, 187-25

Doughty, Francis Worcester, his dime novel stories, by Ross Crauford, 521-106

Ellis, Edward S., bibliography, 529-2

Fantasy, Science-Fiction and Lost Race Adventures in the Street & Smith Paperback Volumes, by Stuart A. Teitler, 442-71

FIFTEEN CENT ROMANCES (Ornum & Co.), (partial), 20-4

FIRESIDE SERIES, 541-25

FIVE CENT WEEKLY LIBRARY, (partial), 12-5

Checklist (cont.)

GARFIELD LIBRARY, THE, (bibliographic), by Denis R. Rogers, 471-138

Hancock, H. Irving, boys' series books, by Bob Chenu, 538-64

Hanshew, T.W. (Hamilton Cleek, Detective), by J. Randolph Cox, 487-44; 490-81

Hardy Boys, boys' series by F.W. Dixon, bibliography, by Robert V.Riordan, 530-35

Henty, G.A., bibliography, by Stanley A. Pachon, 195-97; 196-1

HILTON'S PRIZE ROMANCE, 534-125

HILTON'S TEN CENT NOVELS, (partial), 14-5

HUB 10 CENT NOVELS, THE, by Edward T. LeBlanc, 232-3

LIVES OF GREAT AMERICANS, 539-76

Merriwell, Frank, stories, bibliography with story synopsis, by Gerald J. McIntosh, 474-34

MORRISON'S SENSATIONAL SERIES, (partial), 9-7

Movies featuring real and fictional characters made famous by dime novels, by Arthur N. Carter, 520-91

Munro, George, Publications, 378-23

NEW BUFFALO BILL WEEKLY, bibliographic listing, by J. Edward Leithead, 452-SS

NEW NICK CARTER WEEKLY, bibliographic listing, by J. Randolph Cox, 516-SS

NEW SENSATION, THE, and THE SPORTING NEW YORKER, bibliographic listing, by Ross Crafurd, 521-SS

NEW YORK BOYS LIBRARY, (partial), 6-3

NEW YORK BOYS WEEKLY (and OUR BOYS), The Great Tousey-Munro Rivalry, bibliographic listing, by Ross Craufurd, 535-SS

NICK CARTER LIBRARY, bibliographic listing, by J. Randolph Cox, 502-SS

Optic, Oliver, chronological list of books, by Janet R. Lillibridge, 517-28

Optic, Oliver, definitive checklist, by S.E.Wallen, 511-26

Optic, Oliver (a/ Wm. Taylor Adams) listing of works, by Peter C. Walther, 548-26

OUR BOYS (and NEW YORK BOYS WEEKLY), The Great Tousey-Munro Rivalry, bibliographic listing, by Ross Crauford, 535-SS

Patten, Gilbert, writings prior to Frank Merriwell, by Donald L. Steinhauer and Edward T. LeBlanc, 410-118

PETERSON'S ILLUMINATED SERIES, 532-91

Checklist (cont.)
    Police Gazette Series of Famous
        Criminals, (partial), 7-9
    RAILROAD READING, 535-13
    RED WOLF SERIES, 533-108
    Reynolds, G.W.M., Novels, 536-34
    Rolt-Wheeler, Francis, boys'
        series books, by John T. Dizer,
        Jr., 500-59
    ROUGH RIDER WEEKLY, by J. Edward
        Leithead and Edward T. LeBlanc,
        478-3
    SERIES OF SEA TALES, list of titles,
        531-75
    SPORTING NEW YORK (and THE NEW
        SENSATION), bibliographic listing,
        by Ross Carufurd, 521-SS
    Standish, Vurt L., Short Short
        Stories, by Gerald J. McIntosh,
        391-34
    Starr Gang in Dime Novels, by
        J. Edward Leithead, 290-87
    Stratemeyer, Edward, boys books first
        published as serials, by John T.
        Dizer, Jr., 515-118
    Stratemeyer, Edward, early writings,
        by John T. Dizer, Jr., 549-50
    Stratemeyer, Edward, serials and
        boys books, by John T. Dizer, Jr.,
        516-126
    Street & Smith Dime Novels and
        Related Publications, by Edward T.
        LeBlanc and Ralph Adimari, 299-60
    Strong, Ted, series in dime novels,
        by J. Edward Leithead and Edward
        T. LeBlanc, 478-3
    Swift, Tom, series, boys books, biblio-
        graphic list, by William R.Gowan,
        536-22
    Swift, Tom, Jr., bibliography, by
        William R. Gowan, 538-56
    Swift, Tom (Sr. & Sr.), by John T.
        Dizer, Jr., 520-88
    TALES OF BORDER ADVENTURE, 538-67
    TALES OF CELEBRATED HIGHWAYMEN, list
        of titles, 528-126
    TIP TOP WEEKLY, bibliographic listing,
        by Robert McDowell, 532-SS
    Trowbridge, J.T., works, by Gil O'Gara,
        544-69
Chenu, Julius R., Bill Bruce Books Back-
    ground, (Bill Bruce series boys' books
    by Maj. Henry Arnold), 474-41
Chenu, Julius R., Books of William
    Heyliger, (boys' series books), 519-62
Chenu, Julius R., Boy Scouts in a Great
    Tangle, or Unraveling the Saalfield
    Puzzle, (Boy Scouts boys' books),
    499-42; 505-124
Chenu, Julius R., The Boy Scout Series
    Book Mess (the various Boy Scout boys'
    series books), 486-34
Chenu, Julius R., The First Tom Slade
    Book, or Movies to Print (Tom Slade
    Boy Scout boys' series books), 514-83
Chenu, Julius R., G & D Every Boys
    Library Boy Scout Editions (boys'
    books), 536-33

Chenu, Julius R., Garden City Publishing
    Company's Paperback Juveniles, (boys'
    series boys), 531-72
Chenu, Julius R., Hard Ones to Find -
    Do They Really Exist? (scarce or
    non-existent boys' books), 468-107
Chenu, Julius R., Harrie Hrving Hancock's
    Boys Series Books (discussion with
    checklist), 538-64
Chenu, Julius R., HIKE AND THE AEROPLANE,
    (discussion on this rare boys' book
    by Tom Graham), 550-81
Chenu, Julius R., The Lawrenceville
    Series by Owen Johnson, (boys' series
    books), 517-11
Chenu, Julius R.; letter of comment,
    410-123; 435-125; 526-92; 549-66
Chenu, Julius R., Magazine Serial and
    Book Relationships in Leo Edwards
    Books (discussion), 534-122
Chenu, Julius R., The Most Popular Boys
    Series of Books (discusses various
    series), 540-98
Chenu, Julius R., Notes on One of Gilbert
    Patten's Less Well Known Hard Cover
    Books: THE DEADWOOD TRAIL, 449-20
Chenu, Julius R., Optics Serials as Books
    (Oliver Optic), 518-50
Chenu, Julius R., Scout Master G. Harvey
    Ralphson's Triplets (Boy Scout boys'
    series books pub. by Donohue Co.,
    with checklist), 498-32
Chenu, Julius R., Winning World I (the
    exploits of war in boys' books)
    543-50
Chester Gard Mayo - An Appreciation
    (on Mayo's collection of dime novels,
    books, story papers), by John T. Dizer,
    Jr., 530-48
Chicago Dime Novels, (with Chicago locales
    by Edwin Brooks, 108-3
(CHILDREN'S LITERATURE: A HISTORICAL AND
    CONTEMPORARY BIBLIOGRAPHY, by Irving
    P. Leif), Review by John T. Dizer,Jr.,
    530-53; 531-77
CHILDRENS MAGAZINE, (1st American juvenile
    periodical, 1789), 7-9
CHING CHING'S OWN, 119-10; 132-4; 132-5
(Chipman, William P.), Rev. William P.
    Chipman, Writer of Boys Books,
    obituary, 71-2
(Christmas issues), Old English Journals
    for Boys: Those Special Christmas
    Issues, by William M. Burns, 326-92
Chronological Listing of Boys Books by
    Edward Stratemeyer first published as
    Serials, by John T. Dizer, Jr.,
    515-118
Circus clowns in comeback, news item,
    203-66
Circus is Coming to Town, The, (verse),
    132-1
Circus News 1864, 210-19
CIRCUS TOM WEEKLY, by Kenneth Daggett,
    141-4
Circus Yarns and Circus Programmes,
    (reminiscences), by "Taffy" Harris,
    167-1

(circus), The Anatomy of Dime Novels,
No.12: Novels of the Circus,
(discussion), by J. Edward Leithead,
432-88; 433-96
(circus), My Pal the Elephant, (circus
reminiscences), by Joe Gantner,
179-1
(circus), Tanbark and Spangles in the
Five-Cent Libraries, (circus theme
stories), by J. Edward Leithead,
223-25; 265-76; 266-84
Civil War in Dime Novels, The, (Civil
War theme stories), by J. Edward
Leithead, 275-62
(Civil War), The Anatomy of Dime Novels,
No.8: Civil War Novels, (discussion),
by J. Edward Leithead, 422-106;
423-114
Claggett, William M.: Cousin of Buffalo
Bill Dies After Long Illness, (the
obituary of Arthur P. Cody), 72-2
Clark, Bill: letter of comment, 381-51
(Clark, Charles: AMAZING ADVENTURES OF
LYIN' BOB HAGIN AND FIDDLIN' JIM)
Review by Edward T. LeBlanc, 390-30
Clark, Ida C.: The Dime Novel Friend
(verse), 171-2
CLAUDE DUVAL SERIES, 25-8
Clay, Bertha M.), The Bertha M. Clay
Mystery Cleared Up (identity of
author shown to be William J.
Benners), 95-3
(Clay, Bertha M.), Dime Novel Daze,
112-3
(Clay, Bertha M.), For Bertha M. Clay,
(verse), by Lynne Gray, 300-80
(Clay, Bertha M.), William J. Benners
The First Historian of the Dime
Novel, by Ralph Adimari, 312-123
Clayton Corral, The, (Clayton magazines),
15-7; 16-7; 17-7; 18-7; 19-9
(Clayton, Jeff, Detective), Jeff Clayton-
Sexton Blake, or Another Mystery
Solved (Clayton of Arthur Westbrook
Co. paperback books, and Sexton
Blake), by J. Edward Leithead,
449-21
(Clayton Magazines), The Clayton
Corral, 15-7; 16-7; 17-7; 18-7; 19-9
Clayton Magazines, list, 17-8
Cleek and His Forty Faces, or T.W.
Hanshew, a Dime Novelist Who Made
Good (Hamilton Cleek, Detective,
discussion), by J. Randolph Cox,
487-41; 490-81
Close, Stuart, The Beadle's Dime Novel,
(verse), 20-3
CLUES, 15-7
Cobb, Sylvanus, Jr., (author), 16-2;
88-3
(Cobb, Sylvanus, Jr.), Sylvanus Cobb,
Jr., (early author), by William
Berry Lapham, 51-3
Cobwebbed Bookshelf, The, (older books
still available), by Michael L.
Cook, 551-104

(Cody, Arthur P.), Cousin of Buffalo
Bill Dies After Long Illness,
(obituary), by William M. Claggett,
72-2
Cody, Buffalo Bill, mention, 26-3;
111-4; 151-2
(Cody, Buffalo Bill), Alas, That Truth
Must Prevail, (comments), by "Seajay,"
158-4
(Cody, Buffalo Bill), The Anatomy of
Dime Novels, No2: Buffalo Bill
Stories, by J. Edward Leithead,
389-10; 390-22
(Cody, Buffalo Bill), The Battle for
Buffalo Bill's Bones, newspaper item,
363-111
(Cody, Buffalo Bill), Buckskin Bill Recalls
Famous Iowa Neighbors and a Trip to Old
Missouri, (reminiscences, Buffalo Bill
and the James Gang), by J. Edward Leit-
head, 291-94
(Cody, Buffalo Bill), Buffalo Bill and Ned
Buntline, (relationship), by Sam E.
Conner, 161-1
(Cody, Buffalo Bill), Buffalo Bill in Bound
Book Fiction, by Don Russell, 320-40
(Cody, Buffalo Bill), Buffalo Bill Reprints
by J. Edward Leithead, 342-18; 343-26
(Cody, Buffalo Bill), Buffalo Bill Slept
Here, (reminiscences), by Joseph Myler,
388-1
(Cody, Buffalo Bill), Buffalo Bill's
Benevolence, or Col. Cody's Church
Dollar, (spiritual life of Cody), by
Gerald J. McIntosh, 484-2
(Cody, Buffalo Bill), Buffalo Bill's Life
on the Border, (reminiscences), by
Paul T. Nolan, 383-68
(Cody, Buffalo Bill), Buckskin Men of
Forest and Plain, by J. Edward Leithead,
246-18; 248-33; 249-43; 250-50; 253-74;
254-86
(Cody, Buffalo Bill), "By the Author of
Buffalo Bill," (various authors who
wrote Cody stories), by J. Edward Leit-
head, 308-34; 309-42; 310-100
(Cody, Buffalo Bill), English Reprints of
Buffalo Bill Novels, by J. Edward Leit-
head, 392-44; 393-56
(Cody, Buffalo Bill), Facts About the "Two
Bills" and Buntline, (Wild Bill, Buffalo
Bill, and Ned Buntline), by Roland D.
Sawyer, 160-4
(Cody, Buffalo Bill), Gen. Phil Sheridan's
Words on Buffalo Bill, 295-31
(Cody, Buffalo Bill), How I Met Buffalo
Bill, (reminiscences), by G.H.Cordier,
167-3
(Cody, Buffalo Bill), How Ned Buntline
Turned from Runaway Boy to Writing
Genius: His Relations with Buffalo Bill
and the "Know Nothings," by Leon Mead,
101-1
(Cody. Buffalo Bill), Movies: Checklist,
by Arthur N. Carter, 520-92

(Cody, Buffalo Bill), My Meeting With Buffalo Bill, (reminiscences), by Willis E. Hurd, 136-2

(Cody, Buffalo Bill), Nick Carter and Buffalo Bill Items, by J. Edward Leithead, 61-1

(Cody, Buffalo Bill), Review of THE LIVES AND LEGENDS OF BUFFALO BILL by Don Russell; by J. Edward Leithead, 340-2

(Cody, Buffalo Bill), Rome Bans Nick Carter, Buffalo Bill and Lincoln, news item, 89-1

(Cody, Buffalo Bill), The Wild West in England, (English reprints of dime novel westerns), by Ralph F. Cummings, 61-2

(Cody, Buffalo Bill), The Wild West Shows Pass in Grand Review, (survey and review of the wild west shows), by J. Edward Leithead, 264-65; 265-75; 266-84

Coincidence?, (reminiscences dime novel period), by George French, 247-26

Cole Younger, James Bandit, Dies Reformed, news item, 117-8

Coleman, Lucile: letter of comment, 375-113

(collecting), A Book Grabber's Gripes, (collecting experiences), by Jack R. Schorr, 475-50

(collecting), A Few Do's and Don'ts, (collecting advice), by Don S. Learned, 342-22

(collecting), A Lurid Record, (collecting experiences), by W.E.Bennett, 60-1

(collecting), A Vacation Trip 1973, (collecting experiences, boys books), by Jack Schorr, 495-137

(collecting), Advice to Collectors, by Charles Bragin, 245-14; 342-21; 405-63

(collecting), Ah, Those Golden Years, (collecting experiences, boys' books), by Jack Schorr, 508-5

(collecting), The Book I Had the Hardest Time Finding, (experiences of var. collectors, boys' books), by Jack R. Schorr, 444-95

(collecting), Browsing Around, (boys' books collecting experiences), by Jack R. Schorr, 473-23

(collecting), Collecting Books for Your Kids to Read, (difficulty in pleasing present generation), by Jack R. Schorr, 463-40

(collecting), Collecting for Fun or Profit, (collecting advice), by Jack R. Schorr, 460-2

(collecting), Collecting Our Favorites, (experiences and advice), by E.T. Gossett, 84-1

(collecting), Collection of Horror and Thrills, (experiences, collecting dime novels) by L. Morgan, 118-1

(collecting), Collector Averages Out, (experiences, collecting dime novels) by Fred T. Singleton, 19-5

(collecting), Collectoritis, (comments on collecting), by "Dr.Stackumup," 496-12

(collecting), Collectors Dime Novel Bookshelf, (publications), by Edward T. LeBlanc, 491-95; 495-138; 496-3; 499-46; 501-71; 502-81; 504-114; 505-126; 507-139; 510-22; 512-47; 514-88; 515-117; 517-27; 521-123; 523-21; 524-50; 535-15; 536-35

(collecting), Dime Novel Bonanza, (collecting experiences), by J. Edward Leithead, 65-1

(collecting), Dime Novel Collector's Bookshelf, (publications), by Edward T. LeBlanc, 363-112; 364-2; 365-18; 370-66; 376-7; 381-50; 382-64; 385-89; 389-17; 391-41; 392-52; 402-29; 405-63; 406-71; 407-83; 410-117; 411-133; 413-20; 419-81; 425-22; 429-65; 437-27; 438-37; 441-63; 452-58; 453-65; 459-126; 470-133; 471-151; 477-69; 484-14; 485-24; 486-36

(collecting), Dime Novel and Boys Book Collecting Bookshelf, (publications), by Edward T. LeBlanc, 537-48; 538-68; 544-74; 547-17; 548-40

(collecting), Dime Novel Collecting, by Charles Bragin, 365-12; 402-28

(collecting), Dime Novel Collecting, by "Deadwood Dick, Jr." 64-1

(collecting), Dime Novel "Daze", (collecting experiences and reminiscences), by Gerald J. McIntosh, 448-3

(collecting), Dime Novels Exhibited in the Express Window, (reminiscences), 125-1

(collecting), Dime Novel Prices Hold, (values in collecting), by Charles Bragin, 19-4

(collecting), Dime Novel Round-Uppers, (experiences and reminiscences), by F.P.Pitzer, 19-4

(collecting), Dime Novel Sidelights, (misc. bibliographical data), by Ralph P. Smith, 479-72

(collecting), Displaying Your Collection, (boys' books series), by Jack R. Schorr, 465-57

(collecting), Disposal of a Book Collection, (problems inherent), by Denis R. Rogers, 546-98 (See also letters on subject 549-66, 549-67)

(collecting), Disposing of Your Collection, by Jack R. Schorr, 503-103

(collecting), The Elusives, (hard-to-find boys' books), by Jack Schorr, 494-130

(collecting), Exasperations of a Book Collector, (boys' books), by Jack R. Scorr, 448-2

(collecting), Foolish Buying, (comments) by Walt Mason, 71-3

(collecting), 4500, All Mint, (boys' book collecting), by Jack R. Schorr, 469-118

(collecting), From Boxes to Shelves or How to Know What You Have, (boys' books), by Jack R. Schorr, 479-76

(collecting), Girls' Books Should Be Collected, (girls' series books as desirable as boys' books), by Harlan Miller, 470-133

(collecting), Going, Going, Gone, (boys' book collecting), by Jack Schorr, 488-56

(collecting), Hang On To Your Old Dime Novels, (values increasing, more scarce), by "Nameless Joe," 209-13

(collecting), Happyhours Brotherhood on the Loose, or: Leave Your Wives at Home, (report of meeting of the dime novel collectors club), by "Miles Behind," 230-63

(collecting), How to Get Dime Novels for Nothing, (advice), by Ralph F. Cummings, 86-3

(collecting), Hunting for Novels is Fun, (dime novel collecting experiences), by George Flaum, 180-2

(collecting), Hybrids, Oddities and Freaks, (variations in editions of dime novels and boys' books), by Denis R. Rogers, 475-46; 476-56

(collecting), In Defense of Listing Current Alger Values (discussion on scarcity and values), by Ralph D. Gardner, 472-2

(collecting), Is Interest in Dime Novels Dying?, by George T. Flaum, 247-27

(collecting), Long Stories in My Collection, by William M. Burns, 273-47

(collecting), My Adventures Into Book Collecting, by W.B.Poage, 189-4

(collecting), My Collection of Beadles Half Dime Library, by William M. Burns, 164-1

(collecting), My Search for Old Nick Carters, by Joe Gantner, 111-1

(collecting), 19th Century Peep-Show, (collecting dime novels rewarding), by Fred T. Singleton, 225-41

(collecting, Odds 'n' Ends, (boys' books collecting), by Jack Schorr, 451-45; 452-57; 455-88; 456-96

(collecting), Old Bowery Days in the Dime Novel, by Fred T. Singleton, 9-3

(collecting), The Old Guard, (dime novels), 263-62

(collecting), On the Trail of Novel Hunters, (collecting experiences), by Fred T. Singleton, 6-2; 8-5; 9-7

(collecting), Over My Shoulder, (caution in mail order collecting of dime novels), 204-75

(collecting), Prize Packages of Nickel Novels, by Frank T. Fries, 5-4

(collecting), Protect Your Novels, (preservation of dime novels), by Charles Bragin, 340-7

(collecting), Recently Published Articles Concerning Dime Novel Collecting, (bibliography), by Edward T. LeBlanc, 381-52; 390-30; 392-51; 395-84; 402-30; 408-90; 409-109; 412-11; 413-20; 415-43; 416-51; 425-22; 427-40; 428-50; 429-64; 430-76; 431-82; 432-94; 435-125; 437-27; 438-46; 441-63; 443-85; 447-131; 448-4; 449-21; 451-46; 452-57; 453-68; 454-75; 455-89; 457-106; 459-126; 461-19; 463-41; 465-58; 467-86; 469-119; 470-132; 472-16; 473-31; 474-43; 475-52; 477-69; 479-74; 480-92; 482-116; 483-127; 485-24; 486-38; 489-66; 490-76; 500-60; 502-88; 505-126; 507-139; 508-6; 509-14; 511-33; 514-85; 515-121; 517-26; 518-53; 519-65; 520-96; 521-124; 522-143; 523-21; 525-72; 526-91; 528-133; 529-28; 530-49; 531-75; 532-93; 533-110; 534-124; 535-10d; 536-35

(collecting), Recently Published Articles Concerning Dime Novels & Boys' Books Collecting, (bibliography), by Edward T. LeBlanc, 537-46; 538-68; 540-97; 542-43; 544-74; 543-59; 545-86; 547-21; 549-65

(collecting), Reckless Ralph Tracks 'em Down, (dime novel collecting experiences), by "Miss Larel," 29-1

(collecting), Six Hundred Dime Novels for Fifteen Dollars (collecting experiences, reminiscences), by "Jack Harkaway," 9-5

(collecting), Standard Library Reference Books for the Book Collector, (bibliography), by Jack Bales, 504-112

(collecting), "Strikes" That I Have Made in Noveldom, (dime novels collecting experiences), by William M. Burns, 4-1

(collecting), That Little Gem - The Dime Novel Roundup, (comments on periodical) 222-18

(collecting), To Collectors of Frank Reade Stories, (collecting comments), by William M. Burns, 322-62

(collecting), Travels of a Book Collector, (boys' books collecting experiences), by H.W.Miller, 483-121

(collecting), Travels of a Book Collector, (boys' books collecting experiences), by Jack R. Schorr, 483-120

(collecting), Treat 'em Tenderly, Pard, (preservation of dime novels), by Fred T. Singleton, 5-1

(collecting), Used Book Prices (values of books; why) by Denis R.Rogers, 469-114

(collecting), Voice of the Collector, (advice and experience), by Charles Bragin, 12-3

(collecting), Wake Up, (urges collectors to seek items), by Ralph F. Cummings, 100-3

(collecting), We Plead Guilty, It's the War, (collecting comments), anon., 108-3

(collecting), What Will You Do?, (comments on collecting situations), by Edward G. Ingraham, 366-27

(collecting) Why the High Cost of Novels in Poor Condition?, by Frank Cummings, 8-3

(collecting), Willard Thompson, Book Dealer, (biog. sketch), by John Guernsey, 480-90

(collecting), With the Novel Stackers, (collecting reminiscences), by "Deadwood Dick, Jr.," 19-6

(collecting), Your Wife and Your Collection, (collor's dilemna), by Jack Scorr, 458-115

Colleting Books for Your Kids to Read, (difficulty in pleasing present generation, boys' books), by Jack R. Schorr, 463-40

Collecting for Fun or Profit, (boys' book collecting), by Jack R. Schorr, 460-2

Collecting Our Favorites, (dime novel collecting comments), by E.T.Gossett, 84-1

Collection of Horror and Thrills (dime novel collecting comments), by L. Morgan, 118-1

(collections), The Austin Collection, by Robert H. Smeltzer, 41-1

(collections), Beadle Stories of Roland D. Sawyer Collection on Display, 363-111

(collections), Charles Austin, 178-53

(collections), Charles Rothstein Collects Florida Dime Novels (those with Florida locales), by Jane Hamlin, 434-115

(collections), Chester Gard Mayo - An Appreciation (collector of dime novels, books, story papers), by John T. Dizer, Jr., 530-48

(collections), Dime Novel Exhibit, Brooklyn Public Library, 1948, 184-3

(collections), Displaying Dime Novels, by Howard Silsbee, 279-104

(collections), Displaying One's Collection (on the boys' books collection of Willis Pothoff), by Edward T. LeBlanc, 518-46

(collections), Hess Collection Acquires Complete Set of AMERICAN BOY, 515-120

(collections), News Notes from the Univ. of Missouri, (boys' book collection), 437-26

(collections), On the Track of Popular Culture, (the Hess Collection of dime novels and related) by J. Randolph Cox, 495-134

(collections), Ralph F. Cummings Collection, (dime novels, story papers), 51-1

(collections), Ray Mengar and His Dime Novel Collection, by Joe Stone, 431-84

(collections), Reckless Ralph's Frightful Apparition, (visit with Ralph Cummings and his collection), 513-50

(collections), The Ryerson Collection, (dime novels), 123-1

(collections), Scientist Collects Dime Novels, (the dime novel collection of Albert Johannsen), by Edwin Brooks, 82-2; 83-1

(collections), Street & Smith Box M58, (discoveries in the Street & Smith collection at Syracuse Univ.), by John T. Dizer, Jr., 526-78

(collections), University of South Florida Has Amassed Fine Dime Novel Collection, news commentary, 521-123

(collections), Western Heritage Center Library, Oklahoma City, Collection, (dime novels), by Gerald J. McIntosh, 397-107

Collector Averages Out, (collecting experiences), by Fred T. Singleton, 19-5

Collector's Items, (verse), by Eva Dubonnet, 111-6

Collectors and the English Penny Dreadful, (historical review), by Charles W. Daniel, 131-1

Collectoritis, (collecting experiences), by"Dr. Stackumup" 496-12

(Collier, Old Cap, Detective), Old Cap Collier and Norman L. Munro, by L.H. Lahmon, 64-3

Collins, E. Burke: William James Benners, Jr., (historian and author), 108-1

Colonel Prentiss Ingraham, (author), by J. Edward Leithead, 376-1; 377-10

(COLUMBIA LIBRARY), Dime Novel Sketches #219, 547-1

Columnists and Commentators Who "Knew" Merriwell, (on Frank Merriwell tales), by Gerald J. McIntosh, 445-105

(Comfort, Lucy R.), obituary of early author, 101-21

(COMIC LIBRARY), Dime Novel Sketches #94, 421-93

(comics), Dime Novels in Cartoons, (Jim Williams and other early cartoonists), by Gerald J. McIntosh, 412-2

(comics), Maw Green on the Dime Novel, 82-2

(comics), The Merriwell Newspaper Comic Strip, (1930's), by Gerald J.McIntosh, 400-2

(comics, American), Local Boys Make Good? Or?, by Arthur Moyse, 322-59

Comic Book Code Pledged, (by manufacturers) 191-68

(comic books), Dime Novels versus Modern Fiction (dime novels, comic books, true det. mag.),by Charles Duprez, 279-105

(comic-strip detectives), Fair Enough,
by Westbrook Pegler, 135-1
(comic strips: "Just Kids" by Ad
Carter), Too Much Blood and Thunder,
and A Matter of Price, (two episodes),
2-7; 3-3
COMRADES, 81A-11
(COMRADES), Dime Novel Sketches #8,
326-91
(COMRADES), Old English Journals for
Boys: COMRADES, (historical
discussion), by William M. Burns,
323-66
COMRADES WEEKLY, by Harold C. Holmes,
103-1
Concerning Old Authors, (general
discussion), by Hermon Pitcher,
109-5
Confessions of a Dime Novelist, The,
(Eugene T. Sawyer) as told to
Gelett Burgess (author of many
Nick Carter stories), 105-2
Conner, Sam E.: Buffalo Bill and
Ned Buntline, 161-1
Conner, Sam E.: Gilbert Patten, (a
memorial article), 150-3
Conrad, Bud: letter of comment,
539-82
Conroy, Jack: letter of comment,
437-26
CONSTANCE LIBRARY, THE, 142-4
(Converse, Frank H.), Writers for
GOLDEN DAYS, No.1: Frank H. Converse,
by Stanley A. Pachon, 333-52
Cook, Fred: letter of comment, 430-73
Cook, Michael L.: The Cobwebbed Book-
shelf, (older books still available),
551-104
(Cook, William Wallace), Letters from
Street & Smith 1927 and THE POPULAR
MAGAZINE, 518-51
(Cook, William Wallace), William Wallace
Cook, (biog. sketch, with pseudonyms),
by Stanley A. Pachon, 300-67
(Cook, William Wallace), William Wallace
Cook - The Marshall Years, (early
years of this author in Marshall,
Michigan), by Mabel Cooper Skjelver,
with checklist, 518-34
(Coomer, George H.), Who Was George H.
Coomer?, (dime novels author and poet,
biog. sketch, with checklist), by S.E.
Wallen, 502-74; 503-90; 504-106
(Coomes, Oll), A Novelist in the Legis-
lature, 85-1
(Cooper, J. Fenimore), biographical
sketch, by Hermon Pitcher, 124-2
(Cooper, J. Fenimore), J. Fenimore Cooper,
Pupil in Military Academy, 90-3
Cordier, George H.: A Curiosity of Horror,
(horror aspects, dime novels), 47-1
Cordier, George H.: THE BOYS OF NEW
YORK, (literary discussion), 133-1
Cordier, George H.: The Duval Series,
(Claude Duval; dime novels), 142-1
Cordier, George H.: English Boys Magazines,
(survey and discussion), 120-1

Cordier, George H.: Favorite Stories,
(boyhood reading reminiscences),
147-1
Cordier, George H.: The Great FIVE
CENT WIDE-A-WAKE LIBRARY, (literary
discussion), 75-1
Cordier, George H.: How I Met Buffalo
Bill, 167-3
Cordier, George H.: How I Met the Steam
Man of the Plains, (dime novel
character), 186-1
Cordier, George H.: The Leslie Publications,
(survey and discussion), 203-65
Cordier, George H.: The Mysteries of
Chinatown, (dime novel reminiscences),
127-1
Cordier, George H.: Old King Brady, (notes
on this detective in dime novels),
42-5; 46-3; 48-5; 50-2; 81A-1
Cordier, George H.: Popular Story Papers
of Other Days, 88-1
Cordier, George H.: Popular Songs of the
Dime Novel Times (w/song words), 113-1
Cordier, George H.: San Francisco in Dime
Novel Days (reminiscences), 119-1
(Corelli, Marie), Faborites of Yesterday:
Marie Corelli, (20th century author),
by Hermon Pitcher, 186-1
Cornelius Shea, An Old Scout, (frontier
reminiscences), by Gerald J. McIntosh,
401-20
(correspondence columns in dime novels),
The Applause Column in TIP TOP WEEKLY,
by J.P.Guinon, 328-2
(COSMOPOLITAN MAGAZINE), Old Cosmopolitans,
(literary reminiscences), by Joe Gantner,
189-1
Couch, M. Bertrand: Blood and Thunder
Novels for Boys, 68-1
Couch, M. Bertrand: The Golden Days of
'49, (reminiscences), 121-1
Couch, M. Bertrand, My Adventures With a
Snake, (humorous reminiscences), 202-59
(Couch, M. Bertrand), Rootin' Tootin'
Shootin' Frisco Bert, (biog. sketch),
by Charles Duprez, 290-85
(couch, M. Bertrand), obituary, 446-116
Couperie, Frank: letter of comment,
425-19
Cousley, Sam A.: letter of comment, 405-62
(cover art: nickel novels) An Artist
Recalls Nickel Novel Days (Charles L.
Wrenn), by J. Edward Leithead, 87-1
COWBOY STORIES, 15-7; 17-8
Cox, J. Randolph: Boxes L-179 and L-180,
(publishing records of Street & Smith),
551-94
Cox, J. Randolph: Chapters from the
Chronicles of Nick Carter (discussion
of detective exploits), 500-50; 501-62
Cox, J. Randolph: Cleek and His Forty
Faces, or T.W.Hanshew, a Dime Novelist
Who Made Good, (Hanshew's dime novel
detective, Hamilton Cleek, master of
disguise), with checklist, 486-30;
487-42; 490-81

Cox, J. Randolph: The Detective-Hero in the American Dime Novel (extensive survey and discussion), 547-2 (See response by David Anderson)

Cox, J. Randolph: Dime Novel Reviews: The Coming of Dr. Quartz (villain in Nick Carter stories), 522-130

Cox, J. Randolph: Dime Novel Reviews: Diamond Dick, 523-2

Cox, J. Randolph: Jesse James Rides Again, (review of stage production "Jesse"), 523-20

Cox, J. Randolph: letter of comment, 393-65; 398-121; 446-116; 482-115; 490-81; 530-51; 549-67

Cox, J. Randolph: Merriwell Apocrypha ("Frank Merriwell in the White House"), 491-93

Cox, J. Randolph: NEW NICK CARTER WEEKLY, (bibliographic listing), 516-SS

Cox, J. Randolph: Nick Carter in the Movies, (discusses various film productions), 534-114

Cox, J. Randolph: NICK CARTER LIBRARY, (bibliographic listing), 502-SS

(Cox, J. Randolph), Nick Carter 100th Anniversary Book, (with biog. sketch of Cox), by Edward T. LeBlanc, 511-33

Cox, J. Randolph: NICK CARTER STORIES and Other Series containing stories about Nick Carter, (bibliographic listing), 526-SS; 542-SS

Cox, J. Randolph: Nick Carter Studies, (exploits of the Great New York Detective), 517-22

Cox, J. Randolph: On the Track of Popular Culture, (the Hess Collection of Dime Novels, story papers, and related newsstand literature), 495-134

Cox, J. Randolph: Some Notes Toward a Study of Nick Carter, 439-44

Cox, J. Randolph: Strange Encounters, (with Nick Carter?), 394-70

Crandall, Rick: Early Juvenile Aviation Fiction, (boys' books aviation tales) 545-82

Crandall, Rick: Notes on World Syndicate Juvenile Aviation Fiction (discusses var. series, boys' books), 552-124

Craufurd, Ross: The Early Doughty - Master of Mysteries and Wonders (Francis Worcester Doughty, author), with checklist, 521-106

Craufurd, Ross: The English Giant, (E. Harcourt Burrage, early author, biog. sketch), 12-2

Craufurd, Ross: Fred Fearnot was There, (dime novel character discussed), 519-58

Craufurd, Ross: Gallows-Fruit, (on English Penny Dreadfuls), 18-2

Craufurd, Ross: Jean Ray, Last and Greatest of the Dime Novelists, (literary biog. sketch), 537-40

Craufurd, Ross: letter of comment, 391-39; 409-108; 516-150; 517-28; 518-51; 519-66; 523-23; 543-58

Craufurd, Ross: THE NEW SENSATION (and THE SPORTING NEW YORKER), (bibliographic listing), 521-SS

Craufurd, Ross: OUR BOYS and NEW YORK BOYS WEEKLY: The Great Tousey-Munro Rivalry, (bibliographic listing), 535-SS

(Crawford, John Wallace), Captain Jack: The Relentless Foe of the Dime Novel, by Paul T. Nolan, 374-102

(Crawford, Will), artist, obituary, 144-3

Crazy Horse and Spotted Tail, (reminiscent sketch), by W.B.McCafferty, 2-5

Creator of Diamond Dick, (dime novel character), by J. Edward Leithead, 335-66

(CRICKET LIBRARY), Dime Novel Sketches #86, 415-33

(Crockett, Col. David), Biographies of Pioneers: Col. David Crockett, (biog. sketch), by Arlie Kinkade, 3-4

(Crockett, Davy), Buckskin Men of Forest and Plain, by J. Edward Leithead, 246-18; 248-33; 249-43; 250-50; 253-74; 254-86

(Crockett, Davy), Movies, Checklist, by Arthur N. Carter, 520-93

(Cummings, Ernest W.), obituary, 62-11

Cummings, Frank: Why the High Cost of Novels in Poor Condition? (comments on collecting), 8-3

Cummings, Ralph: A Little Dime Novel Chat, (reminiscences), 22-3

Cummings, Ralph: Booklet Novels versus Black and Whites, (discussion on pocket size and dime novel size dime novels), 52-1

Cummings, Ralph: BOYS OF AMERICA: A Twentieth Century Story Paper (literary discussion), 7-2

Cummings, Ralph: DEWITT'S NIGHTSHADE SERIES, (discussion), 25-7

Cummings, Ralph: Diamond Dick Creator Left Only $300, news item, 58-12

Cummings, Ralph: Diamond Dick, Jr. (on DIAMOND DICK WEEKLY), 32-1

Cummings, Ralph: The English Novels of Today, (dime novels type of the period) 21-1

Cummings, Ralph: First Dime Novel to be Reprinted After 69 Years (MALESKA), news item, 91-1

Cummings, Ralph: Grand Conflagration at the Munro Plant in 1876 (fire at publishers) 81-2

Cummings, Ralph: The Great Bracebridge Hemyng, (author of Jack Harkaway and Scapegrace series, dime novels), 67-1

Cummings, Ralph: The History of Old Story Papers of Long Ago (NEW YORK WEEKLY STORY TELLER), 216-66

Cummings, Ralph: History of the Happy Hours Brotherhood and the DIME NOVEL ROUNDUP, 430-74; 432-93

Cummings, Ralph: How to Get Dime Novels for Nothing, (collecting advice), 86-3

Cummings, Ralph: If Dreams Were Only
True, (reminiscences), 73-1
Cummings, Ralph: The James Boys Stories,
117-1
Cummings, Ralph: Kirk Munroe and His
Books for Boys, 79-5
Cummings, Ralph: letter of comment,
94-4
Cummings, Ralph: The Life of Happy Hours
Magazine and DIME NOVEL ROUNDUP, Also
Happy Hours Brotherhood, 300-81
Cummings, Ralph: The Life of W. Clark
Russell, (dime novel author), 213-44
Cummings, Ralph: Memorial Notes on
Gilbert Patten, (author), 150-7
Cummings, Ralph: Mr. Edward Harrigan, of
Harrigan & Harts, 80-1
Cummings, Ralph: My First Novel, (dime
novel reading reminiscences), 40-2
Cummings, Ralph: New Interests of the
Juvenile Reader, 72-1
Cummings, Ralph: Odds and Ends, (dime
novel bits of infirmation), 58-9
Cummings, Ralph: Oliver Optic: Centenary
of Birth, 201-52
Cummings, Ralph: Review of HOUSE OF
BEADLE AND ADAMS AND ITS DIME AND
NICKEL NOVELS of Albert Johannsen,
213-43
Cummings, Ralph: Wake Up, (collecting
advice, dime novels), 100-3
Cummings, Ralph: When Dime Novels Were
in Their Glory, (reminiscences), 10-3
Cummings, Ralph: The Wide Awake (WIDE-A-
WAKE LIBRARY notes), 75-12
Cummings, Ralph: The Wild West in England,
(Buffalo Bill and dime novels), 61-2
(Cummings, Ralph), Book Hunting with
Reckless, (novel hunting adventures
and experiences), by Eli A. Messier,
73-9
(Cummings, Ralph), The Dime Novel Friend,
(verse), by Ida C. Clark, 171-2
(Cummings, Ralph), The Most Reckless
Ralph, (biog. sketch, Ralph Cummings)
by Charles Duprez, 348-98
(Cummings, Ralph), Nuther Biography - By
Cracky, (biog. sketch of Cummings), by
Charles Duprez, 270-20
(Cummings, Ralph), Ralph F. Cummings Dime
Novel Collection, 51-1
(Cummings, Ralph), Reckless Ralph and
Wild Bill Visit the Grave of General
Henry Knox, 170-1
(Cummings, Ralph), Reckless Ralph Tracks
'em Down, (collecting experiences), by
Miss Larel, 29-1
(Cummings, Ralph), Reckless Ralph's
Frightful Apparition, (visit with
Cummings and his collection), by
Robert Jennings, 513-60
Cunningham, Eugene, mention, 2-6
Current English Story Papers, by Robert
H. Smeltzer, 49-1
(Custer, General), Bibliography of Custer
Dime Novels, by Brian W. Dippie and
Edward T. LeBlanc, 442-66

(Custer, Gen.) Movies, Checklist,
(featuring Gen. George A. Custer),
by Arthur N. Carter, 520-92
(CUSTER'S LIST: A CHECKLIST OF PICTURES
RELATING TO THE LITTLE BIG HORN: Don
Russell), Review by J. Edward Leithead,
457-106
(Cutpurse, Moll), The Roaring Girl,
(famous English thief, essay), by
W.O.G.Lofts, 473-18

Daggett, Kenneth: CIRCUS TOM WEEKLY,
(discussion), 141-4
Dahl, Marge: Two Boys' Books Writers from
Wisconsin, (biog. discussion of Leslie
Quirk and Everett McNeil), 494-131
Dalton Relatives Visit James Home (Jesse
James home, St.Joseph, Mo.), 178-52
(Dalton, Emmett), The Last of the Dalton
Boys, obituary, 65-5
(Dalton Gang), Outlaw Trails in Indian
Territory, (in dime novel stories), by
J. Edward Leithead, with checklist,
289-78; 290-87
(Dalton, J. Frank), Civil War Vet of
Jesse James Case is dead at 109, news
item, 217-75
Dangers of Wild West Recalled by Old
Letter, by Willard Jaffray, 92-4
Daniel, Charles W.: Collectors and the
English Penny Dreadful, (English
equivalent of dime novel), 131-1
"Dare Devil Dave": That Old Noyhood
Thrill, (verse), 161-2
Darling of the Mob, (Jack Sheppard,
"Prince of Prison Breakers"), by Fred
T. Singleton, 283-30
(Dartt, Dr. Robert), obituary, 496-11
(Davis, Frederick W.), Davis, Nick
Carter's Ghost Writer, Dies in New
Bedford, news item, (1933), 35-1
(Davis, Frederick W.), F.W.Davis obituary,
(Nick Carter writer), 449-19
(Davis, Frederick W.), Notice of Death,
58-10
Davis, Mrs. Marjorie F.: letter of
comment, 377-16
Davis, Nick Carter's Ghost Writer Dies
in New Bedford, news item, (1933),
35-1
(DAWLEY'S CAMP & FIRESIDE LIBRARY), Dime
Novel Sketches #176, 504-105
(DAWLEY'S CAMP & FIRESIDE LIBRARY), Rare
Dime Novels #6: DAWLEY'S, with check-
list, by Edward T. LeBlanc, 238-49
(DAWLEY'S NEW WAR NOVELS), Dime Novel
Sketches #178, 506-129
(DAWLEY'S NEW WAR NOVELS), sketch, 5-7
(DAWLEY'S TEN PENNY NOVELS), Dime Novel
Sketches #161, 489-59
DAY'S DOINGS, photo, 224-33
DAYS OF FORTY NINE, 119-3
Days of 76, The, (verse), by Col. Charles
D. Randolph, 95-6
(Dazaar Series), Doctor Quartz and Other
Nine-Lived Villains, (villains in the
dime novels),by J.Edward Leithead,
380-40; 381-48

Deadshot Dan, the Boy Scout, (verse), by H.O.Rawson, 108-4

Deadwood Dick, Jr. Stories Not Written by Wheeler, with checklist, by Albert Johannsen, 298-54

(Deadwood Dick), A Monument for Deadwood Dick, news item, 31-1

Deadwood Dick, Jr.: Beadles Pocket Library, Reprint of Beadles Boys Library, 117-3

(Deadwood Dick, Jr.), Boy Detectives, (discussion), by J. Edward Leithead, 240-66; 241-74; 242-85

(Deadwood Dick, Jr.), The Creator of Deadwood Dick, by J. Edward Leithead, 335-66

Deadwood Dick Again, (comments), 53-1

(Deadwood Dick,Jr.) Deadwood Dick Forgotten, 325-86

(DEADWOOD DICK, JR.), Dime Novel Sketches #15, 335-65

DEADWOOD DICK in Congress, (file in Library of Congress), 28-1; 31-3

(Deadwood Dick), The Passing of Deadwood Dick, (verse), by William Burton McCafferty, 94-2

(Deadwood Dick), Restoration of Cabin, news item, 320-46

(DEADWOOD DICK LIBRARY), Dime Novel Sketches #66, 393-55

"Deadwood Dick, Jr.": Dime Novel Collecting, (collecting comments), 64-1

"Deadwood Dick, Jr.": The Novels of Edward L. Wheeler, (dime novels), 94-1

"Deadwood Dick, Jr.": Retrospection, or Leaves from the Past (reminiscences) 81A-6

de la Ree, Gerry: letter of comment, 369-58

(DeMorgan, John), John DeMorgan, Author, by Harry A. Weill, 295-30

Derring-Do of the Diamond Dicks (bibliography), by J. Edward Leithead, 187-25

DETECTIVE DIME NOVELS, Novel News, 94-3

Detective-Hero in the American Dime Novel, (survey and discussion), by J. Randolph Cox, 547-2. (See also David Anderson's response)

(DETECTIVE LIBRARY), Dime Novel Sketches #85, 412-1

Detective Stories in Dime Novels, 112-6

DETECTIVE WEEKLY, THE, 21-1; 49-2

(Detectives, bootblack), The Anatomy of Dime Novels No.11: Bootblack Detectives, (survey & discussion), by J. Edward Leithead, 431-78

(detectives in dime novels), This "Sleuth" Business, by J. Edward Leithead, 369-50; 370-62

(detectives in dime novels), The Two King Bradys and Their Girl Detectives, by J. Edward Leithead, 372-80; 373-90

Deutsch, James I.: Jesse James in Dime Novels: Ambivalence Towards An Outlaw, (literary discussion, hero material), 517-2

Deutsch, James I.: letter of comment, 522-142

DeVean, Ross: letter of comment, 381-52

DeWitt Information, (DEWITT'S NIGHTSHADE SERIES), by Patrick Marshall, 34-3

DEWITT'S TEN CENT NOVELS, by Roland D. Sawyer, 148-4

(DEWITT'S CLAUDE DUVAL SERIES), Dime Novel Sketches #152, 480-79

DEWITT'S GOOD BOOK SERIES, 123-4

DEWITT'S GOOD BOOK SERIES, Checklist of Titles, 515-123

(DEWITT'S GOOD BOOK SERIES), Dime Novel Sketches #187, 515-89

(DEWITT'S HANDSOME JACK SERIES), Dime Novel Sketches #198, 526-77

DEWITT'S HANDSOME JACK SERIES, List of Titles, 526-92

(DEWITT'S JONATHAN WILD SERIES), Dime Novel Sketches #189, 517-1

(DEWITT'S NIGHTSHADE SERIES), (discussion), by Ralph F. Cummings, 25-7

(DEWITT'S NIGHTSHADE SERIES), Dime Novel Sketches #185, 513-49

DEWITT'S ROMANCES, Checklist of Titles, 522-141

(DEWITT'S ROMANCES), Dime Novel Sketches #194, 522-130

(DEWITT'S STORIES OF THE SEA), Dime Novel Sketches #196, 524-25

DEWITT'S STORIES OF THE SEA, List of Titles, 524-49

DEWITT'S TEN CENT ROMANCES, 119-6

(DEWITT'S TEN CENT ROMANCES), Dime Novel Sketches #149, 476-55

(DEWITT'S TWENTY-FIVE CENT NOVELS), Dime Novel Sketches #201, 529-1

DEWITT'S TWENTY-FIVE CENT NOVELS, List of Titles, 529-30

(DeWitt Publications), Checklist of Robert M. DeWitt Publications, (dime novels), by Edward T. LeBlanc, 520-97

(Dexter, Larry, series), Garden City Publishing Company's Paperback Juveniles, (boys' series books), by Julius R. Chenu, 531-72

(Dey, Frederick Van Renselaer), Dime Novel Days: A Philadelphian Who Was a Prolific Writer of That School, (dime novel author), 112-2

(Dey, Frederick Van Rensselaer), Doctor Quartz and Other Nine-Lived Villains, (villains in the dime novels), by J. Edward Leithead, 380-40; 381-48

(Dey, Frederick Van Rensselaer), Frederick Van Rensselaer Dey, (author, dime novels), by J. Edward Leithead, 401-14

(Dey, Frederick Van Rensselaer), On Stage, Mr. Carter, (as writer for Nick Carter stories), by J. Edward Leithead, 314-14; 315-148; 316-9

(Dey, Frederick Van Rensselaer), Supplement to article, by J. Edward Leithead,
404-51
(Dey, Mrs. Haryot Holt), Widow of Frederick Dey Deceased, news item, 214-53
Diamond Dick, (verse), by Col. Charles D.
Randolph, 135-2
Diamond Dick in Schooldays, (verse), by
W. B. McCafferty, 135-2
(Diamond Dick), A Handsome Harry Episode,
(character in Diamond Dick stories),
by Harold C. Holmes, 71-3
DIAMOND DICK, JR., The Boys Best Weekly,
by Homer H. Kurtz, 62-1
(Diamond Dick, Jr./Sr.), The Derring-Do
of the Diamond Dicks, (bibliography),
by J. Edward Leithead, 187-25
Diamond Dick Creator Left only $300, news
item, by Ralph F. Cummings, 58-12
(Diamond Dick), Diamond Dick Dies at
Nebraska Home (Dr. Richard Tanner),
131-3
Diamond Dick, Jr., in DIAMOND DICK
WEEKLY, by Ralph Cummings, 32-1
(Diamond Dick), Dime Novel Reviews, by
J. Randolph Cox, 523-2
(Diamond Dick), The First Diamond Dick
Story, by W.C.Miller, 63-1
Diamond Dick, (on Great Western publi-
cations),by Harold C. Holmes, 86-1
(DIAMOND DICK WEEKLY), Last Issue No.
762, 208-1
(Diamond Dick), Young Diamond Dick,
(literary discussion), by J. Edward
Leithead, 358-68; 359-76; 360-84
(DIAMOND DICK LIBRARY), Dime Novel
Sketches #105, 432-87
DIAMOND DICK WEEKLY, 301-88
(DIAMOND DICK WEEKLY), Diamond Dick,
Jr., (discussion), by Ralph Cummings,
32-1
DICK DOBBS DETECTIVE WEEKLY, 329-13
DICK DOBBS DETECTIVE WEEKLY, by George
French, 42-1
(DICK DOBBS DETECTIVE WEEKLY), Dime
Novel Sketches #67, 394-69
Dick Turpin, The Famous Highway,
(historical discussion), by W.O.G.
Lofts, 441-48
(Dickens, Charles), The Influence of
Charles Dickens on Gilbert Patten
(creator of Frank Merriwell), by
Gerald J. McIntosh, 409-103
Dickinson, D.C.: News Note from the
University of Missouri, (on the
boys' books collection), 437-26
Did Mottern Commit Murder From Reading
Dime Novels?, (influence of dime
novels on possible crime), by
Beatrice Barry, 204-73
Difference Between a Five and Dime Novel,
(dime novels), by "Seajay", 98-5
DIME LIBRARY, 151-2
DIME NOVEL, THE, 2-5
Dime Novels: A Hundred Years Ago,
(reminiscences), 371-76; 372-86;
373-96; 374-104; 375-112; 376-6

Dime Novel Abroad, The, (discussion of
foreign reprints), by Henry Steele,
3-1
Dime Novel Days: A Philadelphian Who Was
a Prolific Writer of That School,
(biog. discussion of Frederick Van
Rensselaer Dey), 112-2
Dime Novels and What They Do to Ye,
(reminiscences), by "Nameless Joe,"
205-83
Dime Novel as an Historian's Tool, The,
(value of dime novels in portraying
history), by William A. Settle, Jr.,
456-92; 457-102
Dime Novel Collecting, (advice and comments),
by Charles Bragin, 365-12; 402-28
Dime Novel Collector's Book Shelf, (books
for collectors and readers), by Edward
T. LeBlanc, (See "collecting")
Dime Novel & Boys Books Collectors Book
Shelf, (books on the subject), by
Edward T. LeBlanc, (See "collecting")
Dime Novel Bonanza, (collecting experiences),
by J. Edward Leithead, 65-1
Dime Novel Collecting, (collecting advice
and experience), by "Deadwood Dick,Jr.",
64-1
Dime Novel "Daze", (reminiscences of
collecting dime novels), by Gerald J.
McIntosh, 448-3
Dime Novel Exhibit, Brooklyn Public Library,
1948, (described), 184-3
Dime Novels Exhibited in the Express
Window (collecting reminiscences), by
Glenn H. Henderson, 125-1
Dime Novel Exhibits, news, 429-65
Dime Novel Friend, The, (verse), by Ida
C. Clark, 171-2
Dime Novels: How One Boy Was Cured of His
Liking for Them, (humorous reminiscences)
191-70
Dime Novels in Cartoons, (discusses Jim
Williams and other early cartoonists),
by Gerald J. McIntosh, 412-2
Dime Novel - Its Place in American Litera-
ture, (historical survey), by Ralph F.
Adimari, 12-6; 13-1; 14-3; 15-2; 16-2;
17-2; 18-4; 19-2; 23-4; 25-3
Dime Novel Must Go, The, (wane of the dime
novel), by William M. Burns, 151-3
Dime Novel Notes, (on various publications),
by Gerald J. McIntosh, 441-62
Dime Novel Prices Hold, (values), by Charles
Bragin, 19-4
Dime Novel Printing, by John C. Kunzog,
428-51
Dime Novel Readers Scrap Book, (advice to a
son who is about to go on his own, 1845),
408-93
Dime Novel Readers Scrap Book, (from TIP
TOP WEEKLY #532), 407-82
Dime Novel Reviews: The Coming of Dr. Quartz,
(Nick Carter villain), by J. Randolph
Cox, 522-130
Dime Novel Reviews: Diamond Dick, (dime
novel character), by J. Randolph Cox,
523-2

52

(DIME NOVEL ROUNDUP), History of the Happy Hours Brotherhood and the DIME NOVEL ROUNDUP, by Ralph F. Cummings, 430-74; 432-93

DIME NOVEL ROUNDUP, Index of Major Subjects, January 1976 to December 1978; 535-10a

DIME NOVEL ROUNDUP, Index to Major Subjects, Issues #1-516, by Edward T. LeBlanc, 529-SS

(DIME NOVEL ROUNDUP), The Life of HAPPY HOURS MAGAZINE and DIME NOVEL ROUNDUP, Also Happy Hours Brotherhood, by Ralph F. Cummings, 300-81

(DIME NOVEL ROUNDUP), New Editor, Edward T. LeBlanc, 238-52

(DIME NOVEL ROUNDUP), Rounding Up the Roundup, or Items You May Have Muffed, (calling attention to past items in DIME NOVEL ROUNDUP), by "Hawknose the Detective", 234-17

(DIME NOVEL ROUNDUP), That Little Gem, THE DIME NOVEL ROUNDUP, 222-18

(DIME NOVEL ROUNDUP), Ye Brotherhood, the Roundup and Its Editor, by Charles Duprez, 274-53

(DIME NOVEL ROUNDUP), Ye Roundup and Its Members, by Charles Duprez, 263-59

Dime Novel Round-Uppers, (collecting comments), by F.P.Pitzer, 19-3

Dime Novel Series Title Changes, by Denis R. Rogers and Edward T. LeBlanc, 488-50

Dime Novel Sidelights, (miscellaneous bibliographical and collecting data), by Ralph P. Smith, 479-72

Dime Novel Sketches, (short surveys of bibliographical data)
No. 1, YOUNG GLORY, 317-13
No. 2, HANDSOME HARRY, 320-39
No. 3, YANKEE DOODLE, 321-49
No. 4, THREE CHUMS, 322-57
No. 5, UP-TO-DATE BOYS' LIBRARY, 323-65
No. 6, PAUL JONES WEEKLY, 324-73
No. 7, PLUCK AND LUCK, 325-83
No. 8, COMRADES, 326-91
No. 9, YOUNG ATHLETE'S WEEKLY, THE 327-99
No.10, DO AND DARE, 329-9
No.11, WIDE AWAKE LIBRARY, 330-17
No.12, BOWERY BOY LIBRARY, 331-33
No.13, BRAVE AND BOLD, 333-49
No.14, RED RAVEN, 334-57
No.15, DIAMOND DICK, JR., 335-65
No.16, FAME AND FORTUNE WEEKLY, 336-73
No.17, BLUE AND GRAY WEEKLY, 337-81
No.18, NICK CARTER STORIES, 338-91
No.19, MIGHT AND MAIN LIBRARY, 340-1
No.20, KLONDIKE KIT LIBRARY, 341-9
No.21, FAR WEST LIBRARY, 342-17
No.22, LOG CABIN LIBRARY, (pocket edition), 343-25

Dime Novel Sketches, (continued)
No.23, FRANK READE WEEKLY, 344-57
No.24, ROUGH RIDER WEEKLY, 345-65
No.25, ADVENTURE WEEKLY, 346-75
No.26, BEADLES AMERICAN LIBRARY, 349-104
No.27, WILD WEST WEEKLY, 350-111
No.28, JESSE JAMES STORIES, 351-119
No.29, BUFFALO BILL STORIES, 352-1
No.30, NICK CARTER DETECTIVE LIBRARY, 353-11
No.31, BEADLES FRONTIER SERIES, 354-19
No.32, NUGGET LIBRARY, 355-27
No.33, THE WAR LIBRARY, 356-35
No.34, NICK CARTER WEEKLY, 357-59
No.35, ALL SPORTS LIBRARY, 358-67
No.36, OLD CAP COLLIER LIBRARY, 359-75
No.37, MOTOR STORIES, 360-83
No.38, BRIGHT DAYS, 361-91
No.39, SATURDAY NIGHT, 363-107
No.40, GOLDEN HOURS, 364-1
No.41, BOYS OF AMERICA, 365-11
No.42, GOLDEN ARGOSY, 366-21
No.43, FRANK LESLIE'S BOYS OF AMERICA, 367-31
No.44, THE HEARTHSTONE, 368-41
No.45, BOYS' WORLD, 369-49
No.46, FRANK LESLIE'S BOYS AND GIRLS WEEKLY, 370-61
No.47, STREET & SMITH'S LITERARY ALBUM, 372-81
No.48, OLD SLEUTH WEEKLY, 372-79
No.49, JAMES BOYS WEEKLY, 373-89
No.50, WIDE AWAKE LIBRARY, 374-100
No.51, SHIELD WEEKLY, 375-107
No.52, THE STARRY FLAG WEEKLY, 376-1
No.53, RED, WHITE AND BLUE, 377-9
No.54, SECRET SERVICE, 378-19
No.55, ARMY AND NAVY WEEKLY, 380-39
No.56, HALF HOLIDAY, 381-47
No.57, YOUNG KLONDIKE, 382-57
No.58, TIP TOP WEEKLY, 383-67
No.59, SNAPS, 384-75
No.60, NEW TIP TOP WEEKLY, 385-83
No.61, WORK AND WIN, 386-93
No.62, BOYS OF NEW YORK, 389-9
No.63, ALL AROUND WEEKLY, 390-21
No.64, OLD BROADBRIM WEEKLY, 391-33
No.65, AMERICAN INDIAN WEEKLY, 392-43
No.66, DEADWOOD DICK LIBRARY, 393-55
No.67, DICK DOBBS DETECTIVE WEEKLY, 394-69
No.68, YOUNG MEN OF AMERICA, 395-77
No.69, GOLDEN WEEKLY, 396-89
No.70, TRUE BLUE, 397-103
No.71, LIBERTY BOYS OF '76, 398-113
No.72, MY QUEEN, 399-125
No.73, FRANK MANLEY WEEKLY, 400-1
No.74, HAPPY DAYS, 401-13
No.75, NEW BUFFALO BILL WEEKLY, 402-23
No.76, YOUNG ROVER LIBRARY, 403-35
No.77, BOYS BEST WEEKLY, 404-47
No.78, BEADLES BOYS LIBRARY, 405-57
No.79, YOUNG BROADBRIM WEEKLY, 406-65

Dime Novel Sketches, (continued)
No.80, BOYS HOME WEEKLY, 407-73
No.81, WESTERN STORY MAGAZINE, 408-85
No.82, WESTERN WEEKLY, 409-95
No.83, TOP NOTCH MAGAZINE, 410-111
No.84, AMERICAN INDIAN SERIES,
    (Westbrook Co.), 411-127
No.85, NEW YORK DETECTIVE LIBRARY-
    DETECTIVE LIBRARY, 412-1
No.86, LOG CABIN LIBRARY - OLD
    LOG CABIN, 413-13
No.87, BOYS STAR LIBRARY, 414-23
No.88, CRICKET LIBRARY, 415-33
No.89, BOB BROOKS LIBRARY, 416-45
No.90, OLD SLEUTH LIBRARY, 417-53
No.91, MORRISON'S SENSATIONAL SERIES,
    418-63
No.92, Dime Novels in French, 419-75
No.93, BEADLES HALF DIME LIBRARY,
    420-85
No.94, COMIC LIBRARY, 421-93
No.95, NEW YORK BOYS LIBRARY, 422-105
No.96, BORDER BOYS LIBRARY, 423-113
No.97, BEADLES DIME LIBRARY, 424-1
No.98, THE PRAIRIE OUTLAWS, 425-11
No.99, NICKEL LIBRARY, 426-23
No.100, NUGGET LIBRARY, 427-33
No.101, FRANK READE LIBRARY, 428-43
No.102, BEADLES POCKET LIBRARY, 429-55
No.103, THE GEM LIBRARY, 430-67
No.104, Pamphlet by Edward S. Ellis as
    Capt. R.M.Hawthorne, 431-77
No.105, DIAMOND DICK LIBRARY, 432-87
No.106, LITTLE CHIEF LIBRARY, 433-95
No.107, BEADLES BOYS LIBRARY (octavo
    edition), 434-107
No.108, GOLDEN LIBRARY, 435-117
No.109, BEADLES POPULAR LIBRARY,
    436-1
No.110, YOUNG SLEUTH LIBRARY, 437-17
No.111, SATURDAY LIBRARY, 438-29
No.112, NEW AND OLD FRIENDS, 439-39
No.113, WIDE AWAKE LIBRARY - SPECIAL,
    440-41
No.114, OWL LIBRARY, 441-49
No.115, NEW YORK COMIC LIBRARY, 442-65
No.116, YOUNG SPORTS FIVE CENT LIBRARY,
    443-75
No.117, BOYS OF NEW YORK POCKET
    LIBRARY, 444-87
No.118, NOVELETTE LIBRARY, 445-99
No.119, 5 CENT WEEKLY LIBRARY, 446-109
No.120, HUB TEN CENT NOVELS, 447-121
No.121, THE NOVELETTE, 448-1
No.122, THE AMERICAN LIBRARY, 449-13
No.123, BEADLE DIME NOVELS, 450-23
No.124, ARMY AND NAVY LIBRARY, 451-39
No.125, YANKEE 5 CENT LIBRARY, 452-49
No.126, THE CHAMPION LIBRARY, 453-59
No.127, NEW YORK BOYS' LIBRARY, 454-71
No.128, THE BOYS OWN LIBRARY, 455-79
No.129, BROADWAY LIBRARY, 456-91
No.130, THE NEW YORK NOVELIST, 457-101
No.131, INDIAN TALES, 458-109
No.132, THE NEW YORK NICKEL LIBRARY,
    459-119

Dime Novel Sketches, (continued)
No.133, THE BOY'S LIBRARY, 460-1
No.134, GOOD NEWS LIBRARY, 461-13
No.135, THE UNION LIBRARY, 462-23
No.136, FACTORY LIFE LIBRARY, 463-35
No.137, LAUGHING STORIES, 464-43
No.138, THE ILLUSTRATED LIBRARY,
    465-51
No.139, YOUTHS LIBRARY
No.140, LIBRARY OF ADVENTURE AND
    ROMANCE, 467-73
No.141, TEN CENT NOVELETTES, 468-89
No.142, IRWIN'S AMERICAN NOVELS,
    469-113
No.143, ORNUM'S INDIAN NOVELS,
    470-123
No.144, MUNRO'S TEN CENT NOVELS,
    471-137
No.145, TEN CENT POPULAR NOVELS,
    472-1
No.146, BEADLE & ADAMS 20 CENT NOVELS,
    473-17
No.147, TEN CENT CLAUDE DUVAL NOVELS,
    474-33
No.148, BEADLES NEW DIME NOVELS,
    475-45
No.149, DEWITT'S TEN CENT ROMANCES,
    476-55
No.150, BEADLES POCKET NOVELS, 477-63
No.151, ORNUM & CO'S FIFTEEN CENT
    ROMANCES, 479-71
No.152, DEWITT'S CLAUDE DUVAL SERIES,
    480-79
No.153, FRANK STARR'S AMERICAN NOVELS,
    481-95
No.154, THE BLACK HIGHWAYMAN NOVELS,
    482-111
No.155, THE BOY'S OWN NOVELS, 483-119
No.156, NEW YORK LIBRARY, 484-1
No.157, CHANEY'S UNION NOVELS, 485-17
No.158, NEW SENSATION TEN CENT NOVELS,
    486-29
No.159, HIGHWAY NOVELS, 487-41
No.160, ADVANCE TEN CENT NOVELS,
    488-49
No.161, DAWLEY'S TEN PENNY NOVELS,
    489-59
No.162, HILTON'S UNION NOVELS, 490-69
No.163, BEADLES CLASSIC STORIES,
    491-85
No.164, RICHMOND'S (SENSATION) NOVELS
    492-97
No.165, BEADLES 15¢ NOVELS, 493-113
No.166, ORIGINAL UNION NOVELS, 494-125
No.167, TEN CENT IRISH NOVELS, 495-133
No.168, HILTON'S TEN CENT NOVELS,
    496-1
No.169, REDPATH'S BOOKS FOR THE CAMP-
    FIRES, 497-13
No.170, PETERSEN'S POPULAR PRIZE
    LIBRARY, 498-29
No.171, CHAMPION NOVELS, 499-37
No.172, NEW YORK FIVE CENT LIBRARY,
    500-49
No.173, IRWIN P. BEADLES TEN CENT
    NOVELS, 501-61

Dime Novel Sketches, (continued)
No.174, HOME LIBRARY/NOVELS, 502-73
No.175, HILTON'S DIME BOOKS, 503-89
No.176, DAWLEY'S CAMP & FIRESIDE
   LIBRARY, 504-105
No.177, BEADLES DIME FICTION, 505-117
No.178, DAWLEY'S NEW WAR NOVELS,
   506-129
No.179, BOYS' BOOKS OF ROMANCE AND
   ADVENTURE, 507-135
No.180, MUNRO'S BACKWOODS SERIES,
   508-1
No.181, AMERICAN TALES, (2nd Series),
   509-9
No.182, HIGHWAY SERIES, 510-18
No.183, PEOPLE'S FIVE CENT NOVELETTES,
   511-25
No.184, BEADLES DIME TALES, 512-37
No.185, DEWITT'S NIGHTSHADE SERIES,
   513-49
No.186, SERIES OF PRIZE NOVELS,
   514-65
No.187, DEWITT'S GOOD BOOK SERIES,
   515-89
No.188, NED BUNTLINE'S OWN, 516-125
No.189, DEWITT'S JONATHAN WILD SERIES,
   517-1
No.190, POPULAR SERIES OF FICTION
   FANCY AND FACT, 518-33
No.191, HOME LIBRARY, 519-57
No.192, THE NIGHTSIDE LIBRARY, 520-73
No.193, BRADY'S CHAMPION SERIES,
   521-105
No.194, DEWITT'S ROMANCES, 522-130
No.195, FRANK LESLIE'S POPULAR LIBRARY,
   523-1
No.196, DEWITT'S STORIES OF THE SEA,
   524-25
No.197, SERIES OF MILITARY NOVELS,
   525-57
No.198, DEWITT'S HANDSOME JACK SERIES,
   526-77
No.199, BRADY'S PEOPLE'S NOVELETTES,
   527-97
No.200, TALES OF CELEBRATED HIGHWAYMEN,
   528-121
No.201, DEWITT'S TWENTY-FIVE CENT
   NOVELS, 529-1
No.202, BRADY'S MERCURY STORIES,
   530-34
No.203, SERIES OF SEA TALES, 531-57
No.204, PETERSON'S ILLUMINATED STORIES,
   532-81
No.205, RED WOLF SERIES, 533-97
No.206, HILTON'S PRIZE ROMANCES,
   534-113
No.207, RAILROAD READING, 535-1
No.208, G.W.M.REYNOLD'S NOVELS, 536-21
No.209, CAPTAIN HERON SERIES OF
   HIGHWAYMAN TALES, 537-39
No.210, TALES OF BORDER ADVENTURE,
   538-55
No.211, LIVES OF GREAT AMERICANS,
   539-73
No.212, CHEAP EDITION OF POPULAR
   AUTHORS, 540-89

Dime Novel Sketches, (continued)
No.213, FIRESIDE SERIES, 541-1
No.214, BEADLES DIME BIOGRAPHICAL
   LIBRARY, 542-33
No.215, FIRESIDE COMPANIONS,
   543-49
No.216, SECRET SERVICE SERIES,
   544-65
No.217, SEA AND SHORE SERIES,
   545-81
No.218, SHIELD SERIES, 546-97
No.219, COLUMBIA LIBRARY, 547-1
No.220, BOY'S HOME LIBRARY, 548-25
No.221, ALGER SERIES, 549-49
No.222, BOUND TO WIN LIBRARY,
   550-73
No.223, SPORT STORIES, 551-93
No.224, NEW FICTION LIBRARY, 552-113
Dime Novels Versus Modern Fiction
   (comparison of dime novels, comic
   books, and TRUE DETECTIVE magazine),
   by Charles Duprez, 279-105
DIME NOVELS, 155-4
Dime Novels and Deviltry, (influence
   claimed on children), 192-73
Dime Novels at Last Recognized in High
   Places, (literary value), by William
   M. Burns, 27-1
Dime Novels in France, (French language
   editions and originals), by George
   Fronval, 379-27
Dime Novels Not Bad, (literary value),
   by James R. Russell, 79-5
Dime Novels - Their Morals and Influence
   (social value and significance),
   203-69
(Dime Novel), Commemorative postage stamp
   for centenary of dime novel urged,
   320-46
(Dime Novels) Odds and Ends, (biblio-
   graphical items), by Ralph F. Cummings,
   58-9
(Dime Novels), Valuable Data, (bibliographical items), by H.O.Rawson,
   58-7
Dinan, John A.: letter of comment,
   516-150; 539-84; 552-127
Dippie, Brian W., & Edward T. LeBlanc:
   Bibliography of Custer Dime Novels
   (featuring General Custer), 442-66
Displaying Dime Novels, (housing the
   collection), by Howard Silsbee,
   279-104
Displaying One's Collection, (boys' books
   collection of Willis Potthoff), by
   Edward T. LeBlanc, 518-46
Displaying Your Collection, (housing
   boys' books collection), by Jack R.
   Schorr, 465-57
Disposal of a Book Collection, (problems
   inherent), by Denis R. Rogers, 546-98,
   see also letters 549-66; 549-67
Disposing of Your Collection, (problems
   and suggestions), by Jack R. Schorr,
   503-103

(Dixon, Franklin W.: Hardy Boys Series),
A Half Century of the Hardy Boys
or Clues to an Obscure Chronology,
(bibliography), by Robert V. Riordan,
530-35

Dizer, John T., Jr.: Boys Books and
the American Dream (appeal of boys'
books), 425-12; 426-29; see also
427-42

Dizer, John T., Jr.: Chester Gard Mayo-
An Appreciation, (collector of dime
novels, books, story papers), 530-48

Dizer, John T., Jr.: Chronological
Listing of Boys Books by Edward
Stratemeyer First Published as Serials,
515-118

Dizer, John T., Jr.: Early Stratemeyer
Writings, with Checklist, 549-50

Dizer, John T., Jr., Land of the Heroes,
(locales of boys' series books),
465-52; 466-62

Dizer, John T., Jr.: Paperbacks, Dime
Novels and the Virtues of Reading
Series Books, 483-122

Dizer, John T., Jr.: Review of CHILDREN'S
LITERATURE: A HISTORICAL AND CONTEM-
PORARY BIBLIOGRAPHY by Irving P. Leif,
530-53; 531-77

Dizer, John T., Jr.: Review of THE GIRL
SLEUTH, A FEMINIST GUIDE by Bobbie
Ann Mason (book on girls' series
books), 530-53; 531-77

Dizer, John T., Jr.: Review of HORATIO
ALGER,JR., AN ANNOTATED BIBLIOGRAPHY
OF COMMENT AND CRITICISM by Gary
Scharnhorst and Jack Bales, 550-74

Dizer, John T., Jr.: The Rolt-Wheeler -
Gilbreth Letters (Francis Rolt-Wheeler
and Lillian M. Gilbreth correspondence;
boys' series books), with checklist
of Rolt-Wheeler works, 500-56

Dizer, John T., Jr.: Serials and Boys
Books by Edward Stratemeyer, 516-126

Dizer, John T., Jr.: Shopton, Home of the
Swifts, (locale of Tom Swift series
books), 449-14

Dizer, John T., Jr.: Stoddard, Saltillo
Boys and Syracuse, (on W.O.Stoddard
and his books for boys), 490-77

Dizer, John T., Jr.: Stratemeyer and
Science Fiction, (discusses Tom
Swift series, early science fiction,
and Stratemeyer's role), 514-66;
520-73

Dizer, John T., Jr.: Stratemeyer and the
Blacks, (attitude toward and treatment
of Blacks by the Stratemeyer Syndicate),
515-90

Dizer, John T., Jr.: Street & Smith Box
M58, (discoveries in the Street &
Smith Collection at Syracuse Univ.),
526-78

(DO AND DARE), Dime Novel Sketches #10,
329-9

DO AND DARE WEEKLY, 115-3

DO AND DARE WEEKLY, (discussion) by
Harold C. Holmes, 114-1

Dobkin, J.B.: letter of comment, 547-18

Doctor Quartz and Other Nine-Lived
Villains, (villains in the dime
novels), by J. Edward Leithead,
380-40; 381-48

(Dome, Marcus), obituary, 5-8

Don on the Farm, (biog. sketch of Don
Learnard), by Charles Duprez, 332-41

Donelson, Ken: Censorship and Early
Adolescent Literature: Stratemeyer,
Mathiews and Comstock, (attempts
to discredit Stratemeyer), 534-119

Donelson, Ken: H. Irving Hancock, A
Romanticized View of Sports and
Boys, (discussion on boy's sports
series books), 522-138

Donelson, Ken: Horatio Alger,Jr. and
Ragged Dick: Reality and Myth,
525-58

Donelson, Ken: Promises, Promises,
Promises, (discusses books mentioned
as promised in boys' series books
but never published), 550-77

Donnelly, T.J.: letter of comment,
118-3

(Donohue, M.A., Co., Publishers),
Edward S. Ellis Stories Published
by the Mershon Complex, by Denis
R. Rogers, 490-70; 491-86; 492-104

Doughty, F.W., author of James Boys
stories in NEW YORK DETECTIVE
LIBRARY, 29-3

(Doughty, Francis Worcester), The Early
Doughty - Master of Mysteries and
Wonders, (dime novel author), with
checklist, by Ross Craufurd, 521-106

(Doughty, Francis Worcester), Francis
Worcester Doughty, Uncrowned King
of the Dime Novel Writers, (biog.
sketch), by Charles Bragin, 44-1

(Doughty, Francis Worcester), From
Movie Picture Stories of Sept.3, 1915,
news item, 293-16

(Doughty, Francis Worcester), obituary,
548-40

(Doughty, Francis Worcester), Retrospect-
Francis Worcester Doughty, by Robert
H. Smeltzer, 343-54

(Doughty, Francis Worcester), The Two
King Bradys and Their Girl Detectives,
(discusses his work in detective dime
novels), by J. Edward Leithead,
372-80; 373-90

Drama of the Seventies, (lurid and sensational plays of 1870's), 39-2

Dreyer, Lou: letter of comment, 416-50;
429-64; 433-104

Driscoll, Dan: letter of comment, 415-41

Dubonnet, Eva: Collector's Items,
(verse), 111-5

(Dumont, Mrs. Nellie), obituary, wife of
Frank Dumont, famous minstrel, 89-2

(Duprez, Charles), see also "Nameless
Joe" and "Ima Tellinya"

Duprez, Charles: A Bangup Vacation,
(reminiscences, dime novel hunting),
313-131

Duprez, Charles: Any You Boys Met George French?, (biog. sketch), 338-89

Duprez, Charles: Boys, Meet Dewey Miller, (biog. sketch), 284-33

Duprez, Charles: Dime Novels versus Modern Fiction, (comparison of dime novels, comic books, TRUE DETECTIVE magazine) 279-105

Duprez, Charles: Don on the Farm, (biog. sketch of Don Learned), 332-41

Duprez, Charles: Great Inventor Tangles with Charlie Miller, the Last of the Pony Express Riders, 252-65

Duprez, Charles: letter of comment, 377-16

Duprez, Charles: The Most Reckless Ralph, (biog. sketch of Ralph F. Cummings), 348-98

Duprez, Charles: Moyse for Choice, (biog. sketch of Arthur Moyse), 339-99

Duprez, Charles: My Boy Harold, (biog. sketch of Harold C. Ingraham), 344-59

Duprez, Charles: MY QUEEN LIBRARY, (data), 249-41

Duprez, Charles: Nuther Biography - By Cracky, (biog. sketch of Ralph F. Cummings), 270-20

Duprez, Charles: Photography in the Raw, (reminiscences), 300-76

Duprez, Charles: The Rockland Terror Carries on Another Biography (biog. sketch of William M. Burns), 268-4

Duprez, Charles: Rootin' Tootin' Shootin' Frisco Bert (biog. sketch of Bertrand Couch), 290-85

Duprez, Charles: Rover Boy Carl Linville, (biog. sketch), 281-10

Duprez, Charles: SNAPS, The Comic Weekly, (discussion and data), 244-1

Duprez, Charles: Today's Children, (reminiscences), 248-38

Duprez, Charles: Ye Brotherhood, The Roundup and Its Editor, (on the Happy Hours Brotherhood, the DIME NOVEL ROUNDUP, and Ralph F. Cummings), 274-53

Duprez, Charles: Ye Roundup and Its Members, (on DIME NOVEL ROUNDUP and some of the Club members), 263-59

Duprez, Charles: YOUNG KLONDIKE, (data and discussion of dime novel), 258-18

Duvall Series of Claude Duvall, by George H. Cordier, (dime novel), 142-1

Dying Cowboy, The, (verse), by Col. Charles D. Randolph, 2-3

Dykes, J.C.: BRADY'S CHAMPION STORIES, (discussion with checklist) of #1-19, 156-1

Dykes, J.C.: In Memorial, Charles Jonas, (memorial tribute), 161-3

Dykes, J.C.: letter of comment, 153-3

E.D.LONG & CO'S DIME ROMANCES, 42-3

Early Adventures with the House of Beadle (early publications), by Roland D. Sawyer, 45-2

Early Bicycling Days, (reminiscences), by J.H.Armbruster, 260-34; 261-45

Early Doughty - Master of Mysteries and Wonders, The, (biog. and literary sketch, Francis Worcester Doughty), by Ross Craufurd, with checklist, 521-106

Early Juvenile Aviation Fiction, (boys' series aviation stories), by Rick Crandall, 545-82

Early Publications of the Aldine Pub. Co. (English publisher, with special interest to Alger Series), by Denis R. Rogers, 532-82; 533-98

Early Stratemeyer Writings, by John T. Dizer, Jr., with checklist, 549-50

Edward L. Wheeler's Own View of Wild Bill Hickok, by "Seajay", 158-3

Edward S. Ellis Stories Published by the Mershon Complex, The, by Denis R. Rogers, 490-70; 491-86; 492-104

Edward Stratemeyer's Appeal to Contemporary Young Readers, (boy's series books), by Peter C. Walther, 535-2

(Edwards, Leo), Magazine Serial and Book Relationships in Leo Edwards Books, (discussion, boys' books), by Julius R. Chenu, 534-122

Eisenberg, Frank: Those Alger Days, (verse), 543-56

(elephant), The Light of Asia, (white elephant imported, news item), 237-41

Ellen Price Wood (1814-1887), English Juvenile Writer, (biog. sketch), by Ralph Adimari, 366-22

ELLERY QUEEN'S MYSTERY MAGAZINE, note, 135-3

Elliott, Thomas & Talbot, Publishers, mention, 144-3

Ellis for Beginners, (bibliography of books of Edward S. Ellis), by Denis R. Rogers, 529-2

Ellis' Ten War Chief Tales, (hardbound Indian Chief novels by Edward S. Ellis), by Denis R. Rogers, 539-74

(Ellis, Edward S.), A Final Word on the Pseudonyms of Edward S. Ellis, by Denis R. Rogers, 363-108

(Ellis, Edward S.), A Publication Pattern of Edward S. Ellis (study of the Porter & Coates/Henry T. Coates/John C. Winston editions of boys' books by Ellis), by Denis R. Rogers and J. Edward Leithead, 480-80; 481-95

(Ellis, Edward S.), Books recorded in "Book Auction Records", 546-102

(Ellis, Edward S.) The Edward S. Ellis Stories Published by the Mershon Complex, by Denis R. Rogers, 490-70; 491-86; 492-104

(Ellis, Edward S.), Ellis for Beginners, (bibliography of books of Ellis), by Denis R. Rogers, 529-2

(Ellis, Edward S.), Ellis' Ten War Chief Tales, (hardbound Indian Chief novels by Ellis), by Denis R. Rogers, 539-74

(Ellis, Edward S.),The Lovell Complex, by Denis R. Rogers, 527-98

(Ellis, Edward S.), Now They're Collectors' Items #1: Edward S. Ellis and Harry Castlemon, (on boys' series books), by J. Edward Leithead, 405-58; 406-66

(Ellis, Edward S.), Pamphlet by Ellis as Capt. R.M.Hawthorne, 431-77

(Ellis, Edward S.), Postscript on the Pen Names of Edward S. Ellis, by Denis R. Rogers, 336-74

(Ellis, Edward S.), Pseudonyms of Edward S. Ellis, by Denis R. Rogers, 267-90; 268-2; 307-25; 315-148; 318-22; 319-30; 320-42; 330-18; 333-58

(Ellis, Edward S.), Statistical Alphabet of Edward S. Ellis (extent of Ellis' works), by Denis R. Rogers, 446-117

(Ellis, Edward S.), Survey of the Probable Publication Pattern of the Books of Edward S. Ellis Under the Imprint of A.L.Burt, by Denis R. Rogers, 524-26

(Ellis, Edward S.: SETH JONES OF NEW HAMPSHIRE), Introduction, (censorship; early dime novel history), 172-1

Elusives, The, (hard to find boys' books), by Jack R. Schorr, 494-130

(Emmett, George: SHOT AND SHELL STORIES), The Rackety Bohemians, (literary discussion), by Patrick Mulhall, 42-3

Emmett Publications, note, 42-4

(Emmett, William L., Publisher), The Rival Rangers of Fleet Street, (publishing history), by A.W. Lawson, 279-102

English Boys Magazines, (discussion), by George H. Cordier

English Giant, The, (biog. sketch of E. Harcourt Burrage), by Ross Craufurd, 12-2

ENGLISH GIRLS' JOURNAL, 279-102

English Novels of Today, The, (English dime novels, contemporary), by Ralph F. Cummings, 21-1

English Reprints of BUFFALO BILL NOVELS, by J. Edward Leithead, 392-44; 393-56

Enslin, Morton S.: A List of Alger Titles, (bibliographic checklist), 467-74; 468-90

Enslin, Morton S.: Horatio Alger, Jr. After Seventy Years, (reminiscences), 451-40; 452-50

(Enslin, Morton S.), obituary, 548-40

(ESQUIRE Magazine), Barred by the Post Office, (rated as obscene, and other postal regulations), by Ralph P. Smith, 145-1

EUREKA DETECTIVE STORIES, 193-83

(Evans, Larry), Larry Evans, A Famous American Novelist, (dime novels), by Roy B. Van Devier, 388-4

EVERY BOYS FAVORITE JOURNAL, 13-5; 21-4

(Every Boys Library), G & D Every Boys Library Boy Scout Editions (boys' books), by Julius R. Chenu, 536-33

EVERY BOYS' MAGAZINE, 14-2

Evidence of Another Stratemeyer Pseudonym (as Ralph Harrington), by Peter C. Walther, 542-41

Exasperations of a Book Collector (boys' series books collecting), by Jack R. Schorr, 448-2

Exit UNION JACK, (cessation), by William M. Burns, 17-5; 23-1

Experiences and Thoughts on Gilbert Patten (biographical notes on author), by Charles Bragin, 409-107

(FACTORY LIFE LIBRARY), Dime Novel Sketches #136, 463-35

Facts About John R. Musick, by Fred T. Singleton, 13-7; 21-5

Facts About "Peter Pad", (dime novel character), by Ralph F. Adimari, 12-3

Facts About the Two Bills and Buntline, (Wild Bill, Buffalo Bill, and Ned Buntline), by Roland D. Sawyer, 160-4

Fahrer, Howard J.: letter of comment, 427-42

Fair Enough, (on comic-strip detectives), by Westbrook Pegler, 135-1

FAME AND FORTUNE, 54-1; 66-6

FAME AND FORTUNE MAGAZINE, 42-3

FAME AND FORTUNE WEEKLY, 42-3; 81A-11; 238-54

(FAME AND FORTUNE WEEKLY), Dime Novel Sketches #16, 336-73

Famous Tousey Story Papers, by Edward T. LeBlanc, 508-2

(fantastic inventions), Today's Facts in Yesterday's Inventions, by Thomas R. Henry, 95-1

Fantasy, Science Fiction and Lost Race Adventures in the Street & Smith Paperback Volumes, checklist, by Stuart A. Teitler, 442-71

FAR WEST LIBRARY, 43-2

(FAR WEST LIBRARY), Dime Novel Sketches #21, 342-17

Favorite Boyhood Characters on the British Screen, by W.O.G.Lofts and D.J.Adley, 525-66; 528-122

Favorite Stories, (reminiscences on boyhood reading), by George H. Cordier, 147-1

Favorites of Yesterday, (biog. sketches of early authors), by Hermon Pitcher,
- Susan Warner, 158-3
- Marie Corelli, 186-1
- E.P.Roe, 191-68
- Rosa N. Carey, 203-66
- Harriet Beecher Stowe, 216-67
- Anna Bartlett Warner, 323-68
- Amelia E. Barr, 326-95

(Fearless, Dave, Series), Garden City Pub. Company's Paperback Juveniles, (boys' series books), by Julius R. Chenu, 531-72

(Fearnot, Fred), Fred Fearnot Was There, (dime novel character discussed), by Ross Craufurd, 519-58

(FICTION FACTORY, THE: Quentin Reynolds), Review of book on history of Street & Smith Publishers by J. Edward Leithead, 282-18

Fifty Years Ago, (on THE GOLDEN ARGOSY), by Patrick Mulhall, 52-4

Figley, Ulysses Grant: The Harkaway Business, (on dime novel character), 124-3

Figley, Ulysses Grant: Harkaway, Merriwell, Etc., (reminiscences and recollections), 115-1

Figley, Ulysses Grant: Old Story Papers, (comments and reminiscences), 115-5

Figley, Ulysses Grant: The Reason Why, (Harkaway novels written by several writers), 118-2

Figley, Ulysses Grant: Well, What Have You? (on old books), 148-2

(Figley, Ulysses Grant), biographical sketch, 135-3

Fink, Clarence M.: letter of comment, 505-127

(firefighters in dime novels), The Anatomy of Dime Novels No.5: The Firefighters, by J. Edward Leithead, 407-74; 407-86

FIRESIDE COMPANION, 6-6

(FIRESIDE COMPANION), Dime Novel Sketches #215, 543-49

FIRESIDE SERIES, Checklist of titles, 541-25

(FIRESIDE SERIES), Dime Novel Sketches #213, 541-1

First Diamond Dick Story, The, by W.C. Miller, 63-1

First Dime Novel to be Reprinted After 69 Years (MALESKA), by Ralph F. Cummings, 91-1

First English Papers for Boys, (historical discussion), by W.O.G.Lofts, 277-84

First Half Year of WORK AND WIN, (discussion), by Harold C. Holmes, 166-1

First Nick Carter, The, by Harold C. Holmes, 79-1

First Nick Carter Story Was Accepted, (Eugene T. Sawyer), 73-7

First Tom Slade Book, or Movies to Print, (Tom Slade Boy Scout series of boys' books), by Julius R. Chenu, 514-83

Fisher, Charles: Merriwell's Out of Date, (fiction), 123-5

FIVE CENT WEEKLY LIBRARY, 58-8

(FIVE CENT WEEKLY LIBRARY), Dime Novel Sketches #119, 446-109

FIVE CENT WIDE AWAKE LIBRARY, 3-6

(flag), Our Flag's Bicentennial (effort of YOUTH'S COMPANION to have flag flown over schools; authorship of Pledge of Allegiance), by Louise Harris, 513-56

(flag), Who Wrote the Pledge of Allegiance? (assertion that James Bailey Upham is true author), by Louise Harris, 528-127

FLAG OF OUR UNION, 15-4; 16-2; 17-4; 175-25

Flaum, George T.: The Art of Repairing Novels, 211-25

Flaum, George T.: Hunting for Novels is Fun, (collecting experiences), 180-2

Flaum, George T.: Is Interest in Dime Novels Dying? (collecting), 247-27

Flaum, George T.: The Prize Plot Story, (Frank Merriwell; TIP TOP WEEKLY), 199-25

Flaum, George T.: Removing Stickers and Labels from Novels with Ease, 238-54

(Florida), Charles Rothstein Collects Florida Dime Novels (with Florida locales), by Jane Hamlin, 434-115

Fogaris, Michael: letter of comment, 381-51; 389-90

Following the Horses Without a Shovel, (reminiscences), by Nameless Joe, 225-43

Following the Merriwell Trail (bibliography with story synopsis), by Gerald J. McIntosh, 474-34

Fond Recollections, (autobiographical reminiscences), by J. Edward Leithead, 287-57

Foolish Buying, (collecting advice), by Walt Mason, 71-3

(Forbes-Lindsay, C.H.), C.H.Forbes-Lindsay, A Famous India Author (biog. sketch) by Roy B. Van Devier, 386-97; 387-104

Foreign Novels, (discussion of foreign dime novels), by Robert H. Smeltzer, 24-3

(foreign editions), Beadles Abroad, (foreign language editions), by Denis R. Rogers, 347-86; 348-96

Forgotten Men of the House of Beadle, The, (little remembered authors), by Roland D. Sawyer, 141-3

FORTUNE STORY MAGAZINE, 62-7; 66-7

Fortunes Left by British Writers, commentary by William J. Benners, 81-5

4500, All Mint, (boys' book collecting) by Jack R. Schorr, 469-118

Foss, Sam Walter: Uncle Seth on the Modern Novel, (verse), 118-6

(Foster, W. Bert), Author and Artist of the Street & Smith Staff - W. Bert Foster and Charles L. Wrenn, by J. Edward Leithead, 361-92; 362-99; 363-110

(Foster, W. Bert), Note on Foster-Wrenn Article, by J. Edward Leithead, 365-17

(Foster, W. Bert), Now They're Collectors' Items, (boys' series books), by J. Edward Leithead, 420-86

(Foster, W. Bert), Pseudonyms of W. Bert
Foster, by J. Edward Leithead, 364-3
Four Footed Friends of Our Dime Novel
Heroes, (animals in the dime novels),
by J. Edward Leithead, 297-2
(Fox, Charles), The Publications of
Charles Fox, by Henry Steele, 13-5;
21-4
(France), Beadles Abroad, (French edns.),
by Denis R. Rogers, 347-88
(France), Dime Novels in France (French
language editions and originals), by
George Fronval, 379-27
(France), Dime Novels in French, Dime
Novel Sketches #92, 419-75
Francis Worcester Doughty, Uncrowned King
of the Dime Novel Writers, (biog.
sketch), by Charles Bragin, 44-1
FRANK LESLIE'S BOYS AND GIRLS WEEKLY,
15-5; 78-1
(FRANK LESLIE'S BOYS AND GIRLS WEEKLY),
Dime Novel Sketches #46, 370-61
FRANK LESLIE'S BOYS OF AMERICA, (data
and discussion), by William M. Burns,
139-1; 141-1; 149-1
(FRANK LESLIE'S BOYS OF AMERICA), Dime
Novel Sketches #43, 367-31
(FRANK LESLIE'S POPULAR LIBRARY), DIme
Novel Sketches #195, 523-1
(Frank Leslie Publishing House), William
J. Benners - The First Historian of
the Dime Novel, by Ralph Adimari,
312-122
Frank Leslie to the Boys and Girls of
America, by Bracebridge Hemyng, 78-1
(FRANK LESLIE WEEKLY), The Leslie
Publications, by George H. Cordier,
203-65
(FRANK MANLEY WEEKLY), Dime Novel
Sketches #73, 400-1
Frank Merriwell at Fardale, by Bob
Smeltzer, 48-1
Frank Merriwell in the Movies, by Gerald
J. McIntosh, 415-39
Frank Merriwell, Life Saver; or, Rescuing
Fair Tip Top Maidens, (discussion),
by Gerald J. McIntosh, 404-48;
405-61
Frank Merriwell on Radio and Television,
(data and discussion), by Gerald J.
McIntosh and Ralph Adimari, 410-112
"Frank Merriwell or Honor Challenged",
Review of stage production, by Frank
C. Acker, 466-68
"Frank Merriwell or Honor Challenged",
Review of stage production, by Edward
T. LeBlanc, 464-48
Frank Merriwell Returns, (discussion on
Merriwell in comic books), by J.P.
Guinon, 273-50
Frank Merriwell, The Unconquerable,
(verse), by Gerald J. McIntosh,
391-38
Frank Merriwell vs. Fred Fearnot, (dime
novel type fiction, pastiche), by
Ralph P. Smith, 493-114

Frank Merriwell's Father, (on death of
creator, Gilbert Patten, and dime
novels in general), by David C. Adams,
150-1
(FRANK MERRIWELL'S FATHER: Gilbert
Patten), comments about book, 384-80
Frank Merriwell's Mottoes, (comments
on Merriwell), by Gerald J. McIntosh,
410-123
Frank Merriwell's Parent, or, Patten
the Paramount, (memorial tribute to
Gilbert Patten), by J.P.Guinon, 150-6
Frank Merriwell's Stage Setback, (review
of "Frank Merriwell or Honor Challenged,
stage production), by Frank C. Acker,
466-68
FRANK READE LIBRARY, 5-4; 6-5
(FRANK READE LIBRARY), Dime Novel Sketches
#101, 428-43
FRANK READE STORIES, 75-8
FRANK READE WEEKLY, 54-2
(FRANK READE WEEKLY), Dime Novel Sketches
#23, 344-57
(FRANK STARR'S AMERICAN NOVELS), Dime
Novel Sketches #153, 481-95
Frank Tousey Authors, The, (discussion of
authors published by Tousey), by
Ralph Adimari, 293-10
Frank Tousey, Newspaper Publisher, 217-74
FRANK TOUSEY'S ILLUSTRATED WAR NEWS,
206-90
Fred Fearnot Was There, (discussion on
dime novel character), by Ross
Craufurd, 519-58
Fred Should Fear Not; or, Nickel Novel's
New Era, (novels in school class), by
Edward G. Ingraham, 340-4
Frederick Van Rensselaer Dey, (biog.
sketch), by J. Edward Leithead,
401-14
(French, George Washington), Any You Boys
Met George French?, (biog. sketch),
by Charles Duprez, 338-89
French, George: Believe It or Not, An
Eye Opener, (visit with Lurana
Sheldon, author), 193-84
French, George: Coincidence?, (reminis-
cences), 247-26
French, George: DICK DOBBS DETECTIVE
WEEKLY, (data, discussion), 42-1
French, George: letter of comment, 373-96;
448-4
French, George: Spring Tonic, (verse),
303-105a
(French, George Washington), Noted Dime
Novel Collector Dies in Towaco, N.J.,
obituary, 456-97
Fries, Frank T.: A Merry Chase After
"Merry", (discussion on Frank Merriwell)
3-5
Fries, Frank T.: Member of James Boys Gang
Now Religious Worker, news, 7-4
Fries, Frank T.: "Noname" Must Have Been
Irish! (on Frank Reade stories), 6-5
Fries, Frank T.: Prize Package of Nickel
Novels, (collecting), 5-4

Frisco Bert: Bang! Bang! Bang!
    (reminiscences), 251-60
Frisco Bert: Blood & Thunder Novels of
    the Gay Nineties Period, (dime
    novels), 105-1
Frisco Bert: Magic California, (extolls
    California), 132-3
From Boxes to Shelves, or How to Know
    What You Have, (housing your boys'
    books collection), by Jack R. Schorr,
    479-76
Fronval, George: Dime Novels in France,
    (French language editions and
    originals, dime novels), 379-27
Fronval, George: Gustave Aimard, (french
    author, biog. sketch), 411-132
(Fronval, George), obituary, 512-47
Front Cover Scenes Repeated, (use of
    same cover art by TIP TOP WEEKLY),
    by Gerald J. McIntosh, 423-118
(frontier stories), The Anatomy of Dime
    Novels No.17: Frontier and Rev. War
    Stories that Missed PLUCK AND LUCK,
    by J. Edward Leithead, 446-110;
    447-122
Frye, Bob: letter of comment, 395-85

G & D Every Boys Library Boy Scout
    Editions, (Boys' books, published
    by Grosset & Dunlap), by Julius R.
    Chenu, 536-33
(G.W.M. REYNOLD'S NOVELS), Dime Novel
    Sketches #208, 536-21
G.W.M. REYNOLD'S NOVELS, Checklist,
    536-34
Gallows-Fruit, (discussion of the
    English Penny Dreadfuls), by
    Ross Craufurd, 18-2
Gannett, Lewis: Review of THE GREAT
    RASCAL, THE LIFE AND ADVENTURES OF
    NED BUNTLINE (by Jay Monaghan),
    235-25
Gantner, Joe: Authors of Old Weeklies,
    (discusses var. authors), 136-1
Gantner, Joe: I Killed Lincoln,
    (fiction, pastiche), 160-1
Gantner, Joe: letter of comment, 153-4
Gantner, Joe: My Pal the Elephant,
    (circus fiction)
Gantner, Joe: My Search for Old Nick
    Carters, (collecting experiences),
    111-1
Gantner, Joe: Nick Carter, Jr. Stories
    Proposed, 153-4
Gantner, Joe: Old COSMOPOLITANS, (comment
    on magazine), 189-1
Gantner, Joe: Old Circuses and Weeklies,
    (reminiscences), 116-1
Gantner, Joe: Old Nick Carters, (dime
    novel reminiscences), 129-1
Gantner, Joe: Was That Jesse James ?,
    128-1
Garden City Publishing Company's Paper-
    back Juveniles, (boys' series), by
    Julius R. Chenu, 531-72

Gardner, Ralph D.: Alger Heroes, The
    Merriwells, etal! (comments),
    445-100
Gardner, Ralph D.: In Defense of Listing
    Current Alger Values, (discussion
    on scarcity and values), 472-2
Gardner, Ralp D.: letter of comment,
    386-96; 410-123
(Gardner, Ralph D.: ROAD TO SUCCESS,
    THE BIBLIOGRAPHY OF THE WORKS OF
    HORATIO ALGER), review by Kenyon C.
    Rosenberg, 488-57
GARFIELD LIBRARY, THE, (English novel
    series), with bibliographic check-
    list, by Denis R. Rogers, 470-124;
    471-138; 472-5
GEM, THE, 49-2
(GEM LIBRARY, THE), Dime Novel Sketches
    #103, 430-67
General Phil Sheridan's Words on
    Buffalo Bill, by Roland D. Sawyer,
    295-31
Genesis of the James Gang, 356-56
GENTLEMAN'S JOURNAL, 16-5
GENTLEMAN'S JOURNAL, THE, (data and
    discussion),by A.W.Lawson, 273-46
George, Bob: letter of comment, 549-67
Germans Burn 40,000 "Thrillers" to
    Save Young, news item, 108-4
(Germany), Beadles Abroad, (German
    editions discussed), by Denis R.
    Rogers, 348-96
(Germany), Notes on German Dime Novels,
    by Oscar C. Pfaus, 433-103
(Geronimo), Geronimo's Widow Dies,
    news item, 216-69
Giants March Past, The, (review of BOYS
    WILL BE BOYS, by E.S.Turner, a history
    of the English boys' papers), by
    J.V.B. Stewart Hunter, 197-9
Gilbert, Dr. Joseph: letter of comment,
    389-17
Gilbert Patten in Clothbound Editions,
    by J. Edward Leithead, 410-116
Gilbert Patten: The Man and the Magic,
    (biog. and literary sketch), by
    Frank C. Acker, 409-96
Gilbert Patten, (memorial tribute) by
    Sam E. Conner, 150-3
(Gilbreth, Lillian M.), The Rolt-Wheeler/
Gilbreth Letters, (correspondence between
    Gilbreth and Francis Rolt-Wheeler,
    boys' book author, with checklist of
    Rolt-Wheeler works), by John T. Dizer,
    Jr., 500-56
(GIRL SLEUTH, A FEMINIST GUIDE: Bobbie
    Ann Mason), review by John T. Dizer,
    Jr., 530-53; 531-77
GIRLS AND BOYS OF AMERICA, 16-5; 147-5
GIRLS AND BOYS PENNY MAGAZINE, 277-84
Girls' Books Should Be Collected, (girls
    series as desirable as boys' as items
    to collect), by Harlan Miller, 470-133
Godey, Louis A.: In Memoriam, (verse),
    101-14

Goggin, Joseph: letter of comment, 459-127

Going, Going, Gone, (comments on boys' book collecting), by Jack R. Schorr, 488-56

Going to New York?, (Dime Novels at New York Public Library), by Alan E. Schaeffer, 86-4

(Gold Rush), The Anatomy of Dime Novels No.16: Stories of the Klondike Gold Rush, by J. Edward Leithead, 443-76; 444-88

(Gold Star Books), Gold Star Books Reprints of Dime Novels, 389-18

Goldberg, Max: In Defense of Horatio Alger, Jr., (discusses the immoral charges against), 552-114

Golden Age of English Literature, (dime novel and boys' books), by William J. Benners, 14-2; 15-5; 16-4

GOLDEN ARGOSY, 52-5

GOLDEN ARGOSY, THE, (discussion), by James E. Knott, 144-1

GOLDEN ARGOSY, THE, (discussion), by Stanley A. Pachon, 382-58; 383-69

(GOLDEN ARGOSY), Dime Novel Sketches #42, 366-21

(GOLDEN ARGOSY), Fifty Years Ago, (reminiscences), by Patrick Mulhall, 52-4

(GOLDEN ARGOSY), The Last Number of THE GOLDEN ARGOSY, by Fred T. Singleton, 10-2; 11-4

(GOLDEN ARGOSY), Our Old Story Papers, GOLDEN ARGOSY No.1, by William M. Burns, 184-1; 185-9

GOLDEN DAYS, 144-3

(GOLDEN DAYS), Writers for GOLDEN DAYS, (biog. discussion and sketch), by Stanley A. Pachon,
No.1, Frank H. Converse, 333-52
No.2, Charles Herbert Heustis, 335-69

Golden Days of '49, The, (reminiscences), by M. Bertrand Couch, 121-1

GOLDEN HOURS - Reminiscences and Reflections, by Harry A. Weill, 137-1

(GOLDEN HOURS), A Lode of GOLDEN HOURS, (on pseudonyms of writers), by Harry A. Weill, 215-59

(GOLDEN HOURS), A Thrice-Told Tale on GOLDEN HOURS, by Harry A. Weill, 148-1

(GOLDEN HOURS), An Open Letter on the Writers of GOLDEN HOURS, by Willis E. Hurd, 130-1

(GOLDEN HOURS), Data on GOLDEN HOURS Nos. 599-780, (bibliographical), 207-98

(GOLDEN HOURS), Dime Novel Sketches #40, 364-1

(GOLDEN HOURS), More on the GOLDEN HOURS, (comments), by Harry A. Weill, 149-5

(GOLDEN HOURS), Nuggets from GOLDEN HOURS, by Harry A. Weill, 171-1

(GOLDEN HOURS), Spanked at Seventeen by the Editor of GOLDEN HOURS, (reminiscences) by Fred T. Singleton, 7-6; 8-4

GOLDEN LIBRARY, 42-2; 144-3

GOLDEN LIBRARY, THE, by E.T.Gossett, 77-5

(GOLDEN LIBRARY), Dime Novel Sketches #108, 435-117

GOLDEN WEEKLY, 26-2

GOLDEN WEEKLY, firefighter stories, 407-76

(GOLDEN WEEKLY), Dime Novel Sketches #69, 396-89

(GOLDEN WEEKLY), Famous Tousey Story Papers, (discussion), by Edward T. LeBlanc, 508-3

Goldsman, Gerald: letter of comment, 389-17; 427-42

(GOOD NEWS LIBRARY), Dime Novel Sketches #134, 461-13

Good Old Dime Novel Days, The, (reminiscences), 365-17; 367-38

Good Old Dime Novel Days - My First Novel, (reading reminiscences), by Albert E. Johnson, 372-86

Gosden, Walter: letter of comment, 444-96

Gossett, E.T.: Collecting Our Favorites, (collecting reminiscences), 84-1

Gossett, E.T.: THE GOLDEN LIBRARY, (discussion), 77-5

Gossett, E.T.: letter of comment, 84-5

Gossett, E.T.: Reminiscences of Our Dime Novel Days, 71-1

Gottesman, Ronald: The Upton Sinclair Novels, (literary discussion), 378-20

Gowan, William R.: The Publication History of Tom Swift, (boys' series books, bibliographic checklist), 536-22

Gowan, William R.: Tom Swift, Jr., (boys' series books, bibliographic checklist of the "new series"), 538-56

(Graham, Tom: HIKE AND THE AEROPLANE), Hike and the Aeroplane, (a rare boys' book discussed), by Julius R. Chenu, 550-81

Grand Conflagration at the Munro Plant in 1876 (fire at publishers; news), by Ralph F. Cummings, 81-2

Grand Old Stories, The, (dime novel reminiscences), by F.N.Wearing, 165-1

Grant, Major A.F., mention, 4-4

Gray, Lynne: For Bertha M. Clay, (verse), 300-80

Graydon, William Murray, mention, 419-82

(Graydon, William Murray), Now They're Collectors' Items, (boys' series books), by J. Edward Leithead, 417-54

Great Bracebridge Hemyng, The, (biog. discussion of author of Jack Harkaway and Scapegrace series), by Ralph F. Cummings, 67-1

Great Five Cent WIDE-A-WAKE LIBRARY,The, by George H. Cordier, 75-1

Great Inventor Tangles With Charlie Miller, The Last of the Pony Express Riders, by Charles Duprez, 252-65

Great North Road, The, (verse), by
Alfred Noyes, 46-2
(GREAT RASCAL, THE: THE LIFE AND ADVEN-
TURES OF NED BUNTLINE by Jay Monaghan),
Review by Lewis Gannett, 235-25
Great Trials of History, The: Trial of
Dick Turpin, (the highwayman), 193-81
(Great Western Publications), Diamond
Dick data, by Harold C. Holmes, 86-1
Greatest Sleuth That Ever Lived (Nick
Carter comments), by J. Edward Leit-
head, 272-38
(Grey, Zane), Zane Grey Dies of Heart
Attack, obituary, 91-2
(Grey, Zane), Zane Grey Estate Earns
$12,000 Year, news item, 92-5
(Grosset & Dunlap, Publishers), Edward
S. Ellis Stories Published by the
Mershon Complex, by Denis R. Rogers,
490-70; 491-86; 492-104
(Grosset & Dunlap, Publishers), G & D
Every Boys Library Boy Scout Editions,
(boys' books), by Julius R. Chenu,
536-33
Gruber, Frank: The Horatio Alger Paper-
back First Editions, 259-26
Guerilla, (fiction about Jesse James),
by Carlee Carlay, 148-3
Guernsey, John: Willard Thompson, Book
Dealer, (biog. comments, pioneer
book dealer), 480-90
Guinon, J.P.: A Memory, (verse), 256-7
Guinon, J.P.: The Admirable Arlington,
(biog.comments, Chester Arlington,
dime novel villain), 70-1; 71-5
Guinon, J.P.: The Applause Column in
TIP TOP WEEKLY, (comments from
readers), 328-2
Guinon, J.P.: Frank Merriwell Returns,
(comments on Merriwell comic book),
273-50
Guinon, J.P.: Frank Merriwell's Parent,
or, Patten, the Paramount, (memorial
tribute to Gilbert Patten, creator
of Merriwell), 150-6
Guinon, J.P.: Gil Patten Vindicated,
381-53
Guinon, J.P.: The Last Days of Billy
the Kid, 104-6
Guinon, J.P.: letter of comment, 381-51;
404-52; 418-69
Guinon, J.P.: Reprints of the Merriwell
Series, (discussion), 271-26
Guinon, J.P.: The Rockspur Series,
(sports series by Gilbert Patten),
304-2
Guinon, J.P.: Stop Thief! (regarding
dishonest dealing in dime novels),
82-1
Guinon, J.P.: Strayed From the Sepulchre,
or, The Tomb-Tamer of TIP TOP, (notes
on stories), 99-1
Guinon, J.P.: The Young Sports Series,
311-112
GUY RAYNER"S BOYS OWN JOURNAL, 116-4;
118-4

H. Irving Hancock: A Romanticized
View of Sports and Boys (on boys'
series books), by Ken Donelson,
522-138
HALF-DIME LIBRARY, 117-4
(HALF-DIME NOVEL), In Praise of the
HALF-DIME NOVEL, by James Wood,
63-1
HALF HOLIDAY, 148-5
(HALF HOLIDAY), Dime Novel Sketches
#56, 381-47
Half Nick Carter and Half Sherlock
Holmes, (Felix Boyd stories in THE
POPULAR MAGAZINE), by Robert Sampson,
552-118
HALFPENNY STANDARD JOURNAL, THE,
13-6; 21-4
Hall, Bill: letter of comment, 404-52
Hall, Edward: letter of comment,
437-26
(Hall, Samuel Stone), Leominster,Mass.
Man Wrote Many Famous Dime Novels,
(discussion, Buckskin Sam), 180-1
Hamilton, C.B.: STREET & SMITH'S
LITERARY ALBUM, 46-2
(Hamilton, Charles), A Tribute to
Charles Hamilton, (author), by
W.O.G.Lofts, 355-33
Hamlin, Edward: A Defense of the Dime
Novel, 151-2
Hamlin, Jane: Charles Rothstein Collects
Florida Dime Novels (with Florida
locales), 434-115
Hammond, E.H.: letter of comment,
386-96
(Hancock, H. Irving), H. Irving Hancock:
A Romanticized View of Sports and
Boys, (boys' series sports books),
by Ken Donelson, 522-138
(Hancock, H. Irving), Harrie Irving
Hancock's Boys Series Books
(discussion with checklist), by
Julius R. Chenu, 538-64
(Hancock, H. Irving), Now They're
Collectors' Items, (boys' series
books by H.Irving Hancock), by J.
Edward Leithead, 420-86
(HANDSOME HARRY), Dime Novel Sketches #2,
320-39
Handsome Harry of the Fighting Belvedere,
(dime novel character), by "Ima
Tellinya", 228-65
(HANDSOME HARRY), A Handsome Harry
Episode, (character in Diamond Dick
stories), by Harold C. Holmes, 71-3
HANDSOME HARRY LIBRARY, 5-4
HANDSOME JACK SERIES, 25-8
Hang On To Your Old Dime Novels, (advice
on collecting), by Nameless Joe,
209-13
(Hanshew, T.W.) The Boy Actor, Author
and Dramatist: Master T.W.Hanshew,
(biog. sketch), 37-1

(Hanshew, T.W.), Cleek and His Forty
Faces, or T.W.Hanshew, a Dime Novelist
Who Made Good, (Hamilton Cleek, dime
novel detective, master of disguise)
with checklist, by J. Randolph Cox,
486-30; 487-42; 490-81

(Hanshew, T.W.), Master T.W.Hanshew,
Boy Actor, Author and Dramatist,
(biog. sketch), 90-3

Happy Birthday, Captain Chester G. Mayo,
(100th Birthday eulogy) (boys' books
author), by Edward T. LeBlanc, 552-126

HAPPY DAYS, 7-2; 42-6; 81A-12; 88-8;
413-16

(HAPPY DAYS), Correction to Bibliography
in letter from Ross Craufurd, 518-51

(HAPPY DAYS), Dime Novel Sketches #74,
401-13

(HAPPY DAYS), Famous Tousey Story Papers,
by Edward T. LeBlanc, 508-3

(HAPPY DAYS), Our Old Story Papers, by
William M. Burns, 214-49

(HAPPY DAYS), PLUCK & LUCK Reprints and
Earlier HAPPY DAYS Stories, (comments
and description), by Robert H. Smeltzer,
149-2

(HAPPY DAYS), Swan Song of HAPPY DAYS,
(cessation), 157-3

(HAPPY DAYS), Up-to-Date History in HAPPY
DAYS, (current evens published), by
William M. Burns, 302-96

Happy Days are Back Again (discussion on
HAPPY DAYS), by W.B.McCafferty, 118-4

Happyhours Brotherhood on the Loose, or:
Leave Your Wives at Home, (humorous
comments on Happy Hours gathering),
by "Miles Behind", 230-83

(Happy Hours Brotherhood), A Plea for
Unity, Brotherhood & Cooperation,
(on the Happy Hours Brotherhood,
dime novel collectors), by William
M. Burns, 54-3

(Happy Hours Brotherhood), History of
the Happy Hours Brotherhood and the
DIME NOVEL ROUNDUP), by Ralph F.
Cummings, 430-74; 432-93

(Happy Hours Brotherhood), The Life of
HAPPY HOURS MAGAZINE and DIME NOVEL
ROUNDUP,(Also Happy Hours Brotherhood),
by Ralph F. Cummings, 300-81

(Happy Hours Brotherhood): note that
lists of members appears in segments
in most issues of early date
particularly

(Happy Hours Brotherhood), Members of
the Happy Hours Brotherhood (essay
on members), by Robert M. Smeltzer,
56-6

(Happy Hours Brotherhood), Memorial
Placque Erected to Gilbert Patten
by H.H.B.), 183-95

(Happy Hours Brotherhood), Whose Pond
Is This?, (humorous comments), by
Edward G. Ingraham, 342-20

(Happy Hours Brotherhood), Ye Brotherhood, the Roundup and Its Editor,
by Charles Duprez, 274-53

(HAPPY HOURS MAGAZINE), The Life of
HAPPY HOURS MAGAZINE, and DIME NOVEL
ROUNDUP, (also Happy Hours Brother-
hood), by Ralph F. Cummings, 300-81

Harbaugh, Tom C., (author) mentioned,
4-4

(Harbaugh, Tom C.), Goods of Noted
Writer Bring $1000, news item,
92-2

Hard-Cover Merriwells, The, (Merriwell
stories in hardbound book editions,
with checklist), by Harry K. Hudson,
541-15

Hard Ones To Find - Do They Really Exist?,
(scarce or non-existent boys' series
books), by Julius F. Chenu, 468-107

Harding, L.: letter of comment, 404-52

(Hardy Boys Series: Franklin W. Dixon),
A Half Century of the Hardy Boys,or,
Clues to An Abscure Chronology,
(bibliography of Hardy Boys books)
by Robert V. Riordan, 530-35

Harkaway Business, The, (comments on
Jack Harkaway stories), by U.G.Figley,
124-3

Harkaway, Jack, (series), mentioned, 15-5

(Harkaway, Jack, series), The Great
Bracebridge Hemyng, (biog. & literary
sketch), by Ralph F. Cummings, 67-1

(Harkaway, Jack, series), Jack Harkaway -
A Pioneer, (comments and discussion),
by Patrick Mulhall, 251-58

(Harkaway, Jack, series), The Reason Why,
(Harkaway novels written by several
writers), by U.G.Figley, 118-2

"Harkaway, Jack": Six Hundred Dime Novels
for Fifteen Dollars, (collecting
experiences), 9-5

(Harkaway, Jack), Novels, mentioned, 157-1

(Harkaway, Jack), Series, mentioned 88-8

(Harkaway, Jack, series), Harkaway,
Merriwell, Etc., (comments on dime novel
heroes), by U.G.Figley, 115-1

(Harkaway, Jack, series), To Reckless
Ralph, The Sleuth of the Sierras,
(comments on dime novels), by J.P.
Quaine, 216-65

Harkaway, Merriwell, Etc., (comments on
heroes, reminiscences, recollections),
by U.G.Figley, 115-1

(Harper Brothers), The Life of John Harper,
60-9

(Harper, John), The Life History of John
Harper, (biog.sketch), 60-9

(Harper, William D.), obituary, 92-5

(HARPERS WEEKLY), Nast and the Harpers
(Theo. Nast, political cartoonist),
184-3

Harrie Irving Hancock's Boys Series Books,
(discussion with checklist), by Julius
R. Chenu, 538-64

(Harrigan, Edward), Mr. Edward Harrigan, of
Harrigan & Harts, by Ralph F. Cummings,
80-1

HARRIGAN & HARTS NEW YORK BOYS PAPER, 26-3

Harrigan & Harts, Publishers, 80-1; 81-3

(Harrington, Ralph), Evidence of Another Edward Stratemeyer Pseudonym, by Peter C. Walther, 542-41

Harris, Louise: letter of comment, 516-150

Harris, Louise: Our Flag's Bicentennial, (YOUTH'S COMPANION's drive to have flag flown over schools, and authorship of Pledge of Allegiance), 413-56

Harris, Louise: Time for the Truth, (on the flag plying over schools, and true author of Pledge of Allegiance), 491-94

Harris, Louise: Who Wrote the Pledge of Allegiance? (assertion that James Bailey Upham is true author), 528-127

Harris, Taffy: Circus Yarns and Circus Programs, (reminiscences), 167-1

Harrison Keith Stories, The, (Harrison Keith, Detective in NEW MAGNET LIBRARY) by J. Edward Leithead, 56-5

(Hart, Tony), Tony Hart of Harrigan & Hart, 81-3

Hassenfeffer, Julius: THREE CHUMS, The Forgotten Weekly, (discussion), 226-52

(Havighurst, Walter: ANNIE OAKLEY OF THE WILD WEST), review, 266-86

HEARTHSTONE, THE, 117-4

(HEARTHSTONE, THE), Dime Novel Sketches #44, 368-41

Heins, Marjorie: Horatio Alger: Symbol for Success, (influence of Alger on his and succeeding generations), 505-118; 506-130

Hemyng, Bracebridge, 311-115

Hemyng, Bracebridge: Frank Leslie to the Boys and Girls of America, 78-1

(Hemyng, Bracebridge), Jack Harkaway - A Pioneer, by Patrick Mulhall, 251-58

(Hemyng, Bracebridge), Now They're Collectors' Items, (boys' series books discussed), by J. Edward Leithead, 420-86

(Hemyng, Bracebridge), To Bracebridge Hemyng, (verse), by P.C.Maroske, 153-3

(Hemyng, Bracebridge), To Reckless Ralph, the Sleuth of the Sierras, by J.P. Quaine, 216-65

(Hemyng, Bracebridge), William Benner Says, 74-3

(Hemyng, Bracebridge), The Works of Bracebridge Hemyng, by William M. Burns, 152-1; 153-1

Henderson, Glenn H.: Dime Novels Exhibited in the Express Window, (collecting reminiscences), 125-1

Henry, Thomas R.: Today's Facts in Yesterday's Fiction, (fantastic inventions), 95-1

Henty Fame and Riches, The, (biog. essay), by W.O.G.Lofts, 526-89

(Henty, G.A.), The Biographical Mysteries of George Alfred Henty (literary essay), by W.O.G.Lofts, 524-44

(Henty, George Alfred), George Alfred Henty, with Checklist, by Stanley A. Pachon, 195-97; 196-1

(Henty, George Alfred), The Henty Fame and Riches, (biog. essay), by W.O.G. Lofts, 526-89

(Henty, George Alfred), Henty Hints, (bibliographical comments and descriptions), by W.B.Poage,
No.1, Redskin and Colonist, 197-10
No.2, 203-71
No.4, 209-13
No.5, 221-13
No.6, 236-33
No.7, 242-84
No.8, 255-98

(Henty, George Alfred), Henty News, by W.B.Poage, 192-74

(Henty, George Alfred), Henty Society, (advertisement), 525-73

(Henty, George Alfred), Now They're Collector's Items, (boys series books) by J. Edward Leithead, 417-54

Henty Hints, (bibliographical comments and descriptions), by W.B.Poage, 197-10; 203-71; 209-13; 221-13; 236-33; 242-84; 255-98

Henty News, (column on G.A.Henty), by W.B.Poage, 192-74

(Hentz, Mrs. Caroline Lee), obituary article 1856, 218-85

Herman, Jack: letter of comment, 396-99; 404-53; 409-108; 493-124; 516-149; 533-110

Hero To Two Generations of Boys, (comments on Frank Merriwell), 109-3

Heroes of Yesterday, (dime novel characters), by Nameless Joe, 199-28

(heroines), Arietta: Heroine of Wild West Trails, (dime novel heroine), by J. Edward Leithead, 367-32

(Hess Collection), Hess Collection Acquies Complete Set of AMERICAN BOY, 515-120

(Hess Collection), On the Track of Popular Culture, (Hess Collection of dime novels, story papers and newstand literature), by J. Randolph Cox, 495-134

(Hess Collection), Research in the Hess Collection, Univ. of Minnesota, 543-56

(Hess, George H., Jr.), see Hess Collection

(Heustis, Charles Herbert), Writers for GOLDEN DAYS, (biog. sketch), by Stanley A. Pachon, 335-69

(Heyliger, William), Books of William Heyliger, (boys' books), by Julius R. Chenu, 519-62

(Hickok, Wild Bill), Biographical Sketches of Famous Frontiersmen #3: James Butler (Wild Bill) Hickok), by Clyde Wakefield, 161-4

(Hickok, Wild Bill), Edward L. Wheeler's Own View of Wild Bill Hickok, by "Seajay", 158-3

(Hickok, Wild Bill), Facts About the "Two Bills" and Buntline, (Wild Bill, Buffalo Bill, and Ned Buntline), by Roland D. Sawyer, 160-4

(Hickok, Wild Bill), Movies, Checklist, by Arthur N. Carter, 520-91

Higgins, Walter A.: letter of comment, 385-89

Highstown, G.W.J.: letter of comment, 96-4

HIGHWAY NOVELS, 116-4

(HIGHWAY NOVELS), Dime Novel Sketches #159, 487-41

(HIGHWAY SERIES), Dime Novel Sketches #182, 510-18

(HIKE AND THE AEROPLANE: Tom Graham), Hike and the Aeroplane, (a rare boys' book discussed), by Julius R. Chenu, 550-81

(Hill, George M., Co., Publishers), Edward S. Ellis Stories Published by the Mershon Complex, by Denis R. Rogers, 490-70; 491-86; 492-104

Hillyer, William Sidney: Blood-and-Thunder Novels Were Well Liked in Last Century, 165-2

(HILTON'S DIME BOOKS), Dime Novel Sketches #175, 503-89

HILTON'S PRIZE ROMANCES, Checklist, 534-125

(HILTON'S PRIZE ROMANCES), Dime Novel Sketches #205, 534-113

(HILTON'S TEN CENT NOVELS), Dime Novel Sketches #168, 496-1

(HILTON'S UNION NOVELS), Dime Novel Sketches #162, 490-69

(historical sources), The Dime Novel as an Historian's Tool, by William A. Settle, Jr., 456-92; 457-102

History of Old Story Papers of Long Ago, The, (on NEW YORK WEEKLY STORY TELLER), by Ralph F. Cummings, 216-66

History of the Happy Hours Brotherhood and the DIME NOVEL ROUNDUP, by Ralph F. Cummings, 430-74; 432-93

Hix, Jihn: The Author Who Lived What He Wrote, (Ned Buntline comments), 77-4

Hoffman, Dick: letter of comment, 465-58

(Hoffman, John M.), Dime Novels Writer's Missing Money, news item, 27-3

(Holland), Beadles Abroad, (Dutch edns.) by Denis R. Rogers, 348-97

(Holmes, Doctor), Who is Doctor Holmes?, 75-12

Holmes, George: letter of comment, 514-87; 522-142; 525-74; 529-29

Holmes, Harold C.: A Bit on NICK CARTER LIBRARY, 90-1

Holmes, Harold C.: A Handsome Harry Episode (Diamond Dick stories character in dime novels), 71-3

Holmes, Harold C.: A Story of India, (dime novel style fiction), 84-2

Holmes, Harold C.: An Open Letter to Mr. Flaum, (dime novel reminiscences) 178-51

Holmes, Harold C.: "Bits" Regarding Dime Novels, 81A-11

Holmes, Harold C.: COMRADES WEEKLY, (discussion), 103-1

Holmes, Harold C.: Diamond Dick Item, (on Great Western Publications), 86-1

Holmes, Harold C.: DO AND DARE WEEKLY, (discussion), 114-1

Holmes, Harold C.: First half year of WORK AND WIN, (discussion), 166-1

Holmes, Harold C.: The First Nick Carter, 79-1

Holmes, Harold C.: letter of comment, 64-3

Holmes, Harold C.: The Merriwell Magazine Stories, 62-4; 66-1

Holmes, Harold C.: My First Novel dime novel reading reminiscences), 49-4

Holmes, Harold C.: NEW MAGNET LIBRARY, No.1036, (descriptive comments), 83-2

Holmes, Harold C.: NEW MAGNET LIBRARY, No.1088, (descriptive comments), 85-1

Holmes, Harold C.: NEW YORK DETECTIVE LIBRARY, No.171, (descriptive comments), 122-1

Holmes, Harold C.: NICK CARTER WEEKLY, Nos.91 and 92, (descriptive comments on these large size issues), 55-1

Holmes, Harold C.: Old King Brady, the Sleuth-Hound (detective in dime novels), 97-1

Holmes, Harold C.: PLUCK AND LUCK, No. 118, (descriptive comments), 188-37

Holmes, Harold C.: SECRET SERVICE, No. 258, (descriptive comments), 154-1; 155-1

Holmes, Harold C.: SHIELD WEEKLY, (comments), 138-1

(Holmes, Sherlock), Odds and Odds on THE BAKER STREET JOURNAL, by W.B.McCafferty, 216-70

(Holmes, Sherlock), Sherlock Holmes, (comments and discussion), 146-1

(Holmes, Sherlock), Sherlock Holmes Exhibit Philadelphia Free Library 1968, including Nick Carter, 429-61

(HOME LIBRARY), Dime Novel Sketches #191, 519-57

(HOME LIBRARY/NOVELS), Dime Novel Sketches #174, 502-73

HOME MONTHLY, 14-5; 205-84

Hon. William Adams Brodribb, Beadle Author, by Denis R. Rogers, (biog. sketch), 353-12

Hopeful Pete: Prowlin' Up Massachusetts Way, (reminiscences), 210-17

Horatio Alger Goes Greeley: From Wretches to Riches, (literary sketch), by David Soibelman, 539-79

Horatio Alger, Jr. After Seventy Years, (reminiscences), by Morton S. Enslin, 451-40; 452-50

(HORATIO ALGER,JR., AN ANNOTATED BIBLIO-
GRAPHY OF COMMENT AND CRITICISM: Gary
Scharnhorst and Jack Bales), review
by John T. Dizer, Jr., 550-74
Horatio Alger, Jr. and Ragged Dick:
Reality and Myth, by Ken Donelson,
525-58
Horatio Alger Paperback First Editions,
The, by Frank Gruber, 259-26
Horatio Alger: Symbol for Success (the
influence of Alger upon his and
succeeding generations), by Marjorie
Heins, 505-118; 506-130
Horatio Alger's Last Hero, (discusses
CAST UPON THE BREAKERS), 495-141
Hospitality on the Range, (reminiscences),
by J.H.Armbruster, 243-90
HOTSPUR, THE, 49-2
(HOUSE OF BEADLE AND ADAMS AND ITS DIME
AND NICKEL NOVELS: Albert Johannsen),
review by Ralph F. Cummings, 213-43
(HOUSE OF BEADLE AND ADAMS AND ITS DIME
AND NICKEL NOVELS: Albert Johannsen),
translations of the foreign quotations
in book, by Albert Johannsen, 215-60
How I Came to Write My First Book, (with
checklist), by Harry Castlemon, 100-1
How I Got Acquainted With the Dime Novel,
anon., 52-8
How I Met Buffalo Bill, by George H.
Cordier, 167-3
How I Met the Steam Man of the Plains,
(dime novel character), by George H.
Cordier, 186-1
How Ned Buntline Turned from Runaway Boy
to Writing Genius: His Relations with
Buffalo Bill and the "Know Nothings",
by Leon Mead, 101-1
How to Become a Ventriloquist, (reminis-
cences), by "Seajay", 100-2
How to Get Dime Novels for Nothing,
(collecting advice), by Ralph F.
Cummings, 86-3
(HUB TEN CENT NOVELS), Dime Novel Sketches
#120, 447-121
(HUB TEN CENT NOVELS), Rare Dime Novels
No.4, with checklist, by Edward T.
LeBlanc, 232-1
Hudson, Harry K.: A New and Interesting
Phantom Title, (boys' book, announced
but not published), 537-47
Hudson, Harry K.: Boys' Book First
Editions, (difficulty in determining),
525-71
Hudson, Harry K.: Changes and additions
to A BIBLIOGRAPHY OF HARD-COVER BOYS
BOOKS, REV. EDN., (by author), 529-31;
531-78; 532-89; 539-82
Hudson, Harry K.: The Hard-Cover Merri-
wells, (merriwell stories in hardbound
editions), with checklist, 541-15
Hudson, Harry K.: letter of comment,
395-86; 525-74; 526-93; 549-66
Hudson, Harry K.: More Gilbert Patten
in Clothbound Editions, 417-60
Hudson, R.B.: letter of comment, 448-4

(HUGH ROY CULLEN: Ed Kilman and Theon
Wright), review, 267-95
Humbarger, Walter: letter of comment,
536-36
(humor), A Sad Calamity, 108-4
(humor), The Many Faceted Alger, (on
his humorous sketches), by Stanley
A. Pachon, 548-37
(humor), Novelnut Nonsense, (humor
among members), 95-5; 96-2; 97-5;
98-3; 99-4; 100-3; 101-9; 102-3;
104-2; 105-5; 106-3; 107-4; 109-4;
112-5; 113-3; 114-9; 115-2; 116-3;
117-5; 118-2; 119-8; 120-5; 121-5
Hunter, J.V.B. Stewart: The Giants March
Past, (review of BOYS WILL BE BOYS,
by E. S. Turner, a history of the
English boys' papers), 197-9
Hunting for Novels is Fun, (collecting
experiences), by George Flaum, 180-2
Hurd, Willis E.: An Open Letter on the
Writers of GOLDEN HOURS, 130-1
Hurd, Willis E.: letter of comment,
131-3
Hurd, Willis E.: More on Pseudonyms, (of
early writers), 214-52
Hurd, Willis E.: My Meeting with Buffalo
Bill, 136-2
Hurd, Willis E.: Those Iver's Reprints
of Beadles Boys Library, 37-1
(Hurst & Company, Publishers), Edward
S. Ellis Stories Published by the
Mershon Complex, by Denis R. Rogers,
490-70; 491-86; 492-104
HUTCHINSON POCKET SPECIAL, 179-4
Hybrids, Oddies and Freaks, (variations
in editions of dime novels and boys'
books), by Denis R. Rogers, 475-46;
476-56
(Hynes, Alfred D.), Alfred D. Hynes,
Beadle and Munro Author, (biog.
sketch), 386-94

I Killed Lincoln, (fiction, pastiche),
by Joe Gantner, 160-1
If Dreams Were Only True, (reminiscences),
by Ralph F. Cummings, 73-1
(ILLUSTRATED AMERICAN LIFE), letter from
Ross Craufurd, 519-66
(ILLUSTRATED LIBRARY, THE), Dime Novel
Sketches #138, 465-51
(illustrations), Old Boys Journals
Illustrations, (comments), by Henry
Steele, 34-1
In and Out of Books: Nostalgia, Ltd.,
(Horatio Alger; reminiscences),
303-105
In Defense of Horatio Alger, Jr., (the
immoral charges against), by Max
Goldberg, 552-114
In Defense of Listing Current Alger
Values, (discussion on scarcity and
prices), by Ralph D. Gardner, 472-2
In Memorial to William James Benners,
Jr., (memorial tribute), 151-1
In Memoriam, (verse), by Louis A. Godey,
101-14

In Memoriam: Charles Jonas, by J.C. Dykes, 161-3

In Praise of the Half-Dime Novel, by James N. Wood, 63-1

In Refutation, (regarding Col. Prentice Ingraham), by William M. Burns, 177-43

In the Mail, (letters), 516-149; 517-28; 518-51; 519-66; 521-125

Index - DIME NOVEL ROUNDUP, January 1976 to December 1978, (index of major subjects), 535-10a

Index - DIME NOVEL ROUNDUP, Issues Nos. 1-516, (major subjects), by Edward T. LeBlanc, 529-SS

(INDIAN TALES), Dime Novel Sketches #131, 458-109

(INDIAN TALES), Rare Dime Novels: INDIAN TALES No.1, (descriptive discussion), by Edward T. LeBlanc, 213-41

(Indians), Crazy Horse and Spotted Tail, biog. sketch), by W.B. McCafferty, 2-5

Influence of Charles Dickens on Gilbert Patten, The, by Gerald J. McIntosh, 409-103

Ingraham, Edward G.: Fred Should Fear Not; or, Nickel Novel's New Era, (novels in school class), 340-4

Ingraham, Edward G.: letter of comment, 372-86; 384-80; 395-86

Ingraham, Edward G.: What Will You Do?, (collecting advice), 366-27

Ingraham, Edward G.: Whose Pond is This?, (Happy Hours Brotherhood activity), 342-20

Ingraham, Edward G.: Young Wild West's Other Pard, or, Arietta's Only Rival, (Mrs. Sarah Thomas), 344-58

(Ingraham, Harold C.), My Boy Harold, (biog. sketch), by Charles Duprez, 344-53

Ingraham, Harold C.: Spacious Living to Come, (predictions), 348-99

Ingraham, Joseph Holt, mention, 15-3

(Ingraham, Col. Prentice, Colonel Prentiss Ingraham, (biog.sketch of author), by J. Edward Leithead, 376-1; 377-10

(Ingraham, Col. Prentice), In Refutation, by William M. Burns, 177-43

(Ingraham, Col. Prentice), My Friend, Col. Prentiss Ingraham, by Gilbert Patten, 140-1

(Ingraham, Col. Prentice), obituary, (1904), 543-57

(Ingraham, Mrs. Rosa L.), obituary, (author), 108-7

Interesting Dime Novel Facts, (misc. data), by Howard R. Silsbee, 282-20; 284-34; 287-64; 288-73; 291-99

Introduction to SETH JONES OF NEW HAMPSHIRE by Edward S. Ellis (discusses censorship), 172-1

IRISH HERALD, THE, 3-1

(IRWIN P. BEADLES TEN CENT NOVELS) Dime Novel Sketches #173, 501-61

(IRWIN'S AMERICAN NOVELS), Dime Novel Sketches #142, 469-113

Is Interest in Dime Novels Dying?, (collecting comments), by George T. Flaum, 247-27

(Ivers, M.J., Co.), Those Ivers' Reprints of Beadles Boys Library, by Willis E. Hurd, 37-1

J. Edward Leithead the Dime Novel King, (verse), by Charles D. Randolph, 458-111

J. Fenimore Cooper, (biog. sketch), by Hermon Pitcher, 124-2

J.T. Trowbridge - A Brief Sketch, (biog./literary sketch), with checklist of books, by Gil O'Gara, 544-66

Jack Harkaway - A Pioneer, by Patrick Mulhall, 251-58

Jacobsen, H.O.: letter of comment, 377-16; 401-21

(Jacobsen, H.O.), obituary, 479-74

Jaffray, Willard: Dangers of Wild West Recalled by Old Letter, 92-4

Jaffray, Willard: Stories I Have Enjoyed Most, (reading reminiscences in dime novels), 89-1

James Ball Naylor: A Famous Ohio Author, (biog. sketch), by Roy B. Van Devier, 369-56

James Boys in the Saddle Again, (discusses Westbrook's Adventure Series), with checklist, by J. Edward Leithead, 280-2; (discusses var. dime novels), 283-26

James Boys Stories, The, by Ralph F. Cummings, 117-1

James Boys Stories in NEW YORK DETECTIVE LIBRARY of F.W.Doughty, 29-3

JAMES BOYS WEEKLY, 54-2; 278-98

(JAMES BOYS WEEKLY), Dime Novel Sketches #49, 373-89

"James Gang" Raids Station, Snatches 7 Mail Pouches, (1939), 92-2

(James, Frank), Frank James, Outlaw, 33-4

(James, Frank), Bandit on the Stand: Frank James Giving Testimony, 326-94

(James, Frank), Death of widow, Mrs. Ann Ralston, 144-4

(James, Frank), Frank James Returns - Moving Picture, (1940), by Eli A. Messier, 98-7

(James, Frank & Jesse), Movies, Checklist, by Arthur N. Carter, 520-91

(James Gang), The Bandit Brothers of Old Missouri, by J. Edward Leithead, 276-70

(James Gang), Buckskin Bill Recalls Famous Iowa Neighbors and a Trip to Old Missouri, by J. Edward Leithead, 291-94

(James Gang), Cole Younger, James Bandit, Dies Reformed, 117-8

(James Gang), Genesis of the James Gang, 356-56

(James Gang), The James Boys Stories, (in dime novels), by Ralph F. Cummings, 117-1

(James Gang), Man Who Prosecuted James Gang is Dead, (William H. Wallace), 71-2

(James Gang), Member of James Gang Now Religious Worker, by Frank T. Fries, 7-4

(James Gang), The Northfield Bank Robbery, by Roy E. Swanstrom, 278-90

(James Gang), Robbers in 1868, 39-1

(James Gang), Some Good Stuff, (dime novel reminiscences), by Walter F. Tunks, 190-57

(James, Jesse), An Interview with Jesse James, by P.J.Moran, 191-66

(James, Jesse), Civil War Vet of Jesse James Case is Dead at 109, 217-75

(James, Jesse), Court Refuses 102 Year Old Man's Plea to Have Name Restored to Jesse James, 217-75

(James, Jesse), Dalton Relatives Visit James Home (1947, St.Joseph, Mo.), 178-52

(James, Jesse), Guerilla, (fiction with Jesse James as character), by Carlee Carlay, 148-3

(James, Jesse), Jesse James in Dime Novels: Ambivalence Towards an Outlaw Hero, (novels present James as hero), by James J. Deutsch, 517-2

(James, Jesse), Jesse James Rides Again, (review of stage production "Jesse"), 523-20

(James, Jesse), "More Proof - Murder of Jesse James a Hoax" in POLICE GAZETTE, 217-77

(James, Jesse), Reappearing Legends About Jesse James, 57-3

(James, Jesse), Was That Jesse James?, by Joe Gantner, 128-1

James Malcolm Rymer and Thomas Pecket Prest, (authors of Gothic "penny bloods" and history of Edward Lloyd and his publications; English), by W.O.G.Lofts, 485-18

James Perkins Tracy - A Self Made Man, (biog. sketch of author), by Ralph Adimari, 277-82

Jay, Frank: Old Boys' Magazines and Journals: The Beeton Publications, 109-1

Jean Ray, Last and Greatest of the Dime Novelists, (biog. & literary sketch), by Ross Craufurd, 537-40

Jeff Clayton - Sexton Blake, or Another Mystery Solved, (Jeff Clayton as detective in Arthur Westbrook paperback books, and Sexton Blake, a comparison), by J. Edward Leithead, 449-21

(Jenks, Charles), Diamond Dick Creator Left Only $300, news item, by Ralph F. Cummings, 58-12

Jenks, George C., mention, 136-1

(Jenks, George C.), obituary, 20-4

(Jennings, Al), Former Badman of Old West Dies, news item, 381-53

Jennings, Robert: letter of comment, 514-86

Jennings, Robert: Reckless Ralph's Frightful Apparition, (visit with Ralph Cummings and his collection), 513-50

(JESSE JAMES STORIES), Dime Novel Sketches #28, 351-119

Johannsen, Albert: Ages of Beadle Authors, 212-39

Johannsen, Albert: Albert Bronaugh Talor, a Beadle Author, (biog. sketch), 303-104

Johannsen, Albert: Beadle Reprints in Iver's and Westbrook's Deadwood Dick and Frontier Novels, 123-6

Johannsen, Albert: Deadwood Dick, Jr. Stories Not Written by Wheeler, with checklist, 298-54

(Johannsen, Albert), Scientist Collects Dime Novels, by Edwin Brooks, 82-2; 83-1

Johannsen, Albert: Translations of the Foreign Quotations in THE HOUSE OF BEADLE AND ADAMS AND ITS DIME AND NICKEL NOVELS (by Johannsen), 215-60

Johannsen, Albert: THE HOUSE OF BEADLE AND ADAMS AND ITS DIME AND NICKEL NOVELS), review by Ralph F. Cummings, 213-43

John H. Whitson, Street & Smith Author, (biog. sketch), by J. Edward Leithead, 69-1

Johnson, Albert E.: Good Old Dime Novel Days - My First Novel, (reading dime novels reminiscences), 372-86

Johnson, Albert E.: letter of comment, 373-96

Johnson, Bill: letter of comment, 488-58

Johnson, Deidre: The Winnetka Graded Book List and Its Supplement (rating childrens books 1924-1925), 549-61

(Johnson, Owen), The Lawrenceville Series by Owen Johnson, (boys' sports series books), by Julius F. Chenu, 517-11

Johnson, W.R.: letter of comment, 380-44; 381-52; 386-96; 417-61; 421-96

Johnson, W.R.: Tip Top & Rough Rider Cards (post cards), 357-65

(Jonas, Charles), In Memoriam, (memorial tribute), by J.C.Dykes, 161-3

(Jones, Clara Augusta), Clara Augusta Jones 1839-1905, (biog. sketch), by Ralph Adimari, 297-5

Jonnie Jones Diary, (humorous fiction), 6-4; 7-3; 8-6; 9-6; 10-5; 11-6

Josephine Chase and Her Pen Names, by
   Roy B. Van Devier, 382-61
Judkins, Esther J.: Charles Asbury
   Stephens, (biog. sketch), 261-41;
   262-50
"Just Kids" Comic Strip, 2-7; 3-3

Kanarr, Dave: letter of comment, 494-131;
   499-46; 515-120
Karsch, Albert: letter of comment,
   404-53
(Keith, Harrison, detective), The
   Harrison Keith Stories, (detective
   tales in NEW MAGNET LIBRARY), by
   J. Edward Leithead, 56-5
(Kellogg, Elijah), letter from publisher,
   (1933), 530-51
(Kilman, Ed & Theon Wright: HUGH ROY
   CULLEN), review, 267-95
King of the Wild West, (discussion on
   ROUGH RIDERS WEEKLY), by J. Edward
   Leithead, 198-17
Kinkade, Arlie: Biographies of Pioneers-
   Col. Daniel Boone, (biog. sketch),
   2-1
Kinkade, Arlie: Biographies of Pioneers-
   Col. David Crockett, (biog. Sketch),
   3-4
Kipp, Richard A.: letter of comment,
   493-124
Kirk Munroe and His Books for Boys,
   (boys' books, adventure), by
   Ralph F. Cummings, 79-5
Kit Carson: An Eye Witness Word, by
   Roland D. Sawyer, 296-40
(Klondike Gold Rush), The Anatomy of Dime
   Novels, No.16: Stories of the Klondike
   Gold Rush, by J. Edward Leithead,
   443-76; 444-88
(KLONDIKE KIT LIBRARY), Dime Novel
   Sketches #20, 341-9
(KLONDIKE KIT LIBRARY), Tales of Klondike
   Gold in Dime Novels, by J. Edward
   Leithead, 301-88
Knott, Frank L.: letter of comment,
   409-108
Knott, James E.: A Tribute to Gil Patten,
   150-4
Knott, James E.: THE GOLDEN ARGOSY,
   (comments and reminiscences), 144-1
Knott, James E.: My Remembrances of
   Gilbert Patten, 288-65
(Knox, General Henry), Reckless Ralph
   and Wild Bill Visit the Grave of
   General Henry Knox, by William M.
   Burns, 170-1
Kohrt, Lou: letter of comment, 377-16;
   382-64; 404-52; 411-133; 454-76;
   539-82; 549-66
Kunzog, John C.: Beadle and His Wooden
   Types, (use of wood print fonts
   by Beadle), 169-1
Kunzog, John C.: The Beadle Brothers,
   Erastus and Irwin, (historical and
   biographical sketch), 415-34; 416-46
Kunzog, John C.: Dime Novel Printing,
   (discussion), 428-51

Kunzog, John C.: letter of comment,
   516-150
Kurtz, Homer H.: DIAMOND DICK, JR., The
   Boys Best Weekly, (discussion and
   reminiscences), 62-1
Kurtz, Homer H.: Public Thanks to Gilbert
   Patten (appreciation tribute), 66-1

Lahart, Mrs. Joe: letter of comment,
   404-53
Lahmon, L.H.: Old Cap Collier and Norman
   L. Munro, (dime novel detective of
   Munro, publisher), 64-3
(Lamb, Charles), Charles Lamb's Fore-
   runners of the Dime Novel, (early
   popular fiction 1805-1808), by
   J.E. Riehl, 533-109
Lanctot, Max T.: letter of comment,
   493-124
Land of the Heroes, (locales of boys'
   book series, various, discussed),
   by John T. Dizer, Jr., 465-52;
   465-62
Lane, Harry L.: letter of comment,
   398-121
Lapham, William Berry: Sylvanus Cobb,
   Jr., Author, (biog. sketch), 51-3
Larel, Miss: Reckless Ralph Tracks 'em
   Down, (collecting by Ralph F.
   Cummings, dime novels), 291-
Larmon, L.H.: NICK CARTER WEEKLY,
   (comments), 59-1
Larry Evans, A Famous American Novelist,
   (literary and biog. sketch), by Roy
   B. Van Devier, 388-4
Last Days of Billy the Kid, The, by
   J.P.Guinon, 104-6
Last Issue of DIAMOND DICK, JR. WEEKLY,
   (No.762), 208-1
Last Number of THE GOLDEN ARGOSY, The,
   (comments), by Fred T. Singleton,
   10-2; 11-4
Last SENSATION, The, 180-5
Last Words Of, (of dime novel heroes),
   by Gerald J. McIntosh, 401-19
Late Robert Louis Stevenson, The,
   (commentary), 75-10
Latimer, Paul: letter of comment, 525-93;
   539-82; 540-97; 551-105
(LAUGHING SERIES), Dime Novel Sketches
   #137, 464-43
Lawrenceville Series by Owen Johnson, The,
   (discusses boys' sports series books),
   by Julius F. Chenu, 517-11
Lawson, A.W.: THE GENTLEMAN'S JOURNAL,
   (comments), 273-46
Lawson, A.W.: The Rival Rangers of Fleet
   Street, (Edwin J. Brett and William
   L. Emmett), 279-102
Lawson, W.B.: BOYS COMIC JOURNAL, 262-52
Learnard, Don S.: A Few Do's and Don'ts,
   (collecting dime novels, advice),
   342-22
Learned, Donald S.: Where is Dot? (dime
   novel reminiscences), 58-2
(Learnerd, Don), A Visit with Don &
   Grace, (reminiscences), by Harold
   Poore, 352-2

(Learnerd, Don), Don on the Farm, (biog. sketch), by Charles Duprez, 332-41

LeBlanc, Edward T.: Checklist of Robert M. DeWitt Publications, (dime novel series), 520-97

LeBlanc, Edward T.: Collector's Dime Novel Bookshelf,. (books of value to collectors), see "Collecting"

LeBlanc, Edward T.: Collectors Dime Novel & Boys Book Bookshelf, (books of value to collectors), see "Collecting"

LeBlanc, Edward T.: Contents and Index of Major Subjects, DIME NOVEL ROUNDUP, Issues Nos. 1-516, 529-SS

LeBlanc, Edward T.: Displaying One's Collection, (boys' book collection of Willis Potthoff), 518-46

LeBlanc, Edward T.: Famous Tousey Story Papers, 508-2

LeBlanc, Edward T.: Happy Birthday, Captain Chester G. Mayo, (100th Birthday eulogy), 552-126

(LeBlanc, Edward T.), New Editor, DIME NOVEL ROUNDUP, July 1952, 238-52

LeBlanc, Edward T.: Nick Carter 100th Anniversary Book, (Nick Carter, Killmaster series paperback books), with biog. sketch by J. Randolph Cox, 511-33

LeBlanc, Edward T.: Rare Dime Novels, (commentary and description)
#1: INDIAN TALES No.1, 213-41
#2: YOUTHS LIBRARY, 215-57
#3: TEN CENT IRISH NOVELS, 218-81
#4: THE HUB TEN CENT NOVELS, with checklist, 232-1
#5: DAWLEYS CAMP & FIRESIDE LIBRARY, with checklist, 238-49

LeBlanc, Edward T.: Review of AMAZING ADVENTURES OF LYIN' BOB HAGUM AND FIDDLIN' JIM by Charles Clark, 390-30

LeBlanc, Edward T.: Review of play, "Frank Merriwell, or Honor Challenged" 464-48

LeBlanc, Edward T. and Ralph Adimari: Checklist of Street & Smith Dime Novels and Related Publications, 299-60

LeBlanc, Edward T. and Brian W. Dippie: Bibliography of Custer Dime Novels (pertaining to Gen. Custer), 442-66

LeBlanc, Edward T. and J. Edward Leithead: ROUGH RIDER WEEKLY and the Ted Strong Saga, with bibliographical checklist, 478-3

LeBlanc, Edward T. and Denis R. Rogers: Dime Novel Series Title Changes, 488-50

LeBlanc, Edward T. and Donald L. Steinhauer: Checklist for writings of Gilbert Patten Prior to his Frank Merriwell work, 410-118

Leckenby, Herbert: A Tribute to Gilbert Patten, 162-1

Leckenby, Herbert, obituary, 331-37

LEDGER, THE, (story paper), 88-2

(Lee, Edward Edson), BOY PARTNERS, An Edward Edson Lee Publication, (index and summary of periodical), by Willis J. Potthoff, 550-83

(Lee, William G.), obituary, 490-80

Leif, Irving P.: letter of comment, 524-51

(Leif, Irving P.: CHILDREN'S LITERATURE, A HISTORICAL AND CONTEMPORARY BIBLIOGRAPHY), review by John T. Dizer, Jr., 530-53; 531-77

Leighter, Learnard C.: Noname, (Lu Senarens, author of dime novels, biographical comments), 56-1

Leithead, J. Edward: Addenda on Robert Emmett Owen, 334-63

Leithead, J. Edward: An Artist Recalls Nickel Novel Days, (Charles L. Wrenn), 87-1

Leithead, J. Edward: The Anatomy of Dime Novels, (survey and discussion),
No.1: Nick Carter, 384-76; 385-85
No.2: Buffalo Bill, 389-10; 390-22
No.3: Railroading, 398-114; 399-126
No.4: Spanish-American War Novels, 402-24; 403-36
No.5: The Firefighters, 407-74; 408-86
No.6: Kit Carson, 413-14; 414-24
No.7: Novels of the American Revolution, 418-64; 419-76
No.8: Civil War Novels, 422-106; 423-114
No.9: Wall Street Stories, 427-34; 428-44
No.10: The Arthur Westbrook Company, 429-56; 430-68
No.11: Bootblack Detectives, 431-78
No.12: Novels of the Circus, 432-88; 433-96
No.13: Temperance Stories, 434-108; 435-118
No.14: West Point and Annapolis Stories, 437-18; 438-30
No.15: Stories of Worldwide Adventure, 440-42; 441-50
No.16: Stories of the Klondike Gold Rush, 443-76; 444-88
No.17: Frontier and Revolutionary War Stories that Missed PLUCK AND LUCK, 446-110; 447-122
No.18: The Alamo and the Mexican War, 450-24
No.19: Stories of Boarding School and College Sports, 454-72; 455-80
No.20: Stories of the Stage, 458-112; 459-120
No.21: Stories of Polar Exploration, 461-14; 462-24

Leithead, J. Edward: Arietta, Heroine of Wild West Trails, (dime novel heroine character), 367-32

Leithead, J. Edward: The Art of Robert Emmett Owen, (cover artist, dime novels), 421-94

Leithead, J. Edward: Author and Artist of the Street & Smith Staff: W. Bert Foster and Charles L. Wrenn, (biog. sketch), 361-92; 362-99; 363-110

Leithead, J. Edward: The Bandit Brothers of Old Missouri, (essay on James-Younger Gang), 276-70

Leithead, J. Edward: Boy Detectives, (in dime novels), 240-66; 241-74; 242-85

Leithead, J. Edward: Buckskin Bill Recalls Famous Iowa Neighbors and a Trip to Old Missouri, (reminiscences regarding Buffalo Bill Cody and the James Gang), 291-94

Leithead, J. Edward: The Buckskin Bill Story, (historical reminiscence & sketch, Col. Charles Daniel Randolph) 270-18

Leithead, J. Edward: Buckskin Men of Forest and Plain, (biog. sketches, survey), 246-18; 248-33; 249-43; 250-50; 253-74; 254-82

Leithead, J. Edward: Buffalo Bill and His Pards of the West, 43-1

Leithead, J. Edward: Buffalo Bill, Multi-Storied Border King, (bibliography of storypaper serials and novels), 168-2; 171-6; 173-1; 174-18; 175-26

Leithead, J. Edward: Buffalo Bill Novels in Paperback Book Format, with checklist, 201-49

Leithead, J. Edward: Buffalo Bill Reprints, 342-18; 343-26

Leithead, J. Edward: "By the Author of Buffalo Bill" (var. other authors), 308-34; 309-42; 310-100

Leithead, J. Edward: The Civil War in Dime Novels, 275-62

Leithead, J. Edward: Colonel Prentiss Ingraham, (biog. sketch of author), 376-1; 377-10

Leithead, J. Edward: The Creator of Diamond Dick, 335-66

Leithead, J. Edward: The Derring-Do of the Diamond Dicks, (bibliography), 187-25

Leithead, J. Edward: Dime Novel Bonanza, (collecting experiences), 65-1

Leithead, J. Edward: Doctor Quartz and Other Nine-Lived Villains, (villains in the dime novels), 380-40; 381-48

Leithead, J. Edward: English Reprints of Buffalo Bill Novels, 392-44; 393-56

Leithead, J. Edward: Fond Recollections (autobiographical reminiscences), 287-57

Leithead, J. Edward: Four Footed Friends of Our Dime Novel Heroes, 297-2

Leithead, J. Edward: Frederick Van Rensselaer Dey, (author sketch), 401-14

Leithead, J. Edward: Gilbert Patten in Clothbound Editions, 410-116

Leithead, J. Edward: The Greatest Sleuth That Ever Lived, (essay on Nick Carter), 272-38

Leithead, J. Edward: The Harrison Keith Stories (detective, in NEW MAGNET LIBRARY), 56-5

(Leithead, J. Edward), J. Edward Leithead, the Dime Novel King, (verse), by Charles D. Randolph, 458-111

Leithead, J. Edward: The James Boys in the Saddle Again, (Arthur Westbrook Co's Adventure Series), with checklist, 280-2

Leithead, J. Edward: The James Boys in the Saddle Again, (on var. dime novels featuring James Gang), 283-26

Leithead, J. Edward: Jeff Clayton - Sexton Blake, or Another Mystery Solved, (detective in Arthur Westbrook Co. paperback books compared to Sexton Blake, English detective), 449-21

Leithead, J. Edward: John H. Whitson, Street & Smith Author, (biog. sketch), 69-1

Leithead, J. Edward: King of the Wild West, (discusses ROUGH RIDERS WEEKLY), 198-17

Leithead, J. Edward: letter of comment, 372-86; 392-52; 396-99

Leithead, J. Edward: THE LIBERTY BOYS OF '76, 229-73

Leithead, J. Edward: More About the Buffalo Bill Stories, 58-1

Leithead, J. Edward: More About the Nick Carter Libraries, 245-10

Leithead, J. Edward: NEW BUFFALO BILL WEEKLY, (bibliographical listing), 452-SS

Leithead, J. Edward: Nick Carter and Buffalo Bill items (re: dime novels) 61-1

Leithead, J. Edward: Nick Carter Detective Tales in MAGNET and NEW MAGNET LIBRARY, (checklist), 212-33

Leithead, J. Edward: Nick Carter in Another Man's Shoes, (Carter stories by Samuel C. Spalding; Sexton Blake) 350-112; 351-120

Leithead, J. Edward: Nick Carter in Print, (bibliography 1886-1936), 181-75

Leithead, J. Edward: Nick Carter Reprints (discussed), 337-82; 338-92

Leithead, J. Edward: The Nickel Novel Almost Everybody Liked: PLUCK AND LUCK, 357-60

Leithead, J. Edward: Now They're Collectors' Items, (boys' series books discussed), No.1, Edward S. Ellis and Harry Castlemon 405-58; 406-66
No.2, various, 411-128
No.3, various, and authors, 417-54
No.4, various, 420-86

Leithead, J. Edward: Notes on Foster-Wrenn Article, 365-17

Leithead, J. Edward: Old Melodramas,
   (discusses old stage productions),
   257-10; 258-20
Leithead, J. Edward: Old Time Boys'
   Books, (early boys' books), 227-58;
   228-69; 231-91; 233-11; 234-22;
   236-35; 238-55; 239-61
Leithead, J. Edward: On Stage, Mr. Carter,
   (Frederick Van Rensselaer Dey as writer
   of Nick Carter stories), 314-140;
   315-148; 316-9
Leithead, J. Edward: Outlaw Trails in
   Indian Territory (in dime novels,
   emphasis on Dalton Gang), with
   checklist, 289-78; 290-87
Leithead, J. Edward: Pseudonyms of
   W. Bert Foster, 364-3
Leithead, J. Edward: Review of CUSTER'S
   LIST, A CHECKLIST OF PICTURES
   RELATING TO THE LITTLE BIG HORN
   by Don Russell, 457-107
Leithead, J. Edward: Review of THE
   FICTION FACTORY by Quentin Reynolds,
   history of Street & Smith, 282-18
Leithead, J. Edward: Review of THE LIVES
   AND LEGENDS OF BUFFALO BILL by Don
   Russell, 340-2
Leithead, J. Edward: Sherlock Holmes
   Exhibit, (Philadelphia Free Library
   1968, including Nick Carter), 429-61
Leithead, J. Edward: Street & Smith
   Item, (Robert Emmett Owen, cover
   artist), 81-4
Leithead, J. Edward: Supplement to Article
   on Frederick Van Rensselaer Dey,
   404-51
Leithead, J. Edward: Tales of Klondike
   Gold in Dime Novels, 301-88
Leithead, J. Edward: Tanbark and Spangles
   in the Five-Cent Libraries, (circus
   theme stories), 223-25; 265-76; 266-84
Leithead, J. Edward: Ted Strong and His
   Rough Rides, (in ROUGH RIDERS
   WEEKLY), 345-66; 346-76
Leithead, J. Edward: This "Sleuth"
   Business, (detectives in dime novels),
   369-50; 370-62; 371-70
Leithead, J. Edward: The Two King Bradys
   and Their Girl Detectives, (detectives
   in dime novels), 372-80; 373-90
Leithead, J. Edward: The Wild West Shows
   Pass in Grand Review, (essay and survey
   on Wild West Shows), 264-65; 265-74;
   266-84
Leithead, J. Edward: Wyoming's Wild Riders
   and Other Hunted Men (Butch Cassidy,
   Billy the Kid, and others in dime
   novels), 294-20
Leithead, J. Edward: Young Diamond Dick,
   358-68; 359-76; 360-84
Leithead, J. Edward: Young Wild West,
   (WILD WEST WEEKLY), 226-49
(Leithead, J. Edward), J. Edward Leithead
   Collection of Pseudonyms, by Ralph
   Adimari, 329-10

(Leithead, J. Edward), Memorial Tribute
   to J. Edward Leithead, by Stanley
   A. Pachon, 458-110
Leithead, J. Edward and Edward T.
   LeBlanc: ROUGH RIDER WEEKLY and the
   Ted Strong Saga, with bibliography
   and checklist, 478-3
Leithead, J. Edward and Gerald J.
   McIntosh: The Merriwells - After
   Tip Top, 354-20; 355-28; 356-36
Leithead, J. Edward and Denis R. Rogers:
   A Publication Pattern of Edward S.
   Ellis (study of the Porter & Coates/
   Henry T. Coates/John C. Winston edns.
   of boys' books by Ellis), 480-80;
   481-95
Leominster, Massachusetts Man Wrote Many
   Famous Dime Novels, (Samuel Stone
   "Buckskin Sam" Hall), 180-1
(Leslie, Frank), Frank Leslie to the
   Boys and Girls of America, by
   Bracebridge Hemyng, 78-1
(Leslie, Frank), The Leslie Publications,
   by George H. Cordier, 203-65
(Leslie, Frank), William J. Benners -
   The First Historian of the Dime Novel,
   by Ralph Adimari, 312-122
Let's Push Back the Clock, (reminis-
   cences), 211-26
Letters, note: frequent letter columns
   from issue No.369 through No.551,
   (letters of comment from readers
   and contributors)
Letters From Dime Novel Publishers, (to
   Will Lisenbee), by Ralph P. Smith,
   209-10
Levy, Edward G.: letter of comment,
   414-32; 421-96
Lewandowski, Joseph: letter of comment,
   550-86
Lewis, Ethel Clark: A Weaver of Romances,
   (Mrs. Alex. McVeigh Miller, early
   author; biog. sketch), 110-1
LIBERTY BOYS OF '76, 296-36
LIBERTY BOYS OF '76, THE, by J. Edward
   Leithead, 229-73
(LIBERTY BOYS OF '76), Dime Novel Sketches
   #71, 398-113
(LIBRARY OF ADVENTURE AND ROMANCE), Dime
   Novel Sketches #140, 467-73
Library of Congress Pseudonyms (as
   recorded by LC), by Ralph Adimari,
   321-50
Life Gits Teejus, Don't It?, (verse),
   202-62
Life History of John Harper, (biog.
   sketch; Harper Bros., Publishers),
   60-9
Life of a Woman Known to Thousnads, The,
   (Mrs. E.D.E.N.Southworth, early
   author, biog. sketch), 192-77
Life of HAPPY HOURS MAGAZINE and DIME
   NOVEL ROUNDUP, Also Happy Hours
   Brotherhood, by Ralph F. Cummings,
   300-81

(THE LIFE OF PETER PAD: Peter Pad),
    (selections from), 9-2; 10-4; 11-3
Life of W. Clark Russell, The, (biog.
    sketch, author), by Ralph F.
    Cummings, 213-44
Light of Asia, The, (news item, white
    elephant imported), 237-41
(Lightbody, Ben, Series), Question on
    existence with comments, (boys'
    books), 514-84
Likes and Dislikes in BRAVE AND BOLD,
    (reading reminiscences), by William
    M. Burns, 368-45
Likes and Dislikes, Then and Now,
    (reading reminiscences), by William
    M. Burns, 102-1
Lillibridge, Janet R.: Chronological
    Checklist of Books of Oliver Optic,
    517-28
Lillibridge, Janet R.: letter of
    comment, 517-28
(Lillie, Maj. Gordon), obituary,
    (a.k.a. Pawnee Bill), by Edwin
    Brooks, 114-9
Lilly, George: Savant Dips Into Dime
    Novels in Library of Congress,
    (commentary), 58-12
(Lincoln, Abraham), Evaluation of
    Abraham Lincoln, (from Frank
    Merriwell story), 414-29
Linville, Carl: letter of comment,
    382-64; 401-21
(Linville, Carl), Rover Boy Carl
    Linville, (biog. sketch), by
    Charles Duprez, 281-10
Lippard, George, (author mentioned),
    115-3
Lippincott, Bill: letter of comment,
    525-75
(Lisenbee, Will, author), Letters
    from Dime Novel Publishers to
    Will Lisenbee, by Ralph P. Smith,
    209-10
Lisenbee, Will: The Little Beadles,
    (verse), 101-10
LITERARY ALBUM, THE, 46-2
Literary Feast, The, (cartoons of
    Webster in NEW YORK WORLD), by
    W.B.McCafferty, 1-1
Little Beadles, The, (verse), by
    Will Lisenbee, 101-10
LITTLE CHIEF LIBRARY, THE, 136-4;
    179-4; 413-16
LITTLE CHIEF LIBRARY, THE, by
    "Seajay", 98-3
(LITTLE CHIEF LIBRARY, THE), Dime
    Novel Sketches #106, 433-95
(LIVES AND LEGENDS OF BUFFALO BILL:
    Don Russell), review by J.
    Edward Leithead, 340-2
LIVES OF GREAT AMERICANS, Checklist,
    (dime novel), 539-76
(LIVES OF GREAT AMERICANS), Dime
    Novel Sketches #211, 539-73
(Livingston, Leon Ray), Leon Ray
    Livingston, Wanderer, Author,
    Orator, (biog.sketch), by Robert
    H. Smeltzer, 259-31

(Lloyd, Edward), James Malcolm Rymer and
    Thomas Pecket Prest, (authors of
    Gothic "penny blooods" and history
    of Edward Lloyd and his publications)
    by W.O.G.Lofts, 485-18
Local Boys Make Good? Or?, (comments
    on the American comics), by Arthur
    Moyse, 322-59
(LOG CABIN LIBRARY), Dime Novel Sketches
    #86, 413-13
(LOG CABIN LIBRARY, pocket edn.), Dime
    Novel Sketches #22, 143-25
LOG CABIN NOVELS, 7-9
(Logan, Herschel C.: BUCKSKIN AND
    SATIN), review, (book on Texas Jack),
    266-86; 268-5
Lofts, W.O.G.: A Tribute to Charles
    Hamilton, (author), 355-33
Lofts, W.O.G.: THE BAD BOYS PAPER,
    313-134
Lofts, W.O.G.: The Biographical Mysteries
    of George Alfred Henty, (biog. essay),
    524-44
Lofts, W.O.G.: Dick Turpin, The Famous
    Highwayman, (essay), 441-48
Lofts, W.O.G.: The First English Story
    Papers for Boys, (historical survey),
    277-84
Lofts, W.O.G.: The Henty Fame and Riches,
    (biog. essay), 526-89
Lofts, W.O.G.: James Malcolm Rymer and
    Thomas Pecket Prest, (authors of
    Gothic "penny bloods", and history
    of Edward Lloyd and his publications),
    485-18
Lofts, W.O.G.:letter of comment,
    408-90; 419-82; 443-84; 475-52
Lofts, W.O.G.: The Real Robin Hood,
    (historical basis of legend),
    502-82; 503-99
Lofts, W.O.G.: The Roaring Girl, (Moll
    Cutpurse, famous English thief),
    473-18
Lofts, W.O.G.: Sexton Blake, (on famous
    detective character), 273-48; 439-40
Lofts, W.O.G.: Spring-Heeled Jack,
    (on colorful English villain),
    489-60
Lofts, W.O.G.: Success and Failure,
    (short history of penny dreadful
    publishers in England), 523-9
Lofts, W.O.C.: The Title Was the Same!
    (English boys' papers with the
    same name), 295-29
Lofts, W.O.G.: Treasure Island, (on
    R.L.Stevenson's TREASURE ISLAND and
    pirate stories in general), 477-64
Lofts, W.O.G. and D.J. Adley: Favorite
    Boyhood Characters on the British
    Screen, 525-66; 528-122
Long, Capt. William F., mention, 6-6
Long Stories in My Collection, (reading
    reminiscences), by William M. Burns,
    273-47
Look Out, Boys, It's a Pinkerton,
    (reminiscences), 8-5
Looking Back...(reminiscences), by
    Harry Pulfer, 406-70

"Lop-Sided Novels", (how to correct the condition), by Robert Smeltzer, 33-1

(Lost race adventures), Fantasy, Science Fiction and Lost Race Adventures in the Street & Smith paperback volumes, (checklist), by Stuart A. Teitler, 442-71

Loucks, Ward G.: letter of comment, 409-108; 414-32

Louis E. Pendleton: A Famous Southern Author, (biog. sketch), by Roy B. Van Devier, 374-100

Lovell Complex, The, (publishing group), by Denis R. Rogers, 527-98

(Lovell, John W., Publisher), The Lovell Complex, by Denis R. Rogers, 527-98

Lunatic Novelist, The, (Gustave Almard), 127-3

Lynn, Frank: The Quatrain, (verse), 101-11

Machen, John W.: letter of comment, 425-19

MADAM LUCIE, THE FRENCH LADY DETECTIVE, 151-2

MAGAZINE FOR BOYS, 14-3

Magazine Serial and Book Relationships in Leo Edwards Books, (boys' books) by Julius R. Chenu, 534-122

Magic California, (reminiscences extolling California), by Frisco Bert, 132-3

(MAGNET LIBRARY), Nick Carter Detective Tales in MAGNET and NEW MAGNET LIBRARY, checklist, by J. Edward Leithead, 212-33

"MALESKA" - Beadles Dime Novel No.1, (commentary), 38-5

"MALESKA" - 1st of the Dime Novels, (commentary), 23-1

Many Faceted Alger, The, (on the humorous sketches of Alger), by Stanley A. Pachon, 548-37

Marchenby, P.D.: letter of comment, 389-17

Maroske, P.C.: To Bracebridge Hemyng, (verse), 153-3

Marsh, M.E.: letter of comment, 36-1

Martin, Walker: letter of comment, 547-19

Mary Roberts Rinehart and the Nickel Novel, by Stanley A. Pachon, 369-55

(Mason, Bobbie Ann: THE GIRL SLEUTH, A FEMINIST GUIDE), review by John T. Dizer, Jr., 530-53; 531-77

Mason, Walt: Foolish Buying, (advice on collecting dime novels), 71-3

Mason, Walt: The Old Book Store, (reminiscences, dime novels), 83-1

Master T.W. Hanshew, Boy Acot, Author, and Dramatist, (biog. sketch), 90-3

Maw Green on the Dime Novel, (on the comic strip), 82-2

MAYME REIDS MAGAZINE, ONWARD, 119-9

(Mayo, Capt. Chester G.), Happy Birthday, Captain Chester G. Mayo, (100th birthday eulogy, boys books author), by Edward T. LeBlanc, 552-126

Mayo, Chester Gard: letter of comment, 381-52

(Mayo, Chester Gard), Chester Gard Mayo - An Appreciation, (collector of dime novels, story papers, books), by John T. Dizer, Jr., 530-48

McArdle, John: letter of comment, 535-15

McCafferty, W.B.: Crazy Horse and Spotted Tail, (Indian sketch), 2-5

McCafferty, W.B.: Diamond Dick in Schooldays, (verse), 98-6

McCafferty, W.B.: Happy Days are Back Again, (on HAPPY DAYS story paper), 118-4

McCafferty, W.B.: The Literary Feast, (cartoons of Mr. Webster, NEW YORK WORLD), 1-1

McCafferty, W.B.: Mr. Merriwell, (verse), 111-3

McCafferty, W.B.: Nassau Street, (reminiscences of Nassau Street, N.Y.C.), 185-13

McCafferty, W.B.: Nick Carter and the Shadow Woman, (commentary), 118-3

McCafferty, W.B.: Odds and Ends, (dime novel miscellany),
- (Thomas Bird Mosher), 199-33
- (Old King Brady), 202-61
- (Maiden St., N.Y.C.), 202-61; 204-75
- (Sherlock Holmes and Baker Street), 216-70

McCafferty, W.B.: The Passing of Deadwood Dick, (verse), 94-2

McCafferty, W.B.: Pawnee Bill, (reminiscences), 152-3

McCafferty, W.B.: The Photo of Billy the Kid, 2-4

McCafferty, W.B.: This and That, (news clipping pertinent), 2-6

(McCafferty, William Burton), Memorial-William B. McCafferty, Dime Novelist, by Gerald J. McIntosh, 408-91

McDowell, Robert: letter of comment, 396-99; 501-70

McDowell, Robert: Merriwells That Might Have Been, (suggested titles for stories), 446-118

McDowell, Robert: Old Dime Novels, (song), 279-106

McDowell, Robert: TIP TOP WEEKLY, (bibliographic listing), 532-SS

McGehee, Lily: letter of comment, 516-149

McIntosh, G.H.: The Old Hen House, (verse), 317-18

McIntosh, G.H.: Sixty Years Ago, (verse), 317-18

McIntosh, Gerald J.: Bruce Browning's Seven Years at Yale in TIP TOP WEEKLY, 390-28

McIntosh, Gerald J.: Buffalo Bill's Benevolence, or, Col. Cody's Church Dollar, (spiritual life of Cody), 484-2

McIntosh, Gerald J.: Captain Walter Wiley, the Windjammer and the Marine Marvel, or, The Terrible and Terrific Teller of Tall Tales in TIP TOP, 435-123

McIntosh, Gerald J.: Columnists and Commentators Who "Knew" Merriwell, 445-105

McIntosh, Gerald J.: Cornelius Shea, An Old Scout, (frontier reminiscences), 401-20

McIntosh, Gerald J.: Dime Novel "Daze" (collecting reminiscences), 448-3

McIntosh, Gerald J.: Dime Novels in Cartoons, (Jim Williams and other cartoonists), 412-2

McIntosh, Gerald J.: Dime Novel Notes, 441-62

McIntosh, Gerald J.: Following the Merriwell Trail, (bibliography, with story synopsis), 474-34

McIntosh, Gerald J.: Frank Merriwell in the Movies, 415-39

McIntosh, Gerald J.: Frank Merriwell, Life Saver, or, Rescuing Fair TIP TOP Maidens, 404-48; 405-61

McIntosh, Gerald J.: Frank Merriwell, The Unconquerable, (verse), 391-38

McIntosh, Gerald J.: Frank Merriwell's Mottoes, 410-123

McIntosh, Gerald J.: Front Cover Scenes Repeated, (duplicate use of covers by TIP TOP WEEKLY), 423-118

McIntosh, Gerald J.: The Influence of Charles Dickens on Gilbert Patten, (Merriwell creator), 409-103

McIntosh, Gerald J.: Last Words, (of dime novel heroes), 401-10

McIntosh, Gerald J.: letter of comment, 390-30; 409-108

McIntosh, Gerald J.: Memorial - William B. McCafferty, Dime Novelist, (tribute) 408-91

McIntosh, Gerald J.: The Merriwell Newspaper Comic Strip, (1930's), 400-2

McIntosh, Gerald J.: Merriwelliana in Cartoons, 442-73

McIntosh, Gerald J.: The Merriwells Under Arrest, or, Dime Novel Heroes Vindicated, (episodes of Merriwells arrested by the law), 395-78; 390-90

McIntosh, Gerald J.: More Books and Stories by Gilbert Patten, 426-24

McIntosh, Gerald J.: More on Gilbert Patten's Pseudonyms, 443-83

McIntosh, Gerald J.: My Visit With Pawnee Bill, 453-66

McIntosh, Gerald J.: Pseudonyms of Gilbert Patten, 436-2

McIntosh, Gerald J.: Real People in the Merriwell Stories, 403-42

McIntosh, Gerald J.: Repetition of Character Names in the Merriwell Stories, 424-2

McIntosh, Gerald J.: Rounded Up for the ROUNDUP, (odd facts on TIP TOP WEEKLY), 421-97

McIntosh, Gerald J.: The Short Short Stories of Burt L. Standish (pseudonym of Gilbert Patten), 391-34; 393-66

McIntosh, Gerald J.: Timothy, Chap.10, 16th Verse, in TIP TOP WEEKLY, 410-117

McIntosh, Gerald J.: "The Wonderful Adventures of Cap't Wiley" ed. by Burt L. Standish (Gilbert Patten), (the "undiscovered" memoirs of dime novel character), 462-31

(McIntosh, Gerald J.), obituary, 484-13

McIntosh, Gerald J. and Ralph Adimari: Frank Merriwell on Radio and Television, 410-112

McIntosh, Gerald J. and J. Edward Leithead: The Merriwells, After TIP TOP, 354-20; 355-28; 356-36

McIntosh, Walter H.: letter of comment, 487-47

McIntosh, Walter H.: You've Told Whoppers - Ever Read One? (humor), 487-46

(McIntyre, John T.), Novelist Fooled by Innocent Face, by B. Benners, 71-2

(McIntyre, John T.), Prize Novelist John T. McIntyre Rises to Defense of Pot-Boilers, by Jean Barrett, 93-1

McNabb, Edward J.: letter of comment, 373-96; 381-51; 394-72; 407-81; 418-69; 444-96; 526-92; 547-20

(McNeil, Everett), Now They're Collectors' Items, (on boys series books), by J. Edward Leithead, 411-128

(McNeil, Everett), Two Boys' Books Writers from Wisconsin, (Leslie Quirk and Everett McNeil), (biog. sketch), by Marge Dahl, 494-131

Mead, Leon: How Ned Buntline Turned From Runaway Boy to Writing Genius-His Relations with Buffalo Bill and the "Know Nothings", 101-1

MEDAL and NEW MEDAL LIBRARIES, by Ralph P. Smith, 98-1

MEDAL LIBRARY, 271-28

(MEDAL LIBRARY), ROUGH RIDER WEEKLY and the Ted Strong Saga, with bibliographic checklist, by Edward T. LeBlanc and J. Edward Leithead, 478-3

Member of James Boys Gang Now Religious Worker, by Frank T. Fries, 7-4

Members of the Happy Hours Brotherhood, (commentary), by Robert M. Smeltzer, 56-5

Memoir of Mayne Reid, (author), by R.H.Stoddard, 205-81

Memorial Tribute to J. Edward Leithead, by Stanley A. Pachon, 458-110

Memorial - William B. McCafferty, Dime Novelist, by Gerald J. McIntosh, 408-91

Memories of the BOYS BEST WEEKLY, (reminiscences and data), by Howard B. Silsbee, 311-116

Mengar, Ray: letter of comment, 458-116

(Mengar, Ray), Ray Mengar and His Dime Novel Collection, by Joe Stone, 431-84

(Merriam Company, The, Publishers), The Edward S. Ellis Stories Published by the Mershon Complex, by Denis R. Rogers, 490-70; 491-86; 492-104

Merriwell Apocrypha, ("Frank Merriwell in the White House"), by J. Randolph Cox, 491-93

MERRIWELL LIBRARY, 271-32

Merriwell Magazine Stories, The, (discussion), by Harold C. Holmes, 62-4; 66-1

Merriwell Newspaper Comic Strip, (1930s) by Gerald J. McIntosh, 400-2

Merriwell Quiz, 481-107

Merriwelliana in Cartoons, by Gerald J. McIntosh, 442-73

Merriwells, The - After TIP TOP, by J. Edward Leithead and Gerald J. McIntosh, 354-20; 355-28; 356-36

Merriwell's Out of Date, (fiction), by Charles Fisher, 123-5

Merriwells That Might Have Been (suggested titles for stories), by Robert McDowell, 446-118

Merriwells Under Arrest, or, Dime Novel Heroes Vindicated, The, (episodes of Merriwells afoul of the law), by Gerald J. McIntosh, 395-78; 396-90

(Merriwells), Alger Heroes, the Merri-wells, Etc!, (commentary), by Ralph D. Gardner, 445-100

(Merriwells), A Quick Synopsis of the Merriwell Saga, (in TIP TOP WEEKLY) by Ralph P. Smith, 537-48

(Merriwells), The Hard-Cover Merriwells, (hardbound Merriwell series boys' books), with checklist, by Harry K. Hudson, 541-15

(Merriwells), The Merriwells - After TIP TOP, by J. Edward Leithead and Gerald J. McIntosh, 354-20; 355-28; 356-36

(Merriwells), The Merriwells Under Arrest, or, Dime Novel Heroes Vindicated, (Merriwells afoul of the law), by Gerald J. McIntosh, 395-78; 396-90

(Merriwells), Paper Back Pulpit, by Noble Tribble, 381-50

(Merriwells), Real People in the Merriwell Stories, by Gerald J. McIntosh, 403-42

(Merriwells), Repetition of Character Names in the Merriwell Stories, by Gerald J. McIntosh, 424-2

(Merriwells), Reprints of the Merriwell Series, by J.P.Guinon, 271-26

(Merriwells), Review of play, "Frank Merriwell or Honor Challenged", by Edward T. LeBlanc, 464-48

(Merriwell, Frank), A Merry Chase After "Merry", by Frank T. Fries, 3-5

(Merriwell, Frank), Adventures of Frank Merriwell (on NBC radio), 175-26

(Merriwell, Frank), Cap'n Wiley, Maine's Merry Muchausen, by Frank C. Acker, 494-126

(Merriwell, Frank), CBS Television Program, 405-63

(Merriwell, Frank), Columnists and Commentators Who "Knew" Merriwell, 445-105

(Merriwell, Frank), Following the Merriwell Trail, (bibliography with story synopsis), by Gerald J. McIntosh, 474-34

(Merriwell, Frank), Frank Merriwell at Fardale, by Bob Smeltzer, 48-1

(Merriwell, Frank), Frank Merriwell in the Movies, by Gerald J. McIntosh, 415-39

(Merriwell, Frank), Frank Merriwell, Life Saver, or, Rescuing the Fair TIP TOP Maidens, by Gerald J. McIntosh, 404-48; 405-61

(Merriwell, Frank), Frank Merriwell on Radio and Television, by Gerald J. McIntosh and Ralph Adimari, 410-112

(Merriwell, Frank), Frank Merriwell Returns, (comic books), by J.P. Guinon, 273-50

(Merriwell, Frank), Frank Merriwell, The Unconquerable, (verse), by Gerald J. McIntosh, 391-38

(Merriwell, Frank), Frank Merriwell's Father, (on death of Gilbert Patten and on dime novels in general), by David C. Adams, 150-1

(Merriwell, Frank), Frank Merriwell's Mottoes, by Gerald J. McIntosh, 410-123

(Merriwell, Frank), Frank Merriwell's Parent, or, Patten, the Paramount, (memorial to Gilbert Patten), by J.P.Guinon, 150-6

(Merriwell, Frank), Frank Merriwell's Stage Setback, (review of Frank Merriwell, or, Honor Challenged, stage production), by Frank C. Acker, 466-68

(Merriwell, Frank), Harkaway, Merriwell, Etc., (miscellany), by U.G. Figley, 115-1

(Merriwell, Frank), Hero to Two Gene-rations of Boys, 109-3

(Merriwell, Frank), Merriwell Apocrypha, ("Frank Merriwell in the White House"), by J. Randolph Cox, 491-93

(Merriwell, Frank), Merriwelliana in Cartoons, by Gerald J. McIntosh, 442-73

(Merriwell, Frank), More Gilbert Patten in Clothbound Editions, by Harry K. Hudson, 417-60

(Merriwell, Frank), Paper Back Pulpit, by Noble Tribble, 402-30

(Merriwell, Frank), Patten vs. Superior Talking Pictures, Inc., (suit by Gilbert Patten regarding copyright of Frank Merriwell story titles), 501-67

(Merriwell, Frank), The Prize Plot Story, (TIP TOP WEEKLY), by George T. Flaum, 199-25

(Merriwell, Frank), The Saga of Frank Merriwell, (TIP TOP LIBRARY No.1), 480 91; (TIP TOP LIBRARY No.2), 482-114; (TIP TOP LIBRARY No.3), 483-126

(Merriwell, Frank), "True Friends", (play adapted from Frank Merriwell stories), by Steve Press, 531-58

(Mershon Co., Publishers), The Edward S. Ellis Stories Published by the Mershon Complex, by Denis R. Rogers, 490-70; 491-86; 492-104

(Messecar, M.L.), obituary, 518-52

Messier, Eli A.: A Memory, (reminiscences), 102-7

Messier, Eli A.: Book Hunting With Reckless, (collecting experiences with Ralph F. Cummings), 73-9

Messier, Eli A.: Frank James Returns, (moving picture, 1940), 98-7

Messier, Eli A.: One for Ripley, (reminiscences), 185-12

(Mexican War stories), The Anatomy of Dime Novels, No.18: The Alamo and the Mexican War, by J. Edward Leithead, 450-24

Meyer, Ernest L.: Alger is Out, (claims Alger no longer popular among readers), 92-1

(MIGHT AND MAIN LIBRARY), Dime Novel Sketches #19, 340-1

(Miller, Mrs. Alex. McVeigh), A Weaver of Romances, (early author), by Ethel Clark Lewis, 110-1

(Miller, Mrs. Alex McVeigh), Biographical Data, (early author), 114-7

(Miller, Charles), Great Inventor Tangles With Charlie Miller, the Last of the Pony Express Riders, by Charles Duprez, 252-65

(Miller, Dewey), Boys, Meet Dewey Miller, (biog. sketch), by Charles Duprez, 284-33

Miller, Harlan: Girls' Books Should be Collected, (girls' books as desirable for collectors as boys' books), 470-133

Miller, H.W.: Travels of a Book Collector, (boys' book collecting experiences), 483-121

Miller, W.C.: The First Diamond Dick Story, 63-1

Mintzer, Maurien: letter of comment, 389-90

Miscellaneous Pseudonyms, (of early authors), by Ralph Adimari, 341-10

Modern Scenic Backgrounds of Old Dime Novels, 157-1

(Monaghan, Jay: THE GREAT RASCAL: THE LIFE AND ADVENTURES OF NED BUNTLINE), review by Lewis Gannett, 235-25

Moore, J.D.: letter of comment, 372-85

Moran, Bob: letter of comment, 395-85

Moran, P.J.: A Meeting With Gilbert Patten, 397-104

Moran, P.J.: An Interview with Jesse James, 191-66

Moran, P.J.: letter of comment, 394-72

(Moran, P.J.), obituary, 516-148

More About the Buffalo Bill Stories, (dime novels), by J. Edward Leithead, 58-1

More About the Nick Carter Libraries, (dime novels), by J. Edward Leithead, 245-10

More Books and Stories by Gilbert Patten, (survey and discussion), by Gerald J. McIntosh, 426-24

More Gilbert Patten in Clothbound Editions, by Harry K. Hudson, 417-60

More on Boston Early Stories and Their Publishers, (dime novels and story papers), by Roland D. Sawyer, 175-25

More on Gilbert Patten's Pseudonyms, by Gerald J. McIntosh, 443-83

More on the GOLDEN HOURS, (storypaper), by Harry A. Weill, 149-5

Morgan, L.: Collection of Horror and Thrills, (dime novel collecting), 118-1

Morgan, L.: My First Novel, (reading dime novel reminiscences), 99-6

Morgan, L.: Old New York After Nightfall, (reminiscences), 114-6

Moriarty, Tom: letter of comment, 382-65; 489-63

Morris, Charles W.: The Rise and Fall of the Dime Novel, (capsule history), 96-1

(MORRISON'S SENSATIONAL SERIES), Dime Novel Sketches #91, 418-63

(Mosher, Thomas Bird), Odds and Ends, (dime novel), by W.B. McCafferty, 199-33

Moskowitz, Sam: letter of comment, 465-58; 545-91

Most Popular Boys Series of Books, The, (discusses var. series), by Julius R. Chenu, 540-98

Most Reckless Ralph, The, (biog.sketch) of Ralph F. Cummings), by Charles Duprez, 348-98

(MOTOR STORIES), Dime Novel Sketches #37, 360-83

Moulton, David: letter of comment, 549-67

(Movie Boys Series, The), Garden City Publishing Company's Paperback Juveniles, (boys' series books), by Julius R. Chenu, 531-72

Movies Featuring Real and Fictional Characters Made Famous by Dime Novels, Checklist, by Arthur N. Carter, 520-91

(movies), Nick Carter in the Movies, (var. film productions), by J. Randolph Cox, 534-114

(movies - British), Favorite Boyhood Characters on the British Screen, by W.O.G.Lofts and D.J.Adley, 525-66; 528-122

Mowry, Russell L.: letter of comment, 535-14

Moyse, Arthur: Local Boys Made Good? Or?, (comments on the American comic), 322-59

(Moyse, Arthur), Moyse for Choice, (biog. sketch), by Charles Duprez, 339-99

Mr. Edward Harrigan, of Harrigan & Harts, by Ralph F. Cummings, 80-1

Mr. Merriwell, (verse), by W.B. McCafferty, 111-3

Mulhall, Patrick: Fifty Years Ago, (THE GOLDEN ARGOSY, comments), 52-4

Mulhall, Patrick: DeWitt Information, (DEWITT'S NIGHTSHADE SERIES), 34-3

Mulhall, Patrick: Jack Harkaway - A Pioneer, (commentary), 251-58

Mulhall, Patrick: The Raketty Bohemians, (George Emmett: SHOT AND SHELL STORIES), 42-3

Mulhall, Patrick: Wanderings of the Dime Novel, (reminiscences), 11-2

Mundell, Elmore H., Jr.: letter of comment, 389-90

Munro, George P., (Publisher), mention, 16-5; 172-3

(Munro, George P.), A Checklist of George Munro Publications, 378-23

(Munro, George P.), This "Sleuth" Business, (detectives in dime novels), by J. Edward Leithead, 369-50; 370-62; 371-70

Munro, Norman L., (Publisher), mention, 30-3

(Munro, Norman L.), Correction of Facts, (as publisher), 30-3

(Munro, Norman L.), Grand Conflagration at the Munro Plant in 1876, (fire), by Ralph F. Cummings, 81-2

(Munro, Norman L.), NEW YORK BOYS LIBRARY Published by Norman L. Munro, (historical commentary), by Rhoda Gay Walgren, 463-36; 464-44

(Munro, Norman L.), Norman L. Munro, Publisher, (essay), by William L. Beck, 25-1

(Munro, Norman L.) Old Cap Collier and Norman L. Munro, (Munro's publishing of Collier tales), by L.H.Lahmon, 64-3

Munro Publications, mention, 147-5; 172-3

(Munro Publications), Alfred D. Hynes, Beadle, and Munro Author, by Denis R. Rogers, 386-94

(Munro Publications), Munro Publishing House, 158-5

(Munro Publications), OUR BOYS and NEW YORK BOYS WEEKLY: The Great Tousey-Munro Rivalry, (bibliographical listing), by Ross Craufurd, 535-SS

(MUNRO'S BACKWOODS SERIES), Dime Novel Sketches #180, 508-1

MUNRO'S GIRLS AND BOYS WEEKLY, 88-10

(MUNRO'S TEN CENT NOVELS), Dime Novel Sketches #144, 471-137

(Munroe, Kirk), Kirk Munroe and His Books for Boys, (literary and biog. sketch), by Ralph F. Cummings, 79-5

(Munroe, Kirk), Now They're Collectors' Items, (boys' series books), by J. Edward Leithead, 417-54

(Munsey Publications), GOLDEN ARGOSY, by Stanley A. Pachon, 382-58; 383-69

(Munsey Publications), The Lovell Complex, by Denis R. Rogers, 527-98

(Murietta, Joaquim, bandit), Wyoming's Wild Riders and Other Hunted Men, (in dime novels), by J. Edward Leithead, 294-20

Musemecke, Rocco: letter of comment, 516-149

(Musick, John R.), Another John R. Musick Item, 14-6

(Musick, John R.), Facts About John R. Musick, by Fred T. Singleton, 13-7; 21-5

(Musick, John R.), J.R.Musick, (biog. sketch), by Ray Caldwell, 90-4

My Adventures With a Snake, (humorous reminiscences), by Bertrand Couch, 202-59

My Adventures Into Book Collecting, (collecting experiences), by W.B.Poage, 189-4

My Boy Harold, (biog. sketch, Harold C. Ingraham), by Charles Duprez, 344-59

My Collection of BEADLES HALF DIME LIBRARY, (collecting experiences), by William M. Burns, 164-1

My First Novel, (dime novel reading reminiscences), by Ralph F. Cummings, 40-2

My First Novel, (dime novel reading reminiscences), by Stewart H.V. Bender, 53-2

My First Novel, (dime novel reading reminiscences), by Harold C. Holmes, 49-4

My First Novel, (dime novel reading reminiscences), by L. Morgan, 99-6

My First Ten Stories, (dime novel reading reminiscences), by Roland D. Sawyer, 69-2

My Friend, Col. Prentiss Ingraham, (biog. reminiscences), by Gilbert Patten, 140-1

My Meeting With Buffalo Bill, by Willis E. Hurd, 136-2

My Pal the Elephant, (circus reminis-
cences), by Joe Gantner, 179-1
My "Pets" in WIDE AWAKE LIBRARY,
(dime novel reading reminiscences),
by William M. Burns, 168-1
(MY QUEEN), Dime Novel Sketches
#72, 399-125
MY QUEEN LIBRARY, (discussion), by
Charles Duprez, 249-41
(MY QUEEN LIBRARY), More About "My
Queen", by Ralph P. Smith, 259-28
My Remembrance of Gilbert Patten, by
James E. Knott, 288-65
My Search for Old Nick Carters,
(collecting experiences), by Joe
Gantner, 111-1
My Surprise Meeting With Gilbert
Patten, by James H. Van Demark,
387-102
My Visit With Pawnee Bill, by Gerald
J. McIntosh, 453-66
Myler, Joseph J.: Buffalo Bill Slept
Here, (frontier reminiscences),
388-1
Mysteries of Chinatown, The, (locale
reminiscences), by George H.
Cordier, 127-1
MYSTERY MAGAZINE, Note on Contents,
(1919), 259-27

"Nameless Joe" (Charles Duprez): The
American Indian, or, Whose Top Is
He Blowing Now, (reminiscences),
217-73
"Nameless Joe" (Charles Duprez): Bowery
Billy's Our Oyster Now, (BOWERY
BOYS LIBRARY), 202-57
"Nameless Joe" (Charles Duprez): Dime
Novels and What They Do to Ye,
(reminiscences), 205-83
"Nameless Joe" (Charles Duprez): Following
the Horses Without a Shovel,
(reminiscences), 225-43
"Nameless Joe" (Charles Duprez): Hang
On To Your Old Dime Novels (values
in collecting), 209-13
"Nameless Joe" (Charles Duprez), Heroes
of Yesterday, (dime novel characters),
199-28
Nassau Street, (New York City reminis-
cences), by W.B.McCafferty, 185-13
Nast and the Harpers, (relation of
Theodore Nast, political cartoonist,
and the Harper Bros.), 184-3
National Cowboy Hall of Fame Opens at
Oklahoma City, and Mammoth Western
Heritage Center Library, by Gerald
J. McIntosh, 397-107
(Naylor, James Ball), James Ball Naylor-
A Famous Ohio Author, (biog.sketch),
by Roy B. Van Devier, 369-56
Ned Buntline's Centennary, by Roland
D. Sawyer, 175-26
NED BUNTLINE'S OWN, 15-4
(NED BUNTLINE'S OWN), Dime Novel
Sketches #188, 516-125

Neetz, C. Arthur and Ralph Adimari:
Wolff and the Tousey Reprints,
(on Tousey Publishing Co.),
332-43
Neglected Weeklies, (YOUNG PEOPLES
WEEKLY and NEW SABBATH LIBRARY)
by Ralph P. Smith, 489-65
(Negro), Stratemeyer and the Blacks,
(attitude toward and treatment
of Blacks by the Stratemeyer
Syndicate), by John T. Dizer, Jr.,
515-90
(NEW AND OLD FRIENDS), Dime Novel
Sketches, #112, 439-39
NEW BUFFALO BILL WEEKLY, (biblio-
graphical listing), by J. Edward
Leithead, 452-SS
(NEW BUFFALO BILL WEEKLY), Dime Novel
Sketches #75, 402-23
(NEW BUFFALO BILL WEEKLY), ROUGH RIDER
WEEKLY and the Ted Strong Saga,
with bibliographical checklist, by
J. Edward Leithead and Edward T.
LeBlanc, 478-3
(NEW FICTION LIBRARY), Dime Novel
Sketches #224, 552-113
New Interests of the Juvenile Reader,
by Ralph F. Cummings, 72-1
NEW MAGNET LIBRARY, 56-5; 83-2; 85-1;
224-37
NEW MAGNET LIBRARY, No.1036, (descript-
ive comments), by Harold C. Holmes,
83-2
NEW MAGNET LIBRARY, No.1088, (descript-
ive comments), by Harold C. Holmes,
85-1
(NEW MAGNET LIBRARY), Nick Carter
Detective Tales in MAGNET and NEW
MAGNET LIBRARY, checklist, by J.
Edward Leithead, 212-33
NEW MEDAL LIBRARY, 3-5
(NEW MEDAL LIBRARY), MEDAL and NEW
MEDAL LIBRARIES, by Ralph P. Smith,
98-1
(NEW MEDAL LIBRARY), ROUGH RIDER WEEKLY
and the Ted Strong Saga, with
bibliographical checklist, by J.
Edward Leithead and Edward T.
LeBlanc, 478-3
NEW NICK CARTER WEEKLY, bibliographical
listing, by J. Randolph Cox, 516-SS
(NEW SABBATH LIBRARY), Neglected
Weeklies, by Ralph P. Smith, 489-65
NEW SENSATION, THE, (and THE SPORTING
NEW YORKER), bibliographical listing,
by Ross Craufurd, 521-SS
NEW SENSATION TEN CENT NOVELS, Dime
Novel Sketches #158, 486-29
NEW TIP TOP WEEKLY, 66-4
(NEW TIP TOP WEEKLY), Dime Novel
Sketches #60, 385-83
(New York), Maiden Street, (locale
reminiscences), by W.B.McCafferty,
202-61; 204-75
(New York), Nassau Street, (locale
reminiscences), by W.B.McCafferty,
185-13

NEW YORK BOYS, 117-7; 117-8
NEW YORK BOYS LIBRARY Published by
    Norman L. Munro, (discussion), by
    Rhoda Gay Walgren, 463-36; 464-44
NEW YORK BOYS LIBRARY, 26-3; 30-3;
    (mentioned)
NEW YORK BOYS LIBRARY, (sketch), 6-3
(NEW YORK BOYS LIBRARY), Dime Novel
    Sketches #127, 454-71; Dime
    Novel Sketches #95, 422-105
NEW YORK BOYS' WEEKLY, 42-7; 117-9
(NEW YORK BOYS' WEEKLY), OUR BOYS and
    NEW YORK BOYS' WEEKLY, The Great
    Tousey-Munro Rivalry, (biblio-
    graphic listing), by Ross Craufurd,
    535-SS
(NEW YORK COMIC LIBRARY), Dime Novel
    Sketches #115, 442-65
NEW YORK DETECTIVE LIBRARY, THE, 3-4;
    133-2
NEW YORK DETECTIVE LIBRARY, No.171,
    (discussion), by Harold C. Holmes,
    122-1
(NEW YORK DETECTIVE LIBRARY), Dime
    Novel Sketches #85, 412-1
(NEW YORK FIVE CENT LIBRARY), Dime
    Novel Sketches #172, 500-49
NEW YORK LEDGER, 119-7
(NEW YORK LIBRARY), Dime Novel Sketches
    #156, 484-1
(NEW YORK NICKEL LIBRARY, THE), Dime
    Novel Sketches #132, 459-119
(NEW YORK NOVELIST, THE), Dime Novel
    Sketches #130, 457-101
(New York Public Library), Going to
    New York? (discusses dime novel
    collection at New York Public
    Library), by Alan E. Schaeffer,
    86-4
(New York Publishing Company, The),
    Edward S. Ellis Stories Published
    by the Mershon Complex, by Denis
    R. Rogers, 490-70; 491-86; 492-104
NEW YORK SATURDAY JOURNAL, 88-4
NEW YORK SATURDAY STAR JOURNAL,
    (story paper), 88-3
NEW YORK SPORTS BUDGET, THE, 117-7
NEW YORK SUN and Those Elusive Alger
    Serials, The, by Stanley A. Pachon,
    492-98
(New York: Wall Street stories), The
    Anatomy of the Dime Novel No.9,
    Wall Street Stories, by J. Edward
    Leithead, 427-34; 428-44
NEW YORK WEEKLY, 79-1; 88-4; 403-36
(NEW YORK WEEKLY), Our Old Story Papers,
    No.3- NEW YORK WEEKLY, by William
    M. Burns, 200-37
(NEW YORK WEEKLY STORY TELLER), The
    History of Old Story Papers of
    Long Ago, by Ralph F. Cummings,
    216-66
NEW YOUTHS MAGAZINE, 277-84
Newsboys Lodging House - Impetus for
    an Immortal, (Alger association
    article), by Jack Bales, 521-116

Nichols, Melvin J.: letter of comment,
    380-45; 401-21
Nick Carter Again, by Robert H.
    Smeltzer, 22-1
Nick Carter and Buffalo Bill Items,
    (relating to dime novels), by J.
    Edward Leithead, 61-1
Nick Carter and the Shadow Woman, by
    W.B.McCafferty, 118-3
Nick Carter Detective Tales in MAGNET
    and NEW MAGNET LIBRARY, (checklist),
    by J. Edward Leithead, 212-33
Nick Carter in Another Man's Shoes,
    (Carter stories by Samuel C.
    Spalding; also on Sexton Blake),
    by J. Edward Leithead, 350-112;
    351-120
Nick Carter in Print, (bibliography
    1886-1936), by J. Edward Leithead,
    181-75
Nick Carter in the Movies, (various
    film productions), by J. Randolph
    Cox, 534-114
Nick Carter? Let 'em Read It, Says
    Scientist, by William J. Benners,
    74-1
Nick Carter Reprints, by J. Edward
    Leithead, 337-82; 338-92
Nick Carter Stories and Other Series
    Containing Stories About Nick
    Carter, (bibliographic listing), by
    J. Randolph Cox, 526-SS; 542-SS
Nick Carter Studies, (exploits of the
    detective in dime novels), by J.
    Randolph Cox, 517-22
(Nick Carter), see also: "Carter, Nick"
(NICK CARTER DETECTIVE LIBRARY), Dime
    Novel Sketches #30, 353-11
NICK CARTER LIBRARY, 90-1; 151-2
NICK CARTER LIBRARY, (bibliographic
    listing), by J. Randolph Cox, 502-SS
(NICK CARTER LIBRARY), The Greatest
    Sleuth That Ever Lived, (discussion),
    by J. Edward Leithead, 272-38
NICK CARTER MAGAZINE, 61-1
(NICK CARTER STORIES), Dime Novel
    Sketches #18, 338-91
NICK CARTER WEEKLY, 81A-11; 301-88;
    429-61
NICK CARTER WEEKLY, by L.H.Larmon, 59-1
(NICK CARTER WEEKLY), Dime Novel Sketches
    #34, 357-59
NICK CARTER WEEKLY, Nos. 91 and 92,
    (discussion, large size issues), by
    Harold C. Holmes, 55-1
NICKEL LIBRARY, THE, by "Seajay", 96-2
NICKEL LIBRARY, THE, 413-16
(NICKEL LIBRARY, THE), Dime Novel
    Sketches #99, 426-23
Nickel Novel Almost Everybody Liked:
    PLUCK AND LUCK, (reminiscent
    discussion), by J. Edward Leithead,
    357-60
(NIGHTSIDE LIBRARY, THE), Dime Novel
    Sketches #192, 520-73
NIGHTSHADE SERIES, 25-8

19th Century Peep-Show, (collecting comments), by Fred T. Singleton, 225-41; 227-57; 232-4; 233-10

(Noel, Mary: VILLAINS GALORE - THE HEYDAY OF THE POPULAR STORY WEEKLY), review, 264-69

Nolan, Paul T.: Buffalo Bill's Life on the Border, (frontier reminiscences), 383-68

Nolan, Paul T.: Captain Jack, The Relentless Foe of the Dime Novel, (John Wallace Crawford), 374-102

Nolan, Paul T.: letter of comment, 389-17; 392-5?

Noname (Lu Senarens), by Learnard C. Leighter, 56-1

"Noname": The Abandoned Farm House, (fictional collecting experiences), 106-1

"Noname" Must Have Been Irish! (on the Frank Reade stories), by Frank T. Fries, 6-5

"Noname", (biog. sketch of Lu Senarens, author and editor), 114-10

Norman L. Munro, Publisher, by William L. Beck, 26-1

(North, Capt. Luther H.), obituary, 42-4

Northfield Bank Robbery, (James Gang), by Roy E. Swanstrom, 278-90

(Norway), Beadles Abroad, (discusses Norwegian editions, reprints), by Denis R. Rogers, 347-86

Notes on Foster-Wrenn Article, (on Charles L. Wrenn, W. Bert Foster), by J. Edward Leithead, 365-17

Notes on World Syndicate Juvenile Aviation Fiction, (var. series, boys' books), by Rick Crandall, 552-124

Noted Dime Novel Collector Dies in Towaco, N.J., (George Washington French, obituary and tribute), 456-97

Notes on One of Gilbert Patten's Less Well Known Hard Cover Books, (THE DEADWOOD TRAIL), by Julius R. Chenu, 449-20

(NOVELETTE, THE), Dime Novel Sketches #121, 448-1

(NOVELETTE LIBRARY), Dime Novel Sketches #118, 445-99

Novelist Fooled by Innocent Face, (on John T. McIntyre), by B. Benners, 71-2

Novelnut Nonsense, (humor among the members of the Happy Hours Brotherhood), 95-5; 96-2; 97-5; 98-3; 99-4; 100-3; 101-9; 102-3; 104-2; 105-5; 106-3; 107-4; 109-4; 112-5; 113-3; 114-9; 115-2; 116-3; 117-5; 118-2; 119-8; 120-5; 121-5

Novels of Edward L. Wheeler, The, by Deadwood Dick, Jr., 94-1

Now They're Collector's Items, (boys' books discussed), by J. Edward Leithead,
  No.1, Edward S. Ellis and Harry Castlemon, 405-58; 406-66
  No.2-4, various authors, 411-128; 417-54; 420-86

Noyes, Alfred: The Great North Road, 46-2

NUGGET LIBRARY, 121-9

(NUGGET LIBRARY), Dime Novel Sketches #32, 355-27; Dime Novel Sketches #100, 427-33

Nuggets From GOLDEN HOURS, (story paper extracts), by Harry A. Weill, 171-1

Nuther Biography - By Cracky, (biog. sketch, Ralph F. Cummings), by Charles Duprez, 270-20

(Oakley, Annie), ANNIE OAKLEY OF THE WILD WEST by Walter Havighurst, review, 266-86

Old Dime Novel Facts, (miscellaneous), by Howard R. Silsbee, 280-5

Oddities of Dime Novel Days, (dime novel bibliographical mysteries), by Denis R. Rogers, 526-85

Odds and Ends, (dime novel miscellany), by Ralph F. Cummings, 58-9

Odds 'n' Ends, (collecting comments), by Jack Schorr, 451-45; 452-57; 455-88; 456-96

O'Desky, L.T.: letter of comment, 387-105; 390-30; 391-40; 452-56

O'Gara, Gil: J.T.Trowbridge, A Brief Sketch, (literary/biog. sketch), with checklist of books, 544-66

O'Gara, Gil: letter of comment, 541-26; 547-19; 547-20

O'Gara, Gil: Poisoning Your Child, (former attitudes and criticism against reading boys' books), 540-91

O'Gara, Gil: Ribbing the Rovers, (book parodies on the Rover Boys), 551-99

(OLD AND NEW MAGAZINE), letter from Tom Moriarty, 489-63

"Old Black Joe", 7-5

Old Book Store, The, (dime novel reminiscences), by Walt Mason, 83-1

Old Bowery Days in the Dime Novel, (collecting reminiscences), by Fred T. Singleton, 9-3

(OLD BOYS JOURNAL), A Partial History of the Brett Publications, by Ralph Adimari, 368-42

Old Boys' Journals Illustrations, (discussion), by Henry Steele, 34-1

Old Boys' Magazines and Journals, The Beeton Publications, by Frank Jay, 109-1

(OLD BROADBRIM WEEKLY), Dime Novel Sketches #64, 391-33

OLD CAP COLLIER, 131-4

OLD CAP COLLIER and Norman L. Munro, (publishing sketch), by L.H.Lahmon, 64-3

(OLD CAP COLLIER), Boy Detectives, (essay, dime novels), by J. Edward Leithead, 240-66

(OLD CAP COLLIER), This "Sleuth"
Business, (detectives in dime novels),
by J. Edward Leithead, 369-50; 370-62;
371-70
OLD CAP COLLIER LIBRARY, 88-5; 151-2;
164-5
(OLD CAP COLLIER LIBRARY), Dime Novel
Sketches #36, 359-75
Old Circuses & Weeklies, (reminiscences),
by Joe Gantner, 116-1
Old Cosmopolitans, (COSMOPOLITAN MAG.),
by Joe Gantner, 189-1
Old Dime Novels, (song), by Robert
McDowell, 279-106
Old English Journals for Boys, (historical
and descriptive discussion), by
William M. Burns,
ALDINES NEW BOYS PAPER, 331-34
THE BOYS LEISURE HOUR, 325-84
BOYS OF THE EMPIRE, 321-52; 322-60
COMRADES, 323-66
Those Special Christmas Issues,
326-92
(Old Ferret, the New York Detective),
Newsy News, (dime novel character),
117-4
Old Guard, The, (collecting comments)
263-62
Old Hen House, The, (verse), 317-18
Old King Brady, (dime novel detective),
by George H. Cordier, 42-5; 46-3;
48-5; 50-2
Old King Brady, the Sleuth-Hound,
(dime novel detective), by Harold
C. Holmes, 97-1
Old King Brady, (dime novel detective)
by George H. Cordier, 81A-1
(Old King Brady), Odds and Ends, by
W.B.McCafferty, 202-61
(Old King Brady), This "Sleuth" Business,
(detectives in dime novels), by J.
Edward Leithead, 369-50; 370-62;
371-70
(Old King Brady), The Two King Bradys
and Their Girl Detective, (detectives
in dime novels), by J. Edward Leithead,
372-80; 373-90
(OLD LOG CABIN), Dime Novel Sketches
#86, 413-13
Old Melodramas, (stage productions),
by J. Edward Leithead, 257-10; 258-20
Old New York After Nightfall, (locale
reminiscences), by L. Morgan, 114-6
Old Nick Carters, (collecting comments),
by Joe Gantner, 129-1
Old Sleuth, (detective), 88-5; 144-4
(OLD SLEUTH), Boy Detectives, by J.
Edward Leithead, 240-66
OLD SLEUTH LIBRARY, 151-2
OLD SLEUTH LIBRARY, by Bob Smeltzer,
167-2
(OLD SLEUTH LIBRARY), Dime Novel
Sketches #90, 417-53
(OLD SLEUTH LIBRARY), This "Sleuth"
Business, (detectives in dime novels),
by J. Edward Leithead, 369-50;
370-62; 371-70

OLD SLEUTH WEEKLY, 240-66
(OLD SLEUTH WEEKLY), Dime Novel
Sketches #48, 372-79
Old Story Papers, (discussion), by
U.G.Figley, 115-5
Old Story Papers: BOYS OF NEW YORK,
(discussion), by William B. Burns,
306-18; 307-28; 308-37
Old Time Authors, (discussion), by
Robert H. Smeltzer, 50-1
Old-Time Boys' Books, (survey and
discussion), by J. Edward Leithead,
227-58; 228-69; 231-91; 233-11;
234-22; 236-35; 238-55; 239-61
Old Werner Publishing Company of Akron,
Ohio, The, (later Saalfield Pub.
Co.), by Roy B. Van Devier,
286-49
Oliver Optic, (discussion), by Roy B.
Van Devier, 298-51
Oliver Optic: Centenary of Birth, by
Ralph F. Cummings, 201-52
Oliver Optic (William Taylor Adams)
As Author and Editor, (with
definitive checklist), by S.E.
Wallen, 511-26; 512-38
Olnhausen, Samuel: Publisher Quits
Pulps and Comic Books Field,
(on Street & Smith), 200-45
(Omohundro, J.B.), BUCKSKIN AND SATIN
by Herschel C. Logan, review of
book on Texas Jack), 266-86;
268-5
On Stage, Mr. Carter, (Frederick Van
Rensselaer Dey as writer of Nick
Carter stories), by J. Edward
Leithead, 314-140; 315-148;
316-9
On the Track of Popular Culture,
(the Hess Collection of dime novels,
story papers and newstand literature)
by J. Randolph Cox, 495-134
On the Trail of Novel Hunters,
(collecting experiences), by Fred
T. Singleton, 6-2; 8-5; 9-7
One for Ripley, (reminiscences), by
Eli A. Messier, 185-12
One Road to Heaven, (fiction), by
William J. Benners, 100-4
Ono, Barry: letter of comment, 24-1
Optics Serials as Books, by Julius R.
Chenu, 518-50
(Optic, Oliver), Chronological Check-
List of Books, by Janet R. Lilli-
bridge, 517-28
(Optic, Oliver), Letter from Publisher,
(1933), 530-51
(Optic, Oliver), Now They're Collectors'
Items, (boys' books), by J. Edward
Leithead, 411-128
(Optic, Oliver), Oliver Optic, by Roy
B. Van Devier, 298-51
(Optic, Oliver), Oliver Optic as Author
and Editor, (with definitive check-
list), by S.E.Wallen, 511-26;
512-38

(Optic, Oliver), Oliver Optic: Centenary of Birth, by Ralph F. Cummings, 201-52
(Optic, Oliver), Optics Serials as Books, by Julius R. Chenu, 518-50
(Optic, Oliver), William Taylor Adams: A Literary Retrospection, (literary discussion), by Peter C. Walther, with checklist, 548-26
(ORIGINAL UNION NOVELS), Dime Novel Sketches #166, 494-125
(ORNUM & CO'S FIFTEEN CENT ROMANCES), Dime Novel Sketches #151, 479-71
Ornum & Company Publications, 26-1
(ORNUM'S INDIAN NOVELS), Dime Novel Sketches #143, 470-123
Orphal, G. Fred: Adventures in Dime Novel Land, (reminiscences), 57-1
Orphal, G. Fred: Yellowstone Bill, (reminiscences), 174-21
Orphal, G. Fred: Obituary of Yellowstone Bill, 207-98
(Orphal, G. Fred), Biographical Sketch, by Charles Duprez, 263-59
(Otis, James), Now They're Collectors' Items, (boys' books), by J. Edward Leithead, 411-128
(Ouida), 19th Century Peep Show, Part V, by Fred T. Singleton, 233-11
OUR BOYS, 58-7; 88-10
OUR BOYS, Index for 1876, 210-21
OUR BOYS' JOURNAL, 16-5
OUR BOYS and NEW YORK BOYS WEEKLY: The Great Tousey-Munro Rivalry, (bibliographic listing), by Ross Craufurd, 535-SS
Our Dear Little Willie, (verse), 303-105a
Our Flag's Bicentennial, (YOUTH'S COMPANION'S drive to have flag flown over schools, and on the authorship of Pledge of Allegiance) by Louise Harris, 513-56
Our Old Story Papers, (descriptive survey), by William M. Burns, No.1, GOLDEN ARGOSY, 184-1 No.2, GOLDEN ARGOSY, 185-9 No.3, NEW YORK WEEKLY, 200-37 No.4, HAPPY DAYS, 214-49
Outlaw Trails in Indian Territory, (outlaws in dime novels; Dalton Gang), with checklist, 289-78; 290-87
Over My Shoulder, (caution in buying dime novels by mail), 204-75
Owen, Maurice: letter of comment. 521-125
(Owen, Robert Emmett), Addenda, by J. Edward Leithead, 334-63
(Owen, Robert Emmett), The Art of Robert Emmett Owen, (dime novel cover artist), by J. Edward Leithead, 421-94
(Owen, Robert Emmett), Report on Robert Emmett Owen, Illustrator of Street & Smith Publications, by Ralph Adimari, 333-50

(Owen, Robert Emmett), Street & Smith Item, (on Owen as cover artist), by J. Edward Leithead, 81-4
(OWL LIBRARY), Dime Novel Sketches #113, 441-49

Pachon, Stanley A.: A Fragment on George A. Amy, Illustrator for YOUNG SPORTS, 371-76
Pachon, Stanley A.: An Overlooked Alger Weekly, (STAR STORIES), 498-30
Pachon, Stanley A.: George Alfred Henty, (biog. sketch with checklist) 195-97; 196-1
Pachon, Stanley A.: GOLDEN ARGOSY, (discussion), 382-58; 383-69
Pachon, Stanley A.: letter of comment, 380-44;384-80; 389-18; 389-90; 394-72; 404-52; 423-120; 489-63; 496-11; 536-36; 548-42
Pachon, Stanley A.: The Many Faceted Alger, (on Alger's humorous sketches), 548-37
Pachon, Stanley A.: Mary Roberts Rinehart and the Nickel Novel, 369-55
Pachon, Stanley A.: Memorial Tribute to J. Edward Leithead, 458-110
Pachon, Stanley A.: THE NEW YORK SUN and Those Elusive Alger Serials, 492-98
Pachon, Stanley A.: Pseudonyms in Popular Literature, (old authors), 207-97; 208-1; 209-10
Pachon, Stanley A.: William Wallace Cook, (literary sketch, with pseudonyms), 300-67
Pachon, Stanley A.: Writers for GOLDEN DAYS, No.1, Frank H. Converse, 333-52; No.2, Charles Herbert Heustis, 335-69
Pad, Peter, 2-5; 21-6; 58-9
(Pad, Peter), Facts About "Peter Pad" by Ralph Adimari, 12-3
(Pad, Peter: THE LIFE OF PETER PAD), selections from, 9-2; 10-4; 11-3
Page, Ernest C.: The Boys of New York, (verse), 235-27
Paging H. Alger - His Stuff Works, (comments on Horatio Alger, Jr.), 94-5
Paper Back Pulpit, (on Frank Merriwell and TIP TOP WEEKLY), by Noble Tribble, 402-30;(on Gilbert Patten and the Merriwells), 381-50
Paperbacks, Dime Novels and the Virtues of Reading Series Books, by John T. Dizer, Jr., 483-122
Passing of Burt L. Standish, The, (memorial tribute to Gilbert Patten), by Robert H. Smeltzer, 150-5
Passing of Deadwood Dick, (verse), by W.B.McCafferty, 94-2
(Patchin, Frank Gee), Now They're Collectors' Items, (boys series books) by J. Edward Leithead, 420-86

84

Patten, J. Alexander: Talked About
People, (Sinclair Tousey, American
News Company), 20-1; 25-5; 27-4
Patten, Gilbert: Pawnee Bill, Another
Friend of Mine, 143-1
Patten vs. Superiod Talking Pictures,
Inc., (suit by Gilbert Patten
regarding copyright to Frank Merriwell
story titles), 501-67
Patten, Gilbert, mention, 2-5; 3-5; 5-7;
5-8; 15-5; 136-1; 140-4; 230-87;
302-99
(Patten, Gilbert), A Meeting With
Gilbert Patten, by P.J. Moran,
397-104
(Patten, Gilbert), A Tribute to Gil
Patten, by James E. Knott, 150-4
(Patten, Gilbert), A Tribute to
Gilbert Patten, by Herbert Leckenby,
162-1
(Patten, Gilbert), Cap'n Wiley, Maine's
Merry Munchausen, by Frank C.
Acker, 494-126
(Patten, Gilbert), Checklist of Writings
of Gilbert Patten Prior to Frank
Merriwell, by Donald L. Steinhauer
and Edward T. LeBlanc, 410-118
(Patten, Gilbert), Dime Novel Reader's
Scrap Book, (extracts from TIP TOP
WEEKLY, No.532), 407-82
(Patten, Gilbert), Experiences and
Thoughts on Gilbert Patten, by
Charles Bragin, 409-107
(Patten, Gilbert), Following the
Merriwell Trail, (bibliography with
story synopsis), by Gerald J.
McIntosh, 474-34
(Patten, Gilbert), Frank Merriwell's
Father, (on death of Patten and
on dime novels in general), 150-1
(Patten, Gilbert), Frank Merriwell's
Mottoes, by Gerald J. McIntosh,
410-123
(Patten, Gilbert), Frank Merriwell's
Parent, or, Patten the Paramount,
(memorial tribute to Patten), by
J.P.Guinon, 150-6
(Patten, Gilbert), Gil Patten Vindicated,
by J.P. Guinon, 381-53
(Patten, Gilbert), Gilbert Patten,
(memorial tribute), by Sam E. Conner,
150-3
(Patten, Gilbert), Gilbert Patten in
Clothbound Editions, 410-116
(Patten, Gilbert), Gilbert Patten- The
Man and the Magic, 409-96
(Patten, Gilbert), Harkaway, Merriwell,
Etc., (discusses dime novel characters)
by U.G.Figley, 115-1
(Patten, Gilbert), The Influence of
Charles Dickens on Gilbert Patten,
by Gerald J. McIntosh, 409-103
(Patten, Gilbert), Letter of Appreciation
by son, H.B.Patten, 182-87
(Patten, Gilbert), Memorial Notes, by
Ralph F. Cummings, 150-7

(Patten, Gilbert), Memorial Placque
Erected to Patten by Happy Hours
Brotherhood, 183-95
(Patten, Gilbert), Merriwells That
Might Have Been, (suggested titles
for stories), by Robert McDowell,
446-118
(Patten, Gilbert), Money Troubles
Solved by Fund, 108-7
(Patten, Gilbert), More Books and
Stories by Gilbert Patten, by
Gerald J. McIntosh, 426-24
(Patten, Gilbert), More Gilbert Patten
in Clothbound Editions, by Harry
K. Hudson, 417-60
(Patten, Gilbert), More on Gilbert
Patten's Pseudonyms, by Gerald
J. McIntosh, 443-83
Patten, Gilbert: My Friend, Col.
Prentiss Ingraham, 140-1
(Patten, Gilbert), My Remembrances of
Gilbert Patten, by James E. Knott,
288-65
(Patten, Gilbert), My Surprise Meeting
With Gilbert Patten, by James H.
Van Demark, 387-102
(Patten, Gilbert), Paper Back Pulpit,
by Noble Tribble, 381-50
(Patten, Gilbert), The Passing of
Burt L. Standish, (memorial tribute
to Patten), by Robert H. Smeltzer,
150-5
(Patten, Gilbert), Patten vs. Superior
Talking Pictures, Inc., (suit by
Patten regarding copyright of
Merriwell titles), 501-67
(Patten, Gilbert), Pseudonyms of Gilbert
Patten, by Gerald J. McIntosh,
436-2
(Patten, Gilbert), Public Thanks to
Gilbert Patten, (for his works), by
Homer Kurtz, 66-1
(Patten, Gilbert), publisher, 288-73
(Patten, Gilbert), The Rockspur Series,
(sports stories), by J.P. Guinon,
304-2
(Patten, Gilbert), The Short Short
Stories of Burt L. Standish, by
Gerald J. McIntosh, 391-34; 393-66
(Patten, Gilbert), Story in SNAPPY
STORIES, (letter from Bob Sampson),
535-14
(Patten, Gilbert), The Wonderful Adven-
tures of Cap't Wiley" ed. by Burt L.
Standish, (the "discovered" memoirs
of dime novel character), 462-31
(Patten, Gilbert: THE DEADWOOD TRAIL),
Notes on One of Gilbert Patten's
Less Well Known Hard Cover Books,
by Julius R. Chenu, 449-20
(Patten, Gilbert: FRANK MERRIWELLS
FATHER), comments on book, 384-80
Patterson, L.S.: A Fine Little
Anecdote, (on dime novels), 186-3
(PAUL JONES WEEKLY), Dime Novel
Sketches #6, 324-73

Pawnee Bill, (reminiscences), by W.B. McCafferty, 152-3

Pawnee Bill - Another Friend of Mine, (reminiscences), by Gilbert Patten, 143-1

(Pawnee Bill), My Visit With Pawnee Bill, (reminiscences), by Gerald J. McIntosh, 453066

(Pawnee Bill), Obituary of Maj. Gordon Lillie, by Edwin Brooks, 114-9

(Pawnee Bill), The Wild West Shows Pass in Grand Review, (historical survey and discussion of Wild West Shows), by J. Edward Leithead, 264-65; 265-75; 266-84

Pegler, Westbrook: Fair Enough, (comments on comic-strip detectives), 135-1

(Pendleton, Louis E.), Louis E. Pendleton A Famous Southern Author, (biog. sketch), by Roy B. Van Devier, 374-100

(Penny Dreadfuls), Collectors and the English Penny Dreadfuls, (comments and discussion), 131-1

(Penny Dreadfuls), The English Giant, E. Harcourt Burrage, (author of the "English dime novels"), by Ross Craufurd, 12-2

(Penny Dreadfuls), Gallows-Fruit, by Ross Craufurd, 18-2

(Penny Dreadfuls), James Malcolm Rymer and Thomas Pecket Prest, (authors of Gothic "Penny bloods" and history of Edward Lloyd and his publications), by W.O.G.Lofts, 485-18

(Penny Dreadfuls), Success and Failure, (history of English penny dreadful publishers), by W.O.G. Lofts, 523-9

PEOPLES FIVE CENT NOVELETTES, 114-12

(PEOPLES FIVE CENT NOVELETTES), Dime Novel Sketches #183, 511-25

Perrigoue, Nell: letter of comment, 320-40

(PETERSEN'S POPULAR PRIZE LIBRARY), Dime Novel Sketches #170, 498-29

Peterson, T.M.: Shaw's Novels, (works by Elmer Shaw discussed), 210-18

PETERSON'S ILLUMINATED SERIES, Checklist of Issues, 532-91

(PETERSON'S ILLUMINATED SERIES), Dime Novel Sketches #204, 532-81

Pfaus, Oscar C.: letter of comment, 433-104

Pfaus, Oscar C.: Notes on German Language Dime Novels, 433-103

Phillips, Thomas E., Jr.: letter of comment, 541-25; 544-74

Photography in the Raw, (reminiscences) by Charles Duprez, 300-76

PILOT, THE, 49-3

(Pinkerton Detective Agency), Look Out, Boys, It's a Pinkerton, (reminiscences), 8-5

(pirates), Treasure Island, (pirate stories in general, and TREASURE ISLAND by Stevenson), by W.O.G. Lofts, 477-64

Pitcher, Hermon: Favorites of Yesterday, (biog. sketches of early authors), Susan Warner, 158-3
Marie Corelli, 186-1
E.P. Roe, 191-68
Harriet Beecher Stowe, 216-67
Rosa N. Carey, 203-66
Anna Bartlett Warner, 323-68
Amelia E. Barr, 326-95

Pitcher, Hermon: J. Fenimore Cooper, (discussion), 124-2

Pitcher, Hermon: letter of comment, 97-7; 99-4

Pitcher, Hermon: World Famous Author, (biog. sketch),Charlotte M. Braeme, 112-3

Pitzer, F.N.: Dime Novel Round-Uppers, (collecting comments), 19-3

(Pledge of Allegiance), Who Wrote the Pledge of Allegiance?, (assertion that James Bailey Upham is true author), by Louise Harris, 528-127

PLUCK AND LUCK, 36-2; 54-1; 81A-11; 133-2; 414-29

PLUCK AND LUCK, by Charles Bragin, 25-2

(PLUCK AND LUCK), Dime Novel Sketches #7, 325-83

PLUCK AND LUCK, firefigter stories, 407-76

(PLUCK AND LUCK), The Nickel Novel Almost Everybody Liked, 357-60

PLUCK AND LUCK, No.118, (discussed), by Harold C. Holmes, 188-37

Poage, W.B.: Henty Hints, (various on G.A.Henty), 197-10; 203-71; 209-13; 221-13; 236-33; 242-84; 255-98

Poage, W.B.: Henty News, (on G.A.Henty) 192-74

Poage, W.B.: My Adventures Into Book Collecting, (collecting experiences) 189-4

Poisoning Your Child, (former attitudes and criticisms against reading boys' books), by Gil O'Gara, 540-91

(Polar explorations), The Anatomy of Dime Novels No.21: Stories of Polar Exploration, by J. Edward Leithead, 461-14; 462-24

POLICE GAZETTE, 169-3

POLICE GAZETTE Passes, (cessation), 16-4

Pollard, John E., Jr.: letter of comment, 375-113;381-52

Poore, Harold: A Visit With Don & Grace, (reminiscences visiting Don Learnard), 352-2

(Popular literature), A Time of Lively Fiction, (survey and discussion of the range of popular literature from dime novels to the present), by Robert Sampson, 540-93; 541-8; 542-33; 543-52; 544-71; 545-87; 546-104

(POPULAR SERIES OF FICTION FANCY AND FACT), Dime Novel Sketches #190, 518-33

Popular Songs of Dime Novel Times, (with song words), by George H. Cordier, 113-1

Popular Story Papers of Other Days, (discussion), by George H. Cordier, 88-1

Porter, R.H.: letter of comment, 402-27

(postal regulations), Barred by the Post Office, (ESQUIRE barred as obscene, and other pertinent regulations), by Ralph P. Smith, 145-1

Postscripts on the Pen Names of Edward S. Ellis, by Denis R. Rogers, 335-74

Potthoff, Willis J.: BOY PARTNERS, An Edward Edson Lee Publication, (index and summary of periodical), 550-83

(Potthoff, Willis J.), Displaying One's Collection, (on the boys' books collection of Potthoff), by Edward T. LeBlanc, 518-46

Potthoff, Willis J.: letter of comment, 519-66; 528-131; 530-50; 548-43; 550-86

(PRAIRIE OUTLAWS, THE), Dime Novel Sketches #98, 425-11

(predictions), Spacious Living to Come, by Harold C. Ingraham, 348-99

Press, Steve: letter of comment, 409-108

Press, Steve: "True Friends", (play for young people adapted from Frank Merriwell stories), 531-58

(Prest, Thomas Pecket), James Malcolm Rymer and Thomas Pecket Prest, (biog. sketch of authors, Gothic "penny bloods", and history of Edward Lloyd and his publications), by W.O.G.Lofts, 485-18

(Price-McGill Company), The Edward S. Ellis Stories Published by the Mershon Complex, by Denis R. Rogers, 490-70; 491-86; 492-104

(printing), Dime Novel Printing, (discussion of methods used), by John C. Kunzog, 428-51

Prize Novelist John T. McIntyre Rises to Defense of Pot-Boilers, (in defense of dime novels), by Jean Barrett, 93-1

Prize Packages of Nickel Novels, (collecting experiences), by Frank T. Fries, 5-4

Prize Plot Story, The, (Frank Merriwell, TIP TOP WEEKLY), by George T. Flaum, 199-25

Promises, Promises, Promises, (mention of forthcoming books in boys' series that were never published), by Ken Donelson, 550-77

Protect Your Nocels, (collecting advice), by Charles Bragin, 340-7

Prowlin' Up Massachusetts Way, (travel and collecting experiences), by Hopeful Pete, 210-17

Pseudonyms of Edward S. Ellis, by Denis R. Rogers, 266-82; 267-90; 268-2; 307-25; 315-148; 318-22; 319-30; 320-42; 330-18; 334-58

Pseudonyms of Gilbert Patten, by Gerald J. McIntosh, 436-2

Pseudonyms in Popular Literature, (older authors), by Stanley A. Pachon, 207-97; 208-1; 209-10

Pseudonyms - More, by Willis E. Hurd, 214-42

Pseudonyms of W. Bert Foster, by J. Edward Leithead, 364-3

(pseudonyms), A Final Word on the Pseudonyms of Edward S. Ellis, by Denis R. Rogers, 363-108

(pseudonyms), A Lode of GOLDEN HOURS, (pen names of authors), by Harry A. Weill, 215-59

(pseudonyms), J. Edward Leithead Collection of Pseudonyms, by Ralph Adimari, 329-10

(pseudonyms), The Library of Congress Pseudonyms, by Ralph Adimari, 321-50

(pseudonyms), Miscellaneous Pseudonyms, by Ralph Adimari, 341-10

(pseudonyms), More on Gilbert Patten's Pseudonyms, by Gerald J. McIntosh, 443-83

(pseudonyms), Pen names, in Newsy Notes, 144-4; 222-21

(pseudonyms), Postscript on the Pen Names of Edward S. Ellis, by Denis R. Rogers, 336-74

(pseudonyms), The Ralph Adimari Collection of Pseudonyms, 324-74

(pseudonyms), The William J. Benners Pseudonyms, by Ralph Adimari, 317-14

(pseudonyms), William Wallace Cook, (pen names used by), by Stanley A. Pachon, 300-75

Public Thanks to Mr. Gilbert Patten, (for his works), by Homer Kurtz, 66-1

Publication History of Tom Swift, (boys' series, bibliographic checklist), by William R. Gowan, 536-22

Publications of Charles Fox, The, by Henry Steele, 13-5; 21-4

Pulfer, Harry: Looking Back... (dime novel reminiscences), 406-70

Pulp Magazines Decline, (Street & Smith, other publishers), 200-46

(pulp magazines), A Time of Lively Fiction, (survey and discussion of the range of popular literature from dime novels through pulps to the present), by Robert Sampson, 540-93; 541-8; 542-33; 543-52; 544-71; 545-87; 546-104

Putting Long Trousers on the Eighteenth Century, (discussion of BOYS OF ENGLAND story paper), by Henry Steele, 8-2

Quaine, J.P.: To Reckless Ralph, The Sleuth of the Sierras, (on Bracebridge Hemyng and The Harkaway Series), 216-65
Quatrain, The, (verse), by Frank Lynn, 101-11
Questions and Answers (on dime novels and Story Papers), 514-84; 515-121; 516-152; 517-27; 518-53; 519-65;; 520-96; 521-123; 522-144; 523-22; 524-50
(Quirk, Leslie), Two Boys' Books Writers from Wisconsin, (big. sketch of Leslie Quirk and Everett McNeil), by Marge Dahl, 494-131
(quiz), Merriwell Quiz, 481-107

Ragsdale, W.B.: letter of comment, 394-72; 414-32; 415-41; 417-61; 528-132; 529-29; 533-110
RAILROAD READING, Checklist, 535-13
(RAILROAD READING), Dime Novel Sketches, #207, 535-1
(railroads), The Anatomy of Dime Novels No.3: Railroading, by J. Edward Leithead, 398-114; 399-126
Ralph Adimari Collection of Pseudonyms, The, (of various authors), by Ralph Adimari, 324-74
Ralph F. Cummings Dime Novel Collection, (described), by Ralph F. Cummings, 51-1
RANCH ROMANCES, 15-7
Randolph, Charles D. ("Buckskin Bill"), Buckskin - Identity of Those Using This Name, 245-14
Randolph, Charles D.: Buckskin Bill Gallops Through the Pages of Beadles Dime Novels, (verse), 457-105
(Randolph, Charles D.), The Buckskin Bill Story, by J. Edward Leithead, 270-18
Randolph, Charles D.: Buffalo Bill, Hero of Dime Novels, (verse), 526-94
Randolph, Charles D.: Buffalo Bill's Birthday, (verse), 221-15
Randolph, Charles D.: Buffalo Bill's Wild West Show, (verse), 247-29
Randolph, Charles D.: The Days of '76, (verse), 95-6
Randolph, Charles D.: Diamond Dick, (verse), 135-2
Randolph, Charles D.: The Dying Cowboy, (verse), 2-3
Randolph, Charles D.: J. Edward Leithead the Dime Novel King, (verse), 458-11
Randolph, Charles D.: letter of comment, 514-86; 518-52; 526-93
Randolph, Charles D.: The Round Up At North Platte, (verse), 58-11

Randolph, Charles D.: Those Good Old Dime Novel Days, (verse), 451-47
RANGELAND LOVE STORY, 15-7
Rare Dime Novels, (descriptive discussion), by Edward T. LeBlanc,
No.1, INDIAN TALES, 213-41
No.2, YOUTHS LIBRARY, 215-57
No.3, TEN CENT IRISH NOVELS, 218-81
No.4, THE HUB 10 CENT NOVELS, with checklist, 232-1
No.5, DAWLEY'S CAMP & FIRESIDE LIBRARY, with checklist, 238-49
(Rathborne, Harry St. George), Now They're Collectors' Items, (boys' books), by J. Edward Leithead, 417-54
Rawson, H.O.: The Boy Avenger, (fiction) 126-1
Rawson, H.O.: Bullfrog Ben Describes Yreka Jim, (verse), 157-3
Rawson, H.O.: Deadshot Dan, the Boy Scout, (verse), 108-4
Rawson, H.O.: Valuable Data, (on dime novels), 58-7
(Ray, Jean), Jean Ray, Last and Greatest of the Dime Novelists, (biog./literary sketch), by Ross Craufurd, 537-40
Ray Mengar and His Dime Novel Collection, (discusses), by Joe Stone, 431-84
(Read, Opie), obituary, (author), 93-2
(Reade, Frank, stories), To Collectors of Frank Reade Stories, (advice on collecting), by William M. Burns, 322-62
(Reade, Frank, stories), see also: FRANK READE LIBRARY, FRANK READE STORIES, FRANK READE WEEKLY
(Reade, Frank, stories), "Noname" Must Have Been Irish, (Lu Senarens), by Frank T. Fries, 6-5
Real Americana, (dime novels), 101-21
Real People in the Merriwell Stories, by Gerald J. McIntosh, 403-42
Real Robin Hood, The, (historical basis of the legend), by W.O.G. Lofts, 502-82; 503-99
Reappearing Legends About Jesse James, 57-3
Reason Why, The, (Harkaway Novels written by several authors), by U.G.Figley, 118-2
Reckless Ralph and Wild Bill Visit the Grave of General Henry Knox, by William M. Burns, 170-1
Reckless Ralph's Frightful Apparition, (visit with Ralph F. Cummings and his collection), by Robert Jennings, 513-50
Reckless Ralph Tracks 'em Down, (the collecting experiences of Ralph F. Cummings), by Miss Larel, 29-1
(RED RAVEN), Dime Novel Sketches #14, 334-57

(RED, WHITE AND BLUE), Dime Novel
    Sketches #53, 377-9
RED WOLF SERIES, 25-8
RED WOLF SERIES, Checklist, 533-108
(RED WOLF SERIES), Dime Novel Sketches
    #205, 533-97
(REDPATH'S BOOKS FOR THE CAMP FIRES),
    Dime Novel Sketches #169, 497-13
(Redpath Novels, the), Books for the
    Campfire, by Roland D. Sawyer,
    198-20
(reference), Standard Reference Books
    for the Book Collector, (lists
    and describes), by Jack Bales,
    504-112
(Reid, Captain Mayne), Memoir of
    Mayne Reid, (author, sketch), by
    R.H.Stoddard, 205-81
Reinecke, William: letter of comment,
    434-114
Remarkable Heroes, (dime novel characters)
    222-19
(Remarque, Eric Maria), U.S. Bars
    Authors Wife, news item, 92-5
Remember When, (verse), by H.L.
    Wilson, 109-5
Reminiscences, 57-3
Reminiscences in Novelania Past and
    Present, by William M. Burns,
    183-96; 189-3; 190-58; 193-82
Reminiscences of Our Dime Novel Days,
    by E.T.Gossett, 71-1
(reminiscences), A Bangup Vacation,
    by Charles Duprez, 313-131
(reminiscences), A Dime Novel
    Graduate, by J.H.Armbruster,
    77-1
(reminiscences), A Little Dime Novel
    Chat, by Ralph F. Cummings, 22-3
(reminiscences), A Memory, by Eli A.
    Messier, 102-7
(reminiscences), A Short Short Mystery,
    (on reading dime novels), 111-2
(reminiscences), A Two-Gun Bluff,
    by J.H.Armbruster, 255-94
(reminiscences), Adventures in Dime
    Novel Land, by G. Fred Orphal,
    57-1
(reminiscences), The American Indian,
    Or Whose Top is He Blowin' Now,
    by Nameless Joe, 217-73
(reminiscences), An Open Letter to
    Mr. Flaum, by Harold C. Holmes,
    178-51
(reminiscences), Bang! Bang! Bang!
    by Frisco Bert, 251-60
(reminiscences), Books He Remembers,
    by A. Jay See, 186-2
(reminiscences), Boyhood Heroes,
    by Don Buchan, 422-110
(reminiscences), Coincidence? by
    George French, 247-26
(reminiscences), Dime Novels and
    What They Do to Ye, by Nameless
    Joe, 205-83

(reminiscences), Dime Novel "Daze",
    by Gerald J. McIntosh, 448-3
(reminiscences), Early Bicycling
    Days, by J.H.Armbruster,
    260-34; 261-45
(reminiscences), Following the
    Horses Without a Shovel, by
    Nameless Joe, 225-43
(reminiscences), Fond Recollections,
    (autobiographical), by J. Edward
    Leithead, 287-57
(reminiscences), The Golden Days of
    '49, by M. Bertrand Couch, 121-1
(reminiscences), Golden Hours:
    Reminiscences and Reflections,
    by Harry A. Weill, 137-1
(reminiscences), The Good Old Dime
    Novel Days, 365-17; 367-38;
    372-86
(reminiscences), The Grand Old
    Stories, by F.N.Wearing, 165-1
(reminiscences), Harkaway, Merriwell,
    Etc., by U.G.Figley, 115-1
(reminiscences), Hospitality on the
    Range, by J.H.Armbruster, 243-90
(reminiscences), How I Got Acquainted
    With the Dime Novel, anon.,52-8
(reminiscences), How to Become a
    Ventriloquist, by "Seajay", 100-2
(reminiscences), If Dreams Were Only
    True, by Ralph F. Cummings, 73-1
(reminiscences), Let's Push Back the
    Clock, 211-26
(reminiscences), Likes and Dislikes
    in BRAVE AND BOLD, by William M.
    Burns, 368-45
(reminiscences), Likes and Dislikes,
    Then and Now, by William M. Burns,
    102-1
(reminiscences), Long Stories in My
    Collection, by William M. Burns
    273-47
(reminiscences), Looking Back...,
    by Harry Pulfer, 406-70
(reminiscences), Memories of the
    Boys Best Weekly, by Howard B.
    Silsbee, 311-116
(reminiscences), My Adventure With
    a Snake, by M. Bertrand Couch,
    202-59
(reminiscences), My First Novel,
    (reading), by Ralph F. Cummings,
    40-2
(reminiscences), My First Novel,
    (reading), by Stewart H.V. Bender,
    53-2
(reminiscences), My First Novel,
    (reading), by Harold C. Holmes,
    49-4
(reminiscences), My First Novel,
    (reading), by L. Morgan, 99-6
(reminiscences), My First Ten Stories,
    (reading), by Roland D. Sawyer,
    69-2

(reminiscences), My Visit With Pawnee Bill, by Gerald J. McIntosh, 453-66

(reminiscences), 19th Century Peep Show, by Fred T. Singleton, 225-41; 227-57; 232-4; 233-10

(reminiscences), The Old Book Store, by Walt Mason, 83-1

(reminiscences), Old Circuses and Weeklies, by Joe Gantner, 116-1

(reminiscences), Old New York After Nightfall, by L. Morgan, 114-6

(reminiscences), One for Ripley, by Eli A. Messier, 185-12

(reminiscences), Photography in the Raw, by Charles Duprez, 300-76

(reminiscences), Prowlin' Up Massachusetts Way, by Hopeful Pete, 210-17

(reminiscences), Reminiscences in Newsy Notes, by Howard M. Rentschler, 144-4

(reminiscences), Reminiscences in Novelania, by William M. Burns, 183-96; 189-3; 190-58; 193-82

(reminiscences), Reminiscences of Our Dime Novel Days, by E.T. Gossett, 71-1

(reminiscences), Retrospection, or Leaves from the Past, by Deadwood Dick, Jr., 81A-6

(reminiscences), Reverie, Home on the Range, 225-47

(reminiscences), Today's Children, by Charles Duprez, 248-38

(reminiscences), Wanderings of the Dime Novel, by Patrick Mulhall, 11-2

(reminiscences), Western Pioneer Days, by J.H.Armbruster, 132-2

(reminiscences), When Dime Novels Were in Their Glory, by Ralph F. Cummings, 10-3

(reminiscences), When the Mounties Did Not Get Their Man, by J.H. Armbruster, 107-1

(reminiscences), Where is Dot?, by Donald S. Learned, 58-2

Removing Stickers and Labels from Novels with Ease, by George T. Flaum, 238-54

(repairing), The Art of Repairing Novels, by George T. Flaum, 211-25

(repairing), Removing Stickers and Labels from Novels with Ease, by George T. Flaum, 238-54

(repairing), "Lop-Sided Novels" (how to correct), by Robert Smeltzer, 33-1

Repetition of Character Names in the Merriwell Stories, by Gerald J. McIntosh, 424-2

Report on Robert Emmett Owen, Illustrator of Street & Smith, by Ralph Adimari, 333-50

Reprints of the Merriwell Stories, by J.P.Guinon, 271-26

(reprints), Beadles Dime Novel Library No.204, 406-71

(reprints), Corinth Publications reprinting pulps in pocketbook format, 409-107

(reprints), The Dime Novel Abroad, by Henry Steele, 3-1

(reprints), First Dime Novel to be Reprinted After 69 Years, ("MALESKA"), by Ralph F. Cummings, 91-1

(reprints), Gold Star Books Reprints of Dime Novels, 389-18

(reprints), MAGNET No.1, 395-84

(research), Bibliographic Reflections, (research in the dime novels and story papers), by Denis R. Rogers, 509-10; 510-17

Retrospect: Francis Worchester Doughty, (biog. sketch), by Robert H. Smeltzer, 343-54

Retrospection, or Leaves From the Past, (reminiscences), by "Deadwood Dick, Jr.", 81A-6

Reutschler, Howard M.: reminiscences, in Newsy Notes, 144-4

Reverie, Home on the Range, (reminiscences), 225-47

(Reynolds, G.W.M.), A Lost Novel by G.W.M.Reynolds, (THE GIPSEY CHIEF), by E.F.Bleiler, 499-38

(Reynolds, Quentin: THE FICTION FACTORY), review of book on history of Street & Smith Publishers, by J. Edward Leithead, 282-18

Ribbing the Rovers, (book parodies on The Rover Boys, boys' books), by Gil O'Gara, 551-99

Richardson, Mrs. Buford: letter of comment, 386-96

Rich, Arthur T.: Boys Who Never Grow Up, (dime novel characters), 163-1; 192-75

RICHMOND NOVELS, 52-11; 144-3

(RICHMOND'S SENSATION NOVELS), Dime Novel Sketches #164, 492-97

Riehl, J.E.: Charles Lamb's Forerunners of the Dime Novel (early popular fiction novels 1805-1808), 533-109

(Rinehart, Mary Roberts), Mary Roberts Rinehart and the Nickel Novel, by Stanley A. Pachon, 369-55

Riordan, Robert V.: A Half Century of the Hardy Boys, or, Clues to an Obscure Chronology, (bibliography) 530-35

Rise and Fall of the Dime Novel, The, by Charles W. Morris, 96-1

Rival Rangers of Fleet Street, The, (rival publishers, Edwin J. Brett and William L. Emmett), by A.W. Lawson, 279-102

Roach, Mrs. Joyce: letter of comment, 475-52; 498-36

(ROAD TO SUCCESS: THE BIBLIOGRAPHY OF THE WORKS OF HORATIO ALGER: Ralph D. Gardner), review by Kenyon C. Rosenberg, 488-57

Roaring Girl, The, (Moll Cutpurse, famous English thief), by W.O.G.Lofts, 473-18

Robbers in 1868, (James Gang), 39-1

Robertson, Frank C.: reminiscences, 18-7

ROBIN HOOD SERIES, 2-6

(Robin Hood), The Real Robin Hood, (historical basis for the legend), by W.O.G.Lofts, 502-82; 503-99

Robison, Charles S.: letter of comment, 529-29

Rockland Terror Carries On Another Biography, The, (biog. sketch of William M. Burns), by Charles Duprez, 268-4

Rockspur Series, The, (sports stories by Gilbert Patten), by J.P. Guinon, 304-2

Rodgers, Walter P., Jr.: letter of comment, 526-93

(Roe, E.P.), Favorites of Yesterday: E.P.Roe, (early author, biog.sketch), by Hermon Pitcher, 191-68

Rogers, Denis R.: A Final Word on the Pseudonyms of Edward S. Ellis, 363-108

Rogers, Denis R.: A Statistical Alphabet of Edward S. Ellis, (extent of Ellis' works), 446-117

Rogers, Denis R.: THE ALDINE LIFE AND ADVENTURE LIBRARY, with checklist, 533-98

Rogers, Denis R.: Alfred D. Hynes, Beadle and Munro Author, (biog./literary sketch), 386-94

Rogers, Denis R.: Beadles Abroad, (foreign language editions of Beadles Dime Novels), 347-86; 348-96

Rogers, Denis R.: BEADLE'S FRONTIER SERIES, 507-136

Rogers, Denis R.: Beadles in England, (London publications of Beadle & Co., with checklist), 496-2; 497-14; 498-33

Rogers, Denis R.: Bibliographical Reflections, (research in the story papers and dime novels), 509-10; 510-17

Rogers, Denis R.: THE BOYS OWN LIBRARY, 453-60

Rogers, Denis R.: THE BOYS OWN LIBRARY, Author Index, 453-63

Rogers, Denis R.: Disposal of a Book Collection, (problems inherent), 546-98, (see also 549-66; 549-67)

Rogers, Denis R.: Early Publications of the Aldine Publishing Company (with special interest to Alger Series), 532-82; 533-98

Rogers, Denis R.: The Edward S. Ellis Stories Published by the Mershon Complex, 490-70; 491-86; 492-104

Rogers, Denis R.: Ellis for Beginners, (bibliography of books by Edward S. Ellis), 529-2

Rogers, Denis R.: Ellis' Ten War Chief Tales, (hardbound Indian Chief novels by Edward S. Ellis), 539-74

Rogers, Denis R.: THE GARFIELD LIBRARY, (English novel series with checklist 470-124; 471-138; 472-5

Rogers, Denis R.: Hon. William Adams Brodribb, Beadle Author, (biog. & literary sketch), 353-12

Rogers, Denis R.: Hybrids, Oddities and Freaks, (variations in editions of dime novels and boys' books), 475-46; 476-56

Rogers, Denis R.: letter of comment, 372-86; 393-65; 519-66; 549-68; 551-105

Rogers, Denis R.: The Lovell Complex (publishing history), 527-98

Rogers, Denis R.: Oddities of Dime Novel Days, (dime novel biblio-graphical mysteries), 526-85

Rogers, Denis R.: Postscripts on the Pen Names of Edward S. Ellis, 336-74

Rogers, Denis R.: Pseudonyms of Edward S. Ellis, 266-82; 267-90; 268-2; 307-25; 315-148; 318-22; 319-30; 320-42; 330-18; 334-58

Rogers, Denis R.: Survey of the Probable Publication Pattern of the Books of Edward S. Ellis Under the Imprints of A.L.Burt, 524-26

Rogers, Denis R.: Used Book Prices, (discusses values of books and why), 469-114

Rogers, Denis R. and Edward T. LeBlanc: Dime Novel Series Title Changes, 488-50

Rogers, Denis R. and J. Edward Leithead: A Publication Pattern of Edward S. Ellis, (study of the Porter & Coates/Henry T. Coates/John C. Winston editions of boys' books by Ellis), 480-80; 481-95

Rogers, Ivor A.: letter of comment, 486-36

(Rolt-Wheeler, Francis), Checklist of Boys' Book Titles, by John T. Dizer, Jr., 500-59

(Rolt-Wheeler, Francis), The Rolt-Wheeler/Gilbreth Letters, (correspondence between Rolt-Wheeler and Lillian M. Gilbreth, with checklist of Rolt-Wheeler boys' books titles), by John T. Dizer, Jr., 500-56

Rome Bans Nick Carter, Buffalo Bill, and Lincoln, news item, 89-1

Rootin' Tootin' Shootin' Frisco Bert, (biog. sketch of Bertrand Couch), by Charles Duprez, 290-85

Rosenberg, Kenyon C.: Review of Ralph D. Gardner's ROAD TO SUCCESS, THE BIBLIOGRAPHY ON THE WORKS OF HORATIO ALGER, 488-57

(Rothstein, Charles), Charles Rothstein
Collects Florida Dime Novels (with
Florida locales), by Jane Hamlin,
434-115

(Rough Riders), Ted Strong and His Rough
Riders, by J. Edward Leithead, 345-66;
346-76

ROUGH RIDERS WEEKLY and the Ted Strong
Saga, bibliographical checklist, by
J. Edward Leithead and Edward T.
LeBlanc, 478-3

(ROUGH RIDERS WEEKLY), Dime Novel Sketches
#24, 345-65

(ROUGH RIDERS WEEKLY), King of the Wild
West, by J. Edward Leithead, 198-17

(ROUGH RIDERS WEEKLY), Ted Strong and
His Rough Riders, by J. Edward
Leithead, 345-66; 346-76

(ROUGH RIDERS WEEKLY), Tip Top and
Rough Rider Cards, (post cards
published), by W.R.Johnson, 357-65

Round Up at North Platte, The, (verse),
by Charles D. Randolph, 58-11

Rounded Up for the Round-Up, (odd facts
on TIP TOP WEEKLY), by Gerald J.
McIntosh, 421-97

Rounding Up the Roundup, or Items You
May Have Muffed, (reviews past
items in DIME NOVEL ROUNDUP), by
Hawknose the Detective, 234-17

ROVER, THE, 49-3

Rover Boy Carl Linville, (biog. sketch),
by Charles Duprez, 281-10

Rover Boys, B'Gosh, The, (on the early
Rover Boys stories), by Robert H.
Smeltzer, 50-4

(Rover Boys Series), Ribbing the Rovers,
(book parodies on the Rover Boys),
by Gil O'Gara, 551-99

ROVERS LOG, THE, 279-103

ROVERS OF THE SEA, 279-103

ROVERS OF THE SEA, THE, by "Topchin
Twiddlewinks", 242-82

Rudman, Jack: letter of comment, 482-115

Ruff, John: letter of comment, 36-2

Russell, Don: Buffalo Bill in Bound
Book Fiction, 320-40

Russell, Don: letter of comment, 394-72;
531-76

(Russell, Don: CUSTER'S LIST, A CHECK-
LIST OF PICTURES RELATING TO THE
LITTLE BIG HORN), review by J.
Edward Leithead, 457-106

(Russell, Don: THE LIVES AND LEGENDS
OF BUFFALO BILL), review by J.
Edward Leithead, 340-2

Russell, James R.: Dime Novels Not
Bad, (defends dime novel literature)
79-5

(Russell, W. Clark), The Life of
W. Clark Russell, (early author),
by Ralph F. Cummings, 213-44

Ryan, H.L.: letter of comment, 381-52

Ryerson Collection, The, (comments),
123-1

(Rymer, James Malcolm), James Malcolm
Rymer and Thomas Pecket Prest,
(biog./literary sketch of authors
of Gothic "penny bloods", and
history of Edward Lloyd and his
English publications), by W.O.G.
Lofts, 485-18

(Saalfield Publishing Co.), The Old
Werner Publishing Company of Akron,
Ohio, (predecessor to Saalfield),
by Roy B. Van Devier, 286-49

(Sabin, Edwin L.), Now They're
Collectors' Items, (boys' books
of Sabin), by J. Edward Leithead,
417-54

Saga of Frank Merriwell, The, (in
TIP TOP LIBRARY, Nos.1-3), 480-91;
482-114; 483-126

Sahr, George: letter of comment,
380-45; 390-30; 391-39; 394-72;
398-120

(Sahr, George), obituary, 494-131

(Saltillo Boys), Stoddard, Saltillo
Boys and Syracuse, (on W.O.Stoddard
and his boys' books), by John T.
Dizer, Jr., 490-77

Sampson, Robert: A Time of Lively
Fiction, (survey and discussion of
the range of popular literature
from dime novels to the present),
540-93; 541-8; 542-33; 543-52;
544-71; 545-87; 546-104

Sampson, Robert: Half Nick Carter and
Half Sherlock Holmes, (Felix Boyd
stories in THE POPULAR MAGAZINE),
552-118

Sampson, Robert: letter of comment,
535-14

Samuel, Ray: letter of comment, 453-68

San Francisco in Dime Novel Days,
(reminiscences), by George H.
Cordier, 119-1

Sanford, Ernest P.: letter of comment,
404-52; 409-108

SATURDAY JOURNAL, 14-5

SATURDAY LIBRARY, 152-4

(SATURDAY LIBRARY), Dime Novel Sketches
#111, 438-29

(SATURDAY LIBRARY), correction on dates,
by Ralph P. Smith, 451-46

SATURDAY NIGHT, (story paper), 88-3

(SATURDAY NIGHT), Dime Novel Sketches
#39, 363-107

Savant Dips Into Dime Novels in Library
of Congress, by George Lilly,
58-12

(Sawyer, Eugene T.), Confessions of a
Dime Novelist, (author of many Nick
Carter stories), by Gelett Burgess,
105-2

(Sawyer, Eugene T.), First Nick Carter
Story was Accepted, 73-7

(Sawyer, Eugene T.), obituary, 132-4

(Sawyer Publishing Co.), story require-
    ments, 214-54
Sawyer, Roland D.: THE BEADLES MONTHLY,
    163-2
Sawyer, Roland D.: Beadles STANDARD
    LIBRARY OF ROMANCE, 296-41
Sawyer, Roland D.: Books for the Camp-
    fire, The Redpath Novels, 198-20
Sawyer, Roland D.: Buffalo Bill,
    (comments), 66-12
Sawyer, Roland D.: The DeWitt Ten Cent
    Novels, 148-4
Sawyer, Roland D.: Early Adventures with
    the House of Beadle, (comments on
    early dime novels), 45-2
Sawyer, Roland D.: Facts About the "Two
    Bills" and Buntline, (Wild Bill,
    Buffalo Bill, and Ned Buntline
    relationship), 160-4
Sawyer, Roland D.: The Forgotten Men of
    the House of Beadle, (early authors)
    141-3
Sawyer, Roland D.: Gen. Phil Sheridan's
    Words on Buffalo Bill, 295-31
Sawyer, Roland D.: Kit Carson, An Eye
    Witness Word, 296-40
Sawyer, Roland D.: More on Boston Early
    Stories and Their Publishers, 175-25
Sawyer, Roland D.: My First Ten Stories,
    (dime novel reading reminiscences),
    69-2
Sawyer, Roland D.: Ned Buntline's
    Centennary, 175-26
Sawyer, Roland D.: Two Boston Publishing
    Houses of Stories, (Richmond & Co.,
    and Elliott, Thomas & Talbot), 144-3
(Scharnhorst, Gary and Jack Bales: HORATIO
    ALGER, JR., AN ANNOTATED BIBLIOGRAPHY
    OF COMMENT AND CRITICISM), review by
    John T. Dizer, Jr., 550-74
Schaeffer, Alan E.: Going to New York?,
    (dime novels at New York Public
    Library), 86-4
Schenkel, Joe A.: letter of comment,
    382-65
(school), The Anatomy of Dime Novels
    No.19, Stories of Boarding School
    and College Sports, by J. Edward
    Leithead, 454-72; 455-80
(school), Fred Should Fear Not, or,
    Nickel Novel's New Era, (use of
    dime novels in school class), by
    Edward G. Ingraham, 340-4
SCHOOLBOY SERIES, 179-4
Schorr, Jack R.: A Book Grabber's
    Gripes, (boys' books collecting
    experiences), 475-50
Schorr, Jack R.: A Few of the Less
    Known Series, (discusses boys'
    books), 464-47
Schorr, Jack R.: A Few of the Non-Series
    Books, (boys' books), 467-85
Schorr, Jack R.: A Sketch of Hezekiah
    Butterworth, (early author, boys'
    books), 539-77

Schorr, Jack R.: A Vacation Trip 1973,
    (boys' books collecting experiences)
    495-137
Schorr, Jack R.: Ah, Those Golden
    Years, (boys' book collecting),
    508-5
Schorr, Jack R.: The Book I Had the
    Hardest Time Finding, (comments by
    various collectors), 444-95
Schorr, Jack R.: Browsing Around, (boys'
    book collecting), 473-23
Schorr, Jack R.: Collecting Books for
    Your Kids to Read, (difficulty in
    pleasing present generation), 463-40
Schorr, Jack R.: Collecting for Fun or
    Profit, (boys' book collecting),
    460-2
Schorr, Jack R.: Displaying Your
    Collection, (housing your boys' books
    collection), 465-57
Schorr, Jack R.: Disposing of Your
    Collection, (problems inherent),
    503-103
Schorr, Jack R.: The Elusives, (hard
    to find boys' books), 494-130
Schorr, Jack R.: Exasperations of a
    Book Collector, (boys' books),
    448-2
Schorr, Jack R.: 4500, All Mint, (boys'
    book collecting), 469-118
Schorr, Jack R.: From Boxes to Shelves,
    or How to Know What You Have,
    (housing the boys' books), 479-76
Schorr, Jack R.: Going, Going, Gone,
    (collecting boys' books), 488-56
Schorr, Jack R.: letter of comment,
    521-125; 531-76
Schorr, Jack R.: Odds 'n' Ends (boys'
    book collecting), 452-57; 455-88;
    456-96
Schorr, Jack R.: Some of the Boys'
    Books from England, 471-150
Schorr, Jack R.: Travels of a Book
    Collector, (collecting boys' books,
    experiences), 483-120
Schorr, Jack R.: "Wanted: A Hero"
    (heroes in the boys' books),
    482-112
Schorr, Jack R.: Your Wife and Your
    Collection, (collecting boys' books)
    458-115
Schott, Frank: letter of comment,
    380-44; 382-64; 400-9; 423-119
Schott, Jack: letter of comment, 434-114
Schulze, C. Henry: letter of comment,
    380-44
(science-fiction), Fantasy, Science
    Fiction and Lost Race Adventures
    in the Street & Smith Paperback
    Volumes, (checklist), by Stuart A.
    Teitler, 442-71
(science-fiction), Stratemeyer and
    Science Fiction, (early science
    fiction and Stratemeyer's role) by
    John T. Dizer, Jr., 516-66; 520-73

Scientist Collects Dime Novels, (the collection of Albert Johannsen), by Edwin Brooks, 82-2; 83-1
Scout Master G. Harvey Ralphson's Triplets, (checklist of Boy Scout books published by Donohue & Co.) by Julius R. Chenu, 498-32
(SEA AND SHORE SERIES), Dime Novel Sketches #217, 545-81
"Seajay": Alas, That Truth Must Prevail, (comments on Buffalo Bill), 158-4
"Seajay": An Oddity, (BEADLES HALF DIME LIBRARY No.5), 96-2
"Seajay": The Difference Between a Five and Dime Novel, 98-5
"Seajay": Edward L. Wheeler's Own View of Wild Bill Hickok, 158-3
"Seajay": How To Become a Ventriloquist, (reminiscences), 100-2
"Seajay": Little Chief Library, 98-3
"Seajay": THE NICKEL LIBRARY, 96-2
"Seajay": see also A. Jay See
SECRET SERVICE, 54-1
(SECRET SERVICE), Dime Novel Sketches #54, 378-19
(SECRET SERVICE), The Two King Bradys and Their Girl Detective, (detectives in dime novels), by J. Edward Leithead, 372-80; 373-90
SECRET SERVICE No.258, (discussed), by Harold C. Holmes, 154-1; 155-1
(SECRET SERVICE SERIES), Dime Novel Sketches #216, 544-65
SECRET SERVICE WEEKLY, 42-5
Seddon, Dick: letter of comment, 524-51
See, A. Jay: Books He Remembers, (dime novel reading reminiscences), 186-2
See, A. Jay: see also "Seajay"
Senarens, Lou, 6-5
(Senarens, Lou): Biography of Lu Senarens, author and editor), 114-10
(Senarens, Lou), Noname, (biog. sketch) by Learnard C. Leighter, 56-1
(Senarens, Lou), obituary, 95-4
(Senarens, Lou), obituary corrections, 334-63
(Senarens, Lou), see also "Noname"
Serials and Boys Books by Edward Stratemeyer, by John T. Dizer, Jr., 516-126
(SERIES OF MILITARY NOVELS), Dime Novel Sketches #197, 525-57
(SERIES OF SEA TALES), Dime Novel Sketches #203, 531-57
SERIES OF SEA TALES, list of titles, checklist, 531-75
(SETH JONES OF NEW HAMPSHIRE: Edward S. Ellis), Introduction, (censorship; early history of dime novels), 172-1
Settle, William A., Jr.: The Dime Novel As an Historian's Tool, 456-92; 457-102
Sexton Blake, (English detective character), by W.O.G.Lofts, 439-40
Sexton Blake, Detective, (english detective character), by W.O.G. Lofts, 273-48

SHAMROCK, THE, 3-2
Shaner, Alex T.: letter of comment, 516-149
(Shaw, Elmer), Shaw's Novels, by T.M.Peterson, 210-18
Shaw's Novels, (Elmer Shaw), by T.M.Peterson, 210-18
(Shea, Cornelius), Cornelius Shea, An Old Scout, (frontier biog. sketch), by Gerald J. McIntosh, 401-20
(Sheldon, Laurana), letter by early author, 129-4
(Sheldon, Lurana), Believe It or Not, An Eye Opener, (visit with author), by George French, 193-84
(Sheppard, Jack), Darling of the Mob, ("Prince of the Prison Breakers"), by Fred T. Singleton, 283-30
(Sheridan, General Phillip), Gen. Phil Sheridan's Words on Buffalo Bill, 295-31
Sherlock Holmes, (discussion), by Robert H. Smeltzer, 146-1
Sherlock Holmes Exhibit, (Philadelphia Free Library, 1968; included Nick Carter items), by J. Edward Leithead, 429-61
(SHIELD SERIES), Dime Novel Sketches #218, 546-97
SHIELD WEEKLY, 240-66; 241-75
SHIELD WEEKLY, by Harold C. Holmes, 138-1
(SHIELD WEEKLY), Dime Novel Sketches #51, 375-107
Shopton, Home of the Swifts, (Tom Swift boys' books series, locale) by John T. Dizer, Jr., 449-14
Short Short Stories of Burt L. Standish, The, (Gilbert Patten), by Gerald J. McIntosh, 391-34; 393-66
SHOT AND SHELL, 42-4
Shove, Raymond H.: letter of comment, 380-44
Silsbee, Howard B.: Displaying Your Dime Novels, 279-104
Silsbee, Howard B.: Interesting Dime Novel Facts, (miscellany), 282-20; 284-34; 287-64; 288-73; 291-99
Silsbee, Howard B.: Memories of the BOYS BEST WEEKLY, 311-116
Silsbee, Howard B.: letter of comment, 306-19
Sinclair Tousey's Obituary from FIRESIDE COMPANION (1887), 540-99
Sinclair, Upton, 174-20; 177-44
(Sinclair, Upton), A Letter from Upton Sinclair, (1956), 287-62
(Sinclair, Upton), Hike and the Aeroplane, (rare boys' book by Sinclair as "Tom Graham": HIKE AND THE AEROPLANE), by Julius R. Chenu, 550-81
(Sinclair, Upton), Upton Sinclair, Last of the Dime Novelists, by Ralph Adimari, 285-42; 286-51

(Sinclair, Upton), The Upton Sinclair Novels, by Ronald Gottesman, 378-20

Singleton, Fred T.: Cheap, But Not Trashy, (mail-order periodicals), 224-34

Singleton, Fred T.: Collector Averages Out, (collecting experiences), 19-5

Singleton, Fred T.: Darling of the Mob, (on Jack Sheppard, "Prince of the Prison Breakers"), 283-30

Singleton, Fred T.: Facts About John R. Musick, (author), 13-7; 21-5

Singleton, Fred T.: The Last Number of THE GOLDEN ARGOSY, 10-2; 11-4

Singleton, Fred T.: 19th Century Peep-Show, (collecting comments), 225-41; 227-57; 232-4; 233-10

Singleton, Fred T.: Old Bowery Days in the Dime Novel, (reminiscences), 9-3

Singleton, Fred T.: On the Trail of Novel Hunters, (collecting experiences) 6-2; 8-5; 9-7

Singleton, Fred T.: Spanked at Seventeen by the Editor of GOLDEN HOURS, 7-6; 8-4

Singleton, Fred T.: Treat 'em Tenderly, Pard, (care of your dime novel collection), 5-1

(Singleton, Fred T.), obituary, 331-37

Six Hundred Dime Novels for Fifteen Dollars, (collecting experiences), by "Jack Harkaway", 9-5

Sixty Years Ago, (verse), by G.H. McIntosh, 317-18

SKIPPER, THE, 49-3

Skjelver, Mabel Cooper: letter of comment, 518-51

Skjelver, Mabel Cooper: William Wallace Cook - The Marshall Years, (early years of author in Marshall, Mich.), with checklist, 518-34

(Slade, Tom), The First Tom Slade Books, or, Movies to Print, (Tom Slade Boy Scout boys' series books), by Julius R. Chenu, 514-83

Slepian, Joseph: letter of comment, 522-142; 549-66

SMALL BOYS MONTHLY, 26-2

Small, George C., 2-5; 58-9

(Small, George C.), obituary, 6-3

Smeltzer, Robert H.: The Austin Collection and Exhibit Extraordinary, (dime novels), 41-1

Smeltzer, Robert H.: Current English Story Papers, (survey), 49-1

Smeltzer, Robert H.: Foreign Novels, (dime novels), 24-3

Smeltzer, Robert H.: Frank Merriwell at Fardale, 48-1

Smeltzer, Robert H.: Leon Ray Livingston, Wanderer, Author, Orator, (author discussed), 259-31

Smeltzer, Robert H.: "Lop-Sided Novels" (how to correct condition), 33-1

Smeltzer, Robert H.: Members of the Happy Hours Brotherhood, (var. dime novel collectors), 56-6

Smeltzer, Robert H.: Nick Carter Again, 22-1

Smeltzer, Robert H.: OLD SLEUTH LIBRARY, 167-2

Smeltzer, Robert H.: Old Time Authors, (discussion), 50-1

Smeltzer, Robert H.: The Passing of Burt L. Standish, (memorial tribute to Gilbert Patten), 150-5

Smeltzer, Robert H.: Pluck & Luck Reprints and Earlier Happy Days Stories, 149-2

Smeltzer, Robert H.: Retrospect: Francis Worcester Doughty, (tribute to author), 343-54

Smeltzer, Robert H.: The Rover Boys, B'Gosh, 50-4

Smeltzer, Robert H.: Sherlock Holmes, (discussion), 146-1

Smeltzer, Robert H.: Tip Top Comics, 274-57

Smith, Dwight E.: letter of comment, 432-94

Smith, Ralph P.: A Quick Synopsis of the Merriwell Saga (in TIP TOP WEEKLY), 537-48

Smith, Ralph P.: Barred by the Post Office, (ESQUIRE barred, and other postal regulations pertinent), 145-1

Smith, Ralph P.: Dime Novel Sidelights, (misc. bibliographical and data on collecting), 479-72

Smith, Ralph P.: Frank Merriwell vs. Fred Fearnot, (dime novel type pastiche), 493-114

Smith, Ralph P.: letter of comment, 375-113; 404-52; 428-50; 479-75; 530-50; 550-86

Smith, Ralph P.: Letters from Dime Novel Publishers (to Will Lisenbee, author), 209-10

Smith, Ralph P.: MEDAL and NEW MEDAL LIBRARIES, 98-1

Smith, Ralph P.: More About "My Queen" (MY QUEEN LIBRARY), 259-28

Smith, Ralph P.: Neglected Weeklies, (YOUNG PEOPLES WEEKLY and NEW SABBATH LIBRARY), 489-65

Smith, Ralph P.: SATURDAY LIBRARY, (correction on dates), 451-46

(Smith, Soapy), Soapy Smith ("cheap imitation of a dime novel hero") by J.H.Armbruster, 86-2

(SNAPS), Dime Novel Sketches #59, 384-75

SNAPS, THE COMIC WEEKLY, by Charles Duprez, 244-1

SNAPS WEEKLY, 3-6

Soapy Smith, ("cheap imitation of a dime novel hero"), by J.H. Armbruster, 86-2

Soibelman, David: Horatio Alger Goes Greeley: From Wretches to Riches, (literary sketch), 539-79
Soibelman, David: letter of comment, 483-124; 502-88; 530-50; 533-110; 535-14
Some Good Stuff, (on James Gang), by Walter F. Tunks, 190-57
Some Notes Toward a Study of Nick Carter, by J. Randolph Cox, 439-44
Some of the Boys' Books from Britain, by Jack R. Schorr, 471-150
Song Author Died Before Its Birth, (Jane Brown), 94-3
SONG OF BRITANNIA, THE, 279-103
(songs), Popular Songs of Dime Novel Times, (with song words), by George H. Cordier, 113-1
Southworth, Emma E.D.E.N., 15-3
(Southworth, Mrs. E.D.E.N.), The Life of a Woman Known to Thousands, (biog. sketch, author), 192-77
Spacious Living to Come, (predictions), by H.C.Ingraham, 348-99
(Spalding, Samuel C.), A Letter from the Last of the Nick Carter Authors) 329-11
(Spalding, Samuel C.), Nick Carter in Another Man's Shoes, (Carter stories by Spalding; Sexton Blake), by J. Edward Leithead, 350-112; 351-120
(Spanish-American War), The Anatomy of Dime Novels No.4: Spanish-American War Novels, by J. Edward Leithead, 402-24; 403-36
Spanish reprints, dime novels, 69-1
Spanked at Seventeen by the Editor of GOLDEN HOURS, by Fred T. Singleton, 7-6; 8-4
Specimen Numbers of Bygone Boys Papers, by F.N.Wearing, 176-33
SPIRIT OF THE TIMES, THE, 17-4
(SPORT STORIES), Dime Novel Sketches #223, 551-93
(SPORTING NEW YORKER, THE), THE NEW SENSATION and THE SPORTING NEW YORKER, bibliographical listing, by Ross Craufurd, 521-SS
(sports), The Anatomy of Dime Novels No.19: Stories of Boarding School and College Sports, by J. Edward Leithead, 454-72; 455-80
SPORTS STORY MAGAZINE, 62-6; 66-6
Sprague, Richard S.: letter of comment, 419-82; 434-114
Spring-Heeled Jack, (on colorful English villain), by W.O.G.Lofts, 489-60
Spring Tonic, (verse), by George French, 303-108a
(stagecoach), The Anatomy of Dime Novels No.20 - Stories of the Stage, by J. Edward Leithead, 458-112; 459-120
STANDARD LIBRARY OF ROMANCE, by Roland D. Sawyer, 296-41

Standard Library Reference Books for Collectors, (lists and describes), by Jack Bales, 504-112
Standish, Burt L.: see also Gilbert Patten
Standish, Burt L.: 3-5; 5-8; 15-5
Stangler, Bert: letter of comment, 529-29
(STAR JOURNAL), A Complete File of the STAR JOURNAL, (comments), 217-75
STAR SPANGLED BANNER, THE, 175-25
(STAR STORIES), An Overlooked Alger Weekly, by Stanley A. Pachon, 498-30
(Starr Gang), Outlaw Trails in Indian Territory, (in dime novels), by J. Edward Leithead, 290-87
STARRY FLAG WEEKLY, 402-25
(STARRY FLAG WEEKLY, THE), Dime Novel Sketches #52, 376-1
Statistical Alphabet of Edward S. Ellis, (extent of Ellis' works), by Denis R. Rogers, 446-117
Steele, Henry: A Famous Old English Boys Journal - BOYS OF ENGLAND, 134-1
Steele, Henry: The Dime Novel Abroad, (foreign reprints), 3-1
Steele, Henry: Old Boys Journals Illustrations, (discussion), 34-1
Steele, Henry: The Publications of Charles Fox, 13-5; 21-4
Steele, Henry: Putting Long Trousers on the Eighteenth Century, (BOYS OF ENGLAND story paper), 8-2
Steele, Joan: letter of comment, 415-41
Steinhauer, Donald L. and Edward T. LeBlanc: Checklist of Writings of Gilbert Patten Prior to Frank Merriwell, 410-118
(Stephens, Charles Asbury), Charles Asbury Stephens, (author biog. sketch), by Esther J. Judkins, 261-41; 262-50
Stevens, D.W.: see John R. Musick
(Stevens, D.W.), A Note on D.W. Stevens, by William L. Beck, 12-4
(Stevenson, Robert Louis), The Late Robert Louis Stevenson, (comments) 75-10
(Stevenson, Robert Louis), Treasure Island, (on pirate stories in general and on Stevenson's TREASURE ISLAND), by W.O.G.Lofts, 477-64
(Stinemetts, Henry), Trick and Fancy Roper Now Building Custodian, news item on old time cowboy, 180-3
(Stitt Publishing Co.), Edward S. Ellis Stories Published by the Mershon Complex, by Denis R. Rogers, 490-70; 491-86; 492-104
Stockmesser, Kent L.: letter of comment, 377-16; 527-115

Stoddard, Saltillo Boys, and Syracuse, (W.O.Stoddard and his boys' books) by John T. Dizer, Jr., 490-77

Stoddard, R.H.: Memoir of Mayne Reid, (author biog. sketch), 205-81

(Stoddard, William O.), Now They're Collectors' Items, (boys' book author and books), by J. Edward Leithead, 411-128

(Stoddard, William O.), Stoddard, Saltillo Boys, and Syracuse, (boys' series books author and his Saltillo Boys series), by John T. Dizer, Jr., 490-77

Stone, Joe: Ray Mengar and His Dime Novel Collection, 431-84

Stop Thief! (regarding dishonest mail dealing in dime novels), by J.P. Guinon, 82-1

Stories I Have Enjoyed Most, (dime novel reading reminiscences) by A. Willard Jaffray, 89-1

STORIES OF THE SEA Series, 25-8

(story papers), see "penny dreadfuls" and also individual titles

(story papers), A Famous Old English Boys Journal, (BOYS OF ENGLAND), by Henry Steele, 134-1

(story papers), A Lode of GOLDEN HOURS, (on pseudonyms), by Harry A. Weill, 215-59

(story papers), A Thrice-Told Tale on GOLDEN HOURS, by Harry A. Weill, 148-1

(story papers), An Open Letter on the Writers of GOLDEN HOURS, by Willis F. Hurd, 130-1

(story papers), THE BAD BOYS PAPER, by W.O.G.Lofts, 313-135

(story papers), Blood and Thunder Novels for Boys, by M. Bertrand Couch, 68-1

(story papers), BOYS OF AMERICA - A Twentieth Century Story Paper, by Ralph F. Cummings, 7-2

(story papers), BOYS OF AMERICA, Dime Novel Sketches #41, 365-11

(story papers), THE BOYS OF NEW YORK, by George H. Cordier, 133-1

(story papers), BOYS OF NEW YORK, Dime Novel Sketches #62, 389-9

(story papers), BOYS' WORLD, Dime Novel Sketches #45, 369-49

(story papers), Current English Story Papers, by Robert H. Smeltzer, 49-1

(story papers), Data on GOLDEN HOURS Nos. 599-780, 207-98

(story papers), The Dime Novel Abroad in England and Ireland, by Henry Steele, 3-1

(story papers), English Boys Magazines, by George H. Cordier, 120-1

(story papers), The English Giant, (E. Harcourt Burrage), by Ross Craufurd, 12-2

(story papers), The English Novels of Today, by Ralph F. Cummings, 21-1

(story papers), Exit UNION JACK, (cessation), by William M. Burns, 17-5; 23-1

(story papers), Famous Tousey Story Papers, by Edward T. LeBlanc, 508-2

(story papers), Fifty Years Ago (with GOLDEN ARGOSY), by Patrick Mulhall, 52-4

(story papers), The First English Story Papers for Boys, by W.O.G. Lofts, 277-84

(story papers), FRANK LESLIE'S BOYS OF AMERICA, Dime Novel Sketches #43, 367-31

(story papers), FRANK LESLIE'S BOYS OF AMERICA, by William M. Burns, 139-1; 141-1; 149-3

(story papers), FRANK LESLIE'S BOYS' AND GIRLS' WEEKLY, Dime Novel Sketches #46, 370-61

(story papers), The Golden Age of English Boys' Literature, by William J. Benners, 14-2; 15-5; 16-4

(story papers), THE GOLDEN ARGOSY, by James E. Knott, 144-1

(story papers), GOLDEN ARGOSY, by Stanley A. Pachon, 382-58; 383-69

(story papers), GOLDEN ARGOSY, Dime Novel Sketches #42, 366-21

(story Papers), GOLDEN HOURS, Dime Novel Sketches #40, 364-1

(story papers), THE HEARTHSTONE, Dime Novel Sketches #44, 368-41

(story papers), The History of Old Story Papers of Long Ago, (NEW YORK WEEKLY STORY TELLER), by Ralph F. Cummings, 216-66

(story papers), The Last Number of THE GOLDEN ARGOSY, by Fred T. Singleton, 10-2; 11-4

(story papers), More on the GOLDEN HOURS, by Harry A. Weill, 149-5

(story papers), Neglected Weeklies, (YOUNG PEOPLES WEEKLY and NEW SABBATH LIBRARY), by Ralph P. Smith, 489-65

(story papers), NEW YORK BOYS LIBRARY, Dime Novel Sketches #95, 422-105

(story papers), NEW YORK DETECTIVE LIBRARY/DETECTIVE LIBRARY, Dime Novel Sketches #85, 412-1

(story papers), Nuggets from GOLDEN HOURS, by Harry A. Weill, 171-1

(story papers), Old English Journals for Boys, (ALDINES NEW BOYS PAPER) by William M. Burns, 331-34

(story papers), Old English Journals for Boys, (COMRADES), by William M. Burns, 323-66

(story papers), Old English Story Papers for Boys, (THE BOYS LEISURE HOUR), by William M. Burns, 325-84

(story papers), Old English Journals
for Boys, (BOYS OF THE EMPIRE),
by William M. Burns, 321-52; 322-60

(story papers), Old English Journals
for Boys, (special Christmas issues),
by William M. Burns, 326-92

(story papers), Old Story Papers, (BOYS
OF NEW YORK), by William M. Burns,
306-18; 307-28; 308-37

(story papers), Our Old Story Papers,
(GOLDEN ARGOSY), by William M. Burns,
184-1; 185-9

(story papers), Our Old Story Papers,
(GOLDEN ARGOSY Nos.1 & 2), by
William M. Burns, 184-1; 185-9

(story papers), Our Old Story Papers,
(HAPPY DAYS), by William M. Burns,
214-49

(story papers), Our Old Story Papers
(NEW YORK WEEKLY), by William M.
Burns, 200-37

(story papers), Our Story Papers, by
U.G.Figley, 115-5

(story papers), Popular Story Papers of
Other Days, by George H. Cordier,
88-1

(story papers), The Rival Rangers of
Fleet Street, (rival publishers,
Edwin J. Brett and William L.
Emmett), by A.W.Lawson, 279-102

(story papers), SATURDAY NIGHT, Dime
Novel Sketches #39, 363-107

(story papers), Spanked at Seventeen by
the Editor of GOLDEN HOURS, by Fred
T. Singleton, 7-6; 8-4

(story papers), Specimen Numbers of
Bygone Boys Papers, by F.N.Wearing,
176-33

(story papers), STREET & SMITH'S
LITERARY ALBUM, Dime Novel Sketches
#47, 372-81

(story papers), The Title Was the Same!,
(English boys papers with the same
title), by W.O.G.Lofts, 295-29

(story papers), YOUNG MEN OF AMERICA,
Dime Novel Sketches #68, 395-77

(story papers), YOUTHS COMPANION, by
Kenneth M. Daggett, 322-58

(Stowe, Harriet Beecher), Favorites of
Yesterday, (early author), by Hermon
Pitcher, 216-67

Strange Encounter, (with Nick Carter?),
by J. Randolph Cox, 394-70

Stratemeyer and Science Fiction, (early
science fiction and Stratemeyer's
role; Tom Swift), by John T. Dizer,
Jr., 514-66; 520-73

Stratemeyer and the Blacks, (attitude
toward and treatment of Blacks by
the Stratemeyer Syndicate), by John
T. Dizer, Jr., 515-90

Stratemeyer, Edward, 311-112

(Stratemeyer, Edward), The Alger Fakes,
(Alger books by Stratemeyer), by
Ralph Adimari, 349-105

(Stratemeyer, Edward), Censorship and
Early Adolescent Literature:
Stratemeyer, Mathiews and Comstock,
by Ken Donelson, 534-119

(Stratemeyer, Edward), Chronological
Listing of Boys Books by Edward
Stratemeyer First Published as
Serials, by John T. Dizer, Jr.,
515-118

(Stratemeyer, Edward), Early Stratemeyer
Writings, with checklist, by John
T. Dizer, Jr., 549-50

(Stratemeyer, Edward), Edward Stratemeyer, (biog. sketch), by Roy B.
Van Devier, 305-10; 306-20

(Stratemeyer, Edward), Edward Stratemeyer's Appeal to Contemporary Young
Readers, by Peter C. Walther, 535-2

(Stratemeyer, Edward), Evidence of
Another Edward Stratemeyer Pseudonym
(as Ralph Harrington), by Peter C.
Walther, 542-41

(Stratemeyer, Edward), Now They're
Collectors' Items, (boys' books
discussed), by J. Edward Leithead,
417-54

(Stratemeyer, Edward), Pseudonyms,
305-10; 306-20

(Stratemeyer, Edward), Serials and Boys
Books by Edward Stratemeyer, by
John T. Dizer, Jr., 516-126

(Stratemeyer, Edward), Stratemeyer and
Science Fiction, (early science
fiction and Stratemeyer's role; Tom
Swift), by John T. Dizer, Jr.,
514-66; 520-73

(Stratemeyer, Edward), Stratemeyer and
the Blacks, (attitude toward and
treatment of Blacks by the Stratemeyer Syndicate), by John T. Dizer,
Jr., 515-90

Strayed From the Sepulchre, or, The
Tomb-Tamer of Tip Top, (TIP TOP
WEEKLY), by J.P. Guinon, 99-1

(Straw, Jack, series), Question on
existence, with comments (boys'
series books), 514-84

Street & Smith, Publishers, 3-5

(Street & Smith), Author and Artist of
the Street & Smith Staff: W. Bert
Foster and Charles L. Wrenn, by
J. Edward Leithead, 361-92; 362-99;
363-110

(Street & Smith), THE BOYS OWN LIBRARY,
by Denis R. Rogers, 453-60

(Street & Smith), Building and Premises
of, 154-5

(Street & Smith), Boxes L-179 and L-180,
(publishing records examined), by
J. Randolph Cox, 551-94

Street & Smith Box M58, (discoveries in
the Street & Smith Collection at
Syracuse University), by John T.
Dizer, Jr., 526-78

(Street & Smith), Checklist of Street & Smith Dime Novels and Related Publications, by Edward T. LeBlanc and Ralph Adimari, 299-60

(Street & Smith), Fantasy, Science Fiction and Lost Race Adventures in the Street & Smith Paperback Volumes, (checklist), by Stuart A. Teitler, 442-71

(Street & Smith), The Lovell Complex, (publishing history), by Denis R. Rogers, 527-98

(Street & Smith), Possible Reprints, 214-52

(Street & Smith), as publisher for Gilbert Patten, by Frank C. Acker, 409-99

(Street & Smith), Publisher Quits Pulps and Comic Books Field, by Samuel Olnhausen, 200-45

(Street & Smith), Pulp Magazines Decline, 200-46

(Street & Smith), Report on Robert Emmett Owen, Illustrator of Street & Smith Publications, by Ralph Adimari, 333-50

(Street & Smith), review of THE FICTION FACTORY by Quentin Reynolds, history of Street & Smith, by J. Edward Leithead, 282-18

(Street & Smith), Robert Emmett Owen, Cover Artist, by J. Edward Leithead, 81-4

STREET & SMITH'S LITERARY ALBUM, by C.B.Hamilton, 46-2

STREET & SMITH'S LITERARY ALBUM, 180-5

(STREET & SMITH'S LITERARY ALBUM), Dime Novel Sketches #47, 372-81

"Strikes" That I Have Made in Noveldom, (collecting experiences), by William M. Burns, 4-1

Stroecker, James: letter of comment, 398-121; 452-56

(Strong, Ted, series), ROUGH RIDER WEEKLY and the Ted Strong Saga, with bibliographical listing, by J. Edward Leithead and Edward T. LeBlanc, 478-3

(Strong, Ted, series), Ted Strong and His Rough Riders (in ROUGH RIDERS WEEKLY), by J. Edward Leithead, 345-66; 346-76

"Strong-Arm Sam, the Boy Detective", (dime novel type fiction), 239-58

Success and Failure, (short history of English "penny dreadful" publishers), by W.O.G.Lofts, 523-9

SURPRISE, 21-1

Survey of the Probable Publication Pattern of the Books of Edward S. Ellis Under the Imprints of A.L.Burt, by Denis R. Rogers, 524-26

Swan Song of HAPPY DAYS, 157-3

Swanstrom, Roy E.: letter of comment, 369-58; 384-80

Swanstrom, Roy E.: The Northfield Bank Robbery, (James Gang), 278-90

(Swift, Tom, series), The Publication History of Tom Swift, (boys series books, with bibliographic checklist), by William R. Gowan, 536-22

(Swift, Tom, series), Shopton, Home of the Swifts, (discusses locale of the boys' series books), by John T.Dizer, Jr., 449-14

(Swift, Tom, series), Stratemeyer and Science Fiction, by John T. Dizer, Jr., 520-73

(Swift, Tom, series), Tom Swift, Jr., (bibliography and checklist of the Tom Swift, Jr. books by "Victor Appleton II") by William R. Gowan, 538-56

(Syracuse University), Street & Smith Box M58, (discoveries in the Street & Smith publishing records at the University), by John T. Dizer, Jr. 526-78

TALES OF BORDER ADVENTURE, Checklist, 538-67

(TALES OF BORDER ADVENTURE), Dime Novel Sketches #210, 538-55

(TALES OF CELEBRATED HIGHWAYMEN), Dime Novel Sketches #200, 528-121

TALES OF CELEBRATED HIGHWAYMEN, List of Titles, 528-126

Tales of Klondike Gold in Dime Novels, by J. Edward Leithead, 301-88

Talked About People, (sketch of Sinclair Tousey, American News Company), by J. Alexander Patten, 20-1; 25-5; 27-4

Tanbark and Spangles in the Five-Cent Libraries, (circus theme stories in the dime novels), by J. Edward Leithead, 223-25; 265-76; 266-84

(Tanner, Dr. Richard), Diamond Dick Dies at Nebraska Home, 131-3

Tanner, Richard: letter of comment, 335-67

(Taylor, Albert Bronaugh), Albert Bronaugh Taylor, a Beadle Author, (sketch), by Albert Johannsen, 303-104

Ted Strong and His Rough Riders, (series in ROUGH RIDERS WEEKLY), by J. Edward Leithead, 345-66; 346-76

Teicher, Morris: letter of comment, 385-89; 414-32

Teitler, Stuart A.: Fantasy, Science Fiction and Lost Race Adventures in the Street & Smith Paperback Volumes, (checklist), 442-71

"Tellinya, Ima": Handsome Harry of the Fighting Belvedere, (dime novel character), 228-65

TEMPERANCE LIBRARY, THE, 42-2

(temperance stories), The Anatomy of the Dime Novel No.13: Temperance Stories, by J. Edward Leithead, 434-108; 435-118

TEN CENT CLAUDE DUVAL NOVELS, Dime Novel Sketches #147, 474-33

TEN CENT IRISH NOVELS, 111-4
(TEN CENT IRISH NOVELS), Dime Novel
     Sketches #167, 495-133
(TEN CENT IRISH NOVELS), Rare Dime
     Novels, by Edward T. LeBlanc, 218-81
10¢ MEDAL LIBRARY, 3-5
(TEN CENT NOVELETTES), Dime Novel
     Sketches #141, 468-89
(TEN CENT POPULAR NOVELS), Dime Novel
     Sketches #145, 472-1
(Texas Jack), review of BUCKSKIN AND
     SATIN by Herschel C. Logan, 266-86;
     268-5
That Little Gem - the DIME NOVEL ROUNDUP,
     (collecting aid), 222-18
That Old Boyhood Thrill, (verse), by
     "Dare Devil Dave", 161-2
Thinking About Popular Literature: The
     Example of the Dime Novel, (response
     to J. Randolph Cox article, The
     Detective-Hero in the American Dime
     Novel), by David Anderson, 547-13
This and That, (pertinent news clippings),
     by W.B.McCafferty, 2-6; 3-3; 6-6
This "Sleuth" Business, (detectives in
     dime novels), by J. Edward Leithead,
     369-50; 370-62; 371-70
(Thomas, Mrs. Sarah), Young Wild West's
     Other Pard, or, Arietta's Only Rival,
     (dime novel author), by Edward G.
     Ingraham, 344-58
(Thompson and Thomas, Publishers), The
     Edward S. Ellis Stories Published
     by the Mershon Complex, by Denis R.
     Rogers, 490-70; 491-86; 492-104
(Thompson, Charles C., Company, Publishers),
     The Edward S. Ellis Stories Published
     by the Mershon Complex, by Denis R.
     Rogers, 490-70; 491-86; 492-104
Thompson, J. Currie: letter of comment,
     117-8
(Thompson, Willard), obituary, 515-123
(Thorp, William), Genealogy of William
     Thorp, (family history), by Roy B.
     Van Devier, 394-73; 395-85; 396-101;
     397-110; 398-122; 399-133; 400-10;
     402-32; 403-44; 404-54
Those Alger Days, (verse), by Frank
     Eisenberg, 543-56
Those Good Old Dime Novel Days, (verse),
     by Charles D. Randolph, 451-47
Those Iver's Reprints of Beadles Boys
     Library, by Willis E. Hurd, 37-1
THREE CHUMS, 81A-11
(THREE CHUMS), Dime Novel Sketches #4,
     322-57
THREE CHUMS - The Forgotten Weekly, by
     Julius Hasenfeffer, 226-52
THRILLER, THE, 21-1
Time for the Truth, (on our flag flying
     over schools and the Pledge of
     Allegiance), by Louise Harris, 491-94
Tip Top and Rough Rider Cards, (post
     cards from publishers), by W.R.
     Johnson, 357-65
TIP TOP COMICS, by Robert H. Smeltzer,
     274-57

TIP TOP LIBRARY, 3-5
(TIP TOP LIBRARY), The Saga of Frank
     Merriwell, (in TIP TOP LIBRARY
     Nos. 1-3), 480-91; 482-114; 483-126
TIP TOP SEMI-MONTHLY MAGAZINE, 66-4
TIP TOP WEEKLY, Bibliographic listing,
     by Robert McDowell, 532-SS
TIP TOP WEEKLY Locations, (locales of
     stories), by Arthur N. Carter,
     352-8
TIP TOP WEEKLY No.1, photo article,
     310-100
TIP TOP WEEKLY, 48-1; 151-2; 271-28;
     280-5
(TIP TOP WEEKLY), A Quick Synopsis of
     the Merriwell Saga, (in TIP TOP
     WEEKLY), by Ralph P. Smith, 537-48
(TIP TOP WEEKLY), The Applause Column
     in TIP TOP WEEKLY, (comments from
     readers), by J.P.Guinon, 328-2
(TIP TOP WEEKLY), Bruce Browning's
     Seven Years at Yale in TIP TOP
     WEEKLY, by Gerald J. McIntosh,
     390-28
(TIP TOP WEEKLY), Captain Walter Wiley,
     the Windjammer and the Marine Marvel,
     or, The Terrible and Terrific Teller
     of Tall Tales in TIP TOP, by Gerald
     J. McIntosh, 435-123
(TIP TOP WEEKLY), correction as to last
     published issue, 426-27
(TIP TOP WEEKLY), Dime Novel Readers
     Scrap Book, (items from TIP TOP
     WEEKLY No.532), 407-82
(TIP TOP WEEKLY), Dime Novel Sketches
     #58, 383-67
(TIP TOP WEEKLY), Frank Merriwell, Life
     Saver, or, Rescuing Fair Tip Top
     Maidens, by Gerald J. McIntosh,
     404-48; 405-61
(TIP TOP WEEKLY), Front Cover Scenes
     Repeated, (repetition of same covers)
     by Gerald J. McIntosh, 423-118
(TIP TOP WEEKLY), The Merriwells - After
     TIP TOP, by J. Edward Leithead and
     Gerald J. McIntosh, 354-20; 355-28;
     356-36
(TIP TOP WEEKLY), The Merriwells Under
     Arrest, or, Dime Novel Heroes
     Vindicated, (episodes of Merriwells
     running afoul of the law), by Gerald
     J. McIntosh, 395-78; 396-90
(TIP TOP WEEKLY), Paper Back Pulpit,
     (on Frank Merriwell), by Noble Tribble,
     402-30
(TIP TOP WEEKLY), The Prize Plot Story,
     (Frank Merriwell), by George T. Flaum,
     199-25
(TIP TOP WEEKLY), Rounded Up for the
     Round-Up, (odd facts on TIP TOP
     WEEKLY), by Gerald J. McIntosh, 421-97
(TIP TOP WEEKLY), Strayed From the
     Sepulchre, or, The Tomb-Tamer of
     TIP TOP, by J.P.Guinon, 99-1
(TIP TOP WEEKLY), Timothy, Chapter 10,
     16th Verse in TIP TOP WEEKLY, by
     Gerald J. McIntosh, 410-117

(title changes), Dime Novel Series Title Changes, by Denis R. Rogers and Edward T. LeBlanc, 488-50

Title Was the Same, The, (English Boys' papers with the same title), by W.O.G.Lofts, 295-29

To Bracebridge Hemyng, (verse), by P.C. Maroske, 153-3

To Collectors of Frank Reade Stories, by William M. Burns, 322-62

To Each His Own, (reading choices and reminiscences), 381-51

To Reckless Ralph, The Sleuth of the Sierras, (on Bracebridge Hemyng and the Harkaway series), by J.P. Quaine, 216-65

Today's Children, (reminiscences), by Charles Duprez, 248-38

Today's Facts in Yesterday's Fiction, (inventions seemingly fantastic), by Thomas R. Henry, 95-1

(Todd, Jerry, series), Magazine Serial and Book Relationships in Leo Edwards Books, (boys' books), by Julius R. Chenu, 534-122

Tom Swift, Jr., (boys' series books, with bibliographic checklist), by William R. Gowan, 538-56

(Tomlinson, Everett T.), Now They're Collectors' Items, (boys' books of this author), by J. Edward Leithead, 411-128

TOP NOTCH MAGAZINE, 3-5

(TOP NOTCH MAGAZINE), Dime Novel Sketches #83, 410-111

Tousey, Frank, 3-6

Tousey, Frank, death notice, 156-3

(Tousey, Frank), The Frank Tousey Authors, (dime novel publisher), by Ralph Adimari, 293-10

(Tousey, Frank), Frank Tousey, Newspaper Publisher, 217-74

(Tousey, Frank), 19th Century Peep-Show, by Fred T. Singleton, 233-10

Tousey Publications, 114-11; 117-7; 145-2; 147-5; 398-118; 403-36; 433-96

(Tousey Publications), Building and premises occupied, 154-5

(Tousey Publications), Famous Tousey Story Papers, by Edward T. LeBlanc, 508-2

(Tousey Publications), The Two King Bradys and Their Girl Detective, (detectives in dime novels), by J. Edward Leithead, 372-80; 373-90

(Tousey Publications), OUR BOYS and NEW YORK BOYS WEEKLY: The Great Tousey-Munro Rivalry, (bibliographic listing) by Ross Carufurd, 535-SS

(Tousey Publications), Wolff and the Tousey Reprints, by Ralph Adimari and C. Arthur Neetz, 332-43

(Tousey, Sinclair), Sinclair Tousey, Pres., American News Co., (biog. sketch), 344-60

(Tousey, Sinclair), Sinclair Tousey's obituary from FIRESIDE COMPANION (1887), 540-99

(Tousey, Sinclair), Talked About People, (biog sketch of president of American News Co.), by J. Alexander Patten, 20-1; 25-5; 27-4

(Tracy, James Perkins), James Perkins Tracy - A Self Made Man, (author, biog. sketch), by Ralph Adimari, 277-82

Translations of the foreign quotations in THE HOUSE OF BEADLE AND ADAMS AND ITS NICKEL AND DIME NOVELS, by author, Albert Johannsen, 215-60

Travels of a Book Collector, (boys' books collecting experiences), by H.W.Miller, 483-121

Travels of a Book Collector, (boys' books collecting experiences), by Jack R. Schorr, 483-120

Treasure Island, (on pirate stories in general, and R.L.Stevenson's book, TREASURE ISLAND), by W.O.G.Lofts, 477-64

Treat 'em Tenderly, Pard, (on caring for and preserving dime novels), by Fred T. Singleton, 4-1

(trials), Darling of the Mob - Jack Sheppard, Prince of the Prison Breakers, (notable trial account), by Fred T. Singleton, 283-30

Tribble, Noble: Paper Back Pulpit, (Frank Merriwell and TIP TOP WEEKLY) 402-30; (Gilbert Patten and the Merriwells), 381-50

Tribute to Gilbert Patten, by Herbert Leckenby, 162-1

Trick and Fancy Roper Now Building Custodian, news item, (Henry Stinemetts, old time cowboy), 180-3

(Trowbridge, John Townsend), J.T. Trowbridge - a Brief Sketch, (biog. and literary), with checklist of books, by Gil O'Gara, 544-66

TRUE BLUE, 402-24

(TRUE BLUE), Dime Novel Sketches #70, 397-103

TRUE DETECTIVE, 163-2

(true detective magazines), Dime Novels Versus Modern Fiction, (compares dime novels, comic books, true detective magazines), by Charles Duprez, 279-105

"True Friends", (play for young people adapted from Frank Merriwell stories) by Steve Press, 531-58

Tunks, Walter F.: Some Good Stuff, (comments on James Gang), 190-57

(Turner, Bessie), Miss Bessie Turner, (author, biog. sketch), 81-3

(Turner, E.S.: BOYS WILL BE BOYS), The Giants March Past, a review by J.V.B. Stewart Hunter, 197-9

Turpin, Dick, 64-5
(Turpin, Dick), Dick Turpin, the Famous
   Highwayman, by W.O.G.Lofts, 441-48
(Turpin, Dick), The Great Trials of
   History: Trial of Dick Turpin,
   193-81
(TUTTER BUGLE), Periodical for Leo
   Edwards book fans organized, 424-9
TWENTY-FIVE CENT NOVELS SERIES, 25-8
Two Boston Publishing Houses of Stories,
   (Richmond ¢ Co., and Elliott, Thomas
   & Talbot), by Roland D. Sawyer,
   144-3
Two Boys Book Writers from Wisconsin,
   (biog. sketch of Leslie Quirk and
   Everett McNeil), by Marge Dahl,
   494-131
Two King Bradys and Their Girl Detective,
   The, (detectives in dime novels), by
   J. Edward Leithead, 372-80; 373-90

Uncle Seth on the Modern Novel, (verse),
   by Sam Walter Foss, 118-6
UNION JACK, 124-5
UNION JACK, Detective Supplement, 23-3
UNION JACK HALFPENNY, 153-5
(UNION JACK LIBRARY), Exit UNION JACK,
   (cessation), by William M. Burns,
   17-5; 23-1
(UNION LIBRARY, THE), Dime Novel Sketches
   #135, 462-23
(University of Minnesota), On the Track
   of Popular Culture, (the Hess
   Collection of dime novels, story
   papers and newsstand literature),
   by J. Randolph Cox, 495-134
(University of Minnesota), Research in
   the Hess Collection, (of dime novels
   and related material), 543-56
(University of Minnesota) Hess Collection
   Acquires Complete Set of AMERICAN BOY,
   515-120
(University of South Florida), Fine Dime
   Novel Collection, 521-123
(Upham, James Bailey), Who Wrote the
   Pledge of Allegiance? (assertion that
   Upham is true author), by Louise
   Harris, 528-127
UP-TO-DATE BOYS LIBRARY, 164-5; 279-104
(UP-TO-DATE BOYS LIBRARY), Dime Novel
   Sketches #5, 323-65
Up-to-Date History in HAPPY DAYS,
   (current events published), by William
   M. Burns, 302-96
Upton Sinclair, Last of the Dime
   Novelists, by Ralph Adimari, 285-42;
   286-51
Upton Sinclair Novels, The, by Ronald
   Gottesman, 378-20
Used Book Prices, (discussion on values
   of books and why), by Denis R.
   Rogers, 469-114

Valuable Data, (on dime novels, var.),
   by H.O.Rawson, 58-7

Van Demark, James H.: letter of comment,
   381-52
Van Demark, James H.: My Surprise
   Meeting with Gilbert Patten, 387-102
Van Devier, Roy B.: C.H.Forbes-Lindsay,
   A Famous India Author, (biog.sketch)
   386-97; 387-104
Van Devier, Roy B.: Edward Stratemeyer,
   (biog.sketch and comments), 305-10,
   306-20
Van Devier, Roy B.: Genealogy of William
   Thorp, (family history), 394-73;
   395-85; 396-101; 397-110; 398-122;
   399-133; 400-10; 402-32; 403-44;
   404-54
Van Devier, Roy B.: James Ball Naylor,
   A Famous Ohio Author, (biog.sketch),
   369-56
Van Devier, Roy B.: Josephine Chase and
   Her Pen Names, 382-61
Van Devier, Roy B.: Larry Evans, A
   Famous American Novelist, (biog.
   sketch), 388-4
Van Devier, Roy B.: letter of comment,
   369-58; 382-65
Van Devier, Roy B.: Louis E. Pendleton,
   A Famous Southern Author, (biog.
   sketch), 374-100
Van Devier, Roy B.: The Old Werner
   Publishing Co. of Akron, Ohio, (later
   Saalfield Pub. Co.; publishers history),
   286-49
Van Devier, Roy B.: Oliver Optic, (biog./
   literary sketch), 298-51
Value of Friendship, The, by Louis E.
   Bisch, (essay), 161-1
(Verne, Jules), review of JULES VERNE, THE
   BIOGRAPHY OF AN IMAGINATION by George
   H. Waltz, Jr., by Nat Bengis, 158-1
Vernon, Bert: letter of comment, 485-24
Victor, Orville J. (as "Deadwood Dick,
   Jr."): 98 William Street in 1872,
   (home of Beadle & Adams, Publishers),
   14-4
(VILLAINS GALORE: THE HEYDAY OF THE
   POPULAR STORY WEEKLY, by Mary Noel),
   review, 264-69
(villains), Doctor Quartz and Other
   Nine-Lived Villains, (in the dime
   novels), by J. Edward Leithead,
   380-40; 381-48
Voice of the Collector, (collecting
   advice, dime nsvels), by Charles
   Bragin, 12-3

(Wade, Richard & Bertrand), The Derring-
   Do of the Diamond Dicks, (bibliography), by J. Edward Leithead,
   187-25
Wadleck, Joseph P.: letter of comment,
   402-27; 427-42; 468-106
(Waggaman, Mary T.), obituary, (author)
   447-133
Wake Up, (dime novel colhecting advice)
   by Ralph F. Cummings, 100-3

Wakefield, Clyde F.: Biographical
    Sketches of Famous Frontiersmen,
    No.1, Kit Carson, 158-3
    No.2, James Bridger, 160-4
    No.3, James Butler (Wild Bill)
    Hickok, 161-4
Waldrop, Wallace H.: letter of comment,
    386-96; 398-121; 447-131; 485-24
Walgren, Rhoda Gay: NEW YORK BOYS
    LIBRARY Published by Norman L.
    Munro, 463-36; 464-44
(Wall Street stories), The Anatomy of
    the Dime Novel, No.9: Wall Street
    Stories, by J. Edward Leithead,
    427-34; 428-44
(Wallace, William H.) Man Who Prosecuted
    James Gang is Dead, (obituary), 71-2
Wallen, S.E.: Oliver Optic, (William
    Taylor Adams as author and editor,
    with definitive checklist), 511-26;
    512-38
Wallen, S.E.: Who Was George H. Coomer?
    (dime novels author and poet, sketch,
    with checklist), 503-90; 504-106
Walters, Bob: letter of comment, 524-51;
    547-20
Walther, Peter C.: Edward Stratemeyer's
    Appeal to Contemporary Young Readers,
    535-2
Walther, Peter C.: Evidence of Another
    Edward Stratemeyer Pseudonym, (as
    Ralph Harrington), 542-41
Walther, Peter C.: letter of comment,
    528-131
Walther, Peter C.: William Taylor Adams,
    A Literary Retrospection, (literary
    discussion, Oliver Optic, with check-
    list, 548-26
(Waltz, George H., Jr.: JULES VERNE, THE
    BIOGRAPHY OF AN IMAGINATION), review
    by Nat Bengis, 158-1
(Wanamaker, John, Company, Publishers),
    Edward S. Ellis Stories Published by
    the Mershon Complex, by Denis R.
    Rogers, 490-70; 491-86; 492-104
Wanderings of the Dime Novel, (reminis-
    cences), by Patrick Mulhall, 11-2
"Wanted: A Hero", (heroes in the boys'
    books), by Jack R. Schorr, 482-112
(WAR LIBRARY, THE), Dime Novel Sketches
    #33, 356-35
(Warner, Anna Bartlett), Favorites of
    Yesterday, (biog.sketch, author), by
    Hermon Pitcher, 323-68
(Warner, Susan), Favorites of Yesterday,
    (biog. sketch, author), by Hermon
    Pitcher, 158-3
Warshaw, Irving: letter of comment,
    404-53
Was That Jesse James?, by Joe Gantner,
    128-1
Watkin, Albert: letter of comment,
    373-96; 389-17
We Plead Guilty, It's the War, (dime
    novel collecting experiences), anon.,
    108-3

Wearing, F.N.: The Grand Old Stories,
    (dime novel reminiscences), 165-1
Wearing, F.N.: Specimen Numbers of
    Bygone Boys Papers, 176-33
Weatherbee, Harry: letter of comment,
    375-113; 447-131
(Webster, cartoonist with NEW YORK
    WORLD), The Literary Feast, by
    W.B.McCafferty, 1-1
Webster, John W.: letter of comment,
    499-46
Wedding Bells for J.E.Badger, Jr.,
    (dime novel author), 30-1
WEEKLY STORY TELLER, 124-5
WEHMAN DIME NOVELS, 155-4
Weill, Harry A.: A Lode of GOLDEN HOURS,
    (on pseudonyms of writers), 215-59
Weill, Harry A.: A Thrice-Told Tale
    on GOLDEN HOURS, 148-1
Weill, Harry A.: GOLDEN HOURS,
    Reminiscences and Reflections,
    137-1
Weill, Harry A.: John DeMorgan, (biog.
    sketch, author), 295-30
Weill, Harry A.: letter of comment,
    180-4
Weill, Harry A.: More on the GOLDEN
    HOURS, 149-5
Weill, Harry A.: Nuggets from GOLDEN
    HOURS, 171-1
Well, What Have You?, (comments on
    older books), by U.G.Figley,
    148-2
Wenstrup, Dick: letter of comment,
    550-86
(Werner Publishing Co.), The Old
    Werner Publishing Company of Akron,
    Ohio, (later Saalfield Pub. Co.;
    publishers history), by Roy B.
    Van Devier, 286-49
(West Point stories), The Anatomy of
    Dime Novels No.14: West Point and
    Annapolis Stories, by J. Edward
    Leithead, 437-18; 438-30
(Westbrook, Arthur, Company), The
    James Boys in the Saddle Again,
    (Westbrook reprints in Adventure
    Series), by J. Edward Leithead,
    280-2
Westbrook, Charles F.: letter of
    comment, 390-31; 407-81; 474-43
(Westbrook, Charles F.), obituary,
    475-48
WESTERN ADVENTURES, 15-7
(Western Heritage Center Library),
    National Cowboy Hall of Fame at
    Oklahoma City and Mammoth Western
    Heritage Center Library, by
    Gerald J. McIntosh, 397-107
Western Hero's Hall of Fame, 320-40
(WESTERN STORY LIBRARY), ROUGH RIDER
    WEEKLY and the Ted Strong Saga,
    with bibliographical listing, by
    J. Edward Leithead and Edward T.
    LeBlanc, 478-3
WESTERN LOVE STORIES, 15-7

Western Pioneer Days, (reminiscences), by J.H.Armbruster, 132-2

(WESTERN STORY MAGAZINE), Dime Novel Sketches #81, 408-85

(WESTERN WEEKLY), Dime Novel Sketches #82, 409-95

What Dime Novels Are, (essay), 81-4

What I Know About Assorted Novels, (misc. bibliographical data), by Stewart H.V.Bender, 54-1

What Will You Do?, (collecting dime novels commentary), by Edward G. Ingraham, 366-27

(Wheeler, Edward L.), Edward L. Wheeler's Own View of Wild Bill Hickok, by "Seajay", 158-3

(Wheeler, Edward L.), The Novels of Edward L. Wheeler, by Deadwood Dick, Jr., 94-1

(Wheeler, Florence E.), A Librarian Who Unearthed History, (commentary on Johnny Appleseed, and Florence E. Wheeler's push for his recognition), by Nicholas Zook, 224-38

When Dime Novels Were in Their Glory, (reminiscences), by Ralph F. Cummings, 10-3

When the Mounties Did Not Get Their Man - A Real Dime Novel Story, (like fiction), by J.H.Armbruster, 107-1

Where is Dot?, (reminiscences on dime novels), by Donald S. Learned, 58-2

White, George C., (cover artist, dime novels), 58-8

Whitson, John H., (author), 203-70

(Whittaker, Capt. Frederick), obituary, 190-58

Who is Doctor Holmes?, 75-12

Who Was George H. Coomer?, (dime novels author and poet, biog. sketch with checklist), by S.E.Wallen, 502-74; 503-90; 504-106

Who Wrote the Pledge of Allegiance? (assertion that James Bailey Upham was true author), by Louise Harris, 528-127

Whose Pond is This?, (Happy Hours Brotherhood, members activities), by Edward G. Ingraham, 342-20

Why the High Cost of Novels in Poor Condition, (collecting dime novels, comments), by Frank Cummings, 8-3

WIDE AWAKE LIBRARY, 17-5; 25-2; 58-8; 127-5; 145-3; 147-5; 148-4; 152-4; 413-16

WIDE AWAKE LIBRARY, firefighter stories, 407-76

(WIDE AWAKE LIBRARY), Dime Novel Sketches #50, 374-100

(WIDE AWAKE LIBRARY - SPECIAL), Dime Novel Sketches #113, 440-41

WIDE AWAKE WEEKLY, firefighter stories, 407-77

(WIDE AWAKE LIBRARY), The Great Five Cent Wide-A-Wake Library), by George H. Cordier, 75-1

(WIDE AWAKE LIBRARY), My "Pets" in WIDE AWAKE LIBRARY, (favorites, commentary), by William M. Burns, 168-1

(WIDE AWAKE LIBRARY), The WIDE AWAKE, by Ralph F. Cummings, 75-11

(WIDE AWAKE WEEKLY), Dime Novel Sketches #11, 330-17

WILD WEST, 151-2

(Wild West), Dangers of Wild West Recalled by Old Letter, by Willard Jaffray, 92-4

Wild West in England, The, (on Buffalo Bill), by Ralph F. Cummings, 61-2

WILD WEST NOVELS, 54-3

Wild West Shows Pass in Grand Review, The, (survey and discussion of the var. Wild West Shows), by J. Edward Leithead, 264-65; 265-74; 266-84

(Wild West Shows), review of ANNIE OAKLEY OF THE WILD WEST, by Walter Havighurst, 266-86

WILD WEST WEEKLY, 165-4

(WILD WEST WEEKLY), Arietta: Heroine of Wild West Trails, (dime novel heroine), by J. Edward Leithead, 367-32

(WILD WEST WEEKLY), Dime Novel Sketches #27, 350-111

(WILD WEST WEEKLY), ROUGH RIDER WEEKLY and the Ted Strong Saga, with bibliographical checklist, by J. Edward Leithead and Edward T. LeBlanc, 478-3

(WILD WEST WEEKLY), Young Wild West, (dime novel westerns, commentary), by J. Edward Leithead, 226-49

(Wiley, Capt. Walter), Captain Walter Wiley, the Windjammer and the Marine Marvel, or, The Terrible and Terrific Teller of Tall Tales in TIP TOP, (dime novel character), by Gerald J. McIntosh, 435-123

Willard Thompson, Book Dealer, (old-time book dealer, sketch), by John Guernsey, 480-90

William J. Benners, The First Historian of the Dime Novel, by Ralph Adimari, 312-121

William J. Benners Pseudonyms, by Ralph Adimari, 317-14

William James Benners, Jr., (author biog. sketch), by E. Burke Collins, 108-1

William Taylor Adams, A Literary Retrospection, (literary discussion, Oliver Optic's works), with checklist, by Peter C. Walther, 548-26

William Wallace Cook, The Marshall Years, (author's early years in Marshall, Mich.), with checklist, by Mabel Cooper Skhelver, 518-34

(Williams, Jim), Dime Novels in Cartoons, (Jim Williams and other cartoonists discussed), by Gerald J. McIntosh, 412-2

Wilson & Company, (Publishers), 17-2
Wilson, Dencil E.: letter of comment, 409-108
(Wilson, Frank C.), obituary, 331-37
Wilson, H.L.: Remember When, (verse), 109-5
Winnetka Graded Book List and Its Supplement, (rating children's books 1924-1925), by Deidre Johnson, 549-61
Winning World War I, (exploits of boys' books heroes in the war), by Julius R. Chenu, 543-50
With the Novel Stackers, (comments on collecting dime nivels), by Deadwood Dick, Jr., 19-6
WIZARD, THE, 49-3
Wolff - and the Tousey Reprints, (on Tousey Publishing Co.), by Ralph Adimari and C. Arthur Neetz, 332-43
Wonderful Adventures of Cap't Wiley, as edited by Burt L. Standish (Gilbert Patten), (the "discovered" memoirs of a dime novel character) by Gerald J. McIntosh, 462-31
(Wood, Ellen Price), Ellen Price Wood 1814-1887, English Juvenile Writer, (biog./literary sketch), by Ralph Adimari, 366-22
Wood, James N.: In Praise of the Half-Dime Novel, 63-1
WORK AND WIN, 165-4
(WORK AND WIN), Dime Novel Sketches #61, 386-93
(WORK AND WIN), First Half Year of WORK AND WIN, (discussed), by Harold C. Holmes, 166-1
Works of Bracebridge Hemyng, The, by William M. Burns, 152-1; 153-1
(World War I), Winning World War I, (exploits of boys' books heroes in the war), by Julius R. Chenu, 543-50
World Famous Author, (biog. sketch of Charlotte M. Braeme), by Hermon Pitcher, 112-3
(Wrenn, Charles L.), An Artist Recalls Nickel Novel Days, by J. Edward Leithead, 87-1
(Wrenn, Charles L.), Author and Artist of the Street & Smith Staff, W. Bert Foster and Charles L. Wrenn, by J. Edward Leithead, 361-92; 362-99; 363-110
(Wrenn, Charles L.), Note on Foster-Wrenn Article, by J. Edward Leithead, 365-17
Writers for GOLDEN DAYS, (author biog. sketches), by Stanley A. Pachon, No.1, Frank H. Converse, 333-52; No.2, Charles Herbert Heustis, 335-69
Wyoming's Wild Riders and Other Hunted Men,(Butch Cassidy, Billy the Kid, and others in dime novels), by J. Edward Leithead, 294-20

YANKEE DOODLE, 403-39
(YANKEE DOODLE), Dime Novel Sketches #3, 321-49
YANKEE 5¢ LIBRARY, 124-5
(YANKEE 5¢ LIBRARY), Dime Novel Sketches #125, 452-49
Ye Brotherhood, the Roundup, and Its Editor, (on Happy Hours Brotherhood, and its members, and the DIME NOVEL ROUNDUP and editor), by Charles Duprez, 274-53
Ye Roundup and Its Members, (DIME NOVEL ROUNDUP and collectors of dime novels), by Charles Duprez, 263-59
Yellowstone Bill, by G. Fred Orphal, 174-21
(Yellowstone Bill), obituary, by G. Fred Orphal, 207-98
You've Told Whoppers - Ever Read One? (humorous sketch), by Walter H. McIntosh, 487-46
(YOUNG ATHLETE'S WEEKLY), Dime Novel Sketches #9, 327-99
YOUNG BRITON, THE, 11-2; 279-103
YOUNG BROADBRIM WEEKLY, 241-77
(YOUNG BROADBRIM WEEKLY), Dime Novel Sketches #79, 406-65
Young Diamond Dick, (dime novel hero), by J. Edward Leithead, 358-68; 359-76; 360-84
YOUNG ENGLISHMEN'S JOURNAL, 16-5; 279-103
YOUNG FOLKS, 134-2
YOUNG GENTLEMAN OF BRITAIN, 16-5; 279-103
YOUNG GENTLEMANS MAGAZINE, 14-3; 277-84
YOUNG GLORY, 403-38
(YOUNG GLORY), Dime Novel Sketches #1, 317-13
YOUNG IRELAND, 3-2
(YOUNG KING BRADY), The Two King Bradys and Their Girl Detective, (dime novel detectives discussed), by J. Edward Leithead, 372-80; 373-90
YOUNG KLONDIKE, 81A-12
YOUNG KLONDIKE, by Charles Duprez, 258-18
(YOUNG KLONDIKE), Dime Novel Sketches #57, 382-57
(YOUNG KLONDIKE), Tales of Klondike Gold in Dime Novels, by J. Edward Leithead, 301-88
YOUNG MEN OF AMERICA, 26-2; 88-8; 413-16
YOUNG MEN OF AMERICA, firefighter stories, 407-75
(YOUNG MEN OF AMERICA), Dime Novel Sketches #68, 395-77
(YOUNG MEN OF AMERICA), Famous Tousey Story Papers, by Edward T. LeBlanc, 508-3
YOUNG MEN OF AMERICA, photo sketch, 233-9

YOUNG MEN OF GREAT BRITAIN, 16-4; 279-103

(YOUNG PEOPLES WEEKLY), Neglected Weeklies, (commentary), by Ralph P. Smith, 489-65

(YOUNG ROUGH RIDERS WEEKLY), King of the Wild West, (dime novel and characters discussed), by J. Edward Leithead, 198-17

(YOUNG ROVER LIBRARY), Dime Novel Sketches #76, 403-35

(YOUNG SLEUTH LIBRARY), Dime Novel Sketches #110, 437-17

YOUNG SLEUTH LIBRARY, photo sketch, 240-66

(YOUNG SPORTS), A Fragment on George A. Amy, Illustrator for YOUNG SPORTS, by Stanley A. Pachon, 371-76

YOUNG SPORTS 5¢ LIBRARY, 311-112

(YOUNG SPORTS FIVE CENT LIBRARY), Dime Novel Sketches #116, 443-75

YOUNG SPORTS OF AMERICA, 311-112

Young Sports Series, The, by J.P.Guinon, 311-112

Young Wild West, (on WILD WEST WEEKLY), by J. Edward Leithead, 226-49

Young Wild West's Other Pard, or Arietta's Only Rival, (biog. & literary sketch, Mrs. Sarah Thomas, author of dime novels) by Edward G. Ingraham, 344-58

(YOUNG WILD WEST WEEKLY), Young Wild West's Other Pard, or Arietta's Only Rival, (biog. & literary sketch, Mrs. Sarah Thomas, author of dime novels) by Edward G. Ingraham, 344-58

(Younger, Cole), Cole Younger, James Bandit, Dies Reformed, news item, 117-8

(Younger Brothers), The Bandit Brothers of Old Missouri, (outlaw sketch), by J. Edward Leithead, 276-70

(Younger Brothers), Buckskin Bill Recalls Famous Iowa Neighbors and Trip to Old Missouri, (outlaw sketch, James Gang), by J. Edward Leithead, 291-94

Your Wife and Your Collection, (boys' book collecting), by Jack R. Schorr, 458-115

YOUTH MISCELLANY, 277-84

YOUTH'S CASKET, 415-38; 416-46

YOUTH'S COMPANION, 261-43

YOUTH'S COMPANION, by Kenneth M. Daggett, 322-58

(YOUTH'S COMPANION), letter from Louise Harris, 516-150

(YOUTH'S COMPANION), Our Flag's Bicentennial, (effort of YOUTH'S COMPANION to have flag flown over schools; authorship of Pledge of Allegiance) by Louise Harris, 513-56

(YOUTH'S COMPANION), Who Wrote the Pledge of Allegiance?, (assertion that James Bailey Upham was true author), by Louise Harris, 528-127

YOUTHS INSTRUCTOR AND GUARDIAN, 277-84

(YOUTHS LIBRARY), Dime Novel Sketches #139, 466-61

(YOUTHS LIBRARY), Rare Dime Novels - YOUTHS LIBRARY No.2, (descriptive comments), by Edward T. LeBlanc, 215-57

YOUTHS MAGAZINE, THE, 277-84

Zerbe, Andy: letter of comment, 410-123; 515-120; 517-28; 547-19

Zook, Nicholas: A Librarian Who Unearthed History, (Florence E. Wheeler and her push for recognition of Johnny Appleseed), 224-38